The Devil's Brew

by
Jack Treby

Chapter One

I have never been much of a one for beating servants. In my experience, violence only serves to breed resentment and with the serving classes that should be avoided at all costs. The schoolmaster's cane may give much needed direction to the immature mind, but a fully grown man – even a member of the lower orders – should be capable of disciplining himself. If he cannot, he has no business being a servant.

That being said, there are times when I would happily have throttled my man Maurice and Thursday morning was a case in point.

A loud thump from the living room had roused me from my slumber. I had been fast asleep – as any sane person would be at three am – and it took me some time to gather my wits. I pulled a hand from beneath the bed sheets and rubbed my eyes. What the devil was he up to this time? I wondered. The thump was followed by a prolonged and unnatural silence. I lifted myself onto my elbows and peered across the bedroom towards the far door. There was a light flickering beneath the wooden frame; Maurice up and about again for no good reason. I scowled quietly. The man barely seemed to sleep at all. I had almost jumped out of my skin, a couple of weeks earlier, when I had got up in the middle of the night to answer a call of nature and had caught sight of his ghoulish, crumpled face staring up at me from an armchair, a large textbook in his lap. At that time of the morning – four am – anyone with an ounce of sense would have been in the arms of Morpheus, but not my valet. We had had a few words then about his nocturnal activities, but clearly he needed a reminder.

I yawned, stretched myself out and pulled back the bed sheets irritably. I wouldn't be able to get back to sleep now, so I might as well give the fellow a piece of my mind. I did not appreciate being woken up like this, in the middle of the night, especially when I had to be up myself in a few hours time, bright and alert.

I reached across to the bedside lamp and flicked the

switch. Nothing happened. I let out a growl but I was not surprised. Another power cut. The electricity supply here was about as reliable as the plumbing. That was one of the perils of living in such a backwards part of the world. I swung my legs over the side of the bed and my nightshirt snagged on the mattress. I ruffled it out and planted my feet firmly on the floorboards, flinching momentarily at the sudden cold. It could be a little chilly in the early hours, even here in the tropics. The nightshirt was a necessary bulwark and also served to protect my modesty. It was not the done thing for a woman to sleep *au naturel*, even in the relative safety of her own apartment.

I pulled myself up and stood for a moment, gazing across at the light underneath the living room door. It did not have the reassuring flicker of a regular candle. The blasted thing seemed to be darting about all over the place. More like a torch, I thought. But why would Maurice be wandering around the place at this hour with a flash light? It took a few seconds for my befuddled brain to stagger towards the obvious conclusion: it might not be Maurice at all.

I moved back to the bed and sat myself down, shivering again. Good god, it might be a burglar. What if some ruffian had broken into the flat and was even now rifling through my possessions? I gripped my hands on the base of the mattress and took a large gulp of air. If there *was* an intruder, it was probably best not to disturb him. I am no coward – I have faced down all sorts of rogues and scoundrels in my time – but if life has taught me one thing, it is that it is often better not to get involved. There was nothing of any value in the living room. Let the fellow root around if he really wanted to. If I strode out there like some irate landowner, he might well attack me; and burglars in this part of the world were likely to be armed with rather more than the traditional cosh.

The intruder was doing rather a good job of keeping the noise down. Apart from that initial thump, I hadn't heard anything at all. No sloping footsteps, no cupboards being ransacked. In fact, there did not seem to be any noise at all, even out in the street, though my bedroom window was ajar and the blinds were only half drawn. Perhaps he had got in through the living room window. We were only one floor up and even I could probably have managed to shin up that distance. A narrow balcony ran the length of the apartment, encompassing the living room and the bedroom. I just hoped to God he didn't decide to extend his search. Perhaps I ought to cough, make some noise to frighten him off. Or perhaps it would be safer just to lie down and pretend to be asleep.

A low groan sounded from the other room. I shuddered, recognising the voice. It was my man Maurice, out there in the thick of it. He did not sound at all well. And, now that I was more alert, it dawned on me what this must mean. He must have heard a noise and got up to investigate; and then, obviously, someone had clobbered him. That was the thump that had woken me up. Lord. If my valet was lying out there with a sizeable dent in the back of his bonce then I couldn't just ignore it. The burglar might try to finish him off. I had no choice. Somehow, I would have to frighten the blackguard away.

My eyes had now adjusted to the gloom and I glanced around the room for a weapon. Unfortunately, there was nothing suitable to hand. A small silver candle holder next to the lamp shade looked to be my best option. I pulled out the wax stick and grasped the metal disk by the finger hold. That would have to do.

Tentatively, I approached the door. A floorboard creaked beneath me and I cursed it silently. The light from the torch disappeared. I waited a beat, then reached out a hand and grabbed the door handle. I opened it a crack but the living room was in darkness, a much deeper black than the bedroom. The blinds were lowered further out here and I could make out little in the punishing gloom.

Perhaps I had let my imagination run away with me. Maybe my man was up and about on his own and had simply tripped up. If so, I would crucify the fool.

I pulled the door open a little further and then cursed again, realising I would now be visible in silhouette in the doorway. I stepped forward and my foot collided with something solid in front of me. I tripped and stumbled across the carpet, crashing hard into the back of the sofa. My hands grabbed hold of the top of it and I managed to steady myself. At that moment, I heard the door slam on the far side of the living room. Our intruder had fled the scene.

Edging around the sofa, I tottered blindly towards the far wall and searched for a light switch. I flicked the control but nothing happened. Damn it. I had forgotten about the power cut. I cursed a third time and then heard another low moan from behind me. Maurice was lying on the floor between my bedroom door and the sofa. It must have been him I tripped over.

'Morris?' I called out, with some concern. I always called him "Morris" rather than "Maurice". It was a private joke, though more for my amusement than his. The valet let out another groan.

I moved across to the window and grasped for one of the hanging cords. I caught it and pulled the wire taught, rotating the blinds sideways. At last a small shaft of moonlight illuminated the chamber. I glanced around the room. A set of drawers had been quietly ransacked to the right of the windows. Papers were strewn everywhere. I fumbled inside the bureau for a candle and a box of matches. Before I could complete the action, the electric light bulb stuttered into life and the room was bathed in a dim glow.

Maurice was just beginning to rouse himself. He was clutching the back of his head and frowning slightly.

'Morris, are you all right? What happened?'

The man took a moment to recover himself. 'I heard a noise, Monsieur. I came out to investigate.' Maurice was a tall, thickset Frenchman in his mid-fifties. He was dressed in a light but well cut dressing gown. He raised a hand to the back of his head and then, without fuss, examined the residue on his palm. A little blood but nothing serious. 'I believe I may have been struck from behind,' he said. The fellow had a knack for understatement.

'Sit down,' I told him. I moved over to the side table and poured out a glass of whisky. I downed the liquid in one and then dished out a second glass for Maurice. Ordinarily, I would not have allowed him to drink in the flat, but these were exceptional circumstances.

Maurice had been my valet for about a year and a half now. He was a grim, taciturn man with a craggy face and a permanently pained expression. His manner bordered on the surly but, for all that, he was an efficient fellow and not the sort to demand sympathy unnecessarily.

He took the glass and sipped at it gently. 'Thank you, Monsieur,' he said. Even in private, we maintained the forms. It was always 'Monsieur' rather than 'Madame'. I may have been born a woman but I had chosen to live my life as a man. Employing a valet was an important part of that and, for a modest monthly fee, the Frenchman was happy to go along with the charade.

'Did you see who hit you?' I asked him.

'No, Monsieur.'

'Pity.' I poured myself another whisky and had a brief look around. There was no sign of a cosh or any other blunt instrument. 'He must have clambered in through the window,' I guessed. The flat was mercifully small – just a kitchen, a living room and two bedrooms – so there was not much for an intruder to get his teeth into.

Maurice had recovered himself slightly. 'Shall I call the police, Monsieur?'

'Lord, no!' I baulked at that. The last thing I wanted was the local boys crawling all over the place. 'Not before I speak to the minister anyway.' There was nothing of a sensitive nature kept in the apartment, but as a foreign national and an employee of the British legation in Guatemala City, I would require the minister's approval before involving the police. 'We need to see if anything was taken.' I shuffled across the room to examine the open bureau. 'I didn't keep any cash in there. Just a few odds and sods. Certainly nothing valuable.'

'A burglar would not know that, Monsieur.'

'No, I suppose not. The only money in the house is in the drawer next to my bed. Oh, apart from anything you have.' Maurice was given a small allowance for housekeeping, on top of his wages.

5

'A few dollars only, Monsieur. And some local currency.'

'Did he try to come into your room? The burglar?'

'No, Monsieur.'

I downed the second whisky. 'But you heard him moving about?'

'I am a light sleeper Monsieur.' That was certainly true. The man had excellent hearing too. He would know the difference between his master blundering about, answering a call of nature, and some devil of an intruder.

'We've had a lucky escape, Morris. We might have been murdered in our beds.'

'Yes, Monsieur.'

'Oh, how's that head of yours?'

'I will survive, Monsieur.'

I glanced down at the bureau again. One of the drawers had been pulled right out and emptied of its papers. It was an internal drawer, inside the top of the bureau. The flap had been pulled down so that the burglar could look inside. 'That's odd,' I remarked.

'Monsieur?'

I peered at it closely. 'There's a second drawer here. I never noticed that before.'

Maurice rose up from the sofa and came across to take a look.

'You see? It's inside the first one.' I thrust a hand into the larger drawer and slid the tiny compartment back inside the first. 'Good lord,' I exclaimed. 'You wouldn't even know it was there.' I stared down at the thing. 'How do you even open it?'

'A catch, Monsieur.' The valet indicated a slight irregularity in the wood.

I pressed against it, but nothing happened. Then I caught a fingernail on the edge and teased it back. The hidden drawer popped out again. 'Some kind of spring.'

'The burglar knew what he was looking for, Monsieur.'

I stepped back and digested the implications of that. I had been living in this flat for about eight weeks now. Before that, so far as I knew, the place had been empty. 'What on earth

6

could have been in there?' I wondered.

'That was where your predecessor was sitting when he shot himself,' David Richards pointed out maliciously. He was a tall, solidly built man with jet black hair and a pug nose. 'You can still see the bullet hole in the wall behind you.' Richards was our head of mission at the legation. He spoke like an aristocrat but looked like a boxer. It was only the second time he had deigned to speak to me. On the first occasion, in the main building, he had made his disapproval evident. 'I don't like spies,' he had informed me testily. 'My job is to establish cordial relations with the new government and promote British interests in Guatamala. If you do anything to jeopardize that mission, you will be on the first boat back to Blighty.' Officially, Richards was my boss. I was the new head of passport control at the legation – in reality, me and two secretaries – and he was my immediate superior; but we both knew I had other, more shadowy masters back in London, to whom I was ultimately responsible. Richards was unhappy, however, with the idea of anything happening outside of his direct control. 'Mr Markham overstepped the mark,' he continued now, referring to my unfortunate predecessor. 'Got involved with people he had no business getting involved with. And now we see the consequences.' Giles Markham had committed suicide at the end of March, a fact no-one had bothered to inform me of before I had accepted the job. Something to do with gambling debts, apparently. Markham had been creaming off some of the visa receipts collected by the passport office, presumably to pay off his creditors, and it had all got out of hand.

'And you think that might have something to do with the robbery?' I asked.

Richards shook his head. 'Don't be absurd, man. If Giles Markham had left anything important in that apartment, someone would have been in there long before now. It must be over three months since he died. In any case, the place was given a thorough going over at the time. Are you sure this burglar of yours didn't look anywhere else, apart from the bureau?' I had given Richards a full account of the break-in.

'No. And so far as I know, there was nothing of any value in there; or in the whole flat. All the sensitive material – the code books, passports, money – they're all with you at the legation or in the safe over there.' I gestured to a strong box in the corner of the room. The passport control office was a couple of doors down from the legation itself. 'Whoever broke in last night, they were only after one thing. Though what that might be, I have no idea.'

'Have you spoken to Miss Bunting?'

'Yes, of course.' Emily Bunting was one of the clerks in my office. 'I spoke to her first thing this morning.' Miss Bunting was a bubbly young thing in her early twenties. She had started work at the legation a few weeks before me. Apparently, she had arrived in Guatemala City the week Markham had died. A lack of available accommodation had forced her to take up temporary residence in the flat for the first few weeks before I had turned up at the beginning of May; a fact I had not previously been aware of. 'She never went near the bureau. And she says there was no suspicious activity in the block while she was staying there.'

Richards grimaced. 'I really don't have time for this nonsense. I'm sure you're making a mountain out of a mole hill.'

'I hope you're right,' I said. 'Should I inform the Guatemalan police? As a courtesy?'

'Don't be ridiculous!' He growled. 'We don't want them involved. It was bad enough the last time, when your predecessor put that bullet in his head. The last thing we need is them clomping around again in their size eleven boots. That is exactly the sort of unpleasantness we are looking to avoid. One of our apartments broken into in the dead of night. They'll take it as a personal affront, implying that they can't keep their streets safe at night.'

I laughed. 'Have you been out on the streets at night?' No-one in their right mind would risk venturing out in this city after dark.

'Things are improving,' Richards stated tersely. 'And I don't want to hear you implying anything different. I suggest we draw a veil over this whole matter.' He rose to his feet. 'Now get back to work. I can't afford to waste any more time on this. But bear in mind, Mr Buxton...Mr Bland, whatever you call yourself these days, I have my eye on you. If you cause me any trouble, I'll come down on you like a ton of bricks. Remember, you do not have diplomatic immunity. If you get caught breaking any local law, no matter how trivial, you're on your own. I can do nothing to protect you. Good day.' And with that, he stormed out of the office.

I stared after him, barely managing to contain my own anger. Who the devil did he think he was, talking to me like that? I wasn't his lackey. Richards was a weaselly little bean-counter, putting on airs and graces. I didn't have to take that kind of nonsense from him. If his career had amounted to anything, he wouldn't be a *chargé d'affaires* in such an absurd backwater; he'd be a fully fledged ambassador somewhere important. Oh, I knew Richards type well enough: happy to fawn and ingratiate himself with presidents and foreign diplomats, but showing his true colours closer to home. My father would have taken a whip to him.

'Mr Buxton?' a voice piped up from the doorway.

I frowned. "Henry Buxton." My latest *nom de plume*. I was still getting used to the name. It was the second new identity I had adopted in as many years. It did not have quite the same gravitas as my real name – Hilary Manningham-Butler – but at least I had been able to retain the initials. I had been sorely tempted to restore my title as well, when I had written out the passport using one of the blanks in the office in New York. In a previous life, I had been a baronet and Sir Henry Buxton would have had a nice ring to it. However, some thoughtful soul had pointed out that as the head of mission in Guatemala – Mr Richards – had not yet been knighted, it would not be the done thing to outrank him. I had reluctantly conceded the logic of that. Having met the man in question, however, I was tempted to go back and make one final adjustment to that passport.

9

'Yes, what it is?' I snapped, looking up at the figure in the doorway.

William Battersby, my secretary, did not flinch. He was a slender, quiet fellow in his mid twenties, efficient and anxious to please. 'Didn't go well, sir?' he asked.

'What do you think?' I stood up and marched over to the sideboard. It wasn't ten o'clock yet, but I needed a stiff drink.

William observed me quietly as I filled up the glass. He was carrying a bundle of papers with him. 'We're just about to open up.'

I grimaced. Another working day. That was another thing I was having to get used to: a nine to five job. It wasn't right, a woman of my calibre. Not that William – or anybody else here – had the slightest idea about that. The Foreign Office did not allow women to occupy senior positions. Thankfully, the department was only open to the public between 10am and 1pm. 'Any takers today?' I asked, taking a swig of whisky and slumping back into my chair.

William nodded. 'A couple of people waiting, sir. Smartly dressed, too.' Most of the visa applications we received were from local businessmen. They were the only ones who would have the wherewithal to visit the United Kingdom. 'I've got the files you wanted, sir. And you asked me to remind you about your four o'clock appointment.'

'I haven't forgotten.' I downed the rest of the whisky and William handed the paperwork across. 'Well, better open up then. Oh, and close the door behind you. I'm not to be disturbed.' Better to keep the rabble at a distance while I read through these files. The secretary obediently pulled the door shut behind him. His desk was in the outer room, opposite Miss Bunting. It was there that most of the visa applications would be processed.

My own office was reserved for more serious work. The room was painfully small, with just one grated window, a filing cabinet and a corner safe. A large wooden fan rotated laboriously above my head but all it ever seemed to do was redistribute the dust. I glanced down at the files William had

10

given me. The latest reports from Nicaragua and Honduras. Our office did not just provide visas for rich Guatemalans; we were passport control for most of Central America. And that was only the day job. These reports were of a more sensitive nature.

I scowled. Who was I trying to fool? Nothing that happened in this part of the world was of any interest to the mandarins back home. The Secret Intelligence Service needed a presence in Central America, for form's sake, but the days of British influence in this part of the world were slowly drawing to a close. The highest item on the ministerial agenda was Guatemalan loan repayments. It was a dead end job in a backward country. And the worst of it was, they wouldn't even have offered me this position if my predecessor hadn't taken it upon himself to commit suicide. I was not exactly an experienced field operative. One posting with MI5 in Gibraltar and a couple of years in the back office hardly qualified me for a position of any real responsibility. And so I had ended up here, passport control officer in a banana republic, playing second fiddle to the likes of Mr David Richards.

I poured myself another whisky and opened the first folder.

'You are looking tired, Mr Buxton,' Jorge Navarro observed with some sympathy. He was a handsome, olive skinned man in his early thirties with a tasteful moustache and a comfortably symmetrical face. 'Perhaps we should cut the lesson short?'

Rain was pelting the window of the small south-facing classroom. It always seemed to rain in Guatemala in the afternoons. The country had a more temperate climate than I had expected; but what it lacked in temperature it made up for in precipitation. The rain arrived in short, heavy bursts every afternoon, almost like clockwork. Perhaps my perception was a little skewed. I had made the mistake of arriving at the beginning of the rainy season.

'No, no, we'd better continue.' I smiled grimly at the tutor. I had never had much of an aptitude for languages and a year or so living in Gibraltar had given me barely more than a passing acquaintance with the language. Now that I was living in a Spanish speaking country, however, it was only right that I should make some effort to learn the lingo. 'People will start to notice if I don't get any better fairly soon. I just can't get to grips with these pronouns,' I muttered. 'Damn things are the wrong way around.'

The lecturer nodded sympathetically. 'It is never easy for a man of your age to start learning a language from scratch.'

'I'm not that old,' I said. Forty-two was barely middle aged. I might have developed a few grey hairs and my waistline had probably expanded an inch or two over the last couple of years, but I still had a firm jaw and a pleasingly masculine voice. 'I'm not quite ready for the knackers yard just yet.'

We finished the lesson and I closed up the text book. Navarro was a good teacher but he was probably wasting his time with me. Our regular meetings had, however, served to provide me with a great deal of other information.

'You saw Giles Markham, didn't you?' I asked, finally getting down to the important business. 'A few days before he died?'

'Yes. It was he who recruited me,' Navarro said. The professor had been our mole at the University of San Carlos for some years now. The Guatemalan government had its fair share of spies, in every town and village, so it was only reasonable that we should have a few of our own. The lecturer scratched his moustache and leaned forward. As a professor of Spanish, no-one questioned his right to provide lessons for minor diplomats and functionaries such as myself; and he was young enough and sufficiently charismatic to mix well with the students too. As such, he was well placed to provide the office with advance warning of any potential unrest in the capital. Political change in Central America always begins with the universities and Navarro was a reliable barometer, not just for Guatemala but for the whole region.

Strictly speaking, the internal politics of these tin-pot little countries was of no concern to the SIS. Our remit was to gather information regarding potential threats to the United Kingdom and there were precious few of those on this side of the Atlantic. Even the possibility of communist subversion, which was forever being bandied about by those who had little notion of what it actually meant, was not really within our sphere of reference in this part of the world. But information is power, as some wise old soak once said, and any advance warning of a change in the status quo would always be of value. David Richards had his own lines of intelligence, but I was expected to dig a little deeper and not concern myself too much with protocol.

'How did he seem to you?' I asked, following up the reference to my late, lamented predecessor. Giles Markham had used the same cover story I had to visit the lecturer each week. I had told Navarro about the break in at Markham's old flat.

'A little distracted, but then he always was. I had the impression he was thinking about his next appointment. He was always two steps ahead.'

'But he didn't seem unnecessarily worried?'

'Not that I could tell. I was shocked when I heard he had shot himself.' Navarro shuddered at the memory.

'What did you make of him? Generally, I mean? You must have spent quite a bit of time with him.'

The lecturer considered. 'He was a lively, outgoing man. Not the kind to brood or worry. Why, do you think his death may have had something to do with your break-in?'

'I have no idea,' I admitted. 'But I am staying in the same apartment as him. And it's clear the thief was looking for something in particular.'

Navarro shrugged. 'I wish I could help you.'

'Not to worry.' I stretched my arms above my head and sat back in my chair. 'How are things going here at the university? Has everything quietened down a bit?' There had been some bother back in March when the government had banned a student rally and the youngsters had gone out onto the streets. It had caused a major diplomatic incident, after the police had arrested several dozen students from neighbouring El Salvador.

'Back to normal, I think,' Navarro confirmed. 'The president may not like the new regime in El Salvador but he knows it is not in his interest to upset them.'

'He's barely settling into the role himself.' General Jorge Ubico had come to power in Guatemala at the beginning of February.

'He has a lot of good will on his side. And a popular mandate.'

'So everybody says.' I chuckled. 'But it's not difficult to win an election when nobody's standing against you.'

'He is very popular with the people,' Navarro said. 'They want a strong man in charge, in these difficult times. Someone who can get a grip on the nation's finances and cut down on corruption.'

'He's certainly made a lot of noise about that.' Rumour had it that when the new government had moved in they had found precisely twenty seven dollars in the national kitty. 'It'll be interesting to see if he carries it through. Sounds almost as if you approve of him.'

Navarro smiled slyly. 'Let us say I am reserving judgement. Mr Markham had Ubico down as president, you know, before anyone else had even considered him.'

'Yes. He was quite a bright fellow, by all accounts. I do seem to be living in his shadow rather.'

'I am sure you will make your own mark here.' Navarro smiled again. 'Once you have mastered the language.'

Thursday night was my regular bath night and, after a particularly frustrating day, I always looked forward to a good long soak. Maurice had run the bath for me but had left me to my own devices thereafter. After a hard day, it was pleasant to be able to divest myself of the tight cotton bandages I always wore beneath my shirt. I have never had a particularly full figure but what little I did have needed to be flattened down whenever I was away from the flat.

My valet would help me to wind the bandages into place each morning, seeing far more of me than was strictly decent, but he had never displayed any interest in the physical aspects of my deception. As far as Maurice was concerned, I

14

was a shop window dummy, not a woman pretending to be a man. The peculiarities of my lifestyle were a matter of complete indifference to him and he dealt with the few intractable biological differences with a stoic detachment. He was a true professional and, although I would never have admitted it to his face, I was lucky to have him.

I had barely stripped off and plunged into the steaming hot water when there was a knock at the door of the apartment. I scowled. Who could possibly be calling at this hour? It was almost eight o'clock. I rose up from the bathtub and grabbed a towel, shuffling over to the bathroom door and flicking the lock into place. Whoever it was, Maurice would know to get rid of them. There was no question of anyone catching sight of me here in my native state.

He opened the front door and greeted the visitor. A woman's voice echoed across the entrance hall. It was Emily Bunting, one of my secretaries. What on earth was she doing here? I placed an ear to the bathroom door and tried to hear what the girl was saying. In years gone by, I would get terribly anxious whenever I found myself in a situation like this – and, lord, the number of times it had happened – but now, so long as there was a solid lock on the bathroom door, I was happy to let events play themselves out. No one was expecting to find a naked woman in Henry Buxton's bathroom and no one but Maurice had any business looking.

'I'm awfully sorry to be calling at this late hour,' Miss Bunting burbled away. She had a light chirrup of a voice and a mercifully faint Midlands accent. 'I couldn't talk to Mr Buxton at the office. It's rather a private matter. You say he's in the bath?'

'I'm afraid so, Mademoiselle,' Maurice responded gravely.

'Oh, well, never mind.' She had already moved through into the living room, doubtless without any encouragement from my valet. She was rather a head strong girl, that one. I had had cause to reprimand her before for her over-familiarity. Not with me, of course, but with some of the young men at the legation. Frederick Reeves, the Second Secretary, had his eye

15

on the girl and I didn't want her being led astray.

'I really came to return this,' she said. 'I should never have held onto it for so long.' I couldn't see what the "this" was, unfortunately, and I didn't dare unlock the door to find out. 'But after what happened to you last night, I thought I ought to bring it back. Actually, I'd forgotten all about it until this morning; but I didn't want to mention it in the office, in front of William. Especially not when Mr Richards was about. I thought I had better bring it around here after work.'

'That was very thoughtful, Mademoiselle. I will inform Monsieur Buxton for you.'

'Thank you. How are you settling in here, by the way?'

'Very well, Mademoiselle.'

'It must be very different from home. Will you be joining Mr Buxton this weekend?' I was heading north for a couple of days to visit a coffee plantation, of all things. It was more of a social event than anything official. The Second Secretary had invited me along. He was the only member of the inner sanctum who had shown me any civility since my arrival.

'I will be accompanying him,' Maurice confirmed.

'Freddie – Mr Reeves – has asked me to come too,' Miss Bunting declared, happily. 'So we'll all be there together! It will be nice to get out of the city.'

'Indeed, Mademoiselle.'

I cursed silently. Freddie had not told me he had invited the girl along; and she had kept the fact very quiet too. The man did have an eye for a pretty face, though, so I was not altogether surprised.

There was a brief silence. 'Well, I'll leave you to get on,' she said. And with that, she headed back to the door. 'Good night, Monsieur Sauveterre.'

'Goodnight, Mademoiselle.'

I waited until I heard the front door close and then unlocked the bathroom. I poked my head out tentatively. 'Has she gone?'

Maurice was standing over by the bureau. 'Yes, Monsieur.'

'What on earth did she want?'

16

'To return a key, Monsieur. The Mademoiselle said she had forgotten all about it.'

'Yes, I heard that bit. A key to the flat.' I shook my head, pulling the door fully open. She had taken her time, bringing that back. I had been living here for two months now. 'I can't believe Freddie invited her to the plantation.' I growled. 'I wanted to get away from the office this weekend, not take it with me. And lord knows what William will think.' My other secretary had developed a bit of a crush on his female counterpart. The thought of her going off for the weekend with another man would seriously dampen his spirits. Not that I cared about that, but I knew his work would suffer as a result. The mood in the office on Monday morning would be as black as ice.

Maurice's mind was on more practical matters. 'Do you wish to dress, Monsieur, or will you return to your bath?'

I glanced back into the bathroom. 'Shame to waste it,' I said. 'How long's dinner?'

'Forty-five minutes.'

'Back to the bath then.' I moved across the living room to the drinks table. 'Just pour myself a stiff one, before I get back in.'

'Yes, Monsieur.' Maurice moved past the sofa towards the kitchen.

I grabbed the whisky bottle and poured out a small dram. I confess, I barely heard the key turning in the lock as I filled the glass, but I heard the main door swing open and a voice call out. I swung round in alarm. I was only wearing a towel.

'Only me again!' Miss Bunting declared, moving into the small entrance hall. 'I came all this way to return the key and then I forget to give it to you!' She rounded the corner and stopped dead in her tracks. 'Oh, hello, Mr Buxton. I'm terribly sorry. I didn't realise —' She had taken in my towel without batting an eyelid but then she froze and I looked down in horror. The towel had slipped, exposing my left breast. I reached down hurriedly to pull it up but, in so doing, the other half fell away and I found myself standing on the far side of the living room, all but naked. Miss Bunting's eyes were out on stalks. 'Mr Buxton!' she exclaimed.

'You'd better come in,' I whispered hoarsely.

Chapter Two

A gentle plume of sulphurous cloud rose languidly from the crown of the volcano. The steep slopes dominated the northern edge of the valley, the tree line giving way to the traditional rocky cone, though the volcano itself was dormant. The Finca Weiman plantation was situated in the north central highlands, a few hours trek from Guatemala City. It was a modest enterprise; several dozen acres of forest on the south side of the mountain. The hacienda formed the centrepiece of the estate, a two storey wooden affair in red and white with a tiled roof and an exterior terrace on both floors. Hanging baskets on the upper balcony provided a nice floral garnish and a frothing Italianate fountain on the front lawn completed the display. The sharply angled garden was something of a struggle to traverse but the picturesque setting mitigated somewhat against the effort involved.

We had shut up shop at the office early on Friday afternoon, leaving William Battersby to deal with the last of the paperwork. He was in a sullen mood, observing the small group as we piled into the cramped taxicab, having only just discovered that Miss Bunting would be coming with us. The fact that Frederick Reeves had been the one who had invited her added particular salt to the wound.

Emily Bunting did not help matters with her breezy manner. She was a solid, attractive girl in her early twenties, cheerful and well-turned out, with a fluff of curly blonde hair and a button nose. It was no surprise that William, who had led a rather sheltered life, had fallen under her spell. 'We'll bring you back a sack of coffee,' she teased through the open window, as we settled into the back of the decrepit automobile.

Freddie Reeves was in equally good spirits as we arrived at the train station. He was a slim, fair-haired fellow, some years older than Miss Bunting, with a smooth, inoffensive face and a cheerfully relaxed manner. He looked rather dapper today in a light suit, brogues and a broad-brimmed hat. Freddie had done well for himself in his diplomatic career, reaching the dizzy heights of Second Secretary in his early thirties; not bad for a grammar school boy from a red brick university. 'You'll like Gunther,' he told me, as the train chugged away from the station. 'He's got a well-stocked bar.'

Gunther Weiman was the owner of the plantation we were visiting.

'It was kind of him to invite me,' I said, settling back into my seat, which was barely more than a plank of wood. The railroad was owned by United Fruit – the banana people – and paying passengers were something of an afterthought. 'There's nothing like playing second fiddle to a crate load of bananas!' I muttered, shifting my backside uncomfortably.

A tarantula was hanging from the luggage rack on the far wall. I had made sure to sit well away from it, but Miss Bunting was peering up at the odious creature with undisguised fascination. She had foregone her usual work clothes – the formal white blouse and dark skirt – in favour of a pleasant summer dress, which Freddie was already eyeing up appreciatively.

The railway could only take us so far, however. A horse and cart were waiting at the far station and, from there, it was a bumpy and tortuous ride up into the mountains. The clouds opened as we made our way along the dirt track but we had come prepared and by the time we arrived in the rather muddy village adjacent to the Weiman estate the sky had cleared completely. A few other guests had arrived at the same time as us and were busily surveying the rustic scene; the water pump and low houses of a typically small mountain community.

Our driver hopped down from his cart and gestured across to a parade of small horses which had been prepared for us. We took a moment to stretch out our legs before mounting up. Miss Bunting was already cooing with delight at the thought of a bit of horse riding. I was less enthusiastic. I have ridden my fair share of horses over the years but I have never been much of an equestrian. I struggled up as best I could onto my allotted horse, a surly brown beast who took an instant dislike to me. Freddie gamely helped Miss Bunting into her saddle before grabbing his own mount.

We left Maurice behind in the village to sort out another cart for the luggage while the rest of us trotted off on the final leg of our journey.

The road up to the hacienda was new and only partially dug out. We followed a line of telegraph poles for a mile or so before a second dirt track arced right and up a steep incline. This road, it transpired, was also a work in progress. It stretched for a couple of hundred yards and then stuttered to a halt.

A group of labourers were busily working to level the surface. A white supervisor in a straw hat stood watching idly as the coloured men toiled with their picks and shovels, digging out rocks and shifting the earth. It was back breaking work, in the blistering heat of the late afternoon, and most of the negroes were barefoot and stripped to the waist. Miss Bunting averted her gaze, in an uncharacteristic display of modesty.

If only she had shown me the same courtesy, I thought, when she had burst into my apartment last night. It had been an awkward encounter for both of us.

It was not the first time I had been caught in such a compromising position. My double life had been discovered once before, back in England – albeit in slightly less embarrassing circumstances – and that had led to my speedy departure to the continent and an abrupt change of identity. The possibility of it happening a second time had always seemed rather remote to me. Perhaps I was becoming a little complacent, but with my bandages in place and having a fairly masculine aspect, I doubted anyone would ever simply guess the truth. It had certainly never occurred to me that I might be discovered coming out of my own bathroom dressed in nothing but a towel. Such is life, I suppose.

I felt oddly calm, standing over by the drinks table, adjusting my towel and looking back across the living room at Miss Emily Bunting, whose eyes were still boggling. 'Goodness!' she exclaimed. 'You're...'

'A woman, yes,' I responded briskly. There was no point in dissembling. 'I...have been for some time.'

Miss Bunting blinked and then frowned, her face a

picture postcard of confusion. 'Does Mr Richards know?' she asked at last.

'No. Nobody knows, apart from Maurice and I. And now you.'

Miss Bunting was having some difficulty digesting the fact. 'All this time...' she breathed, incredulously. 'You've been living as a man? *Pretending* to be a man?'

I nodded, gazing at the girl intently, trying to guess how she would react when the idea had properly settled in. Would she be appalled? Horrified?

Her mouth expanded into a broad smile. 'That's absolutely marvellous!' she declared; and, all at once, she began to laugh. That was the last reaction I had been expecting. Now I was the one on the back foot. 'I would never have believed it,' she exclaimed, chuckling heartily, as if it were some silly prank. 'Crumbs, I had you down as a grumpy old stick in the mud. Oh, no offence, Mr....*Mrs* Buxton?'

I pursed my lips. 'Mr Buxton will do.'

She laughed again, her eyes twinkling with pleasure. 'Mr Buxton. I think I could do with a drink, if you don't mind.' She gestured to the glass in my hand and moved forward into the room.

Events were not flowing in quite the way I had anticipated. Not that I had anticipated this at all. 'Yes, well, help yourself,' I said. 'I'd...better put on some clothes. Then perhaps we can talk properly. I was going to have dinner shortly. There'll be enough for two, won't there, Morris?'

'Yes, Monsieur,' the valet confirmed.

I hurried into my bedroom to change and Miss Bunting poured herself a drink.

Supper was a peculiar affair. The girl was full of questions, naturally enough, and I had little choice but to answer some of them. I told her about my father and the bizarre set of circumstances which had led me to become, in effect, a male impersonator. I explained how, as an adult, I had gradually come to accept the situation and outlined the considerable advantages I had found in living my life as a man. There were things a man could do, I told her, even in this day and age, that were denied to a woman. Miss Bunting listened intently, her initial surprise giving way over the course of the soup dish to a burgeoning sense of admiration.

'I wish I had the nerve to do what you're doing,' she told me seriously, setting down her soup spoon as Maurice cleared away the first course. As a modern, emancipated woman, Miss Bunting had some sympathy for my position. 'Men can do whatever they like. They can be diplomats, ambassadors, spies. But women...what can we do? I've got as far as I can go in the civil service already.'

Maurice moved in to serve the main course.

'You haven't done too badly,' I suggested, 'for a young slip of a thing.'

'I suppose so,' she said, eyeing up the meat and two veg. The girl had an admirably healthy appetite. 'Crumbs, my parents would be so shocked, if they knew what I really did.' She giggled. 'Working for the secret service, on the other side of the world.' Miss Bunting, like Freddie Reeves, was a grammar school girl. Her parents were domestic servants, according to her file. 'It's all such a long way from Northampton. I wish I could tell them the truth! Sending coded messages and compiling secret reports for the government.'

'You see?' I said. 'It's not all bad.'

She shook her head sadly. 'But there's nowhere left for me to go, is there? At best, if I work really hard, I might become an office manager, and then only if I give up any hope of marriage and children. That's why I think you've got the right idea, Mr Buxton. Dressing up as a man and beating them at their own game.' She grinned. 'Showing them what a bunch of clots they are, ignoring the potential of half the population.' She picked up her fork. 'You never know, you could be the head of the secret service one day.'

I spluttered in surprise. 'I don't think that's very likely. Even if I had the aptitude, I certainly don't have the inclination.'

'So that's not why you do it?' she asked, peering across at me with curiosity. She popped a small chunk of meat into her mouth.

'Not for the career, no. I'd sooner not work at all. How's the lamb?'

She took a moment to digest it. 'Very nice, thank you. Your valet's a smashing cook.'

I peered down at my plate. 'I'm not sure I would agree with that.' I grunted. 'He's always trying to sneak in lots of herbs and spices. That's the Frogs for you. I keep telling him, plain and simple.'

'Has he been with you long, Monsieur Sauveterre?'

'No, not that long. About eighteen months, I think. To be honest, I'm still breaking him in.'

There was a half smile on Miss Bunting's lips. 'And does he...dress you and everything?' She had noticed Maurice entering my bedroom earlier on, when I was getting changed.

'It's a purely professional relationship,' I assured her hastily. 'I'm just a sack of potatoes, as far as he's concerned. Isn't that right, Morris?'

'Yes, Monsieur,' the valet agreed.

Miss Bunting laughed. 'I believe you,' she said, cutting a potato in half.

'I assure you it is.' I stabbed my fork into a chunk of lamb. 'But, as I've said, it's not about my career. There are just so many advantages to living as a man. One is afforded so much more latitude.'

Her eyes gleamed. 'You mean you can get away with more.'

'Well, quite. Look, Miss Bunting, I dare say this has come as quite a shock to you.'

'I'll say!' She grinned again.

'And I realise it's probably a lot to ask...'

The girl was ahead of me. 'You want me to keep quiet about it.'

'Er...yes, if you would. I would be very grateful. This job, it's a new start for me.' I put down my fork. 'It's not exactly where I wanted to find myself, but if I do all right here, it might lead to better things.' Maybe a posting back in Europe. 'If the truth about my sex were to come out, it would mean the end of my career.'

'Yes, I do see that.' She nodded seriously.

'Oh, I dare say I could start again, if I needed to.' I had a couple of spare passports written out, in case of emergencies. 'But, given the choice, I would much rather not.' I dabbed my lips with a napkin. 'I'm sure you understand.'

'Of course,' Miss Bunting agreed. 'I do understand.' She reached a hand across the table and placed it gently on top of mine. I bit my lip and ignored the over familiarity. 'You can rely on me, Mr Buxton. Or whatever your real name is.'

'Hilary,' I said.

'You can rely on me, Hilary. I won't say a word. All girls together, eh?'

'Er...well, yes.' I coughed. 'Although I think perhaps we should stick to more formal titles in public.'

'Of course, Mr Buxton.' She sat back in her chair and took a moment to reflect upon the situation. 'Crumbs! What would William say if he knew the truth? Or Mr Richards?'

'I sincerely hope they never find out.'

'Well, they won't hear it from me. Oh!' she exclaimed, suddenly remembering the purpose of her visit. 'I must give you back your key. That was why I came round in the first place.' She pulled the item out of her handbag, which was resting on the floor next to the table, and placed the key in front of me. She smiled as I took it, and glanced around the room. The electric lighting flickered briefly. 'It's a lovely flat, isn't it?'

'It's serviceable,' I agreed, preparing a mouthful of potato. 'How long did you live here, before I arrived?'

'Not long. Just two or three weeks.'

'You took over from Miss...Stanton, didn't you?'

'Yes, she moved on to Mexico City.'

'And did you ever meet Giles Markham?'

'No, he died just before I arrived. William cleaned the flat out. Not that there was much here. I should have gone into digs with the other girls, but as the rent on the place had already been paid they said I might as well stop here instead.' Her gaze fixed mournfully on the bedroom behind me. 'It's much nicer than where I am now.'

'Still a little cramped,' I said. Two bedrooms, a living room, a bathroom and a kitchen. It was not what I was used to. 'And the balcony's next to useless. No room out there at all.'

'Is that how he got in? The burglar?' she asked.

'We think so. The window wasn't locked and the blind was only partway down.'

'I wonder what he could have wanted.'

'I really have no idea,' I admitted.

After the meal, we packed the girl off home and I settled myself on the sofa. Maurice cleared away the dessert bowls and moved into the small kitchenette to begin the washing up. 'Do you think she'll keep her word?' I called out to him. My valet had always been a good judge of character.

'I believe so, Monsieur.'

'I hope so, anyway.' I laughed, suddenly remembering the look on Miss Bunting's face when that towel had slipped. It was the sort of moment I had fretted about so many times in my youth, but now that it had actually happened, I felt strangely light-headed. Exhilarated, almost. It was a surprisingly pleasant experience, being able to talk about it all with somebody. 'You're right, though. She seems a good sort. I think she'll keep quiet.'

'Just so long as she does not let it slip out accidentally, Monsieur.'

Maurice always knew how to spoil the mood.

'That's not a happy thought,' I muttered.

Miss Bunting had proved as good as her word, however. The following day, in the office, she had been her usual efficient self. For all her frivolity in private, she was a steady, reliable worker and had a fine eye for detail. It was only when we were leaving for the train station that that mischievous gleam had returned to her eyes.

Ahead of us, the path was scarcely more than a mud track. The labourers had moved to the side of the road to let the horses through and as soon as we had passed them by, the overseer – an overweight fellow in a casual shirt – had bellowed at them to resume their labour.

The last half mile was an awkward uphill climb, but

26

finally the hacienda and its associated buildings lurched into view, with the volcano bubbling benignly above them. A stable yard off to the right sat parallel to the front lawn, and half a dozen locals arrived to take charge of the horses.

I swung my leg over the top and thumped down onto the gravel with some relief. My thighs were aching badly. It was uncomfortable enough riding on a flat road but the bumps and judders of an uphill trek had left my legs feeling stretched to exhaustion. I would probably have to hobble the last few yards up to the hacienda.

Freddie Reeves handed the reins of his horse to one of the Indians. 'What do you think?' he asked me, gesturing to the estate.

The farm – or "finca" to use the correct term – was spread out over quite a large area. The hacienda was the focal point, but there were buildings all over the place; processing plants, workers' accommodation, administrative shacks. The finca was a small village in its own right. And, all around us, I could see huge trees stretching up the mountainside and away to the east. The waning sun bathed the valley in a warm glow, reinforcing the impression of a rural idyll. I have never been much of a country person, but after several weeks in the fetid sewer of Guatamala City, it was a joy to breathe some clean air. 'Looks very promising,' I said.

'You'll love it,' Freddie assured me, with a grin. The man had an absurdly cheerful demeanour. If the two of us had met back in England, I doubted we would have become friends, but my standards had slipped somewhat of late. Freddie was the only member of the inner sanctum who had been remotely friendly towards me. The rest of the diplomats reserved their charm – what little they had – for the dignitaries. The worst excesses of Freddie's London accent had been beaten out of him by some thoughtful teacher and it was only the occasional dropped "aitch" which betrayed his working class origins. It was a tribute to his skill and diligence that he had managed to rise to the position of Second Secretary at such a young age, though it seemed unlikely that he would progress much further.

'Gunther's a lovely bloke,' he told me again. 'You'll

like him. He's an Anglophile. He can be a bit reserved but he makes a fine host.'

Freddie had promised me a weekend of gambling and drinking, but the guests who were dusting themselves down in the stable yard did not suit that picture at all. There were at least two married couples among them.

'You did say there would be a few games?'

'Don't worry, Henry. There's going to be lots of gambling.' He grinned again. 'You'll have plenty of opportunities to lose your shirt. Oh, here's Steven.' A wiry, middle-aged man had descended the steps from the front terrace. 'He's the estate manager,' Freddie whispered, leaning in. 'Steven Catesby. An Englishman. You remember I told you about him?'

'The...cousin?'

'That's right. On the wife's side.' The owner of the Finca Weiman estate was a German, but his wife was from God's own country.

'Welcome to the farm!' Steven Catesby declared. He was a gaunt looking fellow with rugged black hair and a small moustache. His voice sounded a little strained but he was not unfriendly. 'Nice to see you again,' he said, greeting Freddie and some of the other guests.

The Second Secretary quickly introduced Miss Bunting and I.

'A pleasure to meet you,' Catesby said. 'Glad you could come. Gunther's been held up for a few minutes but he'll be along shortly. In the meantime, I'll take you up to the house. We've got some drinks laid on and then you can settle in.' He glanced across at the horses, which were now being led away. 'Don't worry about the luggage. The boys will bring it up to the house for you.'

'How many people do you have in the office now?' Catesby enquired, as we settled ourselves at the metal tables in the of the patio. The courtyard was completely enclosed, hree internal walls and a couple of archways leading through from the front porch. It was open to the air above, however, and the tiled floor was tilted slightly, so that any rain water would run off to the sides. A balcony encircled the square on three sides and a couple of *"mestizos"* – people of mixed race – were slogging up the stairs to deposit our luggage in the various bedrooms. Maurice, who had arrived shortly after us with the baggage train, had been whisked off out back to sort out his own accommodation for the night. A small cottage a little way from the hacienda served as a bed for the domestic servants.

A large pot of steaming coffee had been produced as soon as we had arrived inside the house. I have to confess, I have never much liked coffee – it is a bitter, depressing drink with none of the flavour or subtlety of honest to goodness tea – but having arrived at a plantation dedicated to its production I could hardly turn my nose up. It would be like refusing a plate of bacon and eggs at a pig farm. The cups were mercifully small, but the coffee was served black. Miss Bunting, who was perhaps a little less socially astute than the rest of us, immediately asked for a touch of milk. The pause that followed would have downed a heavyweight boxer; but the maid recovered her composure and scurried off to the kitchen to find some cream. I stuck with the black stuff, which tasted absolutely vile.

'Just the three of us, as ever,' I replied, in answer to Mr Catesby's question. 'Miss Bunting, myself and a Mr Battersby.' I took another sip of the devil's brew and tried not to grimace.

'The three "B"s,' Freddie pointed out mischievously.

'Yes. The rest of the legation have already started referring to us as "The B Team".' I set down my coffee cup and smiled tightly. 'That's Foreign Office humour for you. Still, it has its advantages, being away from the main building.'

'They don't have to be quite so diplomatic.' Freddie laughed.

'That's the main advantage,' I agreed. 'We don't have to deal with the other legations or any of the local dignitaries, thank goodness.'

'So you haven't met General Ubico then?' Catesby

29

asked.

'The president? No, I haven't had the pleasure. I've heard a lot about him, though. What is he like?'

'I've only met him the once,' Catesby admitted. 'At a trade fair. He gave a short speech. He seemed a little abrupt, but very driven.'

'I've heard he's got a bit of a Napoleon complex.'

Catesby shrugged. 'He admires strong leaders. And he does have quite a commanding presence. With the poor economic conditions at the moment, he's probably what this country needs. Did you see the new roads being built on your way up here?'

'I could hardly miss them. That's his doing, is it?'

'In part. It's a first step, anyway. This country badly needs infrastructure. Ubico understands that. He doesn't have the resources to invest, but he is helping out where he can. He provides the expertise and the workers provide the labour.'

'Yes, we saw a bunch of them hacking away at it on the way up.'

'Gunther applied to have an extra track dug out between the road and our estate. It's a bit tricky getting motor vehicles up here as things stand. We provide the labour, of course.'

'You pay their wages?'

Catesby shook his head. 'We couldn't afford to just at the moment. No, they do the work in lieu of tax. It keeps them busy until the picking season begins next month.'

'Do you have many black workers?' Miss Bunting enquired, placing her coffee cup back down on the table.

'A fair number. We have some living on the estate. Jamaicans mostly. The rest are Indians and *mestizos*. We have to provide separate accommodation for them. The Indians don't like working with *ladinos*.' "Ladino" was the local term for anyone who wasn't an Indian.

'How many workers do you have?' Miss Bunting asked.

'It varies, depending on the season. At the moment, about – oh, here's Gunther.' Catesby pushed back his chair and rose to his feet.

Gunther Weiman was making his way towards us

30

through an archway at the rear of the courtyard. He was a striking figure in his mid fifties, tall and white haired with a neatly trimmed beard. His face was thin but his eyes were alert. He smiled warmly as he arrived at the tables. 'Good evening everyone!' he said, in a light, welcoming voice. 'Hello, George. Arthur. And Mr Reeves, always a pleasure.' His accent was mild and his grasp of English excellent. The advantages of being married to an Englishwoman, I supposed. Mr Catesby made the introductions.

'A pleasure to meet you,' I said, gripping the German's hand firmly. 'It was kind of you to invite us. This is Miss Bunting, one of my clerks.' Miss Bunting and I were the only newcomers. Everyone else seemed to know each other already.

'An enchanting young woman,' Mr Weiman observed. 'My wife Susan is just seeing to the supper. She will be along shortly.' He shifted his gaze to me. 'So you must be the new passport control officer?' He regarded me shrewdly.

'For my sins,' I said. From his amused expression, I gathered Mr Weiman knew rather more about my job than perhaps he should. I hoped to goodness Freddie had not been speaking out of turn. 'I understand you knew my predecessor, Mr Markham?'

The German's face fell. 'Giles, yes. I was sad to hear about his death. He seemed in such good spirits, when I last saw him.'

'When was that?' I enquired.

'At the end of March, I believe. I am sure Freddie must have told you. He came down here, the weekend before he died.'

'Ah, yes,' I said, barely managing to mask my surprise. Freddie had told me no such thing.

Chapter Three

The wooden fans rotated mechanically above the long dining table. The hum of the generator was louder here than in the courtyard and the electric light bulbs flickered occasionally as the home made power supply ebbed and flowed. The dining hall was at the rear of the hacienda. Wide archways led out onto the back terrace and down into the garden, where the generator was situated in its own small outhouse. Windows peppered the length of the room on two sides, but at this hour everything outside the main building was shrouded in darkness. Inside, however, the room was alive with conversation.

A house boy, Moses, was ladling soup from a fine silver bowl. He was a short, rather spindly lad of about fourteen, in a pristine white shirt, high waisted trousers and a black bow tie. A maid, slightly older and also coloured, was cutting up several loaves of fresh bread to go with the soup. She wore a plain brown dress and had her hair neatly tied back away from her face.

I was sitting in the middle of the table, facing the back windows, and was doing my best to make polite conversation with an alarming variety of house guests. A veritable League of Nations had been gathered for supper: German, Italian, American, even a couple of Guatemalans. Since leaving England, I had had to get used to consorting with people of all ranks but this was hitting a new low. A coffee farmer, an engineer, a fruit seller and a bank manager, not to mention several steely wives of varying provenance. The seating had been arranged in the traditional fashion, with no two men sitting next to each other, meaning I had been squeezed between my own Miss Bunting on the one side, in a pretty floral dress, and the banker's wife on the other. She at least was English, a severe looking woman in her mid forties with an aristocratic nose and an abrupt side-parting. Her tongue was rather sharp, however, and her voice cut across the babble of conversation with practised ease.

I was in a foul mood as I took my first sip of the broth.

The weekend was not working out the way I had imagined it at all. Freddie Reeves had promised me a relaxed couple of days away from the city, gambling and drinking with the boys. I had not expected to be part of a full blown dinner party and, much as I missed the country weekends of old England, I had no desire to spend two consecutive evenings making polite conversation with the wives of various local bigwigs. Unfortunately, it appeared, I was not to be given the choice.

That was not the only reason for my ill humour, however. It was this whole business with Giles Markham.

I had had a few words with Freddie about that before we had descended for supper. His bedroom was next door to mine, on the west side of the house. I had been given a front facing room, with Freddie in the middle and Miss Bunting towards the rear on the same landing. I wasn't sure of the wisdom of placing those two quite so close together but the larger bedrooms on the east side had been reserved for the married couples. Freddie had left his door open a crack and, once Maurice had helped me into my best bib and tucker, I had knocked briefly and bustled into his room.

Freddie regarded my entrance with some surprise. He was already in his shirt sleeves but had not yet fastened his cuffs into place. The man was a meticulous dresser – he had a certain vanity, despite his lowly origins – but he did like to take his time about it. 'Everything all right, Henry?' he asked as I stepped through the door.

'No, everything is not all right,' I hissed, keeping my voice low. 'What the devil do you think you're playing at, Freddie? You never told me Giles Markham came here the weekend before he died.'

'Didn't I?' His eyes twinkled. 'I thought I'd mentioned it.'

'You know damned well you didn't.' I closed the door behind me. 'What's going on Freddie? Why did you bring me here? It wasn't just to play cards, was it?'

Freddie sat down quietly on the bed. 'No, it wasn't,' he admitted. He frowned and took a moment to gather his thoughts. 'The thing is, Henry, I was down here that last

33

weekend. I don't know what it was, but there was a strange atmosphere. Oh, everyone was very civil. We played games and we drank. Had a good laugh. But something wasn't right. And then, the next day, Giles shot himself.'

I moved across the room to the bed. I could not pretend I liked what I was hearing. 'You think there was something suspicious about his death? The circumstances of it, I mean?'

Freddie shook his head. 'No, not at all. He took his own life. There's no doubt about that. He shot himself at point blank range. I just haven't the faintest idea why. I mean, all this talk of gambling debts. We did gamble that weekend, but only for pin money. He can't have lost more than ten dollars the whole weekend.'

'He must have had debts of some sort,' I pointed out, sitting myself down on the bed next to him. 'He'd been creaming cash from the visa account for months.'

Freddie grimaced. 'Yes, I know.'

'The accounts were almost two thousand pounds adrift. I've seen the books.'

'But isn't some of that money meant to be diverted?' He scratched his chin. 'I mean, to finance your...extra curricular activities?'

I scowled. 'You're not supposed to know about that.' He was right, though. A sizeable chunk of the visa receipts was routinely appropriated by British Intelligence and used to fund a small network of spies across Central America. I was only just beginning to get to grips with that side of things, but Freddie – as a bona fide diplomat – was not meant to know anything about it.

He grinned mischievously.

'But I assure you, everything of that nature is properly accounted for.' We were, however, straying from the point. 'So what exactly did you hope to achieve by inviting me here this weekend? You weren't just being friendly, were you?'

'Oh, that too. But no, I did have an ulterior motive. Look, Henry. I'm sorry if I invited you here under false pretences. The thing of it is, I really liked Giles. He was a good bloke.' Freddie sighed, glancing down at his neck tie, which was resting on the blanket between us. He stood up, took hold of it and moved across to the bedside mirror. 'I had to clean out his flat after he died, you know. There was nothing there. No sense of a life, after three years out here.'

'In our profession, it doesn't do to put down roots.'

'No. But I just thought, maybe if you had a nose around, well...' He regarded me hopefully in the mirror. 'You might be able to work out what happened to him. See if there was anything amiss.'

My eyes narrowed. 'Why me?'

'Well, after all...' He chuckled quietly, adjusting his tie. 'You did sort out that business on the *Richthofen* earlier this year.'

I rolled my eyes. 'You're not supposed to know about that either.' Maurice and I had crossed the Atlantic from Spain on a Zeppelin airship. En route, my superiors had charged me with the task of recovering some important documents for Scotland Yard; but things had quickly got out of hand and several people had died. It had been in all the papers when we had arrived in New York. Thankfully, I had been travelling under an assumed name. 'What is the point of changing your identity if everybody still knows who you are?'

Freddie grinned. 'You don't have to worry. It's only the top people at the legation who know.'

I raised an eyebrow. 'Oh, only the *top* people?'

'Well, and me too.' He laughed, pulling back from the mirror. 'But we were told to expect a Mr Reginald Bland as our new passport control officer.' That was the name I had been travelling under on the Zeppelin. 'But then you turned up, Mr Henry Buxton. And of course the minister received a report. Nothing confidential. Just the broad strokes of the affair. But from what I hear, it was thanks to you the whole business was sorted out.'

'Don't believe everything people tell you.' I snorted. 'It was a fiasco from start to finish. I was lucky to get out of it alive.'

'But you do have experience as...' He smiled again. 'Well, for want of a better word, as a detective.'

35

That was too much. 'I am *not* a detective!' I exclaimed, jumping angrily to my feet. 'For goodness sake, I don't know one end of a magnifying glass from the other. And this is meant to be my weekend off. The last thing I want to do is get involved in any skulduggery. I've had my fill of that for one life time, thank you very much.'

'But you are...'

'I'm not a policeman,' I insisted. 'I'm just a passport control officer.'

'And a spy!'

'Keep your voice down, for God's sake. Yes, I am a spy. But it's not like I'm any kind of secret agent. Not like you see in the pictures. I'm an administrator. You know that. It's not my job to get my hands dirty. I have other people to do that for me.'

'What, like William Battersby?' Freddie smirked.

'No, outside the office. People you know nothing about. And shouldn't know about.'

'But you must be curious,' he insisted, grabbing hold of the cuff links on the bedside table. 'About what happened to Giles? Why someone would break into his flat after all this time?'

I moved back to the door. 'You know what curiosity did to the cat, Freddie. In any case, you invited me here before any of that happened.'

'I know.' The matter had clearly been stewing in his mind for some time. 'But this is the first chance I've had to get down here since...well, since Giles popped his clogs. It may sound crazy, but I'm convinced this place has got something to do with his death.'

'Why would you think that?'

He shrugged. 'I don't know. It's just a feeling.'

'Look, Freddie.' I sighed. 'I appreciate you want to find out the truth. Giles was a friend of yours. It's all very admirable. But believe me, I am the *last* person you want to get involved in any of this.' If past experience was anything to go by, I would only make the situation a whole lot worse. 'The best thing you can do is forget all about it. If something dreadful is going on here, we'll find out all about it in the fullness of time. And if *nothing* is happening, then we have nothing to concern ourselves with. Now I suggest we go downstairs and get something to eat. And I don't want to hear another bloody word about Mr Giles Markham this whole weekend. Is that clear?'

Frederick Reeves nodded glumly. He clipped the last cuff link into place.

We joined the other house guests at the dinner table. Freddie was seated near the head of the table, next to Mrs Weiman. I was two seats down, on the other side of Mrs Talbot, the banker's wife. Her husband George was sitting directly opposite me, leaving me with little choice but to converse with the two of them. Mr Talbot was a smart, grey haired man in his late fifties, plump faced and sober in manner. He was a director at the Anglo-South American, the biggest bank in the region. He wore a pair of rounded spectacles and had a slow, ponderous voice.

'Of course, being a British banker in this part of the world makes one *persona non grata*,' he declared, stuffily. 'The locals are happy enough to sign on the dotted line and take the money, but when it comes to repaying the loan...' He lifted his soup spoon. 'They resent every shilling.'

'It's the same the world over, I imagine,' I responded politely. Bankers and moneylenders were rarely popular.

'Perhaps. But it is, I am afraid to say, especially true in this part of the world. The people here prefer to have American corporations buying up their land and building their ports and railways for them.' Like United Fruit, I supposed. 'But it's debatable if that is in their long term interests.'

'Dear, you shouldn't talk business over the dinner table,' Jane Talbot admonished her husband, in a clipped, no-nonsense tone. She was the severe looking woman with the nose and the side parting. 'You'll be in danger of boring Mr Buxton.' In that, she was not far wrong.

'How long have you lived in Guatemala?' I asked her.

'About six years, I believe.'

'In the city?' She nodded. I tore off a piece of bread

37

from the communal plate and dipped it in the soup. 'How do you find it?'

Mrs Talbot considered before replying. 'I've got used to it now. It did take us some time to acclimatize.'

'Jane had never been out of England before,' her husband explained.

'There are so many different types of people here,' she observed distastefully. 'Different racial groups, different stratas of society. It can be rather confusing.'

'Lord, yes,' I agreed. 'Difficult to get a handle on where everyone fits in.'

'It's really very simple,' a brash American voice cut in. This was Arthur Montana, an executive from United Fruit. He was a hefty, determined looking fellow in his early forties. He had a rugged face and heavily cropped brown hair which only partially disguised a badly receding hairline. 'It's a basic pyramid structure,' he declared forcefully. 'You've got the negroes in one corner at the bottom, with the Indians on the other side. Then there are the half-breeds, the *mestizos*. They're on the next level up. And above them are the Hispanics, who are nominally in charge.' That notion seemed to amuse him somewhat. 'Although the West Indian negroes often look down on them, for some reason. And then, of course, at the top of the heap you have the whites, the North Americans and the Western Europeans.' His voice boomed across the table and brooked no contradiction.

Mrs Talbot was not in the least intimidated. 'All rather confusing,' she repeated, 'but one does because accustomed to it eventually.'

The mention of Hispanics prompted George Talbot to gesture to the far end of the table. 'Have you met our engineer, Señor Gonzalez?' he asked me, adjusting his spectacles. The little Guatemalan was sitting quietly out of sight a few chairs to my right. 'He's overseeing the road building. Gunther invited him along this evening, as a thank you for all his hard work.' Not the sort of person, I gathered, who would normally receive an invitation to a house party. Talbot turned to his right. 'Oh, and this is his wife, of course, Consuela Gonzalez.'

Mrs Gonzales was a short but striking *mestizo* woman – half Indian, half Hispanic at a guess – with dark penetrating eyes and a slightly sad air about her, for all her comparative youth. She was squeezed uncomfortably between George Talbot on the one side and the American gentleman on the other. She was wearing the same light brown dress she had sported on her arrival that afternoon.

'Yes, we met earlier on,' I said, meeting her eyes with a smile. 'I hope you're enjoying the soup.' I looked down at the pallid broth, which the rough bread was doing nothing to improve. It was thin and reedy with just a few chunks of meat bobbing about below the surface. Hardly the most appetising of starters.

Consuela Gonzales smiled back at me. 'Very much,' she said.

Arthur Montana, who was sitting to her right, had studiously ignored the native woman while the opening course was being served. I could understand his discomfort – he was probably not used to socializing with *mestizos* – but that was no excuse for being rude. One has to be polite on these occasions.

'Do you live near here?' I asked the woman.

'Yes, in the next town.' Mrs Gonzales had a light but surprisingly confident voice. 'My husband works for the Ministry of Agriculture.'

'In the Department of Roads,' the man himself put in.

'Sounds like a responsible job,' I said, dipping another chunk of bread into the soup. On the far side of the table, the house boy Moses was starting to clear away a few of the bowls.

'Not yet, boy!' Arthur Montana snapped.

The lad flinched, as if he had been slapped, and mumbled a quick apology.

Candles and oil lamps were the order of the day as the evening progressed. 'We always switch off the generator at ten o'clock,' Gunther Weiman explained, 'to save fuel in the evenings.' The white haired German smiled warmly. 'And also to facilitate a good night's sleep for those wishing to retire early.' The menfolk had moved out into the courtyard for the brandy and cigars – a welcome relief after the inevitable round of coffee which had followed dessert – while the women congregated in the living room on the east side of the house. To my delight, a deck of cards had been produced and we were soon engrossed in a pleasantly vicious game of pontoon.

'You want to keep an eye on Steven,' Freddie laughed, when Mr Catesby drew the highest card and got the plum job of banker. 'One of his ancestors tried to blow up the Houses of Parliament.'

'I thought that was Guy Fawkes,' I said, as Catesby dealt out the opening hand. I picked up my first two cards and grimaced.

'Him too.' Freddie glanced down at his hand. 'Stick,' he said.

I threw in a small coin. 'Twist. So what brought you to this part of the world, Mr Catesby?'

Steven Catesby was a thin-faced fellow with solid blue eyes and a mop of curly black hair. An unsuccessful moustache hovered above a rather thin mouth but he was well turned out, in a casual evening suit, and had a small flower in his lapel. 'I was born in Cuba,' he said. 'My uncle – Susan's father – owned a sugar plantation there.' He flipped me the queen of spades.

I growled and threw down my cards. 'Bust.'

'After university I got a job working on a banana plantation in Costa Rica, for United Fruit. My wife sadly died a couple of years ago. Malaria. It's endemic there.'

'I'm very sorry,' I said.

'I'll stick,' Arthur Montana declared.

'After that, I needed to get away. Susan and I grew up together, in Havana.' He looked across to the real-life banker.

'Stick,' George Talbot said.

'She suggested I come here and help Gunther run the farm.'

'Twist, please,' Gunther Weiman said. Steven dealt him a card.

'He's often away on business. I thought I'd be here for six months.'

40

'And stick.'

Catesby turned up his own cards – a five and a seven – and dealt himself an eight of clubs. The lucky sod. 'Play twenty-ones,' he declared. 'And here I am, two years later.'

'Nice to be out of the swamp, I shouldn't wonder,' I said.

The other men threw in their cards and Catesby collected his winnings.

'There are noticeably fewer insects at this altitude,' George Talbot agreed. The plump-faced banker sat back in his chair and took a sip of brandy. 'Far less disease as well.'

'Mind you, the blacks are immune to that sort of thing,' Arthur Montana declared, puffing on his cigar.

Catesby shuffled the pack and prepared to deal out the next hand.

'That's the only reason anyone employs them,' Montana added. The American had some experience in this area, I gathered. As an executive for United Fruit, labour relations would be part of his remit. I doubted, however, that he would be a particularly enlightened employer.

'They do have their fair share of illness,' Catesby said, dealing out the second set of cards. 'But they're good workers. Easier to motivate than the indigenous people.'

'That's true,' Montana agreed, tapping out the end of his cigar in an ashtray and picking up the new hand. 'We could do with importing a few more of them. The Indians are useless. They're far too lazy.'

'Twist,' said Freddie, throwing in a coin.

'You prefer the blacks?' I asked. That was a surprise, given his unflattering comments about them at supper. Montana had made it quite clear that he considered negroes to be inherently inferior to anyone of European extraction. It was not a point of view I shared – given a decent education, I supposed a black man would acquit himself as well as anybody else – but it was a common enough belief. I picked up a king and a five.

Catesby tossed out a card to Freddie.

'Bust.'

'They do have several advantages,' Montana admitted.

41

'Unfortunately, the law dictates that seventy-five per cent of all workers have to be native Guatemalans. It's crazy.'

'Er...twist,' I said, throwing in a coin.

'And even United Fruit has to pay lip service to that.'

I scowled as Catesby dealt me out an eight of hearts. I threw down my cards in disgust. 'Bust. Is there much tension, between the negroes and the Indians?'

Arthur Montana grunted. 'Always. I'll stick. The blacks are better workers and they get paid more for it. But it's not all plain sailing. The West Indian blacks, the Jamaicans.' He pursed his lips. 'They don't pay us the proper respect.' By "us", I gathered, he meant white people.

'I'll stick,' George Talbot declared.

'Negroes are built for hard labour. That's why they make such good boxers. But they need to be taught their place; to show respect for their betters.'

'Twist,' said Gunther Weiman. Catesby tossed him a card. The nine of clubs. The German smiled and abandoned his hand. 'Bust.'

'And the Indians,' I said. 'You don't rate them at all?'

The American snorted again.

'They do their fair share of the work,' Catesby put in diplomatically, as he turned up his own cards. A ten and a seven. 'Play eighteens.'

Only George Talbot had a better hand.

'They're...Mayans aren't they?' I enquired.

'That's right,' Catesby said, as he collected his winnings and paid out to Mr Talbot.

I scratched my chin. 'Aren't they the fellows who built the pyramids?'

'That's them.' Catesby took a moment to gather up the cards.

'Have you had a chance to visit the pyramids yet?' Talbot asked me, taking a quick sip of brandy.

'No, I haven't. Rather difficult to get to, so I've heard. But I've seen the photographs. Remarkable buildings.'

'Indeed,' the banker agreed.

'It's always struck me as a bit strange,' Freddie said. 'I

mean, that they had wherewithal to build these enormous great buildings and now they're reduced to manual labour.'

'It was probably manual labour that allowed the pyramids to be constructed in the first place,' Talbot pointed out. 'But yes, they do seem to have regressed rather.'

'Godless heathens,' Montana muttered, stubbing out his cigar. 'Too stupid to build anything on their own. George is right. It was slave labour that built the pyramids. And, you know what?' His eyes gleamed with pride. 'It was our people at United Fruit who put them back together again.'

'Really?' I said. That was interesting.

Steven Catesby smiled slyly. 'As a propaganda exercise.'

The other man shrugged. 'There's nothing wrong in that.'

'Using local labour, I presume?'

'It was a collaboration,' Montana admitted. 'That's what I'm saying. These natives, they have the muscle, but they lack direction. They need a firm hand, from people like us. People who know how to get things done.'

'Firm but fair,' Catesby agreed. 'Like with these new roads. We'll all benefit from that. If they're ever completed.' He smiled again. 'It's early days, of course, and there's no real money about. We're lucky to have Señor Gonzales to help us.'

The engineer had retired to bed shortly after supper, which was probably just as well. I doubted he would have had the wherewithal to join us at the card table, even with the small amounts we were gambling. I was fortunate, as a fellow government employee, in having a couple of annuities to help me out in addition to my regular wage. It wasn't what I was used to, of course, but it meant at least that I could afford to employ a valet and enjoy a few rounds of cards of an evening without fear of bankrupting myself.

'Did you enjoy the coffee at dinner?' Gunther Weiman asked, changing the subject.

'It was superb,' Freddie declared. 'I've said it before, Gunther, and I'll say it again: you've got a marvellous place here.'

43

Catesby shuffled the pack.

'It'll be nice to have a proper wander around tomorrow,' he added. 'Out into the fields. It was raining too much the last time I was here.'

The German smiled. 'I have organised a tour for all of you tomorrow morning,' he explained, for my benefit. 'At nine thirty. It may be a little taxing so I suggest a hearty breakfast before you leave.'

I tried hard not to grimace. The thought of trekking up and down a mountainside first thing in the morning was not in the least bit appealing. I would probably give it a miss if I could. I had already done my duty as a guest, drinking their foul coffee.

'It'll be good exercise,' Arthur Montana said. 'It's one hell of an estate. I've seen it a dozen times but I never grow tired of it.'

Catesby was about to deal out the next hand but he held off as the ladies emerged from the living room. Arthur Montana's wife, an attractive Italian woman called Anita, was laughing loudly at something Emily Bunting had said to her. The men pulled themselves up from their chairs as the women moved out into the courtyard. A few pleasantries were exchanged and then they made their way to the back stairs.

Susan Weiman – our hostess – was the last to leave. 'I hope you've all had an enjoyable evening,' she said. Mrs Weiman was an amiable woman in her early forties with dark, shoulder length hair, pale skin and wide brown eyes. 'Thank you so much for coming. I will see you all in the morning.' We replied effusively in kind. 'Don't stay up too late, Gunther,' she added.

We watched in silence as the group made their way upstairs and then around the upper corridors to the various bedrooms on the first floor.

'I could do with another drink,' Montana said. 'Where is that boy of yours?'

Weiman glanced at his wristwatch. It was gone eleven now. 'He'll have gone to bed, I am afraid. But the drinks are on the table there. Steven, would you mind?'

Catesby rose smoothly to his feet. One of the patio tables had been commandeered as a makeshift bar for the evening. 'Any other takers?' he enquired. The Englishman did not have to ask twice.

I pulled myself up from the table, keen to take advantage of the brief pause in the game. 'Excuse me for a minute.' My stomach was still feeling the after-effects of that soup. 'Won't be two ticks.'

'You know where it is?' Catesby asked.

'Yes, by the front stairs.' I headed quickly through the arches and under the covered way, out into the hallway on the far side. A set of steps ran up from here to the first floor. The bathroom was just behind them. I grabbed an oil lamp from the small table outside and quickly nipped into the WC.

There was no lock on the inside of the door, which was rather worrying, but the flickering lamplight was enough to warn people that the room was occupied. I checked the lavatory bowl for insects and then swiftly completed my ablutions. It was only when I emerged from the closet that I noticed a figure moving about in the gloom of the corridor. 'Who's that?' I called.

It was Moses, the house boy. 'Just me, mister,' he said.

I grunted. 'You shouldn't go creeping about like that.' I had thought he had gone to bed. 'You could give someone a heart attack.'

'Sorry, mister.' There was a small slip of paper in his hand. 'I have a note for you.'

'A note, for me? Who is it from?'

'A friend, mister.' He proffered the piece of paper.

A friend? What the devil was he talking about? I placed the oil lamp down on the table and took hold of the note. Moses scurried away before I had the chance to unfold it. I crouched down next to the lamp to get some decent light. There wasn't much to read there, just an illiterate scrawl in heavy capital letters.

It said: "DO NOT TRUST MR KATEBY. I NOW ABOWT MR MARKUM. COME TO DRY STORR AT 11 TOMORRO MORNING."

'Good lord,' I breathed.

Chapter Four

The first thing I was aware of was a loud clatter, as the wooden shutters were pulled back from the window. The bedroom was south facing but the morning had progressed sufficiently that a shaft of sunlight was cutting across the top of the bed, slapping me hard across the face like an irate nanny. I groaned and turned my head into the pillow. My head was throbbing and my mouth felt as dry as the Peruvian Altiplano. 'Good morning, Monsieur,' Maurice declared, stepping back from the window and moving across to the side of the bed to pour me a glass of water.

'Is it?' I mumbled. I heard the slosh of liquid and managed to pry open a crusted eyelid. As far as I could recall, I had gone to bed at two or three in the morning, after several stiff brandies. In my younger days, it would have been six am and a couple of dozen, but age was catching up with me. 'What time is it?' I asked.

'Ten o'clock, Monsieur.'

I nodded and took the water. 'So I've missed the tour then?'

'Yes, Monsieur.' That was a relief. 'I understood from Monsieur Reeves that you did not wish to join this morning's expedition.'

I downed the water in one. 'No, I didn't.' As if anyone in their right mind would want to trek through a load of coffee fields first thing in the morning. I handed the glass back to Maurice and he poured out another. I was tempted to ask for a whisky – hair of the dog and all that – but I knew I would need a clear head this morning. I drained the second glass and pulled myself up. I was still wearing my shirt sleeves from the night before. I had barely managed to get my jacket off before I had crashed into bed.

Maurice secured the door and closed the blinds, then came across to unfasten my shirt. I slipped out of it gratefully. The valet unwound my bandages, which were beginning to chafe, and then secured a fresh set. I took a moment to wash my face in a bowl, while Maurice laid out my trousers and a clean shirt. The whole ritual was completed in blissful silence. This was one morning when my man's lack of conversational initiative was deeply appreciated. I had managed to avoid a full-blown hangover but I was still feeling a little delicate. Maurice bent down and banged out my shoes on the wooden floor. I did not complain. It was as well to make sure no scorpions or other creepy crawlies had taken up residence during the night. I laced up the shoes as he pulled back the blinds a second time, then stood up and walked over to the chair where I had slung my jacket the night before. I dug inside for the note and handed it across. 'What do you make of this?'

The valet stared down at the scrawled message, his battered face completely unreadable. 'Most peculiar, Monsieur. Do you know who sent it?'

'Haven't the foggiest. It was given to me by the house boy, Moses. Said it was from "a friend". Judging by the spelling, it must be one of the natives.'

Maurice refrained from comment.

It was the reference to Mr Catesby that troubled me the most. Do not trust him, it said. 'You've been back stairs. What's the atmosphere like?'

'Efficient, Monsieur. Perhaps a little strained.'

'Three servants, aren't there? In the house, I mean.'

'Yes, Monsieur. Moses, Isabel and the housekeeper, Greta.'

'Ah yes. She's a Kraut, isn't she?'

'Yes, Monsieur. Of German descent.'

I shuddered. 'That explains the soup. But nothing odd going on, that you're aware of?'

'No, Monsieur.'

'Oh well, just a thought. How is your accommodation, by the way?' Maurice had been berthed with the other servants in a small cottage a little way off from the main house.

'Satisfactory, Monsieur.'

I chuckled. 'Lord, as bad as that, eh?' My valet was never one to complain but his disapproval was evident. 'Well, it's only for a couple of days. You'll just have to put up with it.'

'Yes, Monsieur.' He handed me back the note and I folded it up, slipping it inside my waistcoat pocket. 'Will you go to the dry store at 11 o'clock?'

I nodded. 'I don't see why not. It can't do any harm. Always assuming I can work out where it is. But first things first. A bit of breakfast, I think.'

There were three things I would have preferred to avoid at the breakfast table. The first, inevitably, was the coffee, which festered in a large silver pot at one end of the table. The second was a radiogram in the corner, which was blaring out some light orchestral music. The third was George Talbot, the dreary but fastidious banker. He was alone at the table, examining a copy of El Imparcial, a local rag. He nodded a greeting as I pulled up a chair and gestured to the coffee pot.

'No, thank you,' I said, taking my seat opposite him. 'Don't tell our hosts, but I'm much more of a tea drinker.'

'I do understand,' Talbot replied, dabbing his lips with a napkin. 'I've grown accustomed to the coffee but I can't pretend I enjoy it.'

'Nothing beats a good, honest cuppa,' I declared. 'Well, maybe a shot of whisky, but it's a bit early for that.' It was a bit early, too, for the radiogram. The music was not doing my head any favours.

Talbot folded up his newspaper. He was smartly dressed, even at the breakfast table, and his grey hair and rounded spectacles conveyed an image of calm authority. 'You will have to forgive the music. It was on when I came in.' He discarded the newspaper and glanced at his wristwatch. 'Ordinarily, I would have switched it off, but there's a news broadcast due in a few minutes which I would like to hear. If you have no objections, Mr Buxton?"

'Be my guest.' I grabbed a slice of toast. Talbot was just finishing up his own breakfast. His glass had the dregs of some fruit juice in it but his plate was empty. 'Although I would hardly describe anything broadcast in this country as news.' The radio, like the printed press, was barely more than a mouth-piece for the government. "El Imparcial" indeed!

'No, you're quite right,' Talbot admitted. 'It is government propaganda. But I do find it useful to know what the authorities want us to think. God forbid, however, that it should be our only source of information.'

I buttered my toast and glanced at the crackling radiogram. 'I'm surprised we can receive anything, this far from the capital.' The radio service was a relatively new innovation in Guatemala.

'It isn't that far, in point of fact. Not as the crow flies.' Talbot removed his spectacles and started wiping the lenses with a handkerchief. His face looked rather bland and puffy without them. 'I take it you didn't want to join the tour this morning?'

'Lord, no. Too energetic for me. Didn't fancy clambering halfway up the damned mountainside.' I grabbed the marmalade. 'You weren't keen either?'

'No. I have seen the estate many times before and I have a few papers to look through this morning.'

I chuckled. 'The work of a banker is never done.' I set down my knife and crunched at the toast. The marmalade was tart but not altogether disagreeable.

Talbot put away his handkerchief and slipped his glasses back on. 'My wife has gone with them, though. She likes to stretch her legs.' He smiled quietly at the thought. Perhaps he was grateful for the respite.

The music finished on the radiogram and was replaced by a jabbering native voice. The news broadcast, presumably, though the announcer was talking far too quickly for me to understand anything he said. The bulletin lasted a couple of minutes and Talbot listened in keen silence.

'Anything of interest?' I asked, when it came to an end.

'A new anti-corruption initiative,' the banker declared, with some gravity. 'The president is keen to cut down on bribery and patronage.'

I nodded. The usual hog-wash. 'Do you think he's sincere? The president?'

'I believe he may be.' Talbot rose up from his chair. 'He

has brought in some stringent new rules. It's just a question of whether they are properly enforced. Ubico is putting his own house in order first, which is only right and proper, but there are always difficulties, particularly with regards the army and the police force. He can't govern without their support, but he still needs to take a firm line.'

'Show them who's boss,' I agreed, pouring myself a glass of orange juice from a jug next to the now empty toast rack.

Another announcer came on, to introduce some more music, but Talbot had already moved across to the radiogram. He switched the device off with a grim smile.

'All the modern conveniences here,' I observed, taking a sip of juice. 'I didn't think they'd even have electricity.'

'Many don't. But Gunther lives in the twentieth century.' The banker returned to his seat. 'He had the generator installed some years ago. He is always on the lookout for new technology.'

'That's the Krauts for you,' I suggested. 'Ahead of the game with that sort of thing. You know he's got a pile of technology magazines in the living room?' I had flicked through a couple of them shortly after I had arrived.

George Talbot nodded. 'Yes, he has a definite interest in such things. He was telling me recently about the new televisor sets being developed in America.'

'Good lord.'

'They are next "big thing", apparently.' Talbot did not sound enthused. 'Gunther believes every home will have one by 1950.'

'Good god, I hope not.' I rolled my eyes and gestured across to the wireless. 'It's bad enough people burbling away on the radio all day long without having to *look* at the bloody fools as well.'

'Yes, it can be rather distracting.' Talbot pushed away his plate. 'But I suppose one cannot stand in the way of progress. Gunther hopes to automate the entire plantation one day; to use machinery to pick and clean the produce.'

'Sounds sensible.'

'It would certainly cut down on the labour costs.' There was the bean counter talking, I thought. 'But I don't think it will be happen anytime soon.'

'Trade not good at the moment?'

'Sadly not. The effects of the depression are still being felt quite keenly.'

I took another crunch of toast. 'This marmalade's rather good,' I declared. 'Have you known Mr Weiman long?'

'Oh, indeed. For some years now. We are close friends. And of course I have the privilege of handling his account at the bank.'

'A perfect relationship,' I responded dryly. 'Although I gather Mr Catesby runs the day to day business of the farm?'

'Yes, for the last couple of years. We've also developed a good working relationship.' This comment sounded rather less effusive. 'Indeed, we have a small bit of business to conclude this weekend. And then, next week, I am happy to say, I am off to British Honduras.'

'The Port of Belize? That will be nice for you.'

'Indeed. It is a beautiful spot. My wife enjoys the sea air and the bank has a couple of branches there. Sadly, it will only be for a few days.' He had perked up considerably at the thought, however. 'Now there's a well run society, Mr Buxton.'

'Yes. No need to worry about bribery and corruption there. Not in a British colony. Although I suppose every community has its bad apples.'

'But at least in British Honduras they have the infrastructure and the rule of law to deal with it.' This, I could tell, was an important point for him. He pushed back his chair. 'You must excuse me. I have a few things to do. I hope you don't mind me deserting you.'

'No, of course not. Oh, I was going to ask, though,' I said, as he rose to his feet. 'Did you ever meet my predecessor, Giles Markham?'

Talbot circled his chair and pushed the seat back under the table. 'Yes, several times. He was a regular house guest here. A most amusing man, if a little over-exuberant. I was sorry to hear that he took his own life. A terrible thing for a man to do.'

'He had his reasons,' I said.

'Gambling debts, I understood.'

'So we believe. He liked a bit of a flutter, apparently. But he got caught with his hand in the till. That was what did for him.'

Talbot frowned. 'In the till? You mean he stole money from your office?'

'Quite a large sum, yes. So you see, it's not just the Guatemalans who abuse the system.'

'How much did he steal?' Talbot asked.

'Markham? Almost two thousand pounds.'

'Good gracious!' The banker shook his head. 'I would never have believed it. Not that I knew him that well.'

'I went through the books when I first arrived here. He must have known he wasn't going to be able to hide it much longer. That's why he killed himself, we believe.'

'I had no idea,' Talbot said, just as the far door opened.

Isabel the maid entered, carrying a fresh tray of toast.

'And here I am, filling in his shoes.' I said, grabbing another slice. 'I wonder what *he* thought of the marmalade.'

The stone fountain on the front lawn was now completely dry. Someone somewhere had switched off the tap. I stepped out onto the front terrace, intent on making my way down to the dry store to answer my peculiar hand-written summons. A framed illustration of the estate was hanging on a wall in the entrance hall to the west side of the hacienda – Maurice had drawn my attention to it – and I had done my best to memorise the route across the farm. Down past the stables, take a left along a mud track and stop at a courtyard which had been marked on the picture – in English – as the "drying floor". Despite a German owner and many Spanish-speaking workers, English appeared to be the *lingua franca* of the estate.

Heading towards the lawn, I tipped my hat to a figure resting languidly in a hammock on the front terrace. 'Good morning,' the woman called out. It was Anita Montana, the

American executive's wife. She was a tall, rather buxom woman with long auburn hair and striking blue eyes. Italian by all accounts, though she didn't have much of an accent. She was dressed in a rather tight white blouse and an elegant pleated skirt. 'It's a beautiful day,' she proclaimed, stretching herself out and surveying the scene with apparent delight. Not beautiful enough, however, for her to want to join the rest of the company on a tour of the estate. In that at least, we were of the same mind. She had a book in her left hand, which she was reading instead. A lurid romantic novel, judging by the dust jacket. 'The Good Lord has blessed us with fine weather.'

'Er...quite,' I said. 'Thought I'd go for a quick stroll.'

She smiled up at me from the hammock, a wide beguiling smile. 'A wonderful idea. You have yourself a good time.'

'I...yes, I will, thank you.' I tipped my hat again and moved down the steps.

The stables were barely more than forty yards from the front of the house. There were two short paths here with a small set of trees either side of them. The first one led to the stables. The second was a longer track, which meandered past the yard towards the coffee fields. I glanced around cautiously, making sure no-one was watching me, and then nipped down this second track.

The path ran parallel to the stables and the pasture land beyond it, where the horses were let out during the day to graze. There was a low barn to my right and, a little further on, a rough courtyard off to the north. This was the drying floor I had seen marked on the map. It was not in use at the moment – we were off season – but it was the store itself, away to the right, that I was looking for.

Another building squatted amiably on the far side of the square, with a fence lining the eastern edge of the pasture. A bored looking horse was dangling its head over the fence but otherwise there was no-one about.

I pulled out my pocket watch and checked the time. Five to eleven. I moved off the dirt path and hurried across the yard to a small door in the side of the barn, which I approached with some trepidation.

The door was not locked. Gingerly, I pulled it open and stepped inside. The dry store was a surprisingly bright space, large but not overly burdened with produce. A few storage crates and several piles of solid looking bags enlivened an otherwise dull scene. The building was barely in use at this time of year. There was a curve in the wall off to the right and from behind a pile of boxes a figure emerged, a coloured fellow, tall, muscular but tentative. In his late twenties, perhaps. He had waited a moment to see who had entered the store before presenting himself. I pulled out the note as he moved towards me. 'This was from you, I take it?'

'Yes, mister,' he said, stopping in front of me, his eyes flashing with barely concealed nerves. 'You are Mr Buxton?' He wore a plain white shirt and breeches. On his feet were a crude pair of leather sandals.

'That's right. And who exactly are you?'

'Joseph Green.' The man held out his hand. I stared at it for a moment, then did the polite thing and gave it a firm shake.

'You work here?'

'For Mr Weiman,' Green said. His voice had a light, musical quality. A Jamaican accent, if I wasn't much mistaken.

'And Mr Catesby?'

His face fell. 'Yes, mister.' He didn't sound too keen on the latter gentleman.

It was time to get to the point. 'What is all this about?' I asked him. 'If you're making mischief...'

'No, mister. I needed to speak to you.'

'About Giles Markham?'

'Yes, mister.'

'You knew him?'

'Yes, mister. A little. He came here a few times. He was a friend of Mr Catesby. But it was my brother who used to speak to him.'

'Your brother?'

'Matthew Green. Mr Markham was very kind to him. He would come out into the fields sometimes and talk to people. He would ask our opinions.'

Any opportunity to gauge the mood of the locals. Very sensible, I thought. I really ought be doing the same thing.

'My brother was learning to read,' Green declared proudly. 'Mr Markham promised to help him; to provide books. But Mr Catesby...' Green's face tensed again at the name. 'Mr Catesby did not like my brother talking to Mr Markham. He got very angry. Then, one day, my brother was beaten.'

'I'm sorry to hear that. Though I don't...'

'Mr Catesby beat him so hard that he died.'

'Good lord. I...I'm sorry.' I blinked. 'Mr Catesby *killed* him?'

Green took a gulp of air. 'It was an accident, they said. Matthew should not have been in the house. Mr Catesby was punishing him; but then he fell and banged his head.'

'Lord.' That was awful. 'What was he doing in the house?'

'I...do not know.'

'Didn't you complain? When he died? Did you call the police?'

The labourer shook his head. 'They came. But the police do not interfere when a coloured man dies. Not if a white man is responsible. And Mr Catesby, he is family.'

'I see.' So the owners had banded together. That wasn't too much of a surprise. 'And you stayed here, working for them? When one of them had killed your brother? Why didn't you just leave? You're not a slave.'

'I have no choice, mister. There is not much work around. And Mr and Mrs Weiman...they at least have been kind to me. The rest of the workers...' He grimaced. 'They did not like my brother. They did not care that he had died.'

'That seems a little harsh.' Normally, when someone was badly treated like that, the other labourers would band together and protest. From what I had heard, the West Indian population was not afraid to stand up for itself. 'But look, I don't see what any of this has to do with Giles Markham. Or me, for that matter. I am sorry about what happened to your brother, but...'

Green's attention shifted abruptly. There were voices

outside, people moving about in the yard. 'I should not be here!' he breathed.

'Oh, don't worry,' I said, waving my hand at him; but it was too late. The labourer had already bolted for the far door. I looked out, in the opposite direction, and caught sight of Gunther Weiman and Arthur Montana heading towards the barn, with the rest of the tour party trailing some distance behind them. I whipped my head away from the window as the two men came to a halt outside the building. I don't know why I was hiding – I was not doing anything wrong – but for some reason I did not feel inclined to reveal my presence. Not until Mr Green was well away, in any case. He had already slipped out of the barn on the far side.

None of what the fellow had told me seemed to make any sense. If his brother had been beaten to death, as he had claimed, there would have been an outcry, at least among the other negroes. At the very least, Mr Catesby would have been quietly found another job, family or no family. It did no-one any good to press a lid down on that sort of powder keg. And why had Joseph Green wanted to speak to me in particular? What on earth did he think I could do about any of it?

Arthur Montana, the United Fruit executive, was lighting up a fat cigar on the far side of the window. 'Well, it looks like he's finally got his act together,' he was telling Mr Weiman. The two men were some yards away from the rest of the tour. 'Not before time. I've kept things stewing for far too long already.'

'You have been very tolerant,' the German agreed. 'It has not been an easy time for any of us.'

Montana took a puff of his cigar. 'Well, it'll all be settled this weekend. Just a few papers to sign and then he'll be out of your hair.' I wasn't sure who exactly they were talking about. Mr Catesby, perhaps? Or George Talbot? 'And then, after that...'

The conversation was cut short as the rest of the house guests shuffled towards them across the yard. Steven Catesby was acting as tour guide. 'This is where the coffee is laid out in the sun to dry.' His voice echoed across the courtyard. 'Once the pulp has been removed. It's then stored in that building over there.'

'Can we see inside?' Miss Bunting enquired.

Lord, I thought. Time to make a swift exit.

'There's not much in there now,' Catesby replied. 'You're welcome to take a look, but I was going to show you the warehouse. We have a rather basic filtering machine...' His voice trailed off as the group moved away. Arthur Montana took another puff of his cigar and made to follow them.

I waited a minute and then peered out of the window. The courtyard was deserted. I could nip out now and head back to the house; but if I did someone might still catch sight of me. Better to hang on here for a few minutes, until they had finished in the warehouse. Damnation. Why did I allow myself to get involved in this sort of thing?

I moved across to the far door, tripped down a couple of steps and pulled out a thin cigarette from my case; my first of the day. I lit it quickly and took a slow drag, then coughed irritably. It was some dreadful American brand, which was all I could get in Guatemala City.

I had almost finished the cigarette when I heard a scraping noise coming from the front of the barn. Someone was opening the main door. Luckily I was out of sight and I stifled a laugh when I realised who it was. Freddie Reeves had nipped away from the tour with Emily Bunting and they had slipped inside the dry store together. The two of them were laughing like naughty school children and probably with good reason. His arms were around her waist and he moved in to kiss her. 'Freddie, you mustn't!' she protested, laughingly. 'Someone might see!'

'Rubbish. They're all heading off home!' He winked at her. 'Come on, girl. You know I'm irresistible.'

'A big head more like!' she teased. 'I shouldn't encourage you. Not after the way you were staring at Mrs Montana over breakfast!'

'I could hardly miss her, now could I? She was sat right in front of me.' He grinned. 'But she's got nothing on you.' And with that, he leaned in to kiss her again.

'Frederick Reeves!' I bellowed, in mock horror, from the top of the steps. 'What on earth do you think you are doing with my secretary?' I couldn't resist interrupting the two of them. 'Unhand her at once!' I said. Miss Bunting had already caught me in a compromising position and it was high time I returned the favour.

Freddie leapt away from the girl at the first sound of a raised voice but, as soon as he realised who it was, he relaxed. I stepped forward into the barn.

'Christ, you frightened the life out of me, Henry! You shouldn't creep up on people like that!' He was smiling now but he did at least have the decency to look a little sheepish.

'I saw the door open and heard a noise. If you are going to seduce Miss Bunting, you could at least have the good grace to find somewhere a little more private.'

He raised his hands in mock surrender. 'All right, you've got me. Seriously, though, what are you doing up and about? I thought you'd still be in bed.'

'I would be, if it wasn't for you. You're the one who asked me to poke around out here. Speaking of which, hadn't you better run along? You don't want to miss the end of the tour.'

Freddie nodded, conceding defeat. He knew I wasn't going to leave the two of them alone. He gave Miss Bunting a quick peck on the cheek and then disappeared out the door.

The girl lingered for a moment. 'Crumbs, what must you think of me?' she wondered, patting down her skirt with a mischievous smile.

'You're an adult,' I said. 'Your private life is your own affair.' I was not about to cast any stones. 'So long as you're discreet. And Freddie is quite a dashing young fellow.'

'Isn't he?' She grinned, looking after him through the window. 'Crikey, do you fancy him as well?'

'Good lord, no!' I spluttered. The very idea. 'I'm a bit too long in the tooth for that sort of thing. And, in any case,' I added, 'it wouldn't exactly be practical, now would it? Not with the life I lead.'

Miss Bunting grinned again and took me by the arm. 'I

suppose not.' We moved through the door and out into the square. 'But you are attracted to men?' she asked. It was something the girl had clearly wondered about, though it was not an easy subject to broach. It was not something I particularly wanted to discuss either, but given all she knew about me, I supposed I would have to forgive the impertinence.

'Yes, of course,' I agreed briskly. 'But unlike some people, Miss Bunting, I am capable of controlling my libido.'

She laughed. 'Where's the fun in that?' We stopped halfway across the drying floor and she regarded me seriously. 'You should take a holiday. Go down to the coast where no-one knows you.'

'Put on a frock and find a nice young man?' I pulled a face. 'Don't think it hasn't occurred to me.' Back in England, as a young woman, I had done exactly that, on more than one occasion. I would nip away for the odd few days, set myself up in some seaside town and find myself a likely local fellow. But those days were long gone.

'You could nip over the border to El Salvador,' Miss Bunting suggested.

'I could do,' I agreed, playing along with the idea. 'I do have a couple of spare passports, if I ever feel the urge.' Actually, those were for work, but there was nothing to stop me hopping across the border and finding myself some handsome young man in a neighbouring country, if I ever felt the need. 'But, to be honest, it's all too much bother.'

'Everyone deserves a bit of fun,' Miss Bunting said.

'Within reason,' I agreed. 'Be careful with Freddie, though. He's a decent enough fellow but he does have a bit of a roving eye.'

'Yes, I've noticed,' the girl admitted glumly. She lifted a hand to brush away a stray hair from her face. She was wearing a bit of make up this morning, I noticed, and a rather fetching pair of flower-shaped earrings. That was for Freddie's benefit, no doubt. Such things were not permitted back in the office. 'But he is such a fun person to be around. And I don't think he'd ever try to take advantage.' She changed the subject. 'So what are you doing out here this morning, anyway? I thought you didn't want to see the estate?'

'Never you mind. A bit of private business.' We had reached the pathway leading back to the hacienda. 'And I'm not quite finished yet. Trot along, there's a good girl. I shall see you at lunch.'

'All right.' She squeezed my hand shyly. 'Hilary.'

'Mr Buxton to you.'

She laughed and moved off.

I waited for a moment until she was out of sight and then glanced along the track leading up into the fields. Where had that man Green got to? I wondered. There were still a few questions I wanted to ask him. Perhaps he had followed the path up into the trees. It might be worth having a quick look, I thought.

The track trundled idly for about sixty yards before becoming intolerably steep. The coffee plants here were interspersed with a set of much taller trees, which formed a loose canopy above them, protecting them from the harsh glare of the sun. Not that there was much sun just now. The sky was beginning to cloud over. Clumps of green "cherries" were budding on some of the branches either side of me, but they were still several weeks away from their first picking. The fruits – if indeed they were fruits – would have to turn red first; and then Green and his colleagues would be out in force, alongside the Indians from the village.

I turned back and made my way past the dry store, the pasture and the stables, emerging unobtrusively into the front yard of the hacienda. A further line of trees on the opposite side masked another set of small buildings. This – if I remembered correctly from the map – was the negro accommodation, carefully shielded and out of sight of the rest of the plantation. Another pathway ran down to the makeshift road leading up from the village.

Something rather unpleasant was happening on the near side of the trees. A grim looking man in a straw hat was assaulting Joseph Green; punching him viciously in the stomach. Another fellow was pinning his arms behind his back. The labourer struggled to avoid two or three heavy blows, one

61

of which struck him awkwardly across the face. I could hear snarls and abusive language coming from the man in the hat. Blood started to pour from Green's nose. I brought my hand up to my mouth in horror.

Steven Catesby was striding past the fountain down the lawn towards the three men. 'What in God's name is going on?' he demanded.

I was wondering that, too. The rest of the guests had already made their way back inside the house but Catesby must have heard Green crying out. I hesitated before stepping forward from the pathway, but Catesby had already seen me, as he strode towards the tree line, though he was too intent on the brutal tableaux ahead of him to shoot me even a cursory glance.

The tough looking fellow grabbed the top of Green's head and pulled it up. The man in the hat – who I realised now was the overseer – then turned to address the new arrival. 'I found him skulking in the trees, Mr Catesby.' The man had a puffy face and an over-sized belly. His accent was difficult to place. 'He was meant to be breaking rocks on the road, but he sneaked away just before eleven.'

Catesby regarded the prisoner severely. 'Well, Joseph? Did you sneak away?'

'I was not feeling well, mister,' Green protested. 'I needed to lie down.'

'Did you ask permission to leave the work party?'

'No, mister.'

Catesby bit his lip angrily. 'You do not leave without asking permission!'

'He would not let me!' Green protested again, nodding his head at the overseer.

'Did you *ask* him?'

The man's face dropped. 'No, mister.'

Catesby shook his head and then addressed the fellow in the hat. 'Three lashes.'

The overseer grinned. 'Reckon ten would be more like it,' he suggested.

'I said three, Peter. And then get him back to work.'

The overseer grunted in disappointment. 'You're too

soft, Mr Catesby.'

'You'd beat him half to death if I let you.'

'It's the only language they understand.'

Catesby sighed. 'Do remember, we have guests this weekend. Please keep the workers away from the house. I don't want any more disturbances.'

'Yes, Mr Catesby.' The overseer tipped his hat and then pulled Green away, shoving the poor fellow back along the path towards the road, where the punishment would doubtless be carried out in front of the other labourers. 'Don't you worry, Mr Catesby,' he called back. 'You won't hear a peep out of them.'

The farm manager watched them go. Belatedly, he acknowledged my presence. 'I'm sorry you had to see that, Mr Buxton.'

'Bit impertinent, that fellow of yours,' I observed, coming forward. 'Ten lashes indeed!'

'Oh, that's just his way. He gets results, which is the main thing.' It was not a glowing recommendation and it was clear Catesby had not intended it to be.

'Even three seems a bit harsh,' I added cautiously, 'if you don't mind me saying.' I did feel somewhat responsible for the man's predicament. 'After all, if he wasn't feeling well...'

Catesby shook his head in sudden anger. 'Not feeling well, my foot. Mr Langbroek is right.' Langbroek, I took it, was the name of the overseer. 'He was skiving. These people need a firm hand, Mr Buxton. Mr Montana is right about that. Especially that one.' He gestured down the lane, where Joseph Green was just disappearing from view between a couple of bushes. 'Bad blood in his veins, I'm afraid.' He turned back to the house and we moved off together. 'Bad blood. Just like his brother.'

63

Chapter Five

The question floated awkwardly the length of the dinner table and I winced as soon as I heard it. Ricardo Gonzales, the engineer, had mentioned the fact that his wife would be expecting their first child towards the end of the year and the inevitable congratulations had led on to talk of children and such like. Miss Bunting's question might have seemed a reasonable follow on but an older, more socially astute woman would have realised the perils of such personal enquiries.

Lunch had been served promptly at half past twelve and the house guests had gathered once again in the dining hall. The housekeeper had put on a passable spread – even she could not go wrong with cold meats and a few light vegetables – and I found myself tucking in greedily. It was not that long since breakfast, but I had already managed to work up quite an appetite.

My brain had undergone something of a workout too, courtesy of Joseph Green. I couldn't help but feel responsible for what had happened to him, though in truth the fellow had rather brought it upon himself. He could, after all, have suggested some other time for us to meet up, when he wasn't supposed to be digging out the road. The punishment Catesby had handed down to him, although severe, was not unreasonable. Whatever his private feelings towards Green – and why Catesby would have any feelings about the man at all I had no idea – he had not allowed it to affect his judgement. Despite what the labourer had claimed, I could not picture Steven Catesby losing his rag and beating someone to death. That overseer fellow, certainly – he looked like a nasty piece of work – but the estate manager? He did not strike me as the aggressive type at all.

I still couldn't fathom why Joseph Green had wanted to talk to me in the first place. He didn't know me from Adam and had no reason to think I would have any interest in Giles Markham's death, let alone the death of his brother. So far as I could tell, Green had barely known my predecessor and, at least according to Mr Weiman, Markham had been in good spirits the last time he had been here. Our conversation had been cut short, however, so perhaps Green had not had time to pass on the really important details.

How any of this related to the break-in at my flat, I had no idea. That surely had more to do with Markham's secret service work. And what about the theft of the visa money? Was that really to pay off gambling debts, as everyone at the legation had concluded, or was something else going on? Perhaps Freddie was right, and there was more to it than that. Whatever the truth, something odd was definitely going on here at the farm.

A more pressing concern for me, however, was my secretary's excruciating faux pas. 'Do *you* have any children, Mrs Weiman?' Miss Bunting had asked, to the consternation of the entire room.

Gunther Weiman, who was sat at my end of the table, immediately cut in to save his wife any embarrassment. 'I'm afraid we have not been blessed in that way.'

Miss Bunting's face fell, as she realised her mistake. I suppose it had seemed natural, given our hosts' age, to assume that any children they had would have flown the nest. It had not occurred to her that there would be no children. 'I'm terribly sorry. I didn't...'

'Don't concern yourself, my dear,' Mrs Weiman reassured the girl smoothly. She was a kindly, dark-haired woman with large brown eyes and a pleasantly youthful face. 'We have been blessed in so many other ways, haven't we darling?' Susan Weiman smiled across the table at her husband.

'Indeed,' he agreed, gazing back contentedly at his wife.

'Have you been married long?' I asked, anxious to move the conversation along.

The German smiled. 'It will be eighteen years this September.'

'Good lord,' I exclaimed, setting down my fork. 'That's a good run. You were married before the war, then?'

'Yes, in the autumn of 1913,' Weiman told me. His eyes were still locked on his wife, at the opposite end of the table.

'It must have been a bit tricky, during the war.' A German man married to an Englishwoman.

'We were far enough away not to be affected. And the German community in Guatemala is very supportive.'

'There's quite a sizeable enclave here,' George Talbot put in, by way of explanation. The dull banker was seated opposite me once again, with Mrs Montana to his right. 'They've cornered the market in coffee production.'

'And Germany is our biggest market,' Weiman said. 'Most of our coffee ends up passing through Hamburg.'

'Unfortunately, the price has plummeted these last couple of years,' Steven Catesby lamented. 'And it's still falling.' The depression had hit everybody hard.

'We are hoping for a good harvest this year,' Weiman asserted diplomatically. 'Fortunately, we are well enough established that we can weather a few lean years. But hopefully it will not last forever. What do you think of our coffee?'

This question was aimed squarely at me. I blanched in surprise. 'It was...er...very pleasant.'

Weiman had a mischievous gleam in his eye. 'You are not a coffee drinker, Mr Buxton?' George Talbot must have told him what I had said about the stuff at breakfast and the German, it appeared, was not above a little teasing.

'Er...no, not really,' I admitted, with some embarrassment. 'But if I was, I'm sure this would be the first place I would come to for my supplies.'

Weiman beamed. 'A very diplomatic answer.'

I laughed, despite myself. 'I do my best.'

Jane Talbot, the banker's wife, was seated between me and the German. 'It's good to know standards are not slipping at the Foreign Office,' she declared, with just a twinge of humour. 'One always hopes for decent representation in the far corners of the world.'

'Well, quite,' I said. 'And, of course, if you ever need your passport stamped...'

Anita Montana, the Italian woman, was gazing at me across the table. 'I would *love* to visit England,' she declared dreamily. 'The spires of Oxford. The green and pleasant land.'

Her eyes twinkled seductively.

'Yes, it's...very pretty,' I agreed. 'Can be rather chilly though. Not what you're used to, I expect. Nothing approaching a Mediterranean climate.'

'I'm sure it must be beautiful in summer though,' she said. Her mouth creased into a wide smile. She was rather a striking woman, Mrs Montana; still handsome in her late thirties with thick auburn hair and a pleasingly full figure.

'Whereabouts in Italy are you from?' I asked her.

'I was born in Naples. But my parents moved to South Carolina when I was a little girl. And that was where I met Arthur. Isn't that right, honey?'

The American beamed contentedly. 'It sure is. It was love at first sight.'

'Have you ever been back? To Italy?'

'No, I never have. I would like to, though. I hear it's beautiful at this time of year.'

'What about you, Mrs Talbot?' I turned to face the Englishwoman. 'Any regrets leaving the old country behind?'

'One or two, perhaps,' she admitted.

'I do miss the old place some times,' George Talbot said. 'The drizzle and the snow. It must be, what, six, seven years since we left?'

'Something like that,' his wife agreed, her nostrils flaring. 'We do pop back occasionally. The last time was for Julie's wedding, do you remember, George?'

'Yes,' he recalled sourly. 'It rained the whole time.'

I chuckled. 'Probably better as a fond memory than a holiday destination.'

'How long is it since *you* left Britain?' Mrs Talbot asked me.

'Coming up to two years. I spent a little time in Gibraltar, then arrived here at the beginning of May. I do still get the occasional twinge for the old place.'

Mr Weiman was of a different opinion. 'I am glad to be away from Germany. It has not been a happy place since the war.'

'No, indeed,' I agreed. 'Things haven't been going

well.' Germany had been particularly badly hit by the depression.

Mrs Talbot did not want to get into a discussion of economics. 'Mrs Montana, what do you think of the pâté?' she asked.

The younger woman gazed down happily at her plate. 'It was divine.'

'Coming from an Italian, that's something of a compliment,' Jane Talbot said.

'Indeed,' Weiman agreed. 'Not local produce, I'm afraid. Steven brought the pâté back with him from Guatemala City. Greta gives him a list whenever he goes into town.'

'You were in Guatemala City this week?' I enquired of Mr Catesby. That was a surprise.

'On Wednesday and Thursday,' the German answered for him. 'A business trip.'

'It was nice to get away for a couple of days,' the Englishman said.

Good lord, I thought. Wednesday and Thursday. It had been in the early hours of Thursday morning that some bounder had broken into my flat. I put down my knife and bit my lower lip. I was beginning to think that Joseph Green might have been right about Steven Catesby after all.

'It felt rather leathery,' Frederick Reeves declared. 'A really strong grip. It wasn't about to fall off in a hurry.'

I shuddered. 'A *tarantula*?'

'Hiding in a little rock. Gunther stuck a stick in there, the tarantula came out and he grabbed it from the top. It's his party trick. I've seen him do it a couple of times.'

'And you let him put it on your hand?' I boggled.

Freddie shrugged. 'He said it was perfectly safe. Even if it stings you, it's not likely to be fatal. A baby maybe or an elderly person. But not you or me. In any case...' He grinned. 'Emily was first in line and I could hardly say no after she'd done it, could I?' That made sense, I thought, with a smile.

Freddie and I were walking down from the hacienda to

68

the village. It was a good hour's trek but I had wanted to get the Second Secretary away from the house, so that we could have a proper talk, away from prying ears. There was a lot to discuss. Freddie had got me involved in all this, so the least he could do was listen as I babbled away, trying to make some sense of it.

We passed the road builders shortly after leaving the estate. The overseer tipped his hat to us but his expression was not friendly. Joseph Green was toiling away once again alongside the other negroes. He was stripped to the waist now and I could see the marks on his back, which had already started to scab over. It didn't seem right, sending him back to work so soon after that whipping this morning, even if it was only three lashes. But he was a strong fellow and doubtless he would cope. There were a couple of buckets of water at the side of the road that the labourers could use to refresh themselves and the canopy either side provided some protection from the mid afternoon sun.

'Was that him?' Freddie asked, jerking his thumb back to the work party once we were some way down the road. I nodded sadly. I had told Freddie about our clandestine meeting earlier in the day. 'He must have a hell of a grudge against Steven, to risk getting flogged like that just to talk to you. How did he even know who you were?'

'I'm not sure. I suppose somebody in the house must have overheard us talking last night. The maid, perhaps, or that house boy of theirs. You know how these things travel. Mind you, Green was quick off the mark, sending me that note.'

'And he told you not to trust Steven?'

'That's about the size of it.'

Freddie grimaced. 'An odd thing to say,' he thought.

'Yes. And now I find out Mr Catesby was in Guatemala City last Wednesday, the night my flat was burgled.' I scratched the side of my face. 'You know, ridiculous as it may sound, I'm beginning to think he may have been the one who broke in.'

'What, Steven?' Freddie was sceptical. 'I can't picture him doing anything like that. I mean, the bloke's not afraid to get his hands dirty, but coshing your valet...'

'It does seem unlikely,' I conceded. 'But, all the same,

he did look rather uncomfortable when Mr Weiman mentioned his trip to town. And we know Giles Markham was a house guest here, so there is definitely some connection between the two of them.' I stopped for a moment. A stone had got into my shoe and I leaned a hand on a nearby telegraph pole so I could bend over and remove the offending item. 'You must have seen them together,' I said, looking up. 'Did they get on?'

'Yes, they were great pals. Always laughing and joking.'

I put my shoe back on. 'Catesby doesn't seem much of a joker.'

'No, not this weekend,' Freddie admitted, as the two of us moved off together. 'You're right. He does seem a bit on edge. Not his usual self at all. But Giles, he was such a card.' Freddie grinned. 'He did make me laugh. Bit of a ladies man too. Always chatting up the girls in the typing pool. Mr Richards had to tell him off a few times about that.' He chuckled. 'He brought out the best in people, did Giles. Liked a drink too.'

'And he came here quite often, to the finca?'

'Yes, he was good friends with Steven. He came down here much more than I did. Maybe once a month.'

'And did *you* hear anything about Catesby and this black fellow? About him dying?'

'No. Not a thing. It didn't happen when I was here, that's for sure.'

I frowned. 'But if one of the labourers had been beaten to death, then surely everyone would know about it?'

'You'd think so,' Freddie agreed.

'Not least the head of the household.'

'Gunther.' He nodded. 'Yes, he must have known about it. And he wouldn't bury it under the carpet. I mean, these thing happen, but he'd have done right by the family. He's good like that. He knows how important his workers are. Not like some people hereabouts.'

I smiled quietly. 'You like him? Mr Weiman?'

'Gunther? Yes, he's a good bloke. A gentle soul. Well, you've seen. Quiet but good-humoured. There aren't many like him.'

The village was a single large square surrounded by hills, with a white-washed church, several low buildings – also in white with green windows and doors – and a few narrow paths scattering off in various directions. It was a sleepy looking place, even on a Saturday afternoon. A couple of trees marked the centrepiece of the plaza and a handful of ragged children were playing a game of tag, making use of a dry stone fountain. A trio of elderly men were slumped outside one of the buildings to my left and two women were passing the time of day at the door of the village shop. A wizened old crone sat behind the grill, ready to dole out the necessary supplies.

The new road did not pass directly through the village – it had more important places to go – but a short, knobbly path led up from it to the plaza. Freddie and I were gasping for breath as we arrived at the top. I was beginning to regret having suggested this walk. It had been bad enough on the way down, but the return journey would be murderous. To make matters worse, the sky had clouded over in the last twenty minutes and I had a horrible suspicion we would not be able to get back to the farm before the heavens opened.

'Do they have a telephone anywhere here?' I asked Freddie. In light of everything we had discussed, I had half a mind to phone my secretary, William Battersby. He knew more about the circumstances of Markham's death than I did and it might be worthwhile to get him to rehash a few of the details.

'In the post office, I think. It won't be open now, though.'

'Pity,' I said. 'I'm parched. Is there anywhere we can get a drink?'

Freddie's face lit up. 'Now you're talking! There is one place.' He gestured to the opposite side of the square. The word "BAR" was stencilled on a far wall, with a green arrow pointing around the corner.

There were two customers inside and no-one at the counter. The bar was even deader than the square. It was a dark, dusty place with an unswept floor and heavily shuttered windows. Not the kind of establishment that ever saw much sunlight, I suspected. A lizard flicked up an internal wall and out through a crack in the ceiling.

Freddie banged amiably on the counter and a figure emerged from a small back room. 'Alberto! Long time no see.'

The barman's face lit up. 'Señor Reeves. Welcome!' He raised a hand in greeting. Alberto was a lively bald man with heavy spectacles and a wide smile. 'It is good to see you!' he said. He wore a checked shirt and a set of bright red braces. A couple of drinks were poured out for us and Alberto dusted down a table near the window, pulling back the shutters to allow in some light.

'Alberto's lived here all his life,' Freddie explained. Poor fellow, I thought. But the man himself was grinning animatedly. 'His son's a book-keeper. Works at the finca. I'll have to point him out to you. Pull up a chair, Alberto. Come and join us.'

The barman hesitated, his eyes flicking briefly to me.

'It's all right. He doesn't mind, do you, Henry?'

'Er...no. No, of course not.' Why wouldn't I want to have a drink with some random fellow in a bar?

The man got himself a beer and seated himself opposite us. We exchanged a few pleasantries. I was identified as a work colleague of Freddie's, which was true enough. Finally, the Englishman leaned forward and got to the point. 'We wanted to ask you something.'

'Si, si, if I can help.' Alberto was eager to please.

'What do you know about a man named Matthew Green?'

The barman considered for a moment. 'He was a labourer at the finca. A resident. He is dead now.'

'What do you know about his death?'

'Only what I've heard, señor.' The man leaned in. I had the distinct impression that Alberto was the village gossip. Doubtless everyone passed through his bar at one time or another. 'He was caught stealing, in the house.'

'Stealing?' Green hadn't mentioned that. But then, our

72

conversation had been cut short rather.

'Si, si. It was a Sunday afternoon, when everyone was at church. Señor Catesby – the farm manager – he found Señor Green in one of the bedrooms. He dragged him out and beat him. But Señor Green fell down the stairs and broke his neck. That was the official story, anyway.'

'And unofficially?' I asked.

Alberto took a swig of beer from his bottle and raised a finger. 'Well, señor.' He grinned. 'You did not hear this from me. I only tell you because you are a good friend.' He beamed at Freddie. 'The rumour was – according to my son – that Señor Green was found sharing a bed with a white man. One of the guests.'

'Good lord,' I exclaimed.

'Si, si.' Alberto affirmed. 'That was why Señor Catesby lost his temper. It was a very shameful thing to happen, in his own home. Two men together like that.'

I scoffed. 'What, so he beat him to death?'

'Si. I am afraid so, Señor.'

'And the white man? Do you know who that was?'

'I do not know. He was an Englishman, I think. But the whole thing was...' The barman searched for the right phrase.

'Hushed up?' I prompted.

'Si, si. Señor Weiman and his wife were not at home that weekend. They were visiting friends. Señor Catesby told them about the theft when they returned to the estate. But that was just a story.'

'I see.'

The door to the bar swung open and another customer walked in behind us. Alberto rose to his feet, all smiles again. 'Miguel! Buenas tardes! You will have to excuse me.' He hurried off to grab a beer for the new arrival, a tattered looking farm hand who looked as if he needed a bath more than any refreshment.

Freddie and I remained at our own little table, digesting what Alberto had told us. 'Lord,' I said. 'That wasn't what I was expecting to hear. Was it Giles Markham, do you think? The Englishman?'

'It would have to be, if Gunther was away that weekend. But I can't believe...' He shook his head in disbelief. 'A sodomite! Giles? It can't be true.'

'Would it really be so surprising?'

Freddie took a swig of beer. 'You never met him. He was such a lively bloke. The girls were all over him. I wouldn't have thought for a minute...' He put down his glass and shook his head again.

'It takes all sorts to make a world, Freddie.'

'I know. But sleeping with another man.' Freddie shuddered. 'And a coloured bloke too...'

I lifted a finger. 'What people get up to behind closed doors is their own affair,' I said. I have never really understood why people take such exception to the notion of two men sharing a bed. I have met my fair share of sodomites over the years and, on the whole, they have been a fairly decent bunch. 'But I agree, it was a devil of a risk to take.' I lifted my glass and took a thoughtful sip. 'Markham was a fool, bringing him into the house like that. He should have found somewhere private, where no-one was likely to stumble across them.'

Freddie downed the last of his beer. 'Yes, that's a lesson I learnt this morning.' He grinned, recalling the incident with Miss Bunting.

'You weren't trying hard enough. But it's the timing I don't understand.' I took another swig from my glass. 'Markham came down here the weekend before he died. That can't have been the weekend he was discovered in bed with this labourer.'

'No,' Freddie agreed. 'I was there that weekend. And so was Susan and Gunther. But I think Giles came up here a couple of times in March. It must have been the time before.'

'But that still doesn't make sense. If he'd been found in bed with another man, in the house, why on earth would they have invited him back? They'd have cut him dead, surely? If Catesby was so upset at the idea of two men sleeping together, there's no way Markham would have been allowed back in the house. And if your Mr Weiman found out about it...'

'He must have known,' Freddie said, glancing across

the bar. 'Believe me, if Alberto knows then everyone knows.'
Perhaps that was why the other labourers had not complained.
There was no reason to suppose the workforce at the farm were
any more broad minded than the owners. 'But I suppose it
might have been a while before the whole story came out.
Maybe when Giles killed himself?'

'That still doesn't explain why he was invited back,' I
said. 'Unless Catesby was blackmailing him. "I know what you
did, give me some money." That sort of thing.'

'Could be,' Freddie thought. 'But then, it was Steven
who clobbered Matthew Green, not Giles.'

I sat back on my stool and sighed. 'Well, anyway.
Whatever the truth, it looks like none of this has anything to do
with us. No government secrets gone astray. No foreign agents.
No diplomatic faux pas. Not even gambling debts. Just a sad
man caught with his pants down, suffering the consequences.'

Freddie shook his head again. 'A black man though.'

'We all have our weaknesses, Freddie. Don't think too
harshly of him. You know, I think it might be better for all
concerned if we just forget all about this.'

'You don't think we should investigate further?'

I shrugged. 'It's none of our business. Nothing we can
do can bring Markham back. Or Matthew Green. And there's
no point the two of us stirring up trouble. If Mr Weiman is
aware of what happened, then it's up to him to sort it out. We
should stay well clear.'

'You really think so?' Freddie gazed unhappily at his
empty glass.

'I really do,' I insisted. 'I came here for a quiet
weekend, Freddie. A bit of gambling, a bit of drinking. As far as
I can see, there's no reason for either of us to get involved in
anything else.'

A rather wet weekend, too, as it transpired. Freddie and I had
lingered too long in the village and, as I had feared, the late
afternoon rains had struck before we were within half a mile of
the hacienda. It was quite a steep upward climb, that last part of

the journey, and once we had got beyond the new road the ground became distinctly muddy underfoot. Freddie had brought an umbrella but it was not much help against the heavily slanted rain. My face was protected from the worst of the downpour by the brim of my hat but the rest of my clothes had quickly become sodden. It was with some relief, therefore, that the two of us made our way into the entrance yard and from there across the lawn – one last steep obstacle – onto the front steps of the hacienda.

Jane Talbot, the big-nosed banker's wife, was standing on the terrace, observing our arrival with an amused smile. 'You look drenched,' she said.

'Yes, I am rather,' I admitted tersely. I was not in the mood for banter. I removed my hat and wiped the rain from the brim.

Freddie had already collapsed his umbrella. He was grinning broadly. 'I don't mind the rain out here. It's nice and warm. Like having a shower.'

'I've never liked showers,' I muttered. My jacket was soaked through and my trousers were spattered with mud. I would have to get changed.

Freddie was not much better off, by the look of him.

'My husband was looking for you a little while ago,' Mrs Talbot informed me. 'He wanted to have a word. I told him you had popped down to the village.' I frowned, not quite sure what the dull banker would want to talk to me about. We had pretty much exhausted our conversation at breakfast. 'He's having a siesta at the moment,' she added.

'I'll speak to him later, then. As soon as I've got out of these wet things.'

Freddie had already moved past us and was taking off his boots before entering the hall. I wasn't going to bother with such niceties. I tipped my head to Mrs Talbot and strode through the central arch into the tiled courtyard. From there I nipped left, underneath the covered way and headed for the rear of the house, where a set of stairs ran up to the first floor. Rain was battering the far terrace and, as I made to ascend the stairs, I heard a cry and a sudden, short series of thumps coming from the rear of the hacienda.

I swerved around the staircase and moved through the far door out onto the back terrace. A second set of stairs to my right connected the upper and lower terraces on the outside. The wood here was slippery and damp with rain.

At the foot of the steps, spread out across the wooden slats, was the plump grey figure of George Talbot. I could tell at a glance that his neck was broken.

Chapter Six

I almost slipped as I moved towards him. The floorboards were a death trap because of that damned angular rain and I took a moment to regain my balance before stepping across and crouching down in front of the prone figure. There was no need to take a pulse. I shuddered, staring for a moment at the twisted neck and the broken glasses, which were still vaguely attached to Talbot's puffy face. I have seen quite a few dead bodies in my time but I have never got used to the experience. There is something fundamentally wrong in observing a figure who was alive a moment before but who has now breathed his last. Part of it, I suspect, is the sudden slap of one's own mortality striking one across the face; but a certain natural sympathy for the plight of another is also a factor, even with a comparative stranger like George Talbot. The distinguished grey-haired banker did not deserve such a clumsy, inelegant death. I rose slowly to my feet. There was nothing I could do for him. My only responsibility now was to call the alarm and break the news to the other guests. It was not a task I relished.

A piercing scream from behind saved me the bother. The maid, Isabel, had come out of the kitchen. She raised her hand to her mouth, looking across at the body in horror. Her eyes flicked uncertainly from him to me. I could only confirm the obvious. 'He's dead, I'm afraid.' The maid stood paralysed as I moved across to her. 'There's nothing to be done. You'd better fetch Mr Weiman.'

She nodded numbly, her eyes still fixed on the corpse. 'The poor mister,' she breathed. 'Did he fall down the stairs?'

'I'm afraid so. He wouldn't have felt a thing,' I added, attempting to reassure the girl. 'It would have been over in an instant. Hurry along now.' She regarded me with a blank face. 'Mr Weiman,' I prompted.

'Yes, mister.' She curtsied and scuttled back into the house.

I followed her through the archway into the back hall. A set of heavy stairs to my right led up to the first floor landing.

There were an awful lot of stairs in the hacienda, it struck me now. The back stairs here, the main stairs in the entrance hall and a further two sets connecting the upper and lower terraces outside. It was these external stairs which Talbot had stumbled on.

Ricardo Gonzales, the engineer, was coming down the steps to my right. He started slightly, catching sight of me at the bottom. He had been coming down at such a lick that the two of us had almost collided. 'Is something wrong, señor?' he asked, recovering himself quickly. Gonzales was a short, slender fellow with slicked black hair and a neatly groomed moustache. 'I heard a scream.' He peered over my shoulder into the dining room on the far side of the hall, as if the noise had come from that direction.

I shook my head and gestured towards the terrace. 'There's been an accident,' I told him. Gonzales moved towards the arch.

Steven Catesby was descending the hall stairs, followed closely by Miss Bunting. Freddie Reeves popped up from the side hall at the same moment. All three of them had heard the maid cry out. Catesby was the first to catch my eye. 'What's going on?' he asked.

'An accident,' I said again. 'Mr Talbot has fallen down the stairs.'

'George?' Catesby's eyes widened in alarm.

'He must have slipped in the rain.'

'Good God. Is he all right?'

I hesitated. There was no point beating about the bush. 'No, I'm afraid not.'

Gonzales had stopped dead just beyond the archway. He blinked at the sight of George Talbot's body and crossed himself quickly. 'He is dead,' the engineer confirmed in a whisper.

Miss Bunting, who had just reached the bottom stair, let out a yelp of horror. Catesby swerved past me and joined the engineer on the verandah. The two of them stood for a moment on the wet floorboards, gazing down at the dead banker, who was out of my line of vision. 'The poor chap,' Catesby

79

breathed, turning back to the rest of us. 'This is awful.'

Miss Bunting moved towards him but Freddie put a restraining hand on her shoulder. 'Best not, Emily. It won't be a pretty sight.'

Another sharp voice rebounded across the courtyard. 'Is something the matter?' Jane Talbot was making her way across the patio from the front of the hacienda. I shuddered. It was her husband lying dead at the foot of the stairs. 'What is it?' she enquired, sensing our disquiet. 'What's going on?'

Catesby stepped back into the hallway. 'Jane, I'm so sorry. Something dreadful has happened. There's been an accident.'

'An accident?' She stared at the Englishman for a moment, her brain taking a few seconds to switch into gear. 'George?' she breathed, at last.

The nod from Catesby was barely perceptible. 'I'm afraid so.'

For a moment, Mrs Talbot did not react at all; then she asked the obvious question. 'Is he...?'

There was no need for a reply. The answer was written on all our faces.

'Where is he?' she asked, her voice beginning to falter.

Catesby gestured through the arch. 'You might not want to...'

Mrs Talbot swept past him and onto the terrace before another word could be spoken. Gonzales stepped back to let her through and Catesby followed the Englishwoman out onto the verandah. 'George!' she exclaimed, rushing forward out of sight.

Freddie, to my left, was dumbstruck. 'Did you see what happened?' he asked me.

'No. I just heard a thump. I went out and found him lying there at the bottom of the stairs. He must have slipped.'

'The poor bloke.'

'I heard a scream,' Miss Bunting put in.

'That was the house maid.'

She slid a hand into Freddie's palm and he squeezed it tightly.

At this point, Gunther Weiman arrived from the side hall. Isabel had found him and passed on the news. Susan Weiman was not far behind. Freddie and Miss Bunting stood back to make room for the older couple. 'Where is Jane?' Mr Weiman asked at once.

'Out on the terrace,' Freddie told him quietly.

Catesby was already leading the poor woman back into the house.

Mr Weiman quickly took charge of the situation. 'Susan, take Jane through to the living room. Get her a drink.' His wife nodded and guided Mrs Talbot away.

'You should go with her,' I suggested to Miss Bunting, who was looking every bit as pale as the older woman. 'You too, Freddie.' He could provide the girl with a little moral support.

'Righty-ho.'

As soon as the four of them were gone, Weiman shot a few brief questions in my direction, since I had been first on the scene. I repeated what little I knew and we moved through the arch together, so he could take in the situation for himself. 'This is terrible,' he breathed.

Catesby was hovering behind us. 'I suppose we ought to call a doctor.'

'It's a bit late for that,' I grunted.

'No, I mean to...certify...'

I grimaced. 'Yes, of course.'

'We'll need to inform the police as well,' Weiman said. He closed his eyes and brought a hand up to his face. Mr Talbot had been a good friend of his. 'You didn't actually see him fall?' he asked, dropping the hand.

'No, as I said, I rushed out and found him there. But it can't have been more than a few seconds after it happened.'

The German peered at me then. 'Did you see anyone else about?'

I frowned, not sure what he was getting at. 'No, nobody. I moved across to the body, then your maid came out of the kitchen and screamed and everyone came running.'

'He should have been more careful,' Catesby said.

81

'Those terraces in the rain. I keep telling people. You have to watch your footing.'

'His eyesight was not the best,' Weiman admitted sadly.

We returned to the back hall, where the engineer, Gonzales, was loitering awkwardly.

'We'll call for a doctor,' Catesby resolved. He glanced at his wristwatch. 'I suppose we'll have to send someone down to the village.'

'Don't you have a telephone?' I asked. I was sure I had seen one on the table in the entrance hall.

'Yes, but it's out of order at the moment. There was a storm earlier in the week which knocked the line down. Gunther's been on to the phone company to repair it, but nothing's happened as yet.'

'In this part of the world, these things take time,' the German explained. 'Señor Gonzales, you have a motor-bicycle, do you not?'

'Yes, señor,' the engineer replied.

'I wonder if we could impose on you?'

'You want me to ride to the village?'

'If you would be so kind. To call for a doctor for Mr Talbot.'

Mr Gonzales was happy to oblige.

'Do you *have* a doctor in the village?' I asked, out of curiosity. The place seemed rather small for that.

Catesby shook his head. 'There's a midwife, I think. But no, the nearest doctor must be a good thirty miles away. We'll have to put a call through to Doctor Rubio.'

Weiman nodded his agreement. 'Our family doctor,' he explained to me. 'There is a telephone at the post office. The postmaster will open up for us, when he hears what has happened. I will give you the number, Señor Gonzales.' He put his arm around the engineer and led the man quietly away.

Catesby and I lingered in the hallway, the farm manager scratching at the edge of his moustache. 'It'll be dark soon,' he realised. 'I doubt the doctor will be able to get here until tomorrow. You haven't got a cigarette have you?'

The rain was gradually beginning to ease. I gazed out from the west terrace across the damp grass of the kitchen garden. A low brick wall separated the hacienda from the servants' quarters on the far side. To the left were a series of small administrative shacks and, beyond that, carefully masked by a line of trees, the negro accommodation. The labourers had their own little enclave, set apart from the rest of the estate. Segregation was a way of life here, it seemed. They even had their own path up into the fields.

I took a puff of my cigarette and glanced across at the gaunt figure of Steven Catesby. Despite the riot of curly black hair and the rather jaunty moustache, he was a grim looking fellow just now. 'I thought today was going to be such a good day,' he said, exhaling a cloud of pallid smoke. 'But it's just gone from bad to worse.' His hands were shaking slightly, the enormity of what had happened only now beginning to sink in. 'I can't believe he's dead. Old George. I was just speaking to him a couple of hours ago.'

'Did you see him fall?' I asked. Mr Weiman had not thought to ask but it seemed an obvious question to me. Catesby had been upstairs at around the time of the thump.

'Me? No, I was in my bedroom. I was just coming out onto the landing when I heard Isabel scream.' He took another drag of his cigarette. 'Why didn't he use the stairs in the hallway? That's what I don't understand.'

'Did you know him well?' I asked. 'Mr Talbot?'

Catesby considered for a moment. 'I suppose so. On and off. He was good friends with Gunther. But our dealings were a little more formal. Bank manager and client.' He smiled ruefully. 'He could be rather pig-headed sometimes. Everything had to be done the right way.' Catesby tapped out a little ash from the end of his cigarette. 'We had a bit of a set-to this afternoon, the last time I saw him. He was being insufferable, as always. Digging in his heels. Poor chap. I'd have talked him round but...' He sighed again. 'It's too late now. It's Jane I feel really sorry for. This will hit her hard.'

'Do they have a family? The Talbots?'

'A daughter, I think. In Guatemala City. The poor girl.'

The roar of a motor-bicycle startled us momentarily. A shaft of light cut across the administrative block. 'That'll be Mr Gonzales, off down to the village,' I guessed. Catesby sighed again and the two of us stood in silence, puffing away on our ghastly American cigarettes.

The banker's death had seriously rattled the man, I could see. That was hardly surprising, even if the two of them had not been friends. But it was interesting to hear that they had recently argued. My mind drifted back to the conversation Freddie and I had had with Alberto in the village. He had said Matthew Green had fallen down a set of stairs and that Catesby had been responsible. I wondered idly if it was the same set of stairs. It would be an odd coincidence if it was. Not that I suspected any foul play. Talbot had slipped on a couple of wet floorboards and lost his footing. It was very sad, but there was nothing more to it than that.

Gunther Weiman emerged from the main hall to interrupt our melancholy silence. 'Señor Gonzales has just left,' he informed us.

Catesby found an ashtray and stubbed out the end of his cigarette.

'He should reach the village in about fifteen minutes. I have given him a message for Doctor Rubio. I don't think it would be fair to ask him to come here this evening. It is far too late to travel all this way. I have asked him to call first thing tomorrow morning.'

'What are you going to do about the body?' I enquired, stubbing out my own cigarette with some relief. 'We shouldn't really leave him lying out there on the terrace all night. It feels a bit...disrespectful.'

'You are right,' Weiman agreed. 'We should at least bring him inside the house. But I think perhaps first of all we could all do with a drink. You look as if you need one, Mr Buxton,' he observed kindly.

'I think we all do,' Steven Catesby agreed.

'Everyone else is gathered in the living room. Susan is taking care of Jane.'

'I'll be along shortly,' I said, glancing down at my mud-splattered trousers. 'Just as soon as I've had a change of clothes.'

Maurice adjusted my neck tie with his usual precision. I had found him loitering outside the kitchen and dragged him upstairs. He had heard the news about Mr Talbot's death but did not seem unduly perturbed. The pained expression on his face as we arrived in the bedroom was the same expression he had worn the day we had first met. If anything, I was the one who was a little out of sorts. 'It was just my luck, to be the one to stumble across the body,' I muttered.

'It was most unfortunate, Monsieur,' the valet agreed. He had laid out my dinner jacket on the bed. It was a little early to be changing for supper but I had to get out of my wet clothes and there was no point changing twice. Satisfied with the tie, he grabbed the jacket and helped me into it.

'Odd coincidence, though, him falling down the stairs,' I said. 'After what happened to that other fellow.'

'Yes, Monsieur.'

I had had a little time now to reflect upon the matter and the more I thought about it, the odder it seemed.

'Mr Catesby was telling me he and Mr Talbot had a bit of a barney this afternoon.'

'An argument, Monsieur?'

'Yes. I've no idea what it was about. Some business thing, I imagine.' I dropped my arms and Maurice picked up a brush to give the jacket a quick once over. 'He is the estate manager, after all. Funnily enough, that American fellow was discussing something similar before lunch, with Mr Weiman. I only heard a brief snatch of it. I wonder if it could be the same thing.'

The valet stepped back to examine his handiwork. 'It is not impossible, Monsieur.'

'And, now I come to think of it, Mr Talbot told me he had a bit of paperwork to complete when I spoke to him at breakfast. Isn't that odd? All these heated discussions and then

85

the poor fellow falls down the stairs.' I rubbed an eyebrow. 'It's the devil of a coincidence.'

'Yes, Monsieur.'

I frowned. 'And you know how much I abhor coincidences.'

'Yes, Monsieur. You have said so many times.' Maurice moved across to the bedside table and set down his brush.

I pursed my lips, ignoring the implied criticism. 'I just wish I knew what sort of business it was. Talbot was the family banker. Perhaps he was calling in a loan or something like that?'

'It is possible, Monsieur. Forgive me. You do not believe Monsieur Talbot's death was an accident?'

'I don't know. I mean, it must have been, mustn't it?'

The valet refused to be drawn. 'I could not say, Monsieur. Did you see anyone moving about, at the top of the stairs?'

'What? No, no-one at all. But then he'd already tripped up by the time I got there. It surely can't have been deliberate, though?'

Maurice was keeping an open mind. 'It does not take much to push a man down the stairs,' he pointed out.

'No. No, it doesn't. Oh, lord.' I closed my eyes. 'Please don't let it have been deliberate.' Even the possibility was bringing me out in a cold sweat. 'The last thing I need is to be involved in anything like that again. Not with the minister breathing down my neck back at the legation.'

'Yes, Monsieur. It would be rather inconvenient.'

'It would be a disaster.' I clutched the side of my face and shuddered. Try as I might, however, I could not entirely dismiss the possibility. What if somebody had deliberately pushed George Talbot down the stairs? 'If it wasn't an accident, then Mr Catesby must be involved somehow. He's the one who's meant to be looking after the books.' Perhaps he had been creaming money off the farm accounts, like Giles Markham with the visa money. 'And he did kill that coloured fellow, according to Alberto. Even if it was an accident. I just wish I knew the man a little better. He seems amiable enough to me. He was quite cheerful last night, when we were playing cards.'

'He is not well liked in the house,' Maurice volunteered.

'Not popular below stairs?'

'No, Monsieur. Unlike the master, Monsieur Catesby does not treat the servants well.'

'They *said* as much?' That was interesting.

'Not in so many words, Monsieur. But the atmosphere is unmistakable. However, Monsieur Catesby is not the only person who may have had reason to do harm to Monsieur Talbot.'

'Oh?'

Maurice took a moment to consider his words. 'I believe the American gentlemen also had words with Monsieur Talbot this afternoon.'

'Mr Montana? The United Fruit man?'

'Yes, Monsieur. I was taking in some washing from the kitchen garden earlier this afternoon, just before the rain came. The garden is adjacent to the lawn at the rear of the hacienda.'

'Yes, I've seen it. Get to the point, Morris.'

'I heard raised voices coming from the back lawn. Monsieur Talbot and Monsieur Montana were having an argument. Quite a serious one, I believe.'

'Lord.' I scratched my head. 'Do you know what they were arguing about?'

'I did not stop to listen, Monsieur.'

I growled. 'Fat lot of use you are, Morris.'

'But I do not believe Monsieur Talbot and Monsieur Montana were friends.'

'No. Chalk and cheese, those two.' An English banker and a fast-talking American, it was hardly surprising. 'So it looks like Mr Talbot upset pretty much everybody before he died.' I growled. That was all I needed to hear. I moved across to the bedside table and poured myself a stiff drink. I never travel anywhere without a decent supply of whisky. 'I don't know, Morris. Perhaps we're reading too much into all this. That rain on the terrace, it was pretty lethal. I almost lost my footing myself. He probably did just slip. And why would anyone want to kill a bank manager anyway? It's not as if a bank's going to write off a debt just because the manager pops his clogs. It doesn't make any sense.'

'No, Monsieur,' Maurice agreed.

The guests had scattered across the house. Supper was still some time away and nobody felt much like socializing. The body of George Talbot had been moved into the back hall. Catesby, Freddie and Mr Montana had lifted him onto a table, which had been placed between the back stairs and the kitchen, and then covered him over with a white sheet. It was the quietest decent place they could find, I suppose. In the ordinary course of events, the body should have been left where it was, but if a doctor couldn't get here until morning we could hardly leave the fellow lying prone out on the terrace all night long.

Anita Montana, the attractive Italian woman, was talking to Miss Bunting as I arrived in the living room. Freddie was standing in the far corner, helping himself to a drink from a table by the front windows. I strode over to join him. He gave me a quiet nod and poured me out a brandy. 'Where's Mrs Talbot?' I asked.

'Sitting out on the front terrace with Susan.' He gestured through the windows. 'Oh, Emily said she wanted to have a word with you. I told her what happened this afternoon,' he confided. 'About Giles Markham and that negro bloke. And about you.'

I took a sip of the brandy. 'You mean, that you brought me here under false pretences?'

He chuckled. 'Well, she knew that already.'

'Did she now?' I grunted in disapproval. Freddie was rather too free with that tongue of his. There are some things one should not discuss, even with a sweetheart.

'Well, we could hardly not talk about it, could we,' he protested, 'after that break in at your flat.'

Miss Bunting had by now caught my eye. She waved a hand at me and skilfully disentangled herself from the Italian woman.

Freddie gamely took up the slack. 'Mrs Montana, can I get you another drink?' he asked, marching across. The woman demurred but greeted the blond man with a fair degree of warmth. Freddie, for his part, was all smiles.

Miss Bunting rolled her eyes at the sight of them, but her expression fell as she drew close to me. 'Crumbs, what a dreadful day,' she said. 'That poor man.'

'It's a terrible business,' I agreed, finishing off my brandy in one quick gulp.

'And his poor wife. I was just coming out of my room when he tripped. I heard the thump.' She frowned. 'At the time, I thought somebody must have dropped something.'

'You didn't see it happen?'

'No. At least, not exactly. That was what I wanted to talk to you about.' She kept her voice low and we shuffled carefully away from the windows.

'Go on.'

'Well, I heard the thump and then moved along the balcony, heading for the back stairs. You can see out onto the terrace from there, through the arch. And I thought I saw...well, a flash of something.'

'A flash?'

'A person,' she corrected, 'moving away. Someone at the top of the stairs. Just an impression of them. But after what Freddie told me happened to that other man...'

'You think Mr Catesby might have been involved?' It seemed I was not the only one to have come to that conclusion.

'Well, that's the thing. His bedroom is on the other side of the back stairs, at the rear of the house.'

'Yes, I've seen it.'

'But a moment or two after the thump I saw him coming out of his bedroom and onto the landing. That was when we both heard the scream. And then Señor Gonzales came out of his bedroom.' Which was above the kitchen on the near side of the stairs. 'And he rushed down ahead of us.'

'So if there was a figure out there on the terrace, it couldn't have been Mr Catesby?'

'No.' She hesitated. 'Or at least, I don't think so. Have

you been on the upper terrace?'

'Er...just the bit outside my room, at the front. If the shutters are back, you can step out through the windows.'

'That's just it,' she agreed. 'It's the same all round. I had a bit of a wander after lunch, looking at all the flowers in the baskets. They're very pretty, you know.'

'Er...yes, they are,' I said, not quite sure what she was getting at.

'Did you know it goes right the way around the house? The terrace, I mean. Well, apart from the bit above the kitchen.' She grinned. 'You'll think me silly, but I was so annoyed when I discovered that. I had wanted to walk the whole way around the building. But anyway...' And here at last she came to the point. 'Mr Catesby's room is the same as ours. It has a set of windows leading out onto the terrace.'

I nodded gravely. 'So in theory he could have pushed Mr Talbot down the stairs, rushed into his bedroom and then come out the other side a moment later, looking all sweet and innocent.'

'I suppose so,' Miss Bunting conceded. 'If you really think there may have been foul play.'

'It's a serious possibility, I'm afraid. But if all of the bedrooms have access to that terrace then pretty much anyone could have pushed him down the stairs and rushed around to one of the other bedrooms.' The Weimans' room was the next one along, on the north east corner; then there was Mrs and Mrs Talbot in the middle room on the east side and the Montanas at the front.

'But why would anyone *want* to kill Mr Talbot?' Miss Bunting wondered, quietly. 'Crumbs, he was hardly the most exciting of men.'

'A bit of a bore,' I agreed. 'Poor fellow.' And, come to think of it, none of the people coming downstairs afterwards had looked in the least bit damp. Not that I had bothered to check, of course; and the roof would have protected them from most of the rainfall in any case. 'Perhaps we are reading too much into this,' I said. 'Maybe it was just an accident. These things do happen.' I wasn't convincing anybody, least of all

90

myself. 'It might be worth finding out where everybody was at the time, though. Who did you see upstairs?'

'Well, there was Señor Gonzales. And Mr Catesby. And me, of course. But as soon as we heard that scream, we all headed straight down the stairs.'

'Gonzales looked rather startled,' I recalled, 'when I bumped into him.' I wondered what he had been doing up there; and where his wife had been. I had not seen Consuela Gonzales since lunch time. 'I might just go and have a word with Mrs Gonzales, if I can find her.'

Miss Bunting nodded. 'She's out on the terrace, I think.' She gestured to the side windows. 'And I shall pour myself another drink.'

I left my secretary to her brandy and moved across to the shutters, stepping out onto the east terrace. The engineer's wife was outside, keeping her own company. It was dark now and the only thing visible across the balustrade was the outline of an administrative block a few yards away. 'Not much of a view,' I said, coming to a rest beside her. At this hour, the pasture land on the far side was all but invisible.

Consuela Gonzales dipped her head gently to acknowledge my presence, but did not say anything in reply. She was not a great talker. Probably a bit out of her depth in this environment. I would do my best to put her at her ease.

'Can I get you a drink? This must all be rather distressing for you.'

'No, thank you. You are very kind.' Her accent was milder than her husband's and rather more pleasing to the ear. 'I did not know Mr Talbot. He seemed a nice man. It is terrible that he should die like that.'

'Yes, it is' I agreed. 'These things happen, unfortunately. Your husband looked rather shocked when he tromped down the stairs.'

Mrs Gonzales nodded. 'He has met Mr Talbot before. They are not friends,' she added matter-of-factly, in case I should get that impression. 'We have an account with the bank. My husband pays in his wages every week. Sometimes he would see Mr Talbot. We are doing our best to save a little, but it is not easy.' Her hand dropped unconsciously to her belly. There was no discernible bump that I could see, but it was difficult to tell in the half light coming from the living room.

'When are you expecting?' I asked. It was not a question I would usually ask of a woman but I had the feeling Mrs Gonzales would not mind.

She smiled up at me then. She was rather a short creature – perhaps four feet eleven – but her eyes were dark and full of life. 'Not until January.'

'What are you hoping for? A boy or a girl?'

'Ricardo is hoping for a boy. I do not mind, so long as it is healthy.' She looked out again across the railing. 'I hope he gets back soon. I do not like him being out on his motorbike after dark.'

'Yes, on these roads, always a bit tricky.' It was bad enough on horse back; but at least the motor-bicycle had a decent head lamp. 'I'm sure he'll be back soon. It was very kind of him to volunteer.' Actually, Mr Weiman hadn't given him much choice.

'The señora wanted to go with him to the village.'

'Mrs Talbot?'

'She has a daughter. It is so sad. She will need to tell her what has happened. But Señor Weiman has persuaded her to wait until tomorrow. He will take her down to the village so that she can make a telephone call.'

'Probably sensible,' I agreed. 'Not a good idea for her to be out and about just now. Mind you, it won't be ideal, passing on that kind of news over the telephone. You forget how isolated we are out here, on the farm.'

As if to emphasize the point, a loud clunk sounded off to my left, followed by a vicious juddering noise; and all at once the hacienda was plunged into darkness.

Chapter Seven

The hum of the generator had been a constant presence throughout the evening. The machinery was housed in a small building to the rear of the main house and when it cut out it left behind a deathly silence. 'That sounded nasty,' I muttered. The death throws had been loud but mercifully brief. Behind me, in the living room, some enterprising soul was already grabbing a candle and starting to light it. I was more interested in what had happened to the generator.

I left Mrs Gonzales to rejoin the others and made my way along the side terrace, using the handrail as a guide. The generator house was situated at the far end, a few feet across the lawn on the east side, though all I could see of it at the moment was a black outline in the gloom. As I reached the far corner, I spotted a dark figure moving furtively across the grass, away from the outhouse. The garden was surrounded by trees and all I could make out of the fellow was a deep blur as he moved towards the gate on the opposite side of the lawn. A short uphill path led from there to a longer track running parallel to the back of the hacienda. Another access route to the fields, apparently; a path the West Indians labourers would use to go to work, come picking season. The man – if it was a man – moved swiftly through the gate and disappeared from view.

I stood for a moment with my hand on the balustrade, wondering if I had imagined seeing him. The garden really was as black as pitch. Then, all at once, a light appeared off to my left. Gunther Weiman had emerged onto the terrace, holding a lantern aloft. Steven Catesby was with him. The two men moved down onto the lawn and quickly crossed to the outhouse. The back garden, unlike the front, was more or less on a level. Catesby stopped at the door of the outhouse and grabbed hold of a metal chain hanging down from its front. I wasn't sure if he had noticed me on the terrace. Probably not. The porch was rather dark, with the upper balcony looming over me, and his attention was focused elsewhere. He muttered something I couldn't quite hear, then pulled the door open and disappeared inside. Mr Weiman followed behind, lantern in hand.

I stood watching for some minutes as the light flickered inside the small building. Behind me, the house was gradually lighting up, as the maid rushed to set out lamps in the dining room and light the regular evening candles. A similar process was taking place in the living room. The low hum of conversation resumed. No-one seemed particularly concerned by the abrupt loss of power. Cuts were part of everyday life here and I doubted it was the first time there had been problems with the generator. This time, however, the machine had been deliberately sabotaged. Why else would that man have run away like that?

Raised voices were already floating through the door of the outhouse. Mr Catesby and Mr Weiman had discovered the truth. I strained my ears, trying to make out what they were saying, but without success. An argument was in progress, that much was obvious, and as the minutes passed it showed no signs of letting up. Angry voices spat across the gloom, sometimes dying away but then quickly re-emerging. Finally, Catesby stormed out of the hut. The blind fury on his face was plain to see even in the dim light now emanating from the main house. He barrelled across the lawn and back up into the hacienda. What was that about? I wondered.

A couple of minutes passed and then Gunther Weiman emerged. He turned and calmly locked up the outhouse behind him. Even with the lantern illuminating his face, however, his expression was unreadable.

There was no sign of Catesby at supper that evening and it was a sadly depleted group who gathered in the dining hall. The flickering candles cast a dim glow across our faces as we settled ourselves down. Mrs Talbot had retired to bed, understandably distressed, and both of our hosts were late. Mrs Weiman had taken up some water for the grieving widow and given her something to help her sleep. I don't know what Mr Weiman was doing. Ricardo Gonzales was down in the village, of course, and even the house boy, Moses, was notable by his absence, though he did turn up eventually.

The broth was piping hot but as watery as a duck pond. A couple of bits of carrot were bobbing about in the bowl but there was little else to grab the attention. The failure of the electricity had sadly failed to improve the quality of the food. We waited politely for Mr and Mrs Weiman to join us before tucking in, but once our hosts had settled themselves at either end of the table there was no further excuse to delay.

Freddie, naturally enough, enquired about the state of the generator and Mr Weiman put a brave face on the matter. It was a mechanical failure, he told us with apparent sincerity, but not one that could be repaired this evening. I am not sure how many people believed him. I was not the only one who had heard the disagreement in the outhouse. Nobody felt inclined to challenge the official story, however. The watery soup was consumed in silence, until the sound of a motor-bicycle heralded the return of the engineer.

After dinner, I sat up drinking with Arthur Montana and a rather strained looking Gunther Weiman. Everyone else – even Freddie – had decided to have an early night. In light of all that had happened, I could hardly blame them. I needed a stiff drink, however, and I was not ready for bed just yet. A round of cards was out of the question, so instead the three of us sat out in the courtyard, drinking cognac and reflecting upon the events of the last few hours.

'Doctor Rubio will be here tomorrow morning,' Weiman said, trying his best to strike a positive note. He had poured out a large glass of brandy for himself, though only after he had attended to Mr Montana and I. 'Once the formalities are taken care of, we can arrange for the body to be returned to Guatemala City.'

'What will you do about Mrs Talbot?' I asked. There was still the matter of her daughter, who would need to be informed of the death.

Arthur Montana swallowed a mouthful of cognac. 'Anita and I will accompany her back to town tomorrow afternoon, straight after church.'

'That's kind of you,' I said.

'It's the Christian thing to do.' Montana made it sound more like a duty than an act of compassion, however.

'Did you know Mr Talbot well?' I asked him.

The American pursed his lips. 'Not that well. We've met a few times, through Gunther here. But we weren't friends.'

That I had already surmised. 'My...er...my valet said the two of you had a bit of an argument this afternoon.'

Montana placed his glass down on the table and frowned. 'Did he now?'

'None of my business, of course. I was just curious.'

'You're right,' he said. 'It is none of your business.'

I coughed in surprise at the curt response. 'It's an odd thing, though. Mr Catesby said he'd had a bit of a set-to with him this afternoon as well. The poor fellow does seem to have ruffled a few feathers today.'

'What exactly are you...?'

'Steven and George had a robust relationship,' Weiman cut in diplomatically. 'I believe there was a minor disagreement, yes. They often disagreed on business matters. But it would have been resolved easily enough. George is...was a very reasonable man.'

'I'm sure he was,' I said. 'It just occurred to me, if there was an argument with Mr Montana as well...'

The American scowled. 'What exactly are you implying, Mr Buxton?'

'Oh, nothing at all. I just thought, if Mr Talbot had his head full of business matters, that might explain why he lost his footing like that. He might not have been paying attention to where he was going.'

'I suppose that is possible,' Gunther Weiman conceded, with a frown.

'Especially if he'd just had a blazing row...'

'There was no row!' Montana responded forcefully. 'A civilised disagreement, nothing more.' He glared at me across the table.

'More of a misunderstanding, I believe,' Weiman suggested, anxious to avoid any conflict. 'It was a matter of

96

transportation fees, wasn't it, Arthur?'

Montana hesitated. 'Yes. Yes, that's right.'

'George has been a good friend to me for many years,' the German explained. 'He has always sought to protect my interests, both personally and professionally. He would challenge anyone he thought was acting against me. Isn't that right, Arthur?'

'He thought I was screwing you over,' Montana agreed, with a growl.

I flinched at the crude language, but I could not resist probing further. 'In what way?'

Montana rose up and poured himself another brandy. He offered me a refill, grudgingly, which I was happy to accept. 'United Fruit, the company I work for, has something of a monopoly on transport in this country.'

'Yes, I've noticed that,' I agreed, taking the glass. The American, I was pleased to note, had not been stingy with the measure.

'On the rail roads and the ports. It's only fair that that should be the case. We built them, after all.' He resumed his seat. That was not strictly true, I thought. United Fruit may have provided some of the finance, but it had been the indigenous people – and a fair number of imported West Indians labourers – who had done the hard work. 'But the company's number one priority is the transportation of its own produce. Getting it to the coast and off to America.'

'That seems fair enough,' I agreed.

'If there's any spare capacity we allow other producers to make use of our facilities. Passengers too. But at a fair premium.'

'Transportation costs are very high,' Weiman confirmed. 'They represent a considerable part of our outlay.'

'And with the price of coffee collapsing, it's been a difficult couple of years for independent producers. Gunther and I have been friends for some time, and knowing the difficulties he's had, I've been able to...' He paused to find the right word. 'Ameliorate the cost a little.'

'Waive the fees?' I asked.

97

'Reduce them considerably.'

'That's very decent of you.' I was somewhat surprised that the American would pull his finger out in that way, even for a friend; but I supposed not everybody who worked for United Fruit was a money-grabbing scoundrel.

'It has been of great help to us over the last few months,' Weiman said. 'Arthur has been a great help.'

Montana took another sip of brandy. 'However, the company is now taking a firmer hand, ensuring a little more consistency in the application of fees. There's been a diktat from on high. From now on, no exceptions are allowed. No favoured rates. Everyone has to pay full whack. I had to break the news to Gunther and Steven.'

'This weekend?'

He hesitated. 'That's right.'

'And that was what you were arguing about with Mr Talbot?'

'We often disagreed. He got the wrong end of the stick on that one. He thought I was imposing the new fees unilaterally; that I was just enforcing the company policy, with no thought to Gunther here.'

'He was not aware of how much help Arthur has given me up to now. He thought I was being...what is the phrase?'

'Stabbed in the back,' the American prompted. 'He got real nasty about it.'

'So it wasn't just a "civilised disagreement" then?'

'He was trying to protect my interests,' the German explained, before Montana could shoot back a reply. 'But it was a misunderstanding and I was soon able to put him right.'

'In fairness to the guy, he did apologise. But I have to admit, I came within an inch of thumping the son of a bitch. You English can be so god-damned patronising sometimes.'

I smiled. 'We do our best. So that was all it was? The argument this afternoon?'

'I just said so, didn't I?'

'Of course.' I made a conscious effort not to frown. There was something about his explanation that seemed a little too pat for me.

'I just hope the conversation did not in some way contribute to his death,' Weiman said. 'Poor George. He was meticulous in business but he was always a little clumsy physically. Jane would often berate him for bumping into things or damaging her crockery.' He shook his head. 'I don't know what she will do now. She and her daughter will be all alone in the world.'

'Do you think they'll go back to England?' I asked.

'I don't know. Susan and I will do our best to support them, whatever they decide to do.'

For a moment, the conversation died. I had not had the nerve to ask Mr Weiman about the argument he had had with Steven Catesby in the generator room. Now did not feel like the right time. Mr Talbot's death had cast a shadow over everything. 'I suppose there'll have to be some kind of inquest,' I put in eventually. 'Lord, I suppose I'll have to come back here for that.'

Weiman did not think that would be necessary. 'The police will come tomorrow and they will take statements. After that, everything will be a formality.'

'Who will they send?' I asked. I wasn't particularly keen on the idea of being interviewed by the police. The Guatemalan authorities had a reputation for brutality which had been well earned, though I suspected they would be courteous enough to foreigners. Rich white foreigners, anyway. 'Some local constable?' That would be the best option.

'No.' Weiman rubbed his beard. 'Señor Gonzales tells me we have a rather senior figure coming. An acquaintance of George who has decided to investigate the matter personally. Señor Julio Tejada.'

'The general?' Montana scowled at the name. 'That's all we need.'

I was perplexed. 'A general? What, you mean a soldier?'

'No, not a soldier. He is a senior police officer,' Weiman said.

'Don't let the title fool you,' Montana told me. 'There are dozens of generals in Guatemala. It means nothing. It's

99

practically the default rank.'

'But General Tejada is rather well connected,' Weiman said. 'So we must all mind our manners. We must not do anything to antagonise him.'

'Unpleasant sort, is he?' I asked.

The American laughed humourlessly. 'The worst kind of butcher. An enforcer more than a policeman. A nationalist too. Doesn't like foreign interference in Guatemalan affairs. His brother-in-law is General Roderico Anzueto, director of the Policia Nacional. And *he's* second in command to Ubico himself. A brutal man, Tejada. I wouldn't trust him as far as I could throw him.'

'It would be a good idea to avoid discussing politics tomorrow or anything other than the matter in hand,' Weiman concluded.

'Fair enough,' I agreed. I would have to have a word with Freddie and Miss Bunting; warn them to mind their Ps and Qs.

Montana was not so sanguine. 'Just keep that devil away from me,' he muttered. 'That's all I ask.'

The candle flickered absently, illuminating the cramped downstairs room. I had no idea what the time was; two or three in the morning, perhaps. The house was completely dead, anyway, though the usual cacophony of insects continued to enliven the exterior of the hacienda. I had crept downstairs to answer a call of nature. I rarely slept a whole night through these days. A chamber pot had been provided in the bedroom but I have an aversion to using such things and it was not as if I had been asleep in any case. The mattress I had been given was rather uncomfortable and my mind was too preoccupied to allow me any respite from the waking world. Better to stretch my legs, I decided, and do things properly.

A small gecko was minding its own business on the ceiling of the cubicle. I did not pay it any attention. I was far too busy ruminating.

It was this damned business with Arthur Montana and

George Talbot. The American, I was sure, had lied to me about the nature of their disagreement and it was obvious he had been prompted to do so by Gunther Weiman. The two men had put on a reasonable show, but I had dealt with enough dissembling over the years to know when someone was trying to pull the wool over my eyes. What were they trying to hide? I wondered. Mr Weiman didn't strike me as a naturally deceitful man and I doubted he had told any outright lies; but he had chosen his words carefully. Perhaps he was just trying to downplay the seriousness of the dispute, in the light of what had happened. Or perhaps there was some sensitive business matter – something really confidential – which they did not wish to discuss in front of me. The fact that George Talbot had died, however, and that they were now so obviously withholding the truth, could not help but reflect badly upon the two of them. I was curious to know what the police would make of that in the morning. And what about the earlier argument between Catesby and Talbot? That, according to the man himself, was also a business matter. Could it have been the same sensitive issue? I had no idea. Then of course there was the sabotage of the generator and the death of Matthew Green all those weeks ago; not to mention the death of Giles Markham.

The police would certainly have a lot to investigate; and they would want to talk to me first, since I had discovered Talbot's body. I didn't fancy being the one to broach the matter of raised voices. I had not witnessed either of the arguments the banker had been involved in; and it was the responsibility of Messrs Weiman, Montana and Catesby to outline their dealings with the dead man. Far better for me to keep out of it. If they chose to lie to the authorities, that was their affair. And in any case, whatever my suspicions, I had no concrete evidence that there had been any foul play. If I started throwing accusations around it might get me into all sorts of hot water. I had told Freddie yesterday afternoon that this whole business was best left alone and, despite the death of Mr Talbot, I was still of that opinion. Whatever was going on, it had nothing to do with any of us at the legation. Freddie may have brought me here with some mad notion of investigating the events leading up to Giles

Markham's suicide, but if I tried to ferret around and uncovered something unfortunate, it could well blow up in my face. No, better to let things be, have a nice breakfast in the morning, say nothing of any consequence to the police and then tootle off for the train in the early afternoon. That way, there would be no come back on any of us. David Richards would not be able to take offence at anything I had done and I could get on with my life, hopefully as far away from this damned finca as possible.

The question of Talbot's death still niggled at me, though. Who was it Miss Bunting had seen moving about at the top of the stairs? Was that what Steven Catesby and Gunther Weiman had been arguing about in the generator room? Despite my concerns, a small part of me was still curious to know the truth. Would it really do any harm to ask a few more questions; perhaps have another quiet word with Mr Catesby? I would have a few hours to kill in the morning, between breakfast and lunch, and I would probably never see the man again after tomorrow. I doubted I would have the nerve to ask him directly about the death of Matthew Green, but there was nothing stopping me from probing a little deeper concerning his business arrangements with George Talbot. Then too there was Joseph Green. It was a Sunday tomorrow. He would be off work. Perhaps I could wander over to the workers' cottages and have a quiet word with him, when no one was looking. Our previous conversation had been interrupted and, in light of what I had discovered about his brother's extra-curricular activities, there was clearly a lot more he could tell me; and perhaps some information I could give to him too, about Giles Markham. Presumably that was why he had sent me that note in the first place. Yes, it would do no harm to talk to Green, so long as I was discreet. This Doctor Rubio fellow would be arriving first thing, with the police, so all attention would be focused on him. Once I had made my statement, I could easily slip away for half an hour.

I completed my ablutions and picked up the lamp. The gecko skittered away through a crack in the door as I grabbed the handle. A loud creak sounded from above. I glanced up at the ceiling. Somebody was up and about on the first floor.

Which room would that be? I wondered. Either Freddie's or Miss Bunting's. I cursed, hoping I would not bump into either of them on the way back to my bedroom. I was dressed decently enough, in a long nightshirt, and my bandages were still in place, but there is always something acutely embarrassing about running into someone in the middle of the night, even if neither of you is doing anything wrong.

I returned the lamp to the hall table outside the water closet. The candle had all but burnt out now. A telephone was resting next to the lamp, just below a framed map of the estate. Out of curiosity, I picked up the receiver and held it to my ear, but the line was dead. I moved towards the stairs and heard a door creak somewhere on the upper landing. I peered up into the gloom. The entrance to Freddie's room was at the top of the stairs, set back from the main drag. That door was firmly closed, so it had to be Miss Bunting who was creeping about. Oh well, I thought, there was no avoiding her now. I moved up the stairs. If she was heading for the little girls' room, this was the direction she would come.

Another thought occurred to me, as I reached the top of the stairs. Perhaps she had arranged a night-time rendezvous with Freddie. That thought made me smile, but all at once I caught sight of the girl and, to my surprise, she was heading in the opposite direction, towards the back of the house. Not visiting Freddie, then, or going to the lavatory. She was on the back landing now, to the north of the courtyard. She did not have a lamp with her but the star-spattered sky above the patio gave me just enough light to make out the white of her short-sleeved dress as she tip-toed down the corridor. What was she up to? There was another set of stairs at the rear of the house, leading down to the back hall, but she ignored them as well and veered left into another short hallway heading out onto the far terrace. At this point, she disappeared from view.

I remained where I was for a moment, my curiosity piqued. I was not unduly surprised that Miss Bunting should be up and about at this hour, but I couldn't fathom what she might be doing. Perhaps Freddie was awake as well and the two of them were planning to meet up somewhere, away from the house. But no, leaning in close to his door, I could hear a gentle snore vibrating across the bedroom. Freddie was in the arms of Morpheus. If Miss Bunting had arranged an illicit rendezvous, it was not with him. Who else could it be, though? All of the rooms on the east side were occupied by married couples. Perhaps she was heading out of the house altogether. The terrace stairs were easily accessible.

Freddie had said he had told Miss Bunting all about my inquiries into the death of Giles Markham. Perhaps that was why she was creeping about in the dead of night. It would be just like the damned girl to go off investigating on her own. If so, I would have to put a stop to that at once. Well, perhaps not at once, but certainly first thing in the morning.

I sighed. My feet were getting cold now, lingering in one place. Carpets were an unknown luxury on this floor. I would hurry back to bed. Whatever Miss Bunting was up to, I would find out soon enough.

Maurice was in good spirits the following morning. 'Looking forward to getting home, eh?' I said.

'Indeed, Monsieur.' He had called early – at eight thirty – so I would be up and dressed in plenty of time to join the others for breakfast.

'I can't wait to get out of this place as well. As soon as the formalities are out the way. What time's the train?'

'Four o'clock, Monsieur. We will need to leave by half past one.'

'Very good. Can't come quickly enough, so far as I'm concerned.' Some of the other guests would be heading down to the village ahead of time, to attend the local church service, but I had no intention of joining them. A hearty breakfast would do far more to lift my spirits than some wizened cleric. Besides, it would be a Catholic service and they could go on for hours. 'Have you had breakfast yet?' I asked my man, absently.

The valet frowned. 'Yes, Monsieur.' He did not sound pleased to be reminded.

'Not the world's greatest cook, that German woman.'

'No, Monsieur.'

'Still. You can't go wrong with a few eggs and a bit of toast.'

'You would not think so, Monsieur,' Maurice commented drily.

I laughed. 'Not everyone can be Michelin starred, Morris. Your standards are too high, that's your problem. It's asking for disappointment.'

'Yes, Monsieur.'

'Oh, I'm thinking of having another quick word with that Green fellow after breakfast,' I said. 'If I can find him.'

Maurice had knocked out my shoes and placed them in front of me by the bed. 'Do you think that is wise, Monsieur?'

'Probably not.' I dipped down to ease my feet into the shoes and then quickly tied the laces. 'But it might be the last chance I'll get. I owe it to Freddie to have one last stab at it.'

'Yes, Monsieur.'

I stood up and let Maurice fuss for a moment, removing some imagined dust or hair from the shoulders of my jacket. He stepped back with a nod of satisfaction. I must admit, having the granite faced fellow attending to me as usual made for a welcome start to the day. There is something rather pleasing in a well-oiled routine, especially when one is away from home.

I pulled open the door and stepped out onto the landing. The sun was hovering just above the roof towards the front of the hacienda, sending a wide arc of light down into the courtyard. I raised a hand to shield my eyes. From out in the front yard, I could hear the sound of a motor vehicle pulling up and, as I made my way towards the back stairs, following the smell of warm bread wafting up from the dining room on the far corner, I saw Mrs Weiman crossing the courtyard from the front entrance.

'Good morning, Mr Buxton!' she called up in greeting. 'I hope you slept well.'

'Very well, thank you,' I lied, reaching the far corner and waving a hand down at her. Now was not the time to complain about the mattress.

'You couldn't give Steven a knock, could you?' she

105

asked. 'I think Doctor Rubio has just arrived.'

I stifled a yawn and nodded. Perhaps this would be a good time to have that private word with him. People often tend to be less guarded first thing in the morning. Catesby's bedroom was just past the back stairs, on the other side of that short hallway where Miss Bunting had disappeared last night. 'It's this one, isn't it?' I gestured to the door as I moved onto the far landing.

'That's right,' Susan Weiman agreed, before disappearing out of view below me.

I passed along the corridor to the requisite door and gave a quick but solid knock. It wasn't locked and the door shifted inwards slightly. There was no response from inside, not even a groan. 'Rise and shine, Mr Catesby!' I called out.

I pushed the door open a crack. Light was fluttering in from the far windows. The shutters must have been left open during the night. Not that the room would get much light even during the day. There was nothing but trees and the mountainside to the north of the hacienda.

Behind me, a babble of voices broke out in the courtyard.

Maybe he was awake already, I thought. Perhaps he had opened the blinds, slipped out the far door and headed down to the bathroom.

It was only as I moved forward to get a proper look that I realised my mistake. Steven Catesby was lying in bed, neatly tucked up, his eyes closed and his expression blank. The bedsheets were covered in blood.

Chapter Eight

As I moved further into the room, the gash across his neck became horribly visible. I let out a silent yelp and brought a hand up to my mouth. My God. Catesby's throat had been slit open. For a moment, I simply stopped and stared. I didn't know what else to do. His pyjamas were stained red, as were the sheets and pillows in the area surrounding his head. It was a dreadful sight. The poor man had been butchered in his own bed. A cut throat razor lay abandoned on the wooden floorboards. It too was slicked with blood. I shuddered, looking down at the thing. Someone had crept into his bedroom in the middle of the night and slit his throat. There did not look to have been any sort of struggle. That was odd, I thought, my mind struggling to reassert itself through a fog of incomprehension. Why hadn't Catesby woken up? And, come to that, why hadn't anybody heard his death throes?

I drew in a breath and moved back to the door, cursing the fates that had placed me in this position once again. Why did I have to be the one to discover the body? It was hardly fair. There were lots of other people in the house. But there was no point crying about it now.

I turned to grab the handle of the door, but as I did so a glint of light from the far side of the room attracted my attention. I strode across to the windows to take a look. Something was twinkling up at me from underneath one of the open shutters. I peered down at it and let out a low howl. I recognised the object. It was an earring with a small flower motif. I picked it up without thinking, my mind juddering in sudden horror. The earring belonged to my secretary, Miss Bunting. I had seen her creeping about in this part of the house in the early hours of the morning. My hand went to my mouth again. She must have been in here last night. I stared back at the body and the stained bedsheets. No, it was not possible. Miss Bunting had not met Steven Catesby before this weekend. She could not be responsible for his demise. But the evidence was there in my hand. The girl had definitely been in his room.

I pocketed the earring and crossed numbly back to the door. I don't know why I kept it. Self-preservation perhaps or a feeling that somehow I must have got it all wrong. Perhaps it was somebody else's earring. For all I knew, it might be a common design. But whatever the truth, I did not wish to remain in that bloody room a moment longer.

I stepped out onto the landing. Gunther Weiman was standing in the courtyard below, conversing with two grim looking officials. I peered down at them from the balustrade. One was a policeman, the other a doctor. The latter fellow was carrying a small medical bag in his left hand. A third individual, some distance behind, was peering suspiciously through some of the archways which encircled the plaza; another policeman, judging by the uniform, a strange looking fellow with alarmingly prominent eyeballs.

Gunther Weiman glanced up and raised a friendly hand to me; then he caught sight of my expression. 'Mr Buxton, is everything all right?'

I took a lungful of air. 'No, no I'm afraid it isn't,' I said. I gestured back towards the bedroom. 'You'd better come and see.'

Doctor Manuel Rubio flexed the dead arm and peered down at Steven Catesby's bloodied throat. 'I am not a pathologist,' he confessed, gazing sadly at the corpse. His accent was light, his voice soft but authoritative. 'The time of death is not easy to determine. But rigor mortis has set in, so he has certainly been dead for some hours.'

General Julio Tejada grunted. 'He was killed in the middle of the night?' The policeman was standing at the far end of the bed. He was a large, intimidating fellow with a chubby face, thick eyebrows and slicked back hair. He was dressed in military fatigues and carried a thin wooden cane in his hand.

'It looks that way, general,' Doctor Rubio replied. His tone was deferential, not to say a little nervous in the other man's presence.

Tejada looked away and noticed me hovering by the

door. I had been obliged to remain in the room while a preliminary examination was carried out. 'You!' he snapped, aiming his stick at me. 'What is your name?'

I stepped forward hesitantly. 'Er...Buxton. Henry Buxton.'

'You knew this man?' He gestured to the corpse.

'Mr Catesby? No. Well, I met him on Friday evening. I'm just a house guest.'

The general's bushy eyebrows coalesced into a sceptical frown. 'What were you doing in his room?' Every question was a bark, like a smack to the jaw.

'I was...Mrs Weiman asked me to give him a knock.' The reply sounded flaccid, even to my own ears. 'He was...late for breakfast. The door wasn't locked. I put my head around and saw him lying there.'

General Tejada eyed me suspiciously. 'Why did you enter the room? You could see he was dead from the doorway.'

'I...I don't know.' That was the God's honest truth. 'I suppose I couldn't quite believe it. I just...stepped in, the door closed behind me. And then I was straight out again.'

'You didn't touch anything in here?'

'No, nothing,' I lied.

The general continued to stare but this time I held his gaze. What was he getting at me for? I wasn't the criminal here. I was just reporting what I had found.

'And the shutters were already drawn back?' He swept his swagger stick across to the windows leading out onto the far terrace.

'Yes. I presume he left them open. It was quite a warm night.'

Tejada scrunched his lips. 'That is for me to determine. The other man, the banker. Did you know him?' We had passed the late Mr Talbot on the way up the stairs. Gunther Weiman had been with us at that point, but he had not had the stomach to linger in the bedroom.

'No. At least...'

'Not before this weekend,' the general finished for me. His tone was bordering on the sarcastic. 'Was that an accident?'

'I believe so. He fell down the stairs.'

'And you discovered his body as well?'

'Er...well, yes. I heard him fall.'

'An unfortunate coincidence. Two men dying within a few hours of each other and you discovering both the bodies.'

'Yes, it's been rather an unfortunate weekend, so far.'

The policeman snorted, glancing back at the bed. 'I do not believe in coincidence.' That was one thing at least we had in common.

Doctor Rubio was examining the dead man's eyeballs, though to what end I could not determine. The man had the air of country GP rather than a pathologist. He made quite a contrast to the grim general.

'We will be taking statements from all the house guests shortly,' Tejada barked, without looking back. 'Do not leave the building. That is all.'

'Right,' I agreed, edging towards the door.

The boggle-eyed deputy was crouching down by the side of the bed with a flashbulb camera, taking a photograph of the razor on the floor. The handle was free of blood, I noticed, if not the blade itself. I wondered if they would find any fingerprints on it.

The general caught my gaze and growled. 'You will leave now, señor. This is a crime scene not a circus.'

'Yes, of course.' I spun around and hurried away.

Gunther Weiman was standing in the corridor outside with his back to the door. I brought myself up abruptly. He was gripping the balustrade with both hands but his head was bowed. His face, beneath that striking white hair, seemed pale and withdrawn. I stopped beside him at the rail, looking down across the empty courtyard. The other guests would be settled in the dining room now, having their breakfast. We could hear their voices drifting quietly up through the open doorway out of sight beneath us. 'Does the rest of the household know what's happened?' I asked.

'No, not yet,' he said. But they would have a sense that something was up. They must have seen the policemen clomping up the stairs. 'I should go and tell them.' His voice

110

sounded strained, which was hardly surprising in the circumstances.

'This is a dreadful business,' I muttered.

'All that blood.' He shuddered. I couldn't blame him for not wanting to linger in the bedroom. 'How could somebody do that? To Steven, of all people.'

'I wish I knew.' There was a brief, awkward pause. 'Doctor Rubio seems a little out of his depth in there,' I observed, finally.

Weiman glanced across at me. 'He is a family doctor. He was not expecting this. He came here to provide a death certificate, not to investigate...' His voice trailed away.

'A murder,' I finished for him, reluctantly. That was the truth of the matter. A murder had been committed. I shut my eyes. Another trail of bodies. Why was it that I kept finding myself in the middle of this sort of thing? Bloody Frederick Reeves, dragging me down here. Weiman had more reason to be upset than I did, though. He must have known Catesby for years. 'Come on,' I said. 'We'd better go downstairs. General Tejada asked me to tell everybody they're not to leave the building until the police have taken statements from everyone.'

Weiman nodded and released his grip on the balustrade. We shuffled along the landing towards the back stairs.

'I didn't like him,' he blurted out suddenly. 'Steven. I never liked him. I always tried to, for my wife's sake, but we never really got on.' He came to a halt at the top of the stairs. 'I know it's wrong to say that now, but it is the truth. He was a difficult man to be around. But I would never have wished....' He closed his eyes. '*Mein gott*. What am I going to tell Susan?'

The smell of warm bread would normally have lifted the coldest of spirits; but nothing that morning could have ameliorated the mood of shock and horror at the breakfast table as the guests and staff learnt of the death of Steven Catesby and the gruesome manner of his demise. Susan Weiman was distraught and Jane Talbot, who was already grieving for her own husband, now found herself in the peculiar position of

111

having to comfort our hostess. It didn't help that the man's bedroom was directly above us. We could all hear the heavy, clomping footsteps of Tejada and his underling as they examined the chamber in the finest detail. Arthur Montana shook his head as Gunther Weiman outlined the dreadful truth, but continued with his breakfast regardless. He didn't even flinch at the mention of the razor. I had offered to speak in Weiman's place, but the German had insisted – rightly – that it was his responsibility. Ricardo Gonzales was busily comforting his wife, who was struggling not to cry. I doubted Consuela Gonzales had spoken more than a dozen words to Mr Catesby the entire weekend, but the woman's natural sympathy was showing through and, in the circumstances, I could not blame her for such a public display of grief. As soon as Weiman had finished speaking, I passed on the general's instruction that no-one should leave the house. Any excursions that had been planned for this morning would have to be postponed.

'We should light a candle for him,' Anita Montana declared, at the mention of church. 'We should pray for him.' I hadn't realised the Italian woman had a religious bent. She was not exactly dressed like a nun.

'We will, honey,' Arthur Montana agreed. 'He's with God now.'

The conversation continued in this stilted fashion for several minutes but was finally cut short when the general thumped out of the bedroom and onto the landing above. We listened in silence as he and Doctor Rubio descended the back stairs and stopped in the hallway to examine the second body. Now it was Susan Weiman's turn to provide comfort to Mrs Talbot.

I caught the eye of Freddie Reeves and we moved away from the table. I offered him a cigarette from my case as we shuffled out onto the side terrace. We stood for some moments there, our backs leaning against the outer railing, gently puffing away.

'It really is murder then?' Freddie asked at last.

'No doubt about it,' I confirmed, in a low voice.

'Christ.' He took another drag from his cigarette. 'So

112

someone crept in and slit his throat? With a cut-throat razor?'

'It looks like it.' Had it been his own razor, I wondered now, or had the murderer brought it with him? Doubtless that was something General Tejada would be able to determine. The policeman was moving about on the other side of the dining hall, waving that damned swagger stick of his all over the place. The house guests were doing their best to ignore the activity, as Doctor Rubio set to work examining the body of George Talbot. After a moment, Tejada moved to the far door and gestured for Gunther Weiman to join them. The German took a deep breath, squeezed his wife's shoulder, and strode out into the back hall.

'I'm sure the police will sort everything out,' I said. At the very least, they appeared to be going through all the right motions.

'I wouldn't be too sure about that,' Freddie whispered, tilting his head confidentially. 'General Tejada's not exactly the most helpful bloke I've ever met.'

'You've met him *before*?' I coughed.

The other man gave a half smile. 'Yes. Didn't I tell you? He was the one who investigated Giles Markham's suicide.'

'*Tejada* did?' I boggled in surprise.

'Yes. That's why the minister's so het up about involving the police in anything else. After that business with Giles, he's desperate to keep a low profile.'

'Not much chance of that now,' I muttered. 'Your Mr Richards is going to have a field day when he finds out the two of us are involved in a murder investigation.'

'Three of us,' Freddie said. 'Emily too. But, hey, it's not as if this has got anything to do with us, is it?'

'It won't matter. We're here. We're involved. I'm already on notice. He'll hang me out to dry.' And if Miss Bunting...no, I didn't even want to think about that. 'He'll take great pleasure in dispatching a telegram to London, demanding my dismissal.'

'It won't come to that, surely? He might not even find out.'

I snorted. 'Oh, he'll find out all right. It'll be all over

the press in a few days time. A murder. They're not going to let that go.'

Freddie bit his lip. 'Perhaps we ought to phone him? Get our side in first?'

I tapped away some of the ash from my cigarette. 'That might not be such a bad idea. If we're ever allowed to leave the house.' It was a shame the hall telephone was out of order. 'And you say it was Tejada who investigated Giles Markham's death?'

'Yes. Bit of a coincidence, really.' Freddie scratched his ear. 'But even the minister couldn't cover up somebody committing suicide like that. Poor old Giles shot himself at point black range. It wasn't a pretty sight.' Freddie had been the second person on the scene, after my secretary William Battersby. 'We had to let the local authorities know, just as a courtesy,' he added. The passport control office was in a separate building from the legation and it was not technically British territory. Anything untoward that happened there would always be the business of the local police. 'It was a mad rush to clear out the office, to get rid of anything sensitive before he arrived. God, that was a hell of a morning.'

'But he didn't find anything amiss? About Markham's death?'

'No. He was barely there half an hour. I got the impression he found it all beneath his dignity. You know, investigating a suicide.'

'And did he search the flat as well?'

'Yes, I think so.' Freddie considered for a moment. 'Yes, a day or two later. After we'd given it the once over.'

'Did you see him do it?'

'No, but William was there. Your Mr Battersby.'

I frowned. 'And now he turns up here, to investigate the case of a man who slipped on a wet floorboard and fell down some stairs.'

'It does sound a bit funny, when you put it like that,' Freddie agreed.

'Mr Weiman told me last night that they were friends, Talbot and the general. Well, acquaintances, anyway. I presume that was why he wanted to come here himself, rather than leaving it to some local bod. They would have had to send a policeman, to compile a report for the coroner.'

'Yes, I suppose they would.' Even in a case of accidental death, there were procedures to follow. 'And he couldn't have known what he was going to find this morning. Bloody hell, Henry. That poor bastard, murdered in his bed.' Freddie took another gasp of his cigarette. 'Do you think it might have been an intruder? A burglar or something?'

'I don't know. I don't think so. The room was untouched. There didn't seem to be any sign of a struggle. That's what confuses me. Surely you'd wake up, if someone tried to slit your throat?'

Freddie shuddered, exhaling a cloud of smoke. 'I don't even want to imagine.' He gazed at me thoughtfully for a minute. 'I suppose you're used to this kind of thing, aren't you? After what happened to you on that airship?'

I shook my head. 'You never get used to it.'

He knocked the ash from the end of his cigarette. 'I'm sorry I dragged you out here. It's all my fault. I shouldn't have got you involved in this, Henry.'

I pursed my lips. 'No, you shouldn't. But what's done is done. The important thing now is to try to limit the damage. And the only way we can do that is to find out what really happened to Mr Catesby.'

'Isn't that the police's job, now that they're here?'

'Probably. But from what you say, and what Mr Montana told me last night, I'm not sure we can rely on General Tejada to investigate the matter thoroughly.'

'No, probably not,' Freddie agreed. 'So where do we start?'

'Well, first of all, we need to work out where everybody was last night.'

He shrugged. 'In bed, presumably.'

'You didn't hear anyone creeping about?'

'No, not me. But I was out like a light. I always fall asleep the moment my head hits the pillow.'

I envied him that. 'You didn't get up at all? Any

nocturnal visits I should know about?'

Freddie laughed. 'What, to see Emily, you mean? No, it hasn't quite got to that stage yet. She's quite protective of her reputation.'

'She's knows a scoundrel when she sees one,' I teased. 'But actually, I meant trips to the little boys' room.'

He chuckled again. 'No, some of us have a little self control.'

'I'll remind you of that when you're my age. But, seriously, you didn't hear anyone wandering around?'

'No, I didn't hear anything at all. Steven went to bed early, didn't he? After he'd gone out to look at the generator.' Catesby had not joined us at supper. 'Could he have been done away before the rest of us went to bed?'

'I don't think so. Doctor Rubio wasn't sure of the time of death but it sounds like it was probably in the middle of the night. Which means it might be anyone.'

'What about George? Do you think he was bumped off as well? By the same person?'

'It's a possibility. Lord. Two murders. And the generator sabotaged as well. It must be...'

'Sabotaged?' Freddie's eyes widened. This was the first he had heard of that. He had obviously not been paying attention last night.

'No doubt about it,' I said. 'I saw a fellow running away from the outhouse. Well somebody running away. It was too dark to make out who it was.'

'Why would anyone want to sabotage the generator?'

'Lord knows.'

'It's not as if they need the electricity. They've got plenty of candles lying about.' Freddie took a last drag of his cigarette and then dropped it to the floor, stubbing it out with his foot and kicking it through the balustrade onto the grass.

'Nevertheless, the thing was deliberately put out of action.'

'Out of spite, you think?'

'It looks like it,' I said. But you did not cut someone's throat out of spite.

Maurice removed the clothes peg from his mouth and peered down at the small flower shaped earring in the palm of my hand. 'It is hers, isn't it?' I asked. The manservant had a much better eye for detail than I did and would always take careful note of what people were wearing. It was part of his job, after all.

'Yes, Monsieur,' he confirmed, without hesitation.

I growled and closed my hand, quickly pocketing the errant jewellery. 'So she was definitely in his room.'

Maurice nodded gravely and attached the clothes peg to the fold of my shirt. 'It would appear so, Monsieur.' The valet had come out to the kitchen garden to hang a couple of my shirts on the line. The sun was at its best mid morning and my man was determined to make the most of it.

The interviews had already begun in the main house. General Tejada had finally addressed the household, though only to inform us – in a rather disdainful manner – that his deputy would be taking our statements, while he pursued other lines of enquiry. An estate worker had been despatched to the village to request a truck and some additional personnel. The bodies would need to be removed as well so that a proper post mortem could be conducted. Tejada and his deputy had arrived at the house on a motor-bicycle and that was hardly a suitable means of conveyance for a corpse. The deputy had only come at all because the general needed a driver – Tejada had travelled in the sidecar – which made it all the more galling that this young fellow would be the one conducting the interviews.

Sergeant Velázquez was an odd looking cove, bearded and boggle-eyed, not ugly as such but the kind of fellow you would think twice about letting shine your shoes. Of course, one should never judge a book by its cover, but the malevolent gleam in his eye did not present much cause for optimism.

I had not been in quite the right frame of mind to submit to another interrogation, so I had done my best to melt into the background as the sergeant surveyed the dining hall, searching for his first victim. Happily, after lingering for a moment on

117

Mrs Arthur Montana and her rather revealing dress, his wandering eye had come to rest on Miss Emily Bunting, the prettiest girl in the room. A typical man. The sergeant grinned, taking in her blonde ringlets and bright blue eyes, and then pointed a bony finger. Miss Bunting rolled her eyes but allowed herself to be led away into the living room to be interviewed.

She was not wearing any earrings this morning, I noticed. I had taken a quick peep at her earlobes as she passed me by. Had she been wearing them last night, I wondered, when I had seen her wandering about? I could not be sure.

Breakfast was abandoned at this point, barely eaten, and Isabel and Moses quietly cleared away the plates.

I slipped away up the hall stairs to my bedroom. Tobacco was all well and good but what I really needed was a spot of whisky to steady my nerves. Events were spiralling out of control and I needed time to think. Standing at the west window, looking out across the terrace into the kitchen garden, I had spotted my man heading out with a wash basket. I knocked back the whisky in one gulp and made my way down the hall stairs to join him. For all his many and varied faults, Maurice was a good listener. Whenever I needed to work through a few ideas, he was happy to act as a sounding board.

'Could she really have done it?' I breathed, staring at my oversized underpants as the valet pegged them to the line. 'Could she have crept into his room and slit his throat, in cold blood?'

Maurice bent down to pull out a pair of socks from the basket. 'It does not seem likely, Monsieur.'

'No, it doesn't. But I can't help thinking...well, she did spend a couple of weeks living in my flat, after Giles Markham died. And she did hold onto that key for rather a long time afterwards, for no real reason. That's suspicious in itself.'

'Yes, Monsieur.'

'And of course Mr Catesby was in town on business last week. What if they knew each other, somehow?'

'They did not appear to know each other, Monsieur.'

'No, they didn't.' The two had acted like perfect strangers when they had been introduced late on Friday

118

afternoon. 'But if Catesby was in town, he might have been the one who clobbered you back at the flat and stolen whatever it was that was taken from the bureau. What if she gave him the key? What if she let him in?'

'The window had been opened, Monsieur.'

'Yes, but he could have done that from the inside, to make it look like a proper break in.'

'If Mademoiselle Bunting gave him the key.'

'Well, exactly.' I scratched my head. 'But if the two of them *were* involved, why would she kill him now?'

Maurice considered for a moment. 'Perhaps they had a falling out.'

'That's possible, I suppose. I didn't ever see the two of them talking, though. Not once. If they were...' I gripped my hands. 'Oh, lord. This is awful. If she *is* involved, Morris, it's the end of me. You do realise that?'

'Not necessarily, Monsieur.'

'What do you mean, "not necessarily". Of course it is. That blasted woman knows everything there is to know about me. Which is your bloody fault, I might add, letting her into the flat in the first place while I was having a bath.'

'Yes, Monsieur.'

'If she's carted away, she'll have no reason to hold her tongue. She'll tell them everything. Especially if I'm called to testify against her. She'll spill the beans to Mr Richards and I'll be out on my ear. We both will be.'

'Yes, Monsieur.'

'Unless...' I growled. 'Unless we keep quiet about it. I mean, neither of us knew Catesby from Adam before this weekend. And it's not our responsibility to bring his murderer to justice. That's the general's job. We don't even know if Miss Bunting *is* responsible. What if it was an accident? Or self defence?'

Maurice was dubious. 'Cutting a man's *throat*. Monsieur? That is not self defence.'

'Well, no, but...there might be mitigating circumstances. And she wouldn't get a fair trial, not in this country. Don't look at me like that, Morris. I'm just considering my options.

119

Wouldn't it be better just to keep quiet? To say nothing and let things be?'

The valet was very firm on that point: '*No*, Monsieur.'

I let out a long sigh. 'You're right,' I agreed, a little resentfully. If Miss Bunting *was* a murderess – and, for my own sake, I hoped to God she wasn't – then she would have to be held to account, whatever the inadequacies of the Guatemalan justice system. I would just have to hope I had got the wrong end of the stick, somehow. 'The murder weapon,' I exclaimed, seizing on anything I could think of which might exonerate the girl. 'A cut-throat razor. That can't have been hers. And if it belonged to Mr Catesby, how would she have known he would have it? In his room, I mean, easily to hand. You wouldn't creep into somebody's bedroom on the off-chance they might have a murder weapon lying around that you could use.'

'No, Monsieur.'

'And if she *did* murder Catesby, did she also push that banker down the stairs? Or was that really just an accident? She was very keen last night to suggest that it wasn't. Why would she draw attention to it, if she was involved herself?'

'It is difficult to say, Monsieur.' The valet's attention had been diverted from the washing line to the far corner of the house. The kitchen garden was adjacent to the regular lawn at the rear of the hacienda. General Tejada had stepped out onto the grass with Gunther Weiman. The two men were making their way across to the far side of the garden. After a moment, they disappeared from view, but I knew where they were heading: the outhouse.

'What about that business with the generator yesterday evening?' I had already confided to Maurice some of my suspicions regarding that. 'Miss Bunting couldn't have sabotaged it. She was in the living room with the others at the time. I remember speaking to her, just before the lights went out.'

'Yes, Monsieur.'

'And I saw some blackguard running away from it half a minute afterwards.'

'Yes, Monsieur. You have already told me.'

120

'That couldn't have been Mr Catesby either. He was in the house. I saw him and Mr Weiman walk out together a minute or so afterwards, like the general just now. So neither he nor Miss Bunting could have been involved in damaging the equipment.'

'No, Monsieur. And I believe the damage to the generator was quite substantial.'

'You've had a look at it, have you?' The valet sounded very sure of himself.

'No, Monsieur. But the housekeeper went out this morning. She said a thick branch had been rammed into the mechanism, preventing one of the wheels from rotating. She was in no doubt that it had been done deliberately.'

'Lord. And did she say who she thought might be responsible?'

'No, Monsieur.'

'So we have...what?' I waved my hands in the air. 'Three, four unexplained events. The break in, the generator, and now two murders.'

'Or perhaps one murder and an accident,' Maurice corrected.

'Well, possibly. But it can't all be coincidental, Morris. General Tejada is right. These events must be connected somehow. There can't be two separate murderers, a saboteur *and* a burglar, just happening along all at the same time.'

'It does not seem likely, Monsieur.' The valet finished attaching the last of my socks to the line. He sounded every bit as baffled as I was.

'Perhaps I should just confront Miss Bunting,' I said. 'Show her the earring. See how she reacts. She might give herself away. Then at least we'd know one way or the other.'

'Yes, Monsieur,' Maurice agreed. 'It occurs to me, however, that there may be an innocent explanation as to how that earring arrived in the room.'

'Oh?' I was willing to consider anything.

'Perhaps the Mademoiselle lost it out on the terrace. Someone else might have trod on it later on and inadvertently attached it to their shoe. The pin has been damaged, after all. It

121

might have lodged itself into the sole of a shoe and the murderer might then have inadvertently walked it into the room.'

I laughed. That idea was too ridiculous for words. 'Don't be absurd Morris. You might just as well suggest Catesby cut his own throat. In any case, that doesn't explain why she was creeping about last night.'

'No, Monsieur.' The valet looked past me towards the kitchen. Moses, the house boy, was gesticulating at us across the lawn.

'What the devil does he want?' I wondered.

Maurice had the answer to that. 'I believe it is your turn to be interviewed, Monsieur.'

Chapter Nine

The picture was an informal family portrait, a small group of relatives gathered together on some long forgotten lawn, bathed in glorious sunshine. The men were in their shirt sleeves, the older woman in a pleated skirt. The little girl on the left, with her hair in bunches and a toothy grin, was a young Susan Weiman. 'My mother took that photograph when I was seven year's old,' she told me, her voice wavering slightly. The death of her cousin had hit the woman hard and she was having some difficulty maintaining her composure. The little girl in the picture was holding hands with a tall, elegant looking gentleman. 'That's my father,' she said. 'And that's Uncle Joe next to him, and his wife Anne. And if you look at the tree over there.' She gestured to the far right corner of the photograph. 'You can just see Steven, poking his head out.' A mass of curly black hair framed a scrunched up face, peering mischievously around the trunk of the tree. The boy – who couldn't have been more than eight or nine – was poking his tongue out at the photographer. Susan Weiman smiled sadly. 'He was a precocious boy even then.'

Precocious. It was an odd word to choose. The gaunt-looking man I had met on Friday evening had not struck me as "precocious" at all. But then I had barely known him.

The photograph was hanging in pride of place just above the mantelpiece in the living room. Another picture in a gilt frame was propped up on the shelf below, a faded portrait of a genial elderly couple. Gunther Weiman's parents, at a guess. They had something of a Germanic look to them.

The other house guests had scattered across the hacienda. I had passed Mrs Montana out in the courtyard, on my way to the living room. She was engrossed in that lurid novel of hers, seemingly unaffected by recent events. Her husband was drinking coffee and trying not to scowl.

Susan Weiman was staring at the mantelpiece as I arrived. I was somewhat peeved, having been called away in such haste, to find myself in an otherwise empty room. The police sergeant was sitting out on the front terrace, at a small metal table in full view of the windows, busily interrogating Mrs George Talbot. The nerve of the fellow, I thought. What was the point of him summoning me here with such urgency if he was going to question somebody else first? Susan Weiman would probably be next in line, which meant I might well be kept standing here for the next half an hour.

'Poor Steven,' she mumbled, looking away from the photograph. Her brown eyes were watery and speckled with grief.

'Were you very close to him?' I asked awkwardly. I have never been much good at dealing with other people's grief.

'When we were children. But we barely saw each other as adults. He married and moved away from the farm. That's his father, there. Uncle Joe.' She gestured once again to the picture on the wall. 'He was a farm manager too, in Cuba. And then I met Gunther and we came out here. And living in different countries...'

'Not easy to keep in touch,' I said.

'We wrote, of course. Exchanged Christmas cards. Then when his wife died a couple of years ago and he lost his job, well, it was the least we could do to offer him a home. A bit of shelter, somewhere to lick his wounds.'

'So he came here and worked for you?'

'Yes. It was never intended to be a permanent arrangement. He'd get back on his feet and find himself a new life. But he got caught up in the work here – as one does – and things kept getting put back. He should have moved on, of course, for his own sake. Found a new life for himself. He did have plans and my husband was doing his best to help him. But it's too late now.' She shuddered.

'This has been a terrible shock for you.'

'Not just him dying, but...but murder.' She gulped. 'Somebody creeping into the house in the dead of night.' Her eyes flashed across to the windows. 'You forget how vulnerable we are here, in a foreign country, in the middle of nowhere. We have no locked doors. No protection. Gunther doesn't even allow guns in the house. But we've always got by. And we've never caused any harm to anybody.'

'You think it was an intruder who came in and...and killed your cousin?'

'It must have been,' she said, shivering at the thought. 'Somebody must have broken in. It wouldn't be difficult.'

That sounded a rather dubious proposition to me. 'Was anything stolen?'

'No, not that I'm aware of. But I don't think it was... Steven...' She sighed. 'He had a bit of a temper. He could be quite abrasive sometimes. Not with us, but with suppliers. Business associates. Some of the workers.'

'And you think somebody like that might have...I don't know, crept into the house; or hired somebody to...?'

'I really don't know. Cutting his throat with...with a razor. Such a horrible, vile thing to do. My god. I don't know anyone who would...' Her voice trailed away.

There was an embarrassed pause. 'Well, I'm sure the general will get to the bottom of it,' I suggested, for want of anything more helpful to say.

'I do hope so. Gunther says he's a man who gets results. But he has a reputation for...well, you hear stories. People being tortured. People disappearing.' She shivered again.

'That's just local politics. It's the way these countries are run.' I waved a hand dismissively. 'Secret police. Unexplained disappearances. It's rather unpleasant, but it won't affect a routine investigation like this.'

She nodded. 'I'm sure you are right, Mr Buxton. Even so, it won't bring Steven back.'

'I've had quite enough of your impertinence!' Jane Talbot exclaimed, from out on the terrace. Her chair had scraped back and the woman was glaring across at the policeman on the opposite side of the table. 'I have told you everything you need to know and I will not sit here and listen to such base accusations!' She rounded the table and stormed through the door into the living room. 'That man is an animal!' she declared, her nostrils flaring furiously. 'He all but accused me of...' She stopped. The two of us were regarding her in open-mouthed astonishment. 'Where is General Tejada? I intend to have serious words with him.'

Mrs Weiman tried to dissuade her. 'Jane, I don't think...'

'I will not be spoken to like that!' I had never seen Mrs Talbot in such a temper. It was a magnificent sight. An English gentlewoman in full flow, venting her spleen.

'I think he's out the back,' I said, gesturing to the far door. 'With Mr Weiman, examining the generator.'

'Thank you Mr Buxton.' She took a brief moment to address her friend. 'Don't let that man intimidate you, Susan. Don't tell him anything you don't want to.' And with that she stormed past us and out into the courtyard heading for the back of the house. It was all I could do not to break into applause.

Sergeant Velázquez had risen up from his chair and appeared at the far door of the living room. His boggle eyes were even more pronounced than usual, anger visible in his clenched fists and pressed lips. He pointed a bony finger at me. 'You! Next!' he snapped.

The seat was as uncomfortable as the bulging stare. The young policeman was doing his damnedest to make everybody feel ill at ease. The interview could just have easily have been conducted in the comfort of the living room, or over tea and crumpets in the courtyard, in the unlikely event that such things had been available to us. That's the trouble with petty officials, especially the younger ones; they know they are wasting their lives and they take out their frustration on others. Well, I was damned if I was going to let him get under my skin. I would answer his foolish questions with a calm and studied deliberation. I would not let him rile me, even as I was assaulted with a barrage of inane questions.

What was my name? he demanded. What was my occupation?

His eyes lit up when I told him I was a passport control officer at the British legation in Guatemala City. 'So you are a spy,' he crowed. His voice was rather deep, despite his relative youth, and his accent was thicker than the marmalade at breakfast.

'No, I'm a passport control officer.'

'All diplomats are spies!' he declared.

'In your part of the world, maybe. But I assure you, Sergeant Velázquez, I am not a spy. In point of fact, I am not even a diplomat. I'm an administrator. I stamp passports. My job is to keep *undesirable people...*' I met his eye and emphasised those last two words, '...out of my country.'

He snorted derisively. 'And the woman. She is also a spy?'

'If you mean Miss Bunting, no. She is my secretary.'

His eyes filmed over for a moment and his face cracked into a lopsided smile. 'She is a very pretty girl. You are her boyfriend?'

'Good lord! No, I am not. What the devil has that got to do with anything?'

'She is not married.' He grinned. 'She come here alone?'

'She come...she *came* here with Mr Reeves, if you must know. At his invitation.' Good God, what sort of man was I dealing with here? He was meant to be taking statements, not eyeing up the women. 'If you know what's good for you, sergeant, you will leave her well alone.'

'I do not take orders from you!' he snapped. 'You know the Weiman family? You know Señor Catesby?'

'Not before this weekend, no.'

'So why are you here?' He was getting combative now.

'I was invited. Freddie – Mr Reeves – is a friend of the family. He suggested I come for the weekend. With Mr Weiman's approval, of course.'

'You know Señor Talbot?'

'No, I didn't know him. Not before this weekend.'

'So why you push him down the stairs?'

'Good god! I didn't push him down the stairs, you idiot! I *found* the body. At the *bottom* of the stairs.'

'You see who push him?'

'No. Nobody pushed him. At least not so far as I'm aware. It was raining. He must have slipped on the top step.'

'But you no see?'

'No, I didn't see. But I have no reason to suppose it was anything other than an accident.' I did not feel inclined to confide any of my suspicions to a cretin like this.

'And you also find Señor Catesby?'

'Yes. Look, I went over all this with the general. I was asked to give him a knock for breakfast, and I found him in bed with his throat cut.'

'You know he has a razor with him?'

'No. Well, I mean, I hadn't really thought about it. But he was clean shaven, so I suppose he was bound to have a razor somewhere.'

'*Como*? What is "clean shaven"?' We had reached the limits of the sergeant's English. It had not taken long.

'He didn't have a beard, so obviously he would have had some kind of razor.'

'Did you kill him?'

'No, I didn't kill him!'

'Do you see who kill him?'

I raised my hands in exasperation. 'How could I have seen him? He was killed in the middle of the night. I didn't go anywhere near his bedroom until this morning.'

'You touch nothing in the room?'

'No. I touch nothing,' I growled. I was beginning to understand why Mrs Talbot had lost her rag with the fellow. The man was a blithering idiot.

'What the hell do you think you're playing at!' Arthur Montana declared, his booming American vowels reverberating the length of the hacienda. 'Her husband's just died, for Christ's sake!'

An argument had been brewing for some time on the far side of the house. Jane Talbot had strode out into the back garden and confronted the general with her thoughts regarding the misbehaviour of his deputy. Having observed the man's impertinence first hand, I could hardly blame her for doing so. I had been too absorbed in my own ridiculous interrogation to take much notice of the raised voices out on the lawn; but when I heard a thump and a sudden cry, my ears pricked up. The argument had moved back into the house and the real slanging match had begun.

'What on earth...?' I exclaimed, rising quickly to my feet at the sound of Arthur Montana's voice.

'You sit down!' Velázquez snapped. 'I no finish my questions.'

'To hell with your questions.' I muttered, brushing past the table and stepping through into the living room. Mrs Weiman was already at the far door, peering into the dining hall, where the argument was now taking place. I moved across to join her.

'I do not have to answer to you!' Julio Tejada snapped, responding angrily to Mr Montana. The general's chubby face had turned a bright shade of puce and his eyes were glaring malevolently at the American beneath those bushy eyebrows.

The United Fruit man did not give any ground. 'You have no right to strike a lady!' he snarled. Jane Talbot was standing behind him, pale with shock. My jaw slackened as I took in the bright red mark across the side of her face. My god. Tejada had thumped her. Not with that stick of his, thank heavens, but he had still given her a solid whack across the face. At last, I understood the cause of the American's anger. There is something particularly despicable about a man who strikes a woman. Any hopes the general had had of gaining our cooperation had vanished at that instant.

'I have every right,' Tejada declared. 'She is trying to interfere with my investigation.'

'I was lodging a complaint,' Mrs Talbot asserted. She could no longer bring herself to meet the eye of the policeman, but neither was she going to bow down before him. What a woman, I thought, in admiration. Standing up to a bully like that, even after he had hit her.

The general was having none of it. He was shaking his swagger stick furiously, though Arthur Montana was standing firmly between him and Mrs Talbot. 'You do not question the behaviour of my officers!' he snarled.

'My husband is dead! Does that not give me the right to some consideration?'

'You have no rights! I am the legal authority here. I am sorry that your husband is dead, but his death was an accident and I am investigating a murder. You may think, because you are British or German or American, that you are entitled to special consideration, but you are not. This is my country and this is my investigation. If anyone else tries to interfere with me or my deputy during the course of our work, I will have them placed under arrest. If anyone attempts to resist arrest they will be shot. Do I make myself clear?'

Sergeant Velázquez took that moment to stride past me into the dining room. The guests shrank back as he joined the general on the far side of the table.

'Do I make myself clear?' Tejada repeated, his free hand now hovering over a leather holster hanging from his left hip.

There were reluctant mumbles of agreement.

'Good. The interviews will be resumed and I will continue with my investigation.' He lifted his hand and glanced at his wristwatch. 'It is half past eleven. Señor Weiman.' He pointed his stick. 'You will provide lunch for me and my sergeant at twelve o'clock and the interviews will continue after that. I have other men on their way and they will arrive here shortly.' The overseer had returned to the farm, having passed on the general's demand for reinforcements. 'No-one will leave the house until these men have arrived.'

Lord, I thought. That would make getting home a bit tricky. 'We have a...' I began, before I could stop myself.

Tejada glared at me. 'Well?'

There was no point holding back. 'Some of us have a train to catch, at four o'clock. We need to leave here by half past one if we're to...'

'Did I not make myself clear? No one leaves. Not until this matter has been fully investigated. No one at all.'

Across the room, Freddie caught my eye. There would be no journey home for us this afternoon. It looked like we were here for the duration.

The generator was a monstrous metal creation with two large wheels and a network of thin metal pipes. The frame was in good shape but a hefty branch had been shoved through one of the wheels, presumably while it was still rotating. It was that which had caused the mechanism to come to a shuddering halt. The branch had twisted and torn under the pressure and was now stuck fast between two points. The damage did not look irreparable – it was simply a matter of extricating the wood – but that in itself would take some effort; and with all the electrical equipment housed in this small outhouse, it was not a task I would have relished.

'Someone took a hell of a risk, doing that,' I observed, hovering warily in the frame of the door. Even with the light streaming in through the far window, the outhouse was depressingly gloomy. A single light bulb hung down from the roof on a cord but without the generator it could provide us with no illumination. 'They might easily have been killed.'

'It would have been better for everyone if they had been,' Arthur Montana grunted. The American had joined me out in the garden for a cigarette; or a cigar, in his case. I had been keen to get him well away from the house while the general was eating. For all Montana's unpleasant views on race relations, I had to acknowledge he had done the right thing, standing up for Mrs Talbot like that. But it had also become clear that confrontation was not the way to deal with a man like Tejada. Better for all of us to keep our distance, where we could, and let him get on with it. The sooner he got what he wanted, the sooner he would leave and the sooner we could all go home.

The general and his underling were currently being served a light lunch out in the courtyard.

It was Montana who had noticed that the door to the outhouse was unlocked. We had finished our smoke, grumbling together about the behaviour of the two policemen, and curiosity had got the better of us. I had told him about the raised voices I had heard coming from the shed when Mr Catesby and Mr Weiman had gone to investigate the power cut.

131

Montana was not surprised, but I still found the argument difficult to make sense of. I would certainly have been angry, if I had discovered my generator had been sabotaged, but I wouldn't have taken it out on one of my in-laws, a man who could not conceivably have been responsible for the damage.

The American had his own thoughts regarding the attack on the generator. 'It has to be someone from outside the estate,' he said, surveying the damaged equipment.

'Not a member of the household?' I raised an eyebrow. Montana had obviously been talking to Mrs Weiman.

'Some vagrant,' he concluded, 'with some half-assed idea about robbing the house.'

'That doesn't sound very likely. I don't think anything was stolen.'

'Or somebody from the village with a grudge. One of those damned Indians.' Montana was always keen to blame a local rather than one of his own. 'Or a business associate. Steve rubbed a lot of people up the wrong way.'

'But you think whoever did this...' I gestured to the splintered branch. 'They were the ones who killed Mr Catesby?'

'Makes sense,' the American thought. 'Get all the lights out, then creep up into one of the bedrooms, looking for anything to steal. But Steve must have woken up and confronted him. The son of a bitch panicked and did him in.'

'I don't think that's very likely,' I said. 'You haven't seen the body. There was no sign of a struggle. And besides, there must have been hours between this happening and Mr Catesby dying.'

'I guess so.'

'I think you may be right about the generator, though. It certainly wasn't anybody in the house. I...saw someone running away from here, just after the generator failed.'

Montana's eyes widened in surprise. 'You saw who did it?'

'Not clearly, I'm afraid. I was talking to Mrs Gonzales out on the terrace. As soon as I heard the crack, I ran to the back of the house and saw a figure darting away. Up there,

132

through the gate.'

Montana considered that darkly. 'Like I said. A vagrant.'

'Possibly. But that still doesn't explain why anyone would want to do it. It's an awful lot of bother, dragging that branch in here.'

'They don't need a reason. Some of them are just plain crazy. Did you recognize the guy? Was it a local, an Indian? Or a negro?'

'I couldn't say. It was too dark. To be honest, I couldn't even tell if it was a man or a woman.'

The American scoffed. 'It couldn't have been a woman.' He gestured to the heavy branch. 'And that pathway leads up into the fields. Like I say, it must have been a vagrant.' Montana was unwilling to let go of the idea. 'Intending to rob the place. And none too bright either. Have you told the general? About what you saw?'

I shook my head. 'It slipped my mind. And to be honest, Mr Montana, right now I don't feel inclined to tell that man anything. Not that he's bothered to ask. I did see him coming out of here earlier on, though. He's obviously had a good look at the place.'

'Much good that'll do,' Montana muttered.

'Have you met him before? The general?'

He nodded contemptuously. 'He's a vicious son of a bitch. But, hey, what can you expect from people like that?' He punched his hand. 'Violence is a way of life in this country. The cops are always getting involved in private disputes. You know the kind of thing. Negroes and Indians getting into fights, on the plantations. Hispanics too. Boy, do they have a chip on their shoulder. They like to pretend they're white, like you and me. Sometimes they pick a fight, even with the managers.' The US executives of United Fruit. 'Good American boys. Occasionally it goes too far and somebody dies. But, hey, people have a right to defend themselves. We try not to involve the police but if the blacks or anyone else kick up a fuss, sometimes we have no choice.'

'And Tejada is the man you bring in?'

133

'Not any more. Not with his connections. He's moved up in the world. He doesn't have to deal with that kind of crap any more. Not now his brother-in-law is Ubico's right hand man. He only gets the plum jobs.'

'I thought the president was meant to be cutting down on corruption, nepotism, that sort of thing.'

'He is. But the head of the Policia Nacional is an exception. You can't run a country like this without the police on your side. And the army. Besides, Tejada has more important fish to fry these days. I don't think he'd be here at all if it wasn't for George.'

'Yes, Mr Weiman did say the two of them knew each other. They can't exactly have been friends, though, if he's thumping the fellow's wife shortly after he dies.' Whatever the connection between them was, it had to be purely professional. I could not imagine a mild-mannered banker like George Talbot ever socializing with a brute like Julio Tejada.

Montana agreed with me. 'It does seem unlikely. But one thing I can tell you: if you're looking for justice, Tejada is the last man you'd ever ask.'

'You've been avoiding me,' Emily Bunting teased, stepping out onto the upper terrace at the front of the house. I had a glass of whisky in my hand and had moved out through the open shutters of my bedroom in the hope of a few quiet moments alone. My free hand rested gently on the wooden balustrade as I looked out across the front lawn. Clouds were gathering above us but the rain was a couple of hours off yet. Insects were buzzing around the hanging baskets and I could hear the voice of Doctor Rubio down in the courtyard, talking quietly with Mrs Weiman. The interviews had concluded at last, with Mr and Mrs Gonzales the last in line, and the general had now disappeared off into the grounds, with his deputy in tow. The house was all the better for their departure.

'Not at all,' I said, in reply to Miss Bunting's light-hearted accusation. 'It's just been rather a busy day.' In truth, I *had* been avoiding the woman, in so far as it was possible in a place like this. The issue of that damned earring was still rattling around in my head and I was concerned lest my suspicions should become obvious to her. If she was innocent, she might take offence – which given all she knew about me I was anxious to avoid – but if she was guilty, well then...I had even less reason to let her know that I was onto her.

'It must have been awful, finding Mr Catesby like that,' she declared, sympathetically.

'It was rather a shock,' I agreed, taking another sip of whisky. 'How have you been coping with it all?'

The girl took a breath and considered for a moment. 'I'm just a bit dazed, if I'm honest. It's all too much. I had hoped for an eventful weekend, but nothing like this. I think you've got the right idea.' She eyed up the whisky in my hand. 'A stiff drink. Even if it is a little early.'

'It helps me to think,' I said. 'And it is after lunch.'

'Oh, I'm not criticizing.' She grinned. 'Actually, I thought I might join you. If you don't mind?'

'No, of course not. Help yourself.' On a day like this, even I could not begrudge the girl a little liquid support. 'It's on the bed-side table. I think there's another glass in the drawer. No soda I'm afraid, but there's water in the jug.'

'That's all right. I prefer it neat.' She disappeared inside the room.

My mind flashed back to Thursday evening, when Miss Bunting had discovered me, *sans* towel, in the living room of my apartment. She had knocked back the whisky then, I recalled. If my mind hadn't been elsewhere, I would have been rather surprised at that. In the office, during the day, she was always the picture of sobriety. And, more to the point, the alcohol had not seemed to affect her at all, which suggested it was not an unusual occurrence. I would have to keep an eye on that bottle of mine. I didn't want her finishing it off behind my back.

Miss Bunting emerged from the bedroom with a rather full glass. She raised it up, took a sip, and came to stand beside me, gazing out across the lawn. It was not much of a view. The fountain, the pathway off to the right and the stables to the left;

trees shrouding the workers' quarters and various administrative shacks. Miss Bunting took it all in and sighed again. It was an afternoon for sighing, I thought. 'It's such a dreadful business,' she said, finally. 'You must despise Freddie, for getting you involved in all this.'

'I won't be accepting any further invitations from him,' I asserted dryly. 'But what's done is done. There's no point crying over spilt milk. And it looks like he was right about Giles Markham. There *was* more to his death than meets the eye.'

'Do you think what happened to him might have something to do with Mr Catesby's death?'

'I think it has to,' I said, taking a final gulp of whisky.

'Did you mention him to the sergeant? Mr Markham, I mean.'

'Lord, no. Didn't want to muddy the waters any further. And, to be honest, I didn't feel particularly inclined to be helpful. Not with a brute like that.'

'He was rather sweet with me,' Miss Bunting confessed.

'That doesn't surprise me. You're very pretty, apparently.'

She giggled. 'He said that?'

I nodded absently.

'I thought he was looking at me rather strangely. But he was very polite. He couldn't stop smiling. And staring. Not that there's much to stare at.' She glanced down at her chest. 'I've never had much down there to draw the eye. Not like Mrs Montana. I meant to ask, though...' She looked across at me. 'How do you...how do you keep all that in check?'

'Bandages. And a safety pin. Mind you, I was never particularly blessed in that department either. I'm just glad I don't have to put up with love starved policemen ogling my décolletage when I'm trying to talk to them.'

'Boggle eyed policemen.' Miss Bunting laughed.

'Well, quite. But believe me, for all his youth, that sergeant is a nasty piece of work. He was barely civil with me and goodness knows what he said to Mrs Talbot.'

'Yes, he must have really riled her. Crumbs. I've never

seen her so angry.'

'No. And that fellow Tejada is no better. Oh, speak of the devil...'

The general had emerged on the far side of the lawn and was making his way back up towards the house. He raised a hand to his mouth and bellowed. 'Señor Weiman! Come here! Now!' Miss Bunting and I exchanged puzzled glances, but the policeman did not look up. He was too intent on finding the owner of the estate. 'Señor Weiman!' he called again.

A muted reply sounded from below as the German stepped out onto the verandah.

A small group of men were emerging from a gap between the trees, at the far end of the pathway leading down to the workers' cottages. Two of the men were dragging a third fellow between them.

'We have found your murderer,' Tejada declared triumphantly.

Even at this distance, I recognised the face of the man they had taken into custody. It was Joseph Green.

Chapter Ten

Gunther Weiman stepped down from the terrace and came to a halt in surprise, as he took in the unexpected scene. General Tejada had come to a rest by the fountain in the middle of the lawn, allowing his underlings time to catch him up. One of the two men – the overseer – had a gleam of triumph in his eyes. This was the swine who had taken a whip to Joseph Green yesterday afternoon. The labourer was barely managing to keep his footing as he was dragged out onto the lawn. The group were now within spitting distance of the senior officer and Green was propelled forward onto the grass, his head narrowly missing the base of the fountain.

'That's your murderer!' Tejada declared again, gesturing to the prone figure, who now began scrabbling up onto his knees.

Gunther Weiman was standing a few yards away, on the front steps of the house. 'Joseph?' he gasped, in disbelief.

The coloured man met his master's eye and even from the upper terrace I could see the fear in his face. 'I didn't do it, Mr Weiman. I didn't do nothing.'

Several other labourers had appeared at the far end of the lawn and were regarding the grim tableaux with understandable consternation. Green must have been dragged away right in front of them. A short path between two sets of trees led directly to the workers' cottages and it was from here that the men had emerged.

'Oh, he did it all right,' the general snarled. He at least was in no doubt that he had got his man. 'On your feet, chico!'

Green planted a hand on the ground to steady himself and slowly pulled himself up. The overseer was standing a few feet behind him, a vindictive smile on his face. Sergeant Velázquez, meantime, was reaching down to his waist to grab a pair of handcuffs.

By now, the sounds of the ruckus had filtered through into the house and various people were starting to emerge from the hacienda. Moses, the house boy, gave a cry of horror as he caught sight of Green. He tried to run towards him but the housekeeper, Greta, took a firm hold of the lad's shoulders.

Joseph Green glanced at the two of them, then back at the sergeant, who was stepping forward now, preparing to cuff him. Finally, he took in the stable yard over to his right. Even from my position on the terrace, I could see the desperate calculation in his eyes. Before Velázquez could lay a finger on him, Green bolted. It was a moment of pure insanity. He dodged the fat overseer and sprinted back down the lawn, not towards the stables or to his fellow labourers but to a muddy pathway leading east into the fields. Velázquez let out a cry of anger but Tejada raised a hand. The sergeant hesitated, not daring to disobey his superior. The general unclipped the holster at his waist and calmly pulled out his revolver. Miss Bunting, standing to my left, brought a hand to her mouth as he raised the gun and fired. Green stopped dead in his tracks. Tejada had shot into the air, but the sound of the revolver had been enough to bring the man to an abrupt halt.

'One more step, chico!' the general called out, aiming his gun carefully at the terrified labourer. 'One more step and this ends now. Your choice.'

Green hesitated, looking back towards the fountain.

The overseer was happy to see him shot. 'Run, you little bastard,' he sneered, 'and save us all the trouble.'

Sweat was pouring down the man's face. He had barely got more than ten yards. At that distance Tejada was unlikely to miss him; and even if he did, it was doubtful that Green would get much further, with the others in hot pursuit. The labourer swallowed hard, clenched his fists briefly and then raised his hands.

The general kept his revolver level but nodded the sergeant forward. Velázquez prepared the handcuffs, while the fat overseer strode across and punched Green viciously in the stomach. The man shuddered and collapsed to the ground. The overseer kicked him again and then again and again.

Miss Bunting squealed in horror, covering her eyes with her hands.

'Leave him alone!' Moses yelled angrily from the

terrace. Greta was still gripping the lad firmly by the shoulders but the boy was struggling to break free. Luckily, the housekeeper was stronger than he was.

'Enough!' Tejada declared.

The overseer got in one last kick, then stepped back and allowed the sergeant to bend down and cuff the prisoner. Green wailed as his hands were pulled tightly behind his back and shackled together. His face, looking up from the grass, was a picture of despair.

The other labourers had been observing these events angrily from the far corner of the lawn. Only the gun and the authority of the general had prevented them from interfering.

Tejada returned the weapon calmly to its holster and then turned to face Gunther Weiman. The white haired German had been standing stock still throughout the entire episode. I couldn't see his face, but I knew he would be as shocked as the rest of us. Mrs Weiman was at his side now, an arm around his waist, trying to comfort her husband.

'We'll need somewhere to lock the prisoner up,' the general said. 'Until the rest of my men get here.'

'The store rooms,' Weiman muttered vaguely. 'Around the side of the house.' A small administrative block was situated on the near side of the stables, along the eastern wall of the hacienda. Three small, rough hewn buildings, all in a row, with a narrow grass pathway between them and the house.

'That'll do,' Tejada agreed.

Joseph Green was still whimpering. Velázquez had placed a foot on his back, keeping the man down in the grass until the general gave the order to cart him off.

Weiman was struggling to maintain his composure. 'How...how can you be sure that Joseph was responsible for Steven's death?'

'You can see for yourself the blood on his shirt,' Tejada declared. 'And we have a witness who says he left his room in the early hours of the morning.' The policeman jerked his thumb back to the coloured men gathered on the far side of the garden. One of the labourers was shaking with rage. Another man had to put a hand on his shoulder to hold him back. They all knew what kind of a person the general was. If any of them raised a voice in protest, they would likely be shot. If more than one of them protested, it could well lead to a massacre. 'And an innocent man,' Tejada added forcefully, 'doesn't run.'

Gunther Weiman was utterly bewildered. 'But why would Joseph, of all people...?'

'Revenge,' the general snapped back. 'For the death of his brother.'

'Yes, but...'

'Your cousin killed Matthew Green, after he broke into your house earlier this year. He cannot be blamed for that. He was confronting a thief. Señor Catesby was well within his rights to protect himself. But this one.' He jerked a finger contemptuously at the prisoner. 'He didn't see it that way. He's been brooding about it ever since. Then yesterday, when he left the work party without permission, Steven Catesby had him whipped; and all the resentment and frustration came boiling out. The death of his brother. His own mistreatment, as he saw it. You can't expect an animal like that to act rationally. He sabotaged the generator out of spite. But that wasn't enough. It didn't satisfy his lust for revenge. So he crept into the house in the dead of night and cut Señor Catesby's throat.'

'No, mister!' Green protested, desperately. 'I didn't do it!'

Velázquez lifted his foot and stamped down hard on the man's shoulders. 'Quiet!' he snarled.

Tejada was unperturbed. 'Oh, you did it, chico.' His chubby face cracked into a smile. His teeth, I noticed, were white and rather well formed, unlike those of his deputy. 'And you'll hang for it. Take him away.'

And with that, the pitiful figure was grabbed from behind, lifted up and manhandled across the lawn towards the administrative block, all the while continuing to protest his innocence.

General Tejada strode back into the house, out of sight below us. Gunther Weiman hovered for a moment, looking anxiously across the lawn, where the other labourers were now muttering angrily among themselves. He spoke briefly to his

141

wife, who nodded her agreement, and then moved across to talk to them. The last thing anyone needed right now was any trouble from that quarter; whatever the justification, it could only serve to inflame the situation.

Emily Bunting had already turned away from the garden, unable to witness a moment more. 'That poor man!' she declared, as I followed her through the shutters into the bedroom. 'They shouldn't have treated him like that, no matter what he's done.' The girl took a moment to recover her wits, then glanced over at me in the frame of the window and smiled half-heartedly. 'I think I may need another drink.' She stepped back as I moved across the room and grabbed the bottle of whisky from the bedside table. She handed me her glass and I filled it without a word. Then I replenished my own. Miss Bunting sat down slowly on the bed and took a sip. I was surprised at how shocked she was. But then, I doubted she had ever seen a man being beaten up like that. 'Do you think he did it?' she asked me, seriously.

'I don't know,' I admitted, sitting down next to her. The mattress was as hard as stone. 'I don't know what to think.' I downed the whisky in one.

'If there was a witness. And blood on his shirt...'

'Yes, it does seem pretty damning.' I let out a heavy sigh. I hadn't been able to see the blood clearly but whoever had killed Mr Catesby was bound to have got some of it onto their clothes. 'Mind you, that blood could just have easily have been from the whipping he got yesterday. Those kind of wounds do have a habit of reopening, if you don't look after them properly. And I doubt a man like that would have many clothes to change into.' I stared down at the tumbler in my hand. 'It's strange, though. Green didn't strike me as the violent type at all. Quite a mild mannered fellow, I would have said, when I spoke to him yesterday. I can't picture him creeping into that bedroom in the dead of night. I suppose he might conceivably have mangled the generator.' Green could have been the figure I had seen stealing away from the outhouse, though it might just as easily have been somebody else.

'What about Mr Talbot, falling down the stairs?' Miss

Bunting asked. 'Could he have been responsible for that?'

'No. No, I don't think so. Somebody would have noticed a coloured man wandering around the house. And, now I come to think of it, he wasn't anywhere near the place when it happened.' I had seen him myself, some minutes before. 'He was out working on the road. Freddie and I passed him by when we were coming back from the village. Him and that overseer fellow.' Miss Bunting screwed up her face at the mention of Mr Langbroek. 'And Mr Talbot fell down the stairs shortly after that, so there wasn't time for him to steal away and visit the house. In point of fact, it's only what you saw, coming along the balcony, that gives us any real evidence of foul play where Mr Talbot's concerned.'

'I suppose I might have been mistaken,' Miss Bunting conceded, back-tracking slightly. She too had finished her whisky. 'It might have been an accident after all.'

'General Tejada certainly seems to think so. You notice he didn't blame Green for Mr Talbot's death. But I don't believe it can have been an accident. It's too much of a coincidence, especially with his brother suffering the same fate. Unless of course it was Mr Catesby who pushed Talbot down the stairs.' That had been my first thought, yesterday evening. Maybe it had been a tit for tat thing: Catesby had murdered one man and somebody else had taken revenge for the killing. 'No, there's far more to all this than meets the eye. Did you see how the house boy reacted?'

'Moses? Yes, he was very upset. The poor thing. I suppose any boy would be, seeing something like that.'

'I think there may be more to it than that. Don't forget, he was the one who acted as go between when Green first asked to meet me.'

'Perhaps the two of them are related,' Miss Bunting suggested. 'Do you suppose it was Moses who told him about you in the first place?'

'It must have been. Though how he knew about my connection to Giles Markham I have no idea.'

'Moses was there when we were introduced, on Friday afternoon. He must have overheard us talking.'

143

'And passed it on to Green? Yes, I suppose so.'

'Crumbs. So if Freddie hadn't invited you here, none of this would have happened.' Miss Bunting shuddered. 'Mr Green wouldn't have slipped away from the road, he wouldn't have been whipped and he wouldn't have taken his revenge.'

'If that's what did happen.' I gazed across at the girl suspiciously. She seemed remarkably keen to pin the blame on the coloured man. That in itself could not help but provoke my own suspicions. 'But it doesn't feel right to me,' I said. 'There are far too many random events.'

'I'm sure you'll get to the bottom of it.' She beamed. 'Freddie says you've had quite a bit of experience of this kind of thing.'

I grunted. 'Freddie talks too much.'

'You wouldn't think he was a diplomat.' She laughed. 'But he's a sweetie really. He means well.'

'I wish I could say the same for the other guests. If Green wasn't responsible for Mr Catesby's murder, then it must have been one of them who killed him. It certainly wasn't a burglar.'

'No, I don't suppose it could have been, if nothing was taken.'

And, sad as it was to admit it, my prime suspect was Miss Emily Bunting herself. 'One of the guests must have been clomping about the house last night, in the early hours.'

Miss Bunting had her eyes fixed firmly on her lap. Her hands were gripping the empty whisky glass. 'Yes, very probably,' she agreed.

'You didn't hear anything?'

'No. I slept the whole night through. I did hear somebody snoring rather loudly, but nobody wandering about.'

'And you didn't get up yourself? A call of nature, anything like that?' I peered at her keenly, alert for any signs of falsehood.

'No. No, I rarely do in the night,' she said, her eyes lifting but darting sideways as she spoke. She was a surprisingly bad liar, I thought. That in itself was rather odd. I glanced at her hands. There was no blood there, of course, but it would have been a simple matter to wash it off; and, from what I could remember, she had been wearing a short-sleeved dress last night.

I scratched my cheek, not quite sure how much further I wanted to probe; but there was no point skirting the issue entirely. I slid a hand into my jacket pocket and pulled out the earring. 'I...found this, this morning. On the floor. I wondered if it was yours?' I held out the small, flower shaped earring and Miss Bunting's eyes lit up.

'You found it! You clever thing! I was looking for that this morning. I thought it must have come off somewhere.' She placed her empty tumbler on the bedside table and took the earring from me with every appearance of delight.

'I'm afraid the clasp is a little buckled.'

'Oh, I'm sure I can straighten it out. Where on earth did you find it?'

'Er...out on the landing.' Even now, I did not have the nerve to confront her directly. Some part of me refused to believe the young woman could possibly be a murderess.

'I must have lost it when I came up to bed last night.'

'Easily done, I'm sure. You...didn't pop in to see Freddie at all? Last night I mean?'

Her eyes glittered mischievously. 'Mr Buxton, whatever are you suggesting?'

'Oh, nothing of that sort, I assure you!' I coughed in embarrassment. 'I'm just...I'm trying to get a picture of where everyone was last night. Helps to narrow things down.'

'You really are a detective,' Miss Bunting observed with glee. 'Freddie was right. All that bumbling around is just an act. You know exactly what you're doing!'

I coughed again. 'I only wish I did. Look here, are you absolutely sure you didn't get up at all last night?'

'Yes, I'm sure.' She frowned momentarily, perplexed at the repeated question. For a moment, I thought she might be on the cusp of telling me something; but if she was then she thought better of it.

'He'll hang you know. Mr Green. Whether he's guilty or not.'

Miss Bunting rose to her feet and peered out through the open shutters. 'Yes, I know,' she whispered sadly.

'I wonder who the witness was? The man who saw him leaving his room? I suppose it must have been one of the other labourers.' That was a lead that might be worth pursuing.

'It could be,' she agreed, turning back to me. 'Hilary, you must find out the truth of this.' The girl placed a gentle hand on my arm. 'Find out the truth, for all our sakes.'

The workers' accommodation was crude but solidly constructed, a small row of connected wooden buildings with corrugated iron roofs on the west side of the estate. A small, rather pleasant garden ran the length of the block, with a bed of flowers on one side and a long row of trees on the other. It was Sunday afternoon and several men were sat out under the porch, angrily discussing the events of the last few hours. The dark mood was understandable but I was glad the workers had had the good sense to vent their spleens in private. Whatever Mr Weiman had said to them, it had managed to calm them down, for now. Indeed, but for the raised voices from the men, it would have been rather a tranquil scene. A woman was taking in washing from the line, before the afternoon downpour, and a little boy, no more than four or five, was clinging to her skirt tails.

All eyes turned to look at me as I appeared through the trees. A couple of the men pulled themselves reluctantly to their feet. There was no hostility in their bearing, just concern about who I was and what I wanted. I doubted they would have been anywhere near as calm had I been another one of Tejada's thugs. One of the workers raised a hand in greeting. 'Can I help you, mister?' he asked, as I came forward. He was a burly fellow in a checked shirt.

'Yes. I'm sorry to interrupt. Your day of rest and everything.'

The man frowned, moving forward to meet me. He had a muscular torso but a thoughtful air. 'There hasn't been much rest today. Have they taken Joseph away?'

146

I blinked. 'Er...no. Not yet. They've locked him up in one of the store houses. Sorry, who are you?' I confess, I was not really used to conversing with labourers, especially not in such fraught circumstances as these. But the fellow seemed friendly enough. Despite his thick set frame, his presence was not in the least intimidating, though neither was he overly deferential. Just the type of fellow Mr Montana would really dislike, I thought.

'Nathan,' he introduced himself. He was the man I had seen holding back that other worker out on the lawn. A sensible fellow, by the looks of it. 'Joseph did not kill anyone,' he told me, without preamble. 'He is an innocent man. He would not harm a fly.'

'That's what I've come to find out.'

Nathan looked me up and down with curiosity. 'You're an Englishman?' That much would be obvious from my voice.

'Yes. The name's Buxton. Henry Buxton. It was...my fault Joseph got whipped yesterday afternoon. Well, indirectly. He sent me a note, asking to meet me and then ran away from the work party so we could talk.'

'He should not have done that,' Nathan said. His voice had a deep timbre to it, slow but authoritative. 'Mr Langbroek looks for any excuse to beat us. He is not a kind man.' Langbroek was the overseer, of course, and "not kind" was something of an understatement.

'And Mr Catesby? What did you think of him?'

'God rest his soul. He was not kind either, but he was at least fair. He did not approve of Mr Langbroek.'

'Did he not?' That was interesting.

'Mr Catesby would not see a man beaten for no reason.'

'No. Although he did have Joseph Green whipped.'

'As I said, mister: he was fair but he was not kind.'

'The general...the policeman...he spoke to you? When he came over here?'

Nathan's head dipped briefly. He could not disguise his fear of the man. Tejada had been less than polite to a house full of Europeans and North Americans. How badly would he behave when confronted with men he considered racially

147

inferior? 'He came,' Nathan confirmed unhappily. 'He spoke to Joseph and to me.'

That was the nub of it. 'The general claims that he has a witness, who saw Green leave his room last night. Was that one of the people here?'

Nathan shook his head. '*I* was the witness. We share a room. Four of us. But the general did not understand what I said to him. He did not listen to me. I told him truthfully, Joseph got up once in the middle of the night, to go to the bathroom.' He indicated a small outhouse, attached to the far end of the main property. 'He was gone two or three minutes and then he returned. That is the truth. But all the general wanted to hear was that he had left the room. He had already made up his mind. He said I must have fallen asleep and imagined Joseph had returned quickly, but I did not.' An understandable bitterness had crept into his voice.

'I'm sure you didn't,' I agreed. 'And you shared a room with him? So there's no way Joseph Green could have crept into the main house and killed anyone, without you knowing about it?'

'He could not and would not,' Nathan agreed. 'I do not sleep well. I would have heard him if he had left.'

I nodded unhappily. It was just as I had feared. Tejada had got the wrong man. And, given the conversation I had just had with Miss Bunting – and the fact that she had tried to pin the blame on Green – every indication available to me suggested the real culprit was my own secretary. And if that was the case, then my life – once again – was about to fall apart.

What the hell was I going to do? I rubbed my eyes absently. If I publicly accused Miss Bunting of killing Steven Catesby, or even just laid out the evidence against her, would anyone believe me? They would only have my word about the earring and, if I admitted removing evidence from the crime scene, Tejada would probably lock me up for perverting the course of justice. Even if he did believe me, and Miss Bunting was arrested, it would mean the end of my career. David Richards would not forgive the damaging publicity if one of our own clerks turned out to be a murderess. And if I testified against her, Miss Bunting would have no reason to conceal all that she knew about me – the fact that I was a woman – which would end my career and expose me to public humiliation. Oh, I dare say I would get through it. I could run away and set up a new identity as I had done before; but I was getting too old now to keep going through the same routine. And what would Maurice do? I doubted I would get him on a boat back to Europe. He was terrified of water. So I would lose him too. On the other hand, if I did nothing, then Joseph Green would hang and I knew now without a shadow of a doubt that he was innocent. Could I keep quiet, let him die, just to protect my career; and allow Miss Bunting to go free? It would be easy enough to do. Tejada already had his man, so far as he was concerned. All I needed to do was keep mum and there would be no backlash whatever. No-one would ever guess the truth and my career would be saved. It may sound despicable, even to consider such a course of action, but until you find yourself in such circumstances, you never know for certain how you are going to react. Self-preservation can often take precedence over moral considerations, even with the most upright of citizens. In my case, however, there was a further complication. I had already confided my suspicions to Maurice and I knew exactly what he would expect me to do. I could just picture him, lecturing me sternly; and, even in my head, as the voice of my conscience, I knew he was right. I could not allow an innocent man to hang. Joseph Green could not be made to pay for somebody else's crime. The question was, how the devil could I prevent it? What evidence could I possibly uncover that would satisfy a narrow-minded brute like General Tejada?

'Mister?'

I had been standing silently for some moments in the garden. Nathan had been too polite to interrupt, but now a perplexed voice startled me from my reverie. 'Mister?' he said again, tugging at the sleeve of my jacket. It was the house boy, Moses. I had been so caught up in my own thoughts I had not even seen him arrive.

'Don't bother the nice gentleman,' Nathan scolded him

gently.

I blinked. 'Sorry, I was miles away. That's quite all right. Moses, what are you doing here? Does Greta know you're away from the house?'

The young lad shook his head. 'She will be very angry. I ran away from the cottage. I wanted to see where Joseph was being held. But Mr Langbroek, he would not let me. So I came here.' The boy's eyes were puffy and red, from where he had been crying. A strong bond clearly existed between him and Joseph Green.

Nathan was looking down at the lad disapprovingly.

'You shouldn't have run away,' I scolded him, saving the other man the bother. 'I'd better take him back to the house. You've been very helpful, Mr...' I stopped, suddenly realising I didn't know the man's surname. 'You've been very helpful, Nathan.'

'It was my pleasure.'

'I'll...I'll do what I can for Joseph. But I can't make any promises.'

'I understand.'

'And as for you, young man.' I glanced down at the boy with mock severity. He was small for his age, I thought. At fourteen, he should have been fully grown, but the lad was barely more than five feet tall. Perhaps that was as big as he was going to get. 'You're coming with me.' I grabbed him by the ear, rotated him around and propelled him forward towards the path leading back to the hacienda. He laughed and wriggled free from my grasp, running a few paces ahead and then stopping. He turned back and waited for me to catch him up. I waved a hand to Nathan, who had returned to the porch, and then strode across to join the youngster. Moses stared up at me as the two of us disappeared between the trees. 'You're really going to help Joseph?' he asked me eagerly.

'I don't know if I can,' I admitted. There was no point getting the boy's hopes up. The pathway ahead of us was short and heavily covered. 'But the more I find out about things, the better the chance that we might be able to do something.' I stopped just before the end of the trees and turned to face the boy. 'The best thing you can do, young man...' I wagged a finger at him. 'Is to tell me everything you know about Joseph Green. And about Matthew.'

Moses frowned seriously. He rubbed his eyes, which still looked rather red. 'They were brothers, mister. They were very close.'

That much I already knew. 'And what about you? Are you related to them?'

'No, mister.' He shook his head emphatically. 'But they are my family. I grew up here.' The boy gestured back to the workers' cottages. 'This is my home.' It was obvious he felt a greater affinity to these labourers than he did to anyone at the hacienda. I could hardly blame him for that.

'Your parents worked here, did they?'

'No, mister.' His face fell. 'I am an orphan. My mother died when I was a baby. My father was a vagrant. Mrs Collinson, she looked after me. She brought me up, with Isabel.'

'The housemaid?'

'Mrs Collinson was her mother. She was my mother too.'

'She looked after you?'

'She was very kind, but very ugly.' He smiled at the memory. 'She is dead now.'

'I see. And...Matthew?'

The boy grinned. 'He was my uncle. And Joseph too. They used to play with me. Teach me things. Matthew especially.'

'What sort of things did he teach you?'

Moses grinned again. 'How to fish in the river. How to set traps to catch animals. He was a very clever man.' And a practical sort, too, by the sounds of it. 'He knew a lot of things. He was learning to read. We were helping each other.'

'You can read too?'

'A little,' Moses said. 'Mr Weiman says Isabel and I must both learn.'

'That's very liberal of him,' I thought. But then everyone had said he treated his workers well. Which begged

151

the question, why did he employ a brute like Mr Langbroek? But we were straying from the point: Matthew Green. 'Do you remember the day Matthew died? Back in March?'

'Yes, mister. I remember it well. I was very upset. And Joseph too.'

'Were you in the house when it happened?'

'No, mister. I was at church. Everyone was at church, except Mr Catesby. It was only when we came back that we heard he was...was dead.'

'And how did everyone react? How did the other labourers feel?'

Moses thought for a moment. 'They didn't know what to do. They said he had been stealing. And other people said...said he had done bad things. That he deserved what happened to him. But I did not believe that, mister. He was a good man.'

'I'm sure he was. But tell me: there was another man here that weekend. Giles Markham.'

'I saw him. Many times. He was your friend?'

'Er...no, I never met him, actually.'

'But you took over from him? His job, for the British?'

'Yes, that's right.'

His eyes twinkled. 'I heard you talking to Mr Weiman, when you arrived.'

'You eavesdropped?'

'Yes, mister.' The boy was unrepentant.

'And you told Joseph about me?'

'Yes, mister. I told him you were here to find out about his brother's death.'

'Good lord.' My jaw dropped open. 'How on earth could you know anything about that?' That had certainly not been discussed over coffee on Friday evening.

'I heard your friend talking, with the nice lady, upstairs. They talked about you. He said you were a detective. That you would investigate.'

Damnation. I stared at the boy. So that explained why Green had been so keen to talk to me. That fool Freddie, mouthing off for everyone to hear. I would have to have serious words with him about that. 'So you told Green all about me and that was why he wanted to see me?'

'Yes, mister. He wanted to help you. He thought you could find out what really happened to his brother. If it was true what the others said. Was he really a thief?'

'And so you passed on a note from him, arranging a meeting on Saturday morning.'

'Yes, mister.' His face clouded over. 'It is my fault. If I had said nothing, he would not have been whipped. And now he would not...he would not...' The boy was starting to sniffle again.

I scowled and pulled out my handkerchief, which I handed across. The last thing I needed was waterworks. 'You can't blame yourself,' I told him firmly. 'You weren't to know what would happen. And it's not your fault he was arrested for murder. It's the general who did that; and if an innocent man hangs then it's his fault, not yours.' Moses yelped again and blew hard on the handkerchief. Perhaps I could have chosen those last words better. 'But why did he leave the work party? Why didn't he choose another time to meet me?'

'The men only have one break in the day, the same time we serve you lunch. In the evening, it would have been too dark. He didn't think you would come.'

He had a point there. I wouldn't have fancied traipsing around the estate in the moonlight hours. I might well have ignored the note. Ah well, what was done was done. 'We'd better get you back to the house,' I said. 'Greta will probably be worried.'

Moses nodded, taking another blow on the handkerchief. 'She is very strict,' he lamented. 'And very fat.'

I laughed. 'Yes, she is. But I'm sure she has your best interests at heart.'

Moses was not convinced. 'You will find out who killed Mr Catesby?'

'I don't know, Moses. But I will try.'

'Do you have any suspects?'

I stifled a laugh. 'Er...well, let's just say I have a few ideas. But I'll need time to investigate, to gather evidence.'

He peered up at me then. 'How will you do that?'

'Well, first of all,' I said, 'I need to make a telephone call.'

Chapter Eleven

A battered police truck had pulled up on the edge of the square. It was a large open backed vehicle, sturdy and mud spattered, with thick, heavy tyres and a murky front cabin. Two muscular officers had stepped down from the cab and were having a quiet smoke, having presumably driven some distance to get here. The truck would not get much further, though, even along the newly constructed road. It wasn't worth risking the axle trying to manoeuvre the vehicle all the way up to the hacienda. A couple of horses were tethered outside the post office and I recognised one of them as the surly brown nag I had ridden on Friday afternoon. Tejada must have sent the horses down to the village with Mr Langbroek when he had summoned the reinforcements. I had no idea how the bodies of the deceased would be carried down here when the time came. Not on horse back, presumably. That would be taking things too far. Perhaps the general would requisition a few of the carts Mr Weiman used to transport his coffee. The bodies would be brought down to the village and then loaded onto the truck and driven to Guatemala City for a proper autopsy.

I was surprised to find myself away from the estate this afternoon. I had been prepared for an abrupt rebuff when I had tentatively floated the idea of travelling down to the village to make a phone call. Those of us who had come from the capital had already, in effect, missed the afternoon train, so it wasn't as if we were likely to abscond; and if we had to remain up in the mountains for another day, it was only fair we had the opportunity to pass on the change of plan to everyone back home. General Tejada was not ordinarily a man to be persuaded by anything approaching a logical argument but, luckily for us, he was in a relaxed mood, now that he had caught his man. Having settled down with another pot of coffee in the courtyard, to await the arrival of the reinforcements, he regarded my entreaty with indifference rather than outright scorn.

Gunther Weiman was kind enough to add his support to

the idea and it was this which tipped the balance. 'I did promise that I would take Jane into the village this morning,' the German told him, 'so she could telephone her daughter. Miss Talbot doesn't know her father has passed away.'

Tejada grunted, sipping at his coffee. 'You need to get that telephone of yours fixed, señor. Very well.' He placed his cup down on the table and regarded me with a steely eye. 'You and the señora can go and make your phone calls. Provided you are back here on the estate within the hour.'

I blinked. 'An hour? That...might be a tall order.' It would take that long just to walk down to the village.

'An hour!' Tejada insisted. He gestured across to a second table, where Ricardo Gonzales was sitting with his wife Consuela. 'Señor Gonzales can drive you.'

The engineer started at the sound of his name, but had no objection to the plan, when he realised what we were about. And so the matter was agreed.

It was not until we stepped out of the hacienda, however, that I fully understood what I had agreed to. We would be travelling down to the village on the back of Mr Gonzales' 496cc Victoria. I almost gave up on the idea at that moment. I am not built for motor-bicycles. It was only the general's glaring eyes back in the courtyard that persuaded me it would not be a good idea to have a change of heart, now that he had granted us his permission to leave.

Ricardo Gonzales was an amiable fellow with a neat moustache and a diffident manner. His wife accompanied us as we moved across the lawn, and he took a moment to kiss her goodbye before unlocking the bicycle, a public display of affection which made the rest of us rather uncomfortable, but was typical of his uncomplicated manner.

He helped me onto the back of the bicycle. Once I was in position, he guided Mrs Talbot into the bullet shaped sidecar and pulled on his helmet and goggles. That done, he clambered swiftly into position and kick-started the vehicle. The engine roared into life beneath us.

I closed my eyes as we moved off down the path, consoling myself with the thought that this way we would at least avoid the rains. I would rather my man had been at the wheel, however. Maurice was a competent rider, having owned a motor-bicycle back in France. Gonzales, by contrast, was an absolute demon. For all his mild manners and modest bearing, the man seemed to have no fear of the road at all. My bones ricocheted like sweets in a half empty jar as we began our brutal descent. I cannot say precisely what speed we were going as we hurtled down that hill, except to say that it was at least three times as fast as any sane man would have contemplated. I was sitting behind Gonzales, pressed up uncomfortably close to the diminutive Guatemalan as I straddled the back seat, holding onto the man's waist but not wanting to press against him too tightly. I confess, at times I just closed my eyes and held on for grim death.

Jane Talbot may have had the worst of it, though, in that rickety sidecar. She was clinging tightly to her bonnet the whole way down.

The first smattering of rain was just beginning to fall as we arrived in the village and Gonzales pulled up the motor-bicycle. He lifted the goggles from his face, smoothed down his moustache and stepped off the machine. He looked back and smiled, catching sight of my pale face. 'Are you all right, señor?' he asked, kindly.

'Very well, thank you,' I lied. I moved to swing my leg over the top of the motor, but my foot snagged on the seat and I nearly fell off the side. My thighs were feeling very sore after all that juddering. I might just as well have come down on horse back. I grabbed the leather upholstery and righted myself, before carefully dismounting the vehicle.

Gonzales had moved around the bicycle and was helping Jane Talbot up from the sidecar. She too was a little windswept but her manner was its usual calm self. 'Thank you, Señor Gonzales,' she said, as she stepped out onto the rough cobbles. 'An exhilarating, if rather bumpy, experience.' The engineer beamed with pleasure.

Mrs Talbot took a moment to absorb the quiet, dusty plaza. She tutted at the sight of the police truck and the two men with the cigarettes, then moved grandly around the front of the motor-bicycle, coming to a rest at my side. 'So, Mr Buxton. Where is this telephone of yours?'

'It's just across there.' I gestured to the far side of the plaza. 'There's a bar, just down that alleyway. Freddie and I – Mr Reeves – visited it yesterday afternoon.'

'A bar?'

'Yes. They have a telephone apparently.' Not that I had been aware of the fact the previous day.

'I suppose it was too much to hope for a post office to be open on a Sunday.'

'I'm afraid so.'

'Well, then, Mr Buxton, lead the way.'

I nodded and gestured the woman across the street. Gonzales remained behind to lock up his bicycle as the two of us navigated gingerly around a pile of horse manure and stepped onto the green. The rain was starting to fall quite heavily now, so we quickened our pace, passing the lifeless stone fountain as the engineer hurried to catch us up.

Alberto's bar was just where I had left it the day before, a little way off the main drag. A grubby little boy was squatting in the dirt outside, cleaning his teeth with a small twig. The badly painted door was pulled back, though the shutters were half closed and there was no sign of any customers. I wasn't entirely sure if the place was open. In England, at this time on a Sunday afternoon, everywhere would be shut up, but I had not been in Guatemala long enough to familiarise myself with the licensing laws. Regardless, we stepped through the doorway into the fetid, gloomy interior. The cobwebs around the window frames did not seem to have moved in the last twenty four hours. 'It's a bit dusty in here, I'm afraid,' I said, as my companion took stock of the grim interior.

'It cannot be helped,' Mrs Talbot replied. 'We are not here for the décor.'

I wiped a finger on the dust of a nearby chair. 'Probably just as well.'

There was no sign of activity behind the bar either. 'Anyone at home?' I called through. The saloon was bereft of life. Perhaps the locals were all at home, enjoying a siesta. I heard a short clutter in response to my cry and, a few seconds later, a cheerful figure emerged from the back room, dish cloth in hand. It was the barman, Alberto. 'Good afternoon, Alberto,' I said. 'Sorry to trouble you. You remember me? I was in here yesterday with Freddie Reeves.'

Alberto beamed. 'I remember. Welcome! Ah, Señor Gonzales.' He knew the engineer already. '*Bienvenidos*!'

'And this is Mrs Jane Talbot.'

'*Encantada*, señora!' The balding barman peered happily across at the Englishwoman, his chunky spectacles magnifying his sparkling eyes.

'Pleased to meet you,' Mrs Talbot responded, extending a hand politely. She did not ruffle an eyelid when he took the hand and kissed the back of it, though I doubted she approved of such familiarity.

'Welcome!' Alberto declared again, folding his dish cloth and secreting it behind the bar. It looked like we had interrupted him during his daily chores. He probably had a few glasses to clean up from the night before.

I got straight down to business. 'We were wondering if we might use your telephone? I was told you had one here?'

His face lit up. 'Si, si! Of course!' He gestured enthusiastically to the back room. The man seemed incapable of responding calmly to any statement. One has to make allowances for locals, of course, but Gonzales at least knew how to contain himself in the presence of strangers.

'Mrs Talbot,' I said, nodding in the direction of the back room, where the barman had indicated. 'I think your call is the more urgent.'

She inclined her head. 'Thank you, Mr Buxton. Through here?'

Alberto nodded and escorted the woman eagerly into the far room. 'It is here, on the wall. No coins. It is a private phone!' This last he declared with some pride. I couldn't help smiling at that. It was not something I would ever feel inclined to boast about.

I stood awkwardly for a moment at the bar, with Gonzales to my left, and then turned my attention back to the

159

saloon. There was a table in the far corner which did not look quite as dusty as the others. 'Shall we?' I suggested. He bobbed his head and we moved across. 'It was good of you to bring us down here,' I said, dusting off the seat with my handkerchief before taking my place.

Gonzales shrugged modestly. 'It was no trouble, señor. I could not let the señora wait any longer to pass on her sad news.'

'I really must have a word with Mr Weiman, tell him to get that damned phone fixed up at the hacienda.' The general had been right about that if nothing else. 'Then we wouldn't have to bother with all this.'

'The phone company...it takes time,' Gonzales said diplomatically.

'You don't have to explain. It's the same back in England. Can take weeks to get the damned things installed. Though why anyone would want one in their home is beyond me.' I had always hated telephones. 'You live quite near here, don't you?'

Gonzales smiled. 'Yes. Consuela and I have a small apartment in the next town.'

'Will you be heading home later today?'

'I hope so. My wife, she is very upset by everything that has happened.'

'Hardly surprising.' I sat back in my chair. 'No-one was expecting this.'

'It was kind of Señor Weiman to invite us, but it was a mistake to bring Consuela this weekend.' People hadn't exactly been friendly towards the Guatemalan couple. I suppose it had been a little awkward, breaking bread in a formal setting with people of such low status, but that was no excuse for bad manners. 'It will be good to get home,' he concluded. 'If we leave by four o'clock, we should be able to get there before it gets dark. If the general allows us to leave.'

'No reason why he shouldn't, now his men are here. But you'll be back in a day or two, I presume, to continue on the road?'

The engineer shook his head. 'My work on this section

is nearly complete. I offer advice only.' He smiled shyly. 'The others do the hard work.'

'Men like Joseph Green?'

'Yes.' He looked away.

'That overseer fellow. What's his name? Langbroek? You've worked with him?'

'A little.' Gonzales rubbed his moustache self-consciously. 'He is not an easy man to work with. He has a bit of a temper. He drinks a lot. And...he does not get on with the local people.'

'Bit of a bigot? Yes, so I gathered. There was no need for him to be so rough with that Green fellow, no matter what he might be guilty of.'

'Do you think he killed Señor Catesby?'

'Lord knows.'

Alberto had returned to the bar. He closed the connecting door behind him to give Mrs Talbot a bit of privacy.

'I don't suppose we could get a drink?' I called across to him.

'Si, si, señor!'

'A couple of beers?' I looked to Gonzales. The engineer nodded his agreement. '*Dos cervezas, por favor.*' I am not much of a beer drinker, as a rule, but after the horrors of the motor-bicycle I needed something to quench my thirst. I could order a whisky later on, if there was time.

Alberto came across with the two bottles, which he opened with a bottle opener hanging from his waist. He wiped the table down and placed the bottles in front of us.

'A couple of glasses, too,' I said. 'Well, one for me, anyway.'

'Of course!' Alberto hesitated a moment. 'The señora, she is upset?' The barman's eyes were alive with concern. He must have overheard the start of her telephone call.

I nodded grimly. 'Yes, her...husband died yesterday. She's calling her daughter in Guatemala City to pass on the news.'

The barman's face fell. 'That is very sad,' he said.

'Yes, rather. Did you know her husband? George

161

Talbot?'

Alberto frowned. 'I do not think so, señor. Although the name is familiar.'

'He's a banker. Or was.'

'Ah yes! My nephew has mentioned him.' He paused for a second, glancing across at the shutters. 'The policemen who have arrived in the village.' The ones out in the street. 'They are not here for Señor Talbot. There is something else wrong, at the hacienda?' The question was a tentative one, but the barman could not disguise his curiosity. 'There are rumours that Señor Catesby...'

I rolled my eyes. Trust Alberto to be in the know already. But it was pointless trying to cover the matter up. 'Yes, it's true I'm afraid. Mr Catesby is dead. The poor fellow was murdered in his bed.'

Alberto let out a small cry and crossed himself. 'That is a dreadful thing to happen.'

'You're telling me. And it gets worse, I'm afraid. They've just arrested Joseph Green for his murder.'

The barman stared at me through his thick glasses, his jaw slack. He blinked a couple of times and then pulled himself together. 'I will get you your glass,' he mumbled and headed off to the bar.

Gonzales had already picked up his bottle and was drinking the beer straight. I waited for Alberto to bring the tumbler and then poured out my own. I was willing to make some concessions to local custom but drinking from the bottle was taking things too far. 'I'll be glad to get shot of this place,' I muttered, taking a quick sip from the glass.

Mrs Talbot was on the phone for a good fifteen minutes. Alberto tactfully lingered behind the bar and waited for the woman to emerge from the back room. She had taken a moment to collect herself before coming out. She was one of the old school, determined to maintain her composure in public. Goodness knows what emotions were churning around inside, however. I would certainly not have wanted to pass on that kind of news by telephone.

'All finished?' I rose gently to my feet.

She nodded. 'Yes, thank you, Mr Buxton. Not a happy duty.'

'No, indeed.'

She turned back to the barman. 'Thank you for the use of the telephone. Let me know how much I owe you.'

Alberto waved the matter away. 'Nothing, señora. I am very sorry for your loss.'

She inclined her head once again. 'Thank you. I wonder if I might trouble you for a small sherry?'

'Si, si, señora. Of course!' Alberto leapt across the bar and grabbed a bottle of "jerez" from a shelf. Busily, he prepared the glass, while Mrs Talbot moved across to our table.

'You don't mind waiting for a few minutes, while I...?'

'That is why you are here, Mr Buxton. You have waited for me, very patiently, and I am content to sit and wait for you. Please be seated, Señor Gonzales.' The engineer had risen to his feet as the Englishwoman came over. He was a little bit in awe of her, I suspected, and with good reason. She was an admirable woman. It had taken great courage for her to maintain her cool in such trying circumstances.

I left the two of them together and moved into the back room, closing the door firmly behind me.

The duty officer at the legation was less than helpful. Derek Plumrose was an unfriendly brute at the best of times and was irritated even to have to answer the phone on a Sunday, which I did not entirely blame him for; but he also took unnecessary pleasure in informing me that the minister was not available. He would not be available, Plumrose added pointedly, until nine am the following morning. Office hours, in other words. The man did not have the courtesy to provide even a basic explanation for this and, although I had stressed the urgency, I was loath to press the matter further. In point of fact, I was rather relieved not to have to speak to Mr Richards directly. It was a conversation I had been dreading all the way down the mountainside; and logging a call with the duty officer would at least confirm that I had attempted to contact him, which might mitigate things somewhat. I hung up the receiver with a clear conscience, cleared the line and then placed a second call via the operator to Guatemala City.

William Battersby answered the telephone. 'Mr Buxton!' he exclaimed in surprise when I told him who it was. The young secretary was well aware of my dislike of telecommunication devices – he had seen the expression on my face when he had informed me that he had a telephone installed at his flat – and he knew I was not in the habit of making long distance calls. 'Is something wrong, sir?' he enquired at once. I could picture the frown on his youthful, doe-eyed face. There was a bit of a crackle on the line and I had to press the receiver tightly against my ear to hear him properly.

'I'll say. Something's come up. You'll have to hold the fort tomorrow morning. We've missed the train.'

There was a brief pause. 'The train's not until four o'clock, sir.'

'I'm aware of that, William. But we're a good two hours away from the train station. We're going to have to stay another night at the finca and catch the early train tomorrow.'

'I see. Of course, sir.'

'Lord knows what time we'll have to get up, but we should be back by the early afternoon. I tried to get in touch with Mr Richards, to tell him Freddie wouldn't be in, but it appears he's out for the day.'

'Yes, sir. He's playing golf with the minister from the French legation.'

'That doesn't surprise me.' I grunted. Richards spent more time hobnobbing with other diplomats on the golf course than he ever did working. 'But you'll have to get a message through to him somehow. Not just about his secretary. I'm afraid we've all been caught up in something rather unpleasant.'

'Sir?'

I took a deep breath and briefly outlined the events of the last few hours. I kept away from anything sensitive – the phone line could hardly be considered secure – but there was no harm in passing on the basic facts. The details would be known by everyone soon enough. William listened in horrified silence, the colour doubtless draining from his already pale face as he took in the words 'murder' and 'police investigation'.

'Is Miss Bunting all right?' he asked, with some concern, when I had finished my story. The young fool really did have a crush on that girl.

'Yes, she's fine,' I snapped irritably. 'But we'll all be out of a job come Monday when the minister hears we've been involved in a murder.'

'It's got nothing to do with you, though, sir.'

'No, of course not. But that's not the point. Richards won't believe it's a coincidence, the three of us being here this weekend. And even if I convince him there's no connection to our...well, our other work, there'll still be all the publicity. You know what the minister's like. He'll think the world has fallen in. And I'll be the one to blame. I'm already on notice. You heard what he said to me on Thursday morning.'

'What can I do, sir?'

'Well, we need to give him the head's up. Better he hears it from us rather than reading it in the papers.'

'You want *me* to tell him, sir?' William was alarmed at the prospect.

'Well, I can't do it, can I? The duty officer won't put me through. You'll have to pop across to the legation, when he gets back from his game.'

'He won't be happy to be bothered on a Sunday, sir.'

'No, he won't. But what choice do we have? Put the best spin on it you can. Nothing to do with us.'

'I'll do my best, sir.'

'You certainly can't make the situation any worse. That's not the only reason I'm calling, though.'

'Sir?'

I took a moment to consider my words. 'The thing is, William, there may be some connection between this murder and the death of my predecessor, Giles Markham.' There was another long pause on the far end of the line. 'Are you still there?'

'Yes, sir. I...don't understand.'

165

'That business with the flat the other day.' The break-in. 'Freddie Reeves has got it into his head that it might be connected in some way with events at the Weiman estate. Mr Markham came here the weekend before he died, apparently. That was why Freddie invited me along. Thought I could do a bit of snooping, the clot. He'd heard all about that business with me and...well, the journey over here.' The affair of the "Red Zeppelin", which I had no intention of mentioning on the telephone. 'And needless to say he got completely the wrong end of the stick. But, in fairness, regarding Markham, I have a horrible suspicion he may be right.'

'But Mr Markham's death was a suicide, sir. I found the body myself.'

'I know that. That's why I wanted to talk to you.' William had given me a thorough account of the events of that day shortly after I had arrived in Guatemala. He had queried a small item in the ledger the Friday before Markham had died and it had subsequently transpired that he had been cooking the books. This time, however, I was seeking some rather different intelligence. 'Look, there's no easy way of asking this: when did Miss Bunting arrive in Guatemala?'

'Emily? I don't understand. Why...?'

'Just answer the question, dammit!'

William swallowed hard and tried to remember. 'Well, Miss Stanton, her predecessor, finished on the Friday evening and Miss Bunting must have started on the following Wednesday, I think.'

'Yes, I know that. But when did she arrive in the country? In Guatemala?'

'Oh...erm, well, on Sunday evening, I think.' He took a moment to reflect. 'Yes, that's right. She spent the night in Puerto Barrios.' That was the port town on the east coast. 'It was too late to catch the train. She stayed the night in a hotel and then hopped on the train the following morning. She would have arrived in Guatemala City on Monday afternoon sometime, probably quite late. She had a day to settle herself in and then started work on the Wednesday, as I said. Look, sir, why are you asking me all this? You surely don't think Miss

166

Bunting...?'

'I don't think anything,' I snapped. 'I'm just trying to ascertain everyone's movements that week. Anyone who has the slightest connection to Giles Markham.'

'But Emily *didn't* have a connection to him, sir. She never met him. He committed suicide before she arrived here.'

'But he was the one who approved her appointment, to the office?'

'Not really, sir. He was informed of it, of course, but she was assigned by London. As we all are.'

I pursed my lips. That was true enough. Roles like ours tended to be appointed from on high rather than locally. 'What about this Miss Stanton? Was she close to Mr Markham?'

'Not really, sir. She was a very efficient woman. Quite intimidating.' Miss Stanton had been some years older than William, I recalled. I had looked over her file when I had started working at the legation. 'I think she disapproved of him a little,' the secretary added. 'His drinking and gambling. Not that there's anything wrong with that,' he asserted hastily. William knew that I was partial to both.

'Tell that to Mr Richards. And she was transferred to Mexico City? Miss Stanton?'

'Yes, sir. A step up for her.'

'And what about Miss Bunting? She was previously in Madrid?' It had been a while since I had last looked at her file.

'That's right, sir. Her first posting. As you know, her Spanish is very good.' His voice was full of youthful admiration. 'Much better than mine,' he added.

'And when did she move into Markham's flat?'

'On the Thursday, sir. She stayed a couple of nights in a hotel, to begin with, while we sorted out the accommodation.'

'And she didn't mind moving into a dead man's flat?'

'No, sir. I'd cleared it out by then. Not that there was much to clear. And it wasn't as if he'd shot himself in there. The place was barely lived in.'

'Yes, so you've said before.'

'Sir, is Emily all right? She isn't involved in this in some way? She can't be, surely? She doesn't know any of the people at the farm.'

'Not to my knowledge,' I agreed. 'But we're all involved now, William. The police have made an arrest, but they may have got the wrong man. You might well have heard of the investigating officer. A General Tejada? Julio Tejada?' There was a sharp intake of breath on the other end of the line. 'Yes, Mr Reeves said you would recognise the name.'

'He...he was the investigating officer for Mr Markham's suicide. And he's at the estate?' William was incredulous.

'Yes, he is. Making a damned nuisance of himself.'

'I...I would be very careful what you say about him, sir. He has a reputation for...'

'Yes, I know all about that.' I had seen Tejada's brutality first hand, though I was not about to say so over the telephone. 'But Markham? Did he do a thorough job there? The investigation?'

'Not really, sir. He was only called in as a courtesy. Mr Richards wanted the whole matter kept quiet and General Tejada didn't seem to have much interest in it anyway. He seemed to think it was beneath him.'

'But he did visit the flat?'

'Yes, sir. A day or two later.'

'The Tuesday or the Wednesday?'

'Er...the Wednesday, I think. Yes, the Wednesday. We went in to check the place out on Tuesday, just to make sure Mr Markham hadn't left anything sensitive in there.'

'We?'

'Mr Reeves and I'

'Freddie helped you clear out the flat?'

'Yes, sir.'

I frowned. 'Was he there when Tejada searched the place?'

'No, sir. Just me. I let him in with one of his deputies.'

'Oh, you mean that boggle eyed fellow? Sergeant Velázquez?'

'I don't recall the name. No, that doesn't sound like him.'

'Never mind. And you were there the whole time?'

168

'No, sir. I just let them in. I was running the office single-handedly that week. I'd already spent half a day clearing out the room. I couldn't afford to spare any more time. The office was closed to the public for the week, but there was still a mountain of paperwork to get through.'

'So you left Tejada in the flat?'

'Yes, sir. One of his officers returned the key later that day. That was the last we heard. There was an inquest a couple of weeks later and a typed up report. And that was it.'

'I see.' I paused for a moment, taking it all in. Not that there was much new information. But it did seem like an awful lot of people had been in and around that apartment at one point or another. General Tejada. Freddie Reeves. Miss Bunting. And Catesby himself had been in town on the evening of the burglary. What about the other house guests? I wondered. The Montanas and the Talbots both lived in Guatemala City. And then there was that overseer fellow. If anyone was born to be a burglar it was him. Could he be connected to Giles Markham in some way? 'Have you ever heard of a man named Langbroek?' I asked William. 'I think he may be South African.'

'The name doesn't ring a bell, sir.'

'Just a thought. What about...erm...Montana? Arthur Montana?'

'Montana.' William thought for a while. 'I'm not sure.'

'How can you not be sure? He's a United Fruit executive. One of those damned banana people.'

'No, I don't know him, sir.'

Who else? 'What about George Talbot? He was the one who fell down the stairs. A banker. Worked for Anglo South American.'

'Talbot.' William paused. 'That names does sound familiar. Just a minute.' He considered briefly. 'Yes, Mr Markham used to meet up with him. We've got it on file somewhere. Just an informal thing. He had a few useful connections, in the business world.'

'George Talbot was...was one of our advisers?' I asked, in surprise. 'I've never seen anything in the files about him.' Not that I had read every word.

'Mr Markham liked to keep some things close to his chest. He didn't always keep comprehensive records. Just in case things fell into the wrong hands.'

'But he used to meet up with George Talbot?'

'Yes, I believe so, sir, on occasion. Although as I say, it was just an informal thing. We had him down as quite a straight-laced chap, if I remember rightly. Not that I ever met him. He passed on a few bits of useful informa...er, advice. Had a bit of a bee in his bonnet about corruption, bribery. That sort of thing.'

'Government corruption?'

'Yes, indirectly. Corruption in the banking sector, I think. Misuse of funds, by the government and by the police. You know what they're like, sir.'

'The police?' I felt a sudden shiver of fear.

'I believe so, sir. Protection rackets. Bribery. Some pretty horrendous stuff. Business rivals being made to disappear. Oh, perhaps I shouldn't...'

'And Talbot was passing on information about that, to us?'

'I think so, sir. Not just to us. To his superiors at the bank. I remember Mr Markham saying he was on something of a crusade about it.'

'Good lord.' I shuddered. That was the last thing I needed to hear.

Chapter Twelve

Steven Catesby's body was being carried out on a lightweight stretcher. The corpse was covered respectfully with a sheet, hiding the blood stained pyjamas and the heavy cut across his throat. Gunther Weiman was standing with Mrs Weiman on the front steps of the hacienda, watching mournfully as the body was transported across the lawn towards a rough looking wooden cart. The policemen from the village had been co-opted to carry the wicker stretcher as soon as they had arrived. They were a solid, grim looking pair with hard eyes and weather beaten faces. Against all the odds, they had beaten us back to the estate and were already being put to good use.

By rights, we should have arrived ahead of them. Gonzales' motor-bicycle was a much faster proposition than the policemen's decrepit horses, but the two men had left the village some twenty minutes ahead of us and, when we caught them up, they had refused to let us pass. At my insistence, Gonzales had blown his horn, but that had just annoyed them even more. There was no point trailing behind them at a snail's pace, so we stopped at the intersection between the main road and the side track up to the farm and lit a couple of cigarettes, allowing the policemen to continue on their merry way without us. After we had finished the smoke, we continued uphill on foot. The terrain was a little soggy here, but Ricardo Gonzales made no complaint as he manhandled his pride and joy up the increasingly steep slope. I was relieved just to be out of the sidecar. Mrs Talbot had probably made the right decision, staying behind in the village. The bullet-shaped compartment was lower to the ground than the driver's seat and every minor pebble sent shock waves rattling through the fragile structure.

I must confess, I had been rather taken aback when the Englishwoman had declared her intention to remain behind in the village, against the general's express instructions. 'I should return home,' she said, as we had made our way out into the square. The rain had subsided now but the ground was squelchy underfoot. 'For my daughter's sake. I should be with her now.'

I did my best to disguise my alarm. 'I do understand,' I mumbled, imagining Tejada's fury when I passed on the news. 'But how on earth will you get there? You don't have time to get to the train station.'

Mrs Talbot's nostrils flared in gentle amusement. 'Señor Gonzales has kindly agreed to provide some transport.'

'Gonzales?' I blinked at the man, who was standing several paces behind her. '*He's* going to drive you?' Good lord. Did that mean I would have to walk back to the hacienda?

The engineer shook his head. 'I have a cousin who lives in the village. He has a motor-bicycle also. He is happy to take her.' Gonzales grinned. The arrangements must have all been made while I was on the telephone. 'He likes to ride.'

'What, all the way to Guatemala City?'

'If he can. He often drives there. He knows the way.'

'And I will of course reimburse him fully for his trouble.'

'He will stay with my sister overnight,' the engineer said.

I was more concerned with the people back at the farm. 'But what will I tell the general? He'll hit the roof.'

Mrs Talbot pursed her lips. There was still the echo of a bruise on her face where the policeman had struck her that morning. 'That cannot be helped. I realise it does place you in an awkward position, Mr Buxton. I do apologise for that. I have no wish to inconvenience you. However, after all that has happened, I am sure you will understand why I have no desire to return to the hacienda.'

'Of course,' I agreed, sympathetically. The farm would now be forever associated in her mind with her husband's death. 'Oh, wait a minute, though. If you're going by road, you'll need to have your passport with you.' No-one could travel anywhere in Guatemala without a certain amount of official scrutiny. There would be several check points along the way between here and the capital.

Mrs Talbot was ahead of me. She patted her handbag. 'I always carry my passport with me. George is of the opinion...' She stopped and her face fell momentarily. 'Well, never mind that. Have no fear, Mr Buxton, I will be well looked after. However, I will not be leaving the village until late afternoon, so if General Tejada wishes to talk to me further he can do so on his way back to town. Now his men are here it shouldn't take him long to finish up at the hacienda.'

I was not so sure about that. 'It might be a couple of hours before the police get down here.'

'I am prepared to wait. I would like to speak to the general before I leave. I want to make sure his men take proper care of my husband's remains.'

'Of course.'

'And I am sure Alberto will look after me in the meantime.'

It was a little after four o'clock when Gonzales and I finally arrived back at the hacienda. We had overshot our allotted hour by some considerable margin. The unexpected delay did at least mean that events had moved on somewhat when we arrived. A cart had been prepared and Doctor Rubio was overseeing the movement of the bodies. General Tejada was standing back by the fountain, his arms gripped firmly behind his back, as Gonzales manoeuvred his motor-bicycle around the far side of the cart and onto the grass. Almost at once, the general noticed Mrs Talbot's absence. 'Where is the woman?' he demanded, striding forward and raising his swagger stick to point at the empty sidecar.

I explained as best I could. Gonzales was cowering behind the far wheel, fearful lest the general should take it upon himself to strike us.

To my surprise, Tejada dismissed the matter out of hand. 'I will deal with her later. You will return to the house. Señor Gonzales, you will give me the keys to your motor-bicycle.' The engineer handed them across without a word. The general unbuttoned the breast pocket of his shirt uniform and dropped the keys inside. 'No one else leaves until I say so.'

The body of Steven Catesby was now being slowly hauled onto the back of the cart, with Doctor Rubio supervising the procedure like an anxious mother hen. A groom was feeding the horses at the other end of the vehicle, in anticipation of the journey ahead, but it was likely to be some time before the police departed. There was a second body to come, not to mention the forensic evidence; bed-sheets etc.

Tejada turned his attention back to the cart, making sure that everything was strapped down to his satisfaction. Gonzales and I took our chance and slipped quietly away. We had parked the bicycle on the far side of the lawn and, as we slogged up the garden, I peered right, around the far edge of the hacienda, to where the overseer, Mr Langbroek, was smoking a cigarette, standing guard outside one of the store houses. It was a rough hewn building with a corrugated iron roof, but the door was padlocked and there was little chance of Joseph Green breaking out of his make-shift prison. Not that there would be much point, even if he could. I could just picture the fellow sat in a dark corner, his knees up against his chest, waiting for the inevitable.

Gonzales had moved on ahead, nodding a shy greeting to our hosts as he moved up the steps, before carrying on through the archway into the courtyard. His wife would be waiting for him in the lounge or the dining room. Other guests were sitting on the upper terrace. Arthur Montana and his Italian wife were taking tea up there; or coffee, more likely. Anita Montana gave me a friendly wave.

I smiled tightly and stopped on the verandah to exchange a few words with Mr and Mrs Weiman.

The Englishwoman greeted me warmly. 'Did you have a successful journey?' she asked. Mrs Weiman seemed to have recovered her composure somewhat during the course of the afternoon.

'Yes, I managed to get a call through to the legation. Told them I wouldn't be back until tomorrow. Oh, Mrs Talbot sends her apologies. She managed to get in touch with her daughter. She's decided to stay down in the village and arrange some transport. She won't be coming back here this evening.'

Mr Weiman was rather concerned to hear that. 'Does the general know?'

'He knows. He's not at all happy about it.'

'Jane has always been very headstrong,' Mrs Weiman

observed.

'It's probably for the best,' her husband concluded. 'She needs to be with her daughter at a time like this.'

'I dare say Jane is holding herself together better than I am.'

'She's certainly doing her best to keep up appearances,' I agreed. 'Stiff upper lip and all that. Oh, she did ask: would you be able to collect up her things and send them on? She says there's no hurry. It doesn't have to be this evening or anything.'

'Yes, of course. I'll see to it first thing tomorrow.'

'My man can do it for you, if you like,' I suggested. 'We could carry some of it back with us when we leave in the morning.'

'That would be very kind of you, Mr Buxton.'

'Henry, please.' We had been through enough now to dispense with the formalities.

'That would be very kind of you, Henry.'

The police were returning to the house with their now empty stretcher. I stepped aside to grant the two men access to the courtyard. Tejada was following behind and he wagged a finger at Gunther Weiman, drawing the German away from us and into the house.

'This is all very difficult for you and your husband,' I said eventually, after the men had departed.

'For the staff too,' Mrs Weiman agreed. 'Greta wasn't expecting to cook for so many people today. And Isabel has her hands full preparing the beds. We weren't anticipating having house guests for a third night.'

'Yes, it's kind of you to put us all up again,' I said. 'Not that any of us have much choice. The minister's not going to be at all happy with Freddie, missing work tomorrow morning. I think Mr Gonzales is going to head off today, though, as soon as he gets the nod. He doesn't have as far to go as the rest of us.'

'Ricardo has been very kind,' Mrs Weiman said. 'That's twice he's driven down to the village for us, running errands.'

'Yes, he's a very amenable fellow.' I smiled.

The policemen were clumped around the back stairs, shifting the body of George Talbot from the table onto a stretcher. I ducked left through a doorway into the entrance hall on the west side and used the stairs here to make my way up to the first floor. Frederick Reeves' bedroom was on the left at the top of the steps. The door was ajar so I knocked briefly. 'Only me, Freddie!'

'Come in!' The Second Secretary was sitting up on his bed, his tie loose at his neck, his blond hair slightly ruffled from contact with the headboard. He had a book in his hand and a glass of scotch on the bedside table. A man after my own heart. The bedroom was oddly shaped, thinner than my own room but longer, with the bed against the far wall to the south and just the one set of windows leading out onto the west terrace. The shutters were back and the late afternoon sun, peeping through the last of the clouds, was filtering into the room at a sharp angle, illuminating the dust particles in the air, but completely missing the bed. 'When did you get back?' Freddie asked.

'Just now.' I moved into the room, closing the door behind me. 'You're in hiding are you?'

He grinned, closing up his book and putting it down on the bed beside him. 'Thought it was best. Emily's having a siesta too.' He jerked his thumb at the far wall.

'I'm surprised the two of you aren't together.'

He chuckled. 'You really do have a low opinion of me. No, she's resting. We thought we'd just leave the police to get on with it. Emily was getting a bit fed up of that sergeant drooling over her.'

'Yes, he wasn't exactly subtle. The sooner they're gone, the better for everyone,' I said.

'They're going to cart that black fellow off as well. Get him under lock and key somewhere.'

I frowned at the mention of Joseph Green.

Freddie swung his legs over the side of the bed and peered across at me. 'You don't think he did it, do you?'

I rolled my eyes. 'So you *have* been speaking to Miss

Bunting.'

'Any chance I get.' His eyes twinkled. 'She talks very highly of you, you know. I might be jealous, if I didn't know you so well.'

I laughed. 'She's far too energetic for my taste.' I glanced at the ruffled bedsheets. 'Well, I'm glad to see you've been busy in my absence. Honestly, you bring me all the way out here to investigate a crime and then put your feet up and leave me to get on with it all on my own. It's disgraceful.'

He grinned again. 'I'm no fool! But I haven't been totally idle.' He reached for the whisky and took a hefty swig from the glass. He must have brought the drink up with him. Either that, or he had slipped into my bedroom and stolen some of mine. I would have to check the bottle. 'I did have a talk with Gunther. Asked him about that generator.'

I raised an eyebrow. 'And did he finally admit it had been sabotaged?'

'Well, he could hardly deny it now, could he? He admitted he had a bit of an argument about it with Steven. Said he had stormed off in a huff.'

'Catesby? Yes, I remember seeing him. But did Mr Weiman say what the argument was about?'

'Yes. Gunther thought Joseph Green was responsible for the damage, because of the whipping yesterday afternoon. He said Steven should have been more lenient with the bloke. Especially after what happened to his brother. Steven wasn't having that. He blew his top.'

'Who did *he* think was responsible?' I asked.

'Gunther didn't say. My money's on Mr Langbroek, though. I could just see him doing something like that, out of spite.'

'And pinning the blame on Joseph Green,' I agreed. 'Any excuse for another whipping. I really don't know why Mr Weiman employs a brute like that.'

'Yes, it is a bit odd.' Freddie drained the last of the whisky from his glass. 'So, anyway. If that coloured bloke didn't kill Steven, who do you think was responsible?'

I shrugged. 'I really don't know. Where were you at

three am last night?'

Freddie chuckled, placing the tumbler back on the bedside table. 'Far away in the land of nod. Seriously, though, do you have any suspects?'

I bit my lip. I wasn't sure how much I wanted to confide in Freddie, given his propensity to blab everything to his girlfriend. 'One or two,' I admitted. 'I spoke to William back at the office. He was quite helpful, for a change. Pointed out a few things I didn't know. Not least of all the fact that the late Mr Talbot was a regular contact of our own Giles Markham.'

Freddie's jaw dropped. 'Contact? What, you mean...for your other work?'

'That's exactly what I mean. Oh, he wasn't a spy or anything like that. Just a helpful insider. Gave Markham the occasional briefing, by all accounts. What's going on at the intersection between business and politics. You know the sort of thing. Not much different from your line of work, just less official. And no money changing hands. But it seems Mr Talbot *was* rather close to Giles Markham.'

Freddie shifted back onto the bed. 'First I've heard of it. George didn't strike me as the kind of bloke to mix business with pleasure. Not that I knew him that well.'

'But you had met him before? Before this weekend, I mean?'

The blond man nodded. 'Yes, a couple of times, up here. With Giles. I knew he knew him through Gunther. But I didn't know there was anything else going on between them.' He smiled. 'But then I'm just a lowly diplomat. I don't have access to your confidential files.'

'There's nothing in there worth reading, believe me. It does interest me, though, this connection between the two of them. It might be worth doing a bit of digging. Shame Mrs Talbot stayed in the village really.' I hadn't had the chance to question her about her husband's relationship with Giles Markham. I doubted George Talbot would have discussed business matters with his wife anyway, despite her obvious good sense, but there was always the chance she might know something about his anti-corruption crusade. I wondered now if that could have been what had got him killed. The new administration was firmly committed to cutting down on corruption in public life and I remembered Mr Talbot had been quietly impressed by their efforts. But it had also been observed that the new rules did not seem to apply to the police.

'Well, if her room's empty, perhaps you ought to slip in there and have a poke around,' Freddie suggested.

'What, Mrs Talbot's room?' I considered for a moment. 'Actually, that's not a bad idea.'

'You never know, you might get lucky.'

'The police must have been through it all by now though.'

'Probably,' Freddie agreed. 'They may have had a quick rummage around. But they don't seem that bothered about George's death. They're too focused on Steven. Everyone's convinced George was just an accident.'

'Well, everyone except your Miss Bunting.'

He grinned again. 'Yes, everyone but Emily.'

And she should know, I thought, darkly.

The Talbots' bedroom was on the far side of the courtyard. There were three rooms to the east of the house: Mr and Mrs Weiman to the rear, the Talbots in the middle and the Montanas at the front. Freddie had agreed to keep a look out for me, as I skirted the courtyard on the upper landing. Luckily there was no-one about downstairs. Most of the guests had now settled in the dining hall and the policemen were out front, tying the late Mr Talbot onto the wooden cart next to Steven Catesby. I reached the bedroom door without being seen and grabbed the handle. I could slip inside now and then peer out through a crack when I needed to emerge, with Freddie giving me the nod if the coast was clear. In all likelihood, there would be nothing of any interest in the Talbots' bedroom, but there was no harm in having a quick gander.

The last thing I was expecting to find inside was one of the other guests. Mrs Montana was standing in front of an open suitcase, rifling through the Talbots' clothes. The tall Italian woman had her back to me, bending over the open case, examining the contents in some detail. It was only when I stepped forward and the bedroom door clicked shut behind me that she became aware of my presence. She stiffened abruptly. Anita Montana was a striking woman, even from behind, with long auburn hair and an hourglass figure. I was surprised Sergeant Velázquez had not paid her more attention, but she was older than Emily Bunting and perhaps not quite as pretty. She wore a short sleeved linen dress in light blue which clung rather tightly to her waist.

I cleared my throat and she lifted herself upright. 'Mrs Montana. What are you doing in here?' I asked. The windows were open on the far side of the room. The woman had been sitting out on the upper terrace when I had last seen her. She must have slipped round the side of the house. Oddly, she did not turn at the sound of my voice; but she did reply to my question.

'Why, Mr Buxton, you gave me the fright of my life.' Her voice was rich and full-bodied, her accent American rather than Italian. 'I thought I ought to help gather up a few of Mrs Talbot's things.' Her elbows briefly disappeared from sight. She was doing something rather odd with her hands, though from my position by the door I couldn't tell exactly what. 'I heard she wasn't coming back,' Mrs Montana added.

'That's right.' The woman must have overheard my conversation with Mr and Mrs Weiman. The three of us had been standing directly beneath the balcony where she had been sitting and it was no surprise that our voices had travelled. 'But it's hardly your concern,' I added.

Anita Montana made one final adjustment to her dress and then swung around, a wide smile on her face. 'Honey, don't be cross with me. I was just trying to help.' The smile was a crude attempt to mollify me and it didn't work.

'I'm not your "honey",' I snapped. My eyes flicked down to the front of her dress. As I had suspected, she had been attempting to hide something there, but she had not made a good job of it. A small piece of paper was poking out from the centre of her décolletage. 'What have you got there?' I demanded.

She hesitated, glancing down at her chest. 'It's nothing.'

I stepped forward. 'Then you won't mind me taking a look.'

Her eyes flashed with sudden anger. 'I certainly would. This belongs to me,' she declared, clutching her bosom tightly. 'I was just...'

'Stealing it by the look of thing.'

'I have every right to this, Mr Buxton. I swear to you.' She pressed her hands firmly against her bust, the picture of wounded innocence. But I did not believe a word of it.

'Show it to me,' I insisted, putting out my hand.

Mrs Montana took a step backwards, circling the edge of the bed. 'Honey, I have no intention of showing you anything.'

I strode forward and shot out a hand, grabbing hold of her wrist, to stop her making a dash for the window. Her eyes flared again and she slapped me abruptly across the face with her free hand. I flinched and stared at her in surprise; then I tightened my grip on her wrist. I wasn't willing to play games. She slapped me again, harder this time, all trace of civility gone. That was it, I thought, and in anger I yanked the woman towards me and thrust a hand down the front of her dress. Mrs Montana yelped in surprise, not without good reason. 'Get your paws off me!' she exclaimed. But the blasted woman had just thumped me and I was damned if I was going to give her any special consideration. I tugged out the bit of paper, released her wrist and immediately retreated to the far side of the room. Mrs Montana was too shocked to follow.

I took a moment to recover my composure, then looked down at the document in my hand. It was light brown in colour and had been folded up rather neatly. I unfolded it and scanned the contents. It was a banker's draft, made out by the Anglo-South American bank, for the sum of nine thousand American dollars.

I whistled in surprise, looking up at Anita Montana. She was glaring back at me with undisguised hostility. Nine thousand dollars. That was just under two thousand pounds, in real money. My brain took a moment to digest the information. Giles Markham had embezzled about nineteen hundred pounds from the visa receipts in our office. Lord. This had to be the document that was stolen from the bureau in my flat.

'That cheque belongs to my husband,' Mrs Montana declared. 'It was money due to him. I was merely taking possession of it.'

I shook my head. 'This money belongs to the British government,' I asserted, with dubious authority. 'It was stolen from our office.' If I was right, then Giles Markham hadn't gambled the money away, as had been assumed at the time of his death. Rather, he had laundered it with the Anglo-South American bank, depositing bits and pieces in a private account over many months. George Talbot must have colluded in it with him, for all the man's supposed incorruptibility, and provided him with this draft – sometime back in March, according to the hand-written date – so that Markham could pass the cash on to somebody else. And now Arthur Montana had sent his wife to retrieve it, knowing full well that no-one else would even suspect its existence. Which meant Mr Montana was probably involved in Steven Catesby's murder. I shuddered, clutching the draft tightly in my hand.

'Honey, I don't know anything about that. Just be a sweetheart,' she said, moving around the bed towards me, 'and give me the damned cheque.' The woman had quite an intimidating presence, when she put her mind to it.

I steeled myself to resist. 'The devil I will...'

Before I had even finished the sentence, she launched herself at me, a sudden whirlwind of fury. I felt a knee to the groin and staggered backwards. Had I been a man, that kick would probably have felled me. As it was, the unexpected onslaught caused me to let go of the banker's draft and the damned woman grasped hold of it before it could fall away to the floor. She turned for the window but I grabbed her by the shoulder. She stomped on my foot but I managed to keep my grip as she moved towards the shutters. She twisted around again, slapping me across the face one last time. I fell backwards, releasing my grip, and she moved triumphantly to the window, the draft in her hand. At that moment, she tripped on the frame of the door and stumbled out onto the balcony, completely losing her footing. I watched in horror as she hit the far balustrade and, in less than a second, flipped over the top. Her body plummeted from view and I heard a sickening crunch from below.

I recovered myself, wiping a dribble of blood from my nose, and rushed forward. The banker's draft had settled itself on the balcony. I was more concerned with the view from the railings. I felt a rush of relief when the ground came into focus. The overseer, Mr Langbroek, had broken Mrs Montana's fall. He had been standing guard in that narrow grass pathway between the house and the storage huts. She had knocked him to the ground and was now sprawled out on top of him. Neither were moving. Then I saw the blood oozing from the back of Anita Montana's head. Her skull must have been whipped back when she had collided with the overseer. It had struck against one of the balcony's wooden support struts. That was the cracking sound I had heard. Gazing down at the bloodied figure, I had no idea if she was alive or dead. For a moment I froze, not knowing what to do.

A small head poked out between two of the huts on the far side of the path. It was the house boy Moses. He took in the two bodies on the ground and then looked up at me. Slowly, his face spread into a smile.

Chapter Thirteen

Moses did not waste any time. He darted across the grass towards the crumpled figures. At first, I assumed he was on an errand of mercy, trying to determine what help, if any, was required; but once he had crouched down in front of the overseer, I saw him slide a hand underneath the sprawled body and whip something out of the man's top pocket. Langbroek groaned but did not move. Moses pulled back and brandished a set of keys triumphantly for me to see. He smiled a second time. I shuddered, looking down at him, realising at once what the boy was about: he was going to release Joseph Green. I mouthed a silent 'no' but he was already scurrying across to the hut where the labourer was imprisoned. He found the correct key, unlocked the padlock and threw open the door. Seconds later, a dazed Joseph Green emerged into the daylight. The man blinked, lifting a hand to cover his eyes, then caught sight of the two bodies on the ground. His mouth formed a small 'oh', but Moses did not allow him any time to digest the scene. The boy was already tugging at his shirt sleeve, urging him away. Freedom awaited, or so the youngster seemed to think. It was madness. Green would not be able to escape. There was nowhere for him to run, not in a place like this. He would be hunted down like a dog. Far better for him to stay where he was. But there was no time for a reasoned debate. Moses was already dragging him away, into that gap between the huts, and I was powerless to intervene.

I don't know how long I stood there immobile on the balcony after the two figures had departed. In all probability, it was only a few seconds, but it felt like a lifetime. I stared down at the bodies spread-eagled across the path below me. They were the more pressing concern right now. The overseer might still be alive, judging by the groan I had heard a short while ago, but the jury was out on Mrs Montana. If the Italian woman was dead, then I was in real trouble. No-one would believe the fall had been an accident; and the general would take great pleasure in clapping me in irons. Tejada had no love of foreigners, even affluent foreigners from powerful countries. For all my status and connections to the British government, the authorities would afford me no special consideration. I had no illusions, either, that my boss, David Richards, would intercede on my behalf. The minister had made his position quite clear: if anything embarrassing like this were to happen, he would wash his hands of me and throw me to the wolves.

There was another grunt from Mr Langbroek. He at least was alive. The full weight of the Italian woman was pressing down on him, in that tight blue dress of hers, and all at once her arm shifted to one side, presumably in response to some movement from the dazed figure beneath her. Perhaps she was beginning to wake up, I thought hopefully. But the activity ceased almost at once. If Mrs Montana was alive, she was in a desperate state. That thought brought me back to my senses. The woman needed help, and quickly.

Doctor Rubio! I had to find the doctor and get him to her. If there was any chance of saving her, he would be the one to do it.

I turned back to the shutters, then stopped and knelt down to pick up the paper Mrs Montana had dropped as she had fallen. The banker's draft had caught on the railings and fluttered down onto the balcony. I glanced at it briefly. Was this really what everything was about? Had Steven Catesby been murdered for the sake of nine thousand dollars? And was that the reason Giles Markham had taken his own life? I stuffed the draft inside my jacket and moved quickly through the bedroom, out onto the landing on the far side.

Freddie Reeves was waiting patiently for me on the opposite landing. He did a double take as I emerged. He had been expecting me to sneak out the door, not rush out in a fluster, in full view of the courtyard below. He signalled across to me frantically, letting me know there were people about; but I ignored him. 'Doctor Rubio!' I called out, loud enough for everyone to hear.

The slim, grey haired doctor was making his way across the courtyard from the front of the hacienda. He looked up as I called to him, frowning at the urgency of my tone. 'May I help

185

you, Señor Buxton?' His voice was calm and unruffled.

'There's been a terrible accident,' I shouted down to him.

'What accident?' This time, it wasn't the doctor speaking. I glanced left and caught sight of Arthur Montana framed in the far door. He had been sitting out on the front terrace, reading a book, which he was carrying now in his hand. His wife's book, I think. 'What's going on?' he demanded.

There was no way to sugar coat it. 'Your wife. I'm terribly sorry. There's been an accident.'

Montana flinched. 'What do you mean, an accident?'

'Mrs Montana. She...tripped and fell.' I gestured back into the bedroom. 'From the balcony.'

The American dropped his hands and the book fell to the floor. 'She...she fell?' It was the first time I had heard any uncertainty in his voice.

'I'm afraid so. It all happened so quickly.'

'Is...is she...?'

'I don't know,' I admitted. 'Mr Langbroek broke her fall. He was standing guard by the side of the house. But I don't know if she...'

Montana was already striding along the landing towards me. I moved aside as he barrelled into the bedroom.

'I wouldn't...' I called out after him, but it was too late. Nothing I could say would prevent him from taking in the scene first hand. I turned and placed a hand on the balustrade. Doctor Rubio was still peering up at me from the courtyard. 'Just outside the living room,' I shouted down to him.

The doctor nodded. His medical bag was resting on a table in the centre of the square. He grabbed it and hurried across to the living room. I was already moving towards the back stairs, skirting the far side of the landing.

Freddie met me halfway. 'What on earth is going on?' he asked.

A cry sounded from the east side of the hacienda. Arthur Montana had caught sight of his wife.

'Mrs Montana was searching the Talbots' bedroom,' I explained, breathlessly. 'I caught her rifling through his clothes.

186

There was a bit of a struggle. I think...I think I may have killed her.'

Freddie's eyes boggled. 'Bloody hell!'

'Find my man Maurice will you? Get him to pack up my things. I have a feeling events might start to get a little nasty in the next few minutes. We may need to make a hasty exit.'

'But...'

'Don't argue, Freddie! Just do it. I don't have time to explain!'

The Englishman nodded numbly. I leapt down the stairs, then moved through the arches and across the courtyard into the living room. Doctor Rubio had already hopped over the hand rail at the far end – he was rather sprightly for his age – and was bending down to examine the two bodies spread out across the grass. It took me some moments to follow his example, pulling my legs over the top of the railing and dropping down two or three feet onto the pathway.

'Will you give me a hand, please?' Rubio said. 'Hold her head.'

I did as I was told, despite the blood, while the doctor dragged the overseer carefully out from underneath Anita Montana's prone body. She was looking in a bad way, I thought, her auburn hair sticky and red. Rubio briefly examined the unconscious man and then dismissed him from his mind. 'He will be all right.'

I didn't care about Mr Langbroek. 'What about Mrs Montana?'

The doctor crouched down next to me and his hands skipped across her head and her throat. 'There's a faint pulse. She's still alive.'

'Thank God!' I moved back slightly, allowing Rubio to lower her head gently onto the grass.

Arthur Montana had now arrived on the lower terrace, his face puffed with exertion. He must have bolted down the stairs like a demon, after catching sight of his wife from the balcony.

'She's still alive,' I reassured him, rising to my feet.

The American looked across at me, not quite comprehending; and then the explosion came. 'What the hell happened?' he demanded.

I couldn't think what to say. 'Your wife was in Mrs Talbot's bedroom.'

'Don't be ridiculous!' he snapped, grasping the handrail between us. 'She was having a lie down in our room.'

'I'm only saying what I saw. She was searching through a suitcase. She caught sight of me, panicked and ran for the windows. And then she...she tripped.'

Montana eyed me suspiciously. I wasn't quite sure what state my face was in, after his wife had slapped me a couple of times. My cheeks might still be a little red. It was fortunate for me that he was on the other side of that railing.

Doctor Rubio had no interest in our dispute. 'We need to get her to a hospital as soon as possible,' he stated, authoritatively.

Montana forgot about me and peered down at his wife in despair. For a moment, I confess, I pitied him; but the moment passed as he pointed an accusing finger at me. 'If she dies, Mr Buxton, I will hold you responsible. A hospital?'

'If at all possible,' the doctor said, looking up.

Montana gathered himself together. 'Right.' He wheeled round and hurried across the terrace towards the front of the house. I have never seen a man move so quickly. 'General Tejada! Please come here!' he called out. 'My wife's been injured.'

By now, half the household had appeared at the living room window and were moving out onto the terrace to take in the sorry scene. It was something of a surprise that the general hadn't already joined them; but he was out front, making final preparations for the departure of his men. It did not take him long to respond to the American's cry, however, and barely a minute passed before Montana popped up at the far end of the pathway, with General Tejada steaming behind him.

The policeman strode purposefully towards us across the grass, his thick eyebrows narrowed in anger at the unexpected interruption to his plans. 'What is this?' he demanded, taking in the two bodies. 'What is going on here?'

'An accident,' I said. 'Mrs Montana fell from the balcony.'

He looked up at the terrace. 'From there?' I could see what he was thinking. There was no damage to the balustrade. How on earth had she managed to fall? 'What happened?'

'She was in Mrs Talbot's bedroom. I opened the door, she ran out onto the balcony and tripped.'

Tejada frowned again. 'You saw it happen?'

'Yes.' I brought a hand to my nose and wiped it without thinking.

'What was she doing in the bedroom?'

'General, we don't have time for this!' Arthur Montana growled. 'My wife is desperately ill. We need to get her to a hospital.'

Tejada looked to the medical man. 'Doctor Rubio?'

'She has suffered a severe head injury,' he said. 'She's needs proper medical treatment and quickly.'

The general growled. This was not the sort of problem he wanted to deal with. 'It's a rough journey to the village and a couple of hours to the nearest town. Is she fit to travel?'

'No.' Rubio was unequivocal. 'But if she stays here, she will certainly die.'

The overseer was by now beginning to come round. He groaned and began to pull himself up onto his elbows. The doctor rose to his feet and hopped across to him. 'Don't try to move, señor. You have had a nasty bump.' He helped Mr Langbroek to sit up against the foot of the terrace.

'What happened to him?' Tejada asked.

'He broke Mrs Talbot's fall,' I replied grimly.

'Idiot.' The general turned his attention back to me. 'You seem to have a habit of being in the wrong place at the wrong time, señor.' He grunted. 'You discovered Señor Catesby's body. You were there when Señor Talbot fell down the stairs. And now this...'

'It was an accident,' I protested. 'It wasn't my fault.'

'That is for me to decide. What were you doing in the Talbots' bedroom?'

189

'Mrs Talbot...Jane...she asked me to collect up her things.'

'When you left her behind in the village.'

'Er...yes. I came through the door and found Mrs Montana rifling through her clothes.'

'That's absurd!' Montana growled again. 'My wife was having a lie down in our bedroom.'

'Are you calling me a liar, Mr Montana?'

'I sure am,' the American declared forcefully. 'You were the one looking through Mrs Talbot's things. My wife must have heard the noise. She came out onto the balcony to take a look, then took fright when you stepped out of the bedroom.'

'That's not how it happened.'

Montana's face was reddening now, his eyes blazing with anger. 'It was your fault she fell. I ought to break your god-damned neck, you son of a bitch!'

'Enough!' General Tejada bellowed. A row of people were now gawping at us from behind Mr Montana. 'This is not a freak show.' The general glared at the unwelcome onlookers. 'Back inside, all of you!' The group retreated through the windows into the living room. 'Not you,' he barked at Mr Montana. 'Or you, Señor Buxton.'

Doctor Rubio had now settled Mr Langbroek and moved back to examine the unconscious Anita Montana.

'Why would the señora be searching the Talbots' bedroom?' Tejada asked.

'I'm telling you...' Montana protested.

The general raised his stick. 'One more word from you, señor, and you'll be locked up with the negro.'

I gulped quietly at the mention of Joseph Green. The door of the hut where he had been confined had swung shut after the labourer had departed but the padlock was hanging loose for all to see. Thankfully, nobody had noticed that as yet.

Tejada's gaze was fixed on me. 'Well, Señor Buxton?'

I pulled out the banker's draft from my jacket. 'She was looking for this,' I said. Reluctantly, I handed the piece of paper across.

His eyes narrowed again, scanning the document. 'Nine

190

thousand American dollars. And that's Señor Talbot's bank?'

'Yes. The Anglo South American.'

'That money belongs to me!' Arthur Montana exploded. 'It was money owed to me.'

'I see.' The general gave a nod of satisfaction. 'So your wife went to the Talbots' bedroom to search for this draft?'

'I...' The American hesitated, realising his mistake.

'You will not lie to me, señor. You will never lie to me.'

'She...she may have taken it into her head...'

'So, you were in dispute with Señor Talbot, before he died,' Tejada concluded.

Montana was becoming flustered. 'Well, look, not exactly.'

'Very convenient. Where was this found?' He waved the draft at me.

'In Mrs Talbot's suitcase,' I said. 'Probably in one of the pockets of her husband's clothes.'

The general scowled. 'Velázquez! I thought you searched that room thoroughly.'

The sergeant cowered at his master's voice. 'I do, general. *Muy* thoroughly.'

Tejada's cane whipped out and struck the man across the face. The sergeant let out a yelp and clutched his cheek. 'Not thoroughly enough. I am surrounded by idiots.' The general folded up the draft and placed it in his top pocket, next to the keys he had confiscated from Mr Gonzales. I opened my mouth to protest but then thought better of it. He pointed his swagger stick at me. 'This draft was found in the señora's suitcase?'

'That's right.'

'And you allowed the woman to remain in the village?'

I swallowed awkwardly, grasping the implication. Perhaps Mrs Talbot had murdered her husband and then scarpered. But that was not possible. I had spoken to Jane Talbot a few moments before Mr Talbot had fallen down the stairs. 'I don't think she can be involved in any of this. If Mrs Talbot had known about the money, why would she leave it behind?'

'Perhaps Señor Montana knows the answer to that,' Tejada suggested, glaring at the American.

'Look, general, I beg you,' Montana implored. 'Whatever questions you have, I'll answer them. But my wife. I need to get her to a hospital.'

Tejada considered for a moment. 'Very well. Velázquez! Get the stretcher from the cart. Rubio, you'll have to go with her. Make sure she's comfortable.'

The doctor shook his head sadly. His hand was holding her wrist. 'I'm very sorry, general. Señor Montana. It is already too late.'

Arthur Montana let out a howl and rushed across to his wife. The hefty American crouched down beside her, cradling her lifeless head in despair. 'My sweet darling,' he cooed, tears beginning to run down his face. I looked away in embarrassment. 'This is your fault,' he breathed, glancing up at me for a moment. 'You did this.' But his grief overwhelmed his anger and he howled once again, pressing his face against the forehead of his poor dead wife. I closed my eyes. He was right. I had killed Anita Montana; or at least, I had been responsible for her death. I should never have attempted to take that draft by force.

Mr Langbroek was beginning to recover his senses. 'What...what the bloody hell happened?' he muttered, finding himself propped up against the foot of the terrace.

'Don't try to move,' Doctor Rubio advised him, shifting across. 'You've suffered a heavy blow to the head. You may have concussion.'

'It's not my head,' the overseer muttered. He let out an expletive as a shaft of pain shot through him. 'It's my leg. My god-damned leg!' He clutched the errant limb with both his hands and his podgy face screwed up in pain.

Rubio gave the leg a quick examination. 'It looks like it might be broken. We will need to set it properly. We can't do it out here. We will have to get you into the house. Señor.' He gestured to me. 'If you could give me a hand?'

I did not feel particularly inclined to offer assistance.

'Help him!' Tejada snapped.

I moved across as instructed and reluctantly provided Mr Langbroek with an arm, enabling the beleaguered overseer to rise up without placing any undue pressure on his injured leg.

'We will move him into the living room,' the doctor suggested.

The general regarded Langbroek scornfully. 'You are an idiot, señor. I leave you to do one thing...' He held out a hand. 'Give me the key to the storage hut. Then get out of my sight.'

The overseer was too disorientated to respond.

'Top pocket!' Tejada barked, this time at me.

I slid my hand into Langbroek's breast pocket but I already knew that I would not find anything inside it. 'There's nothing here,' I mumbled, bowing to the inevitable. I had been hoping to get away before the general discovered that Joseph Green had escaped, but it was too late for that now.

The policeman glowered at the three of us. 'Where is the key, chico?'

'I...I...' The overseer did not know.

Sergeant Velázquez had finally noticed something amiss with the hut on the opposite side of the path. 'General! *Mira!*' The padlock was hanging open. 'The building, it is not locked!'

'What!?!' General Tejada exploded. He rushed across to the door of the small outhouse and flung it open. That's torn it, I thought. He could see at a glance that Joseph Green was gone. 'You locked this up?' he snapped at the sergeant, raising his cane again.

'It is locked, general.' Velázquez cowered. 'I swear.'

The policeman glared at the overseer. 'No-one went near this room?'

'Not...no...'

'Someone must have grabbed the key...' I suggested, a little too hastily.

Tejada scowled. 'You were upstairs? When the señora fell?'

'Yes. I...I rushed straight down. I couldn't have been

more than two minutes. And Doctor Rubio arrived here ahead of me.'

The doctor confirmed that with a nod.

'You saw nothing?' the general asked him.

'No, señor.'

Tejada growled again. 'Someone must have been waiting for an opportunity. But whoever it was, they can't have got far.' He reached down and pulled out a whistle. The other two policemen heard it and rushed across from the front lawn. 'The prisoner's escaped,' he said, 'but he can't have been gone more than five minutes. Someone must have helped him. We need to search the grounds while it's still light. Has Weiman got any dogs?'

That question was aimed at me. 'I...I've no idea. I don't think so.'

'Pity.' He pulled out the pistol from his holster and turned his attention back to his men. 'He'll most likely have headed into the fields. There's a path up from the back garden.' He waved one of his underlings in that direction. 'Velázquez, you take the stables. I'll take the other path. You.' He gestured to the last of the policemen. 'Search the negro cottages. He might try to hide out there.'

'And if we find him?' the sergeant asked.

'He's had his chance,' the general said. 'Don't bother taking him alive. Shoot on sight. That goes for his accomplice, if you find him. Whoever he may be.'

Doctor Rubio and I exchanged worried glances.

'Don't move anywhere!' Tejada snapped at me. 'I have a few more questions for you. That goes for you too, Señor Montana.' The American looked up from his bloodied wife, his face stained with tears. 'A curfew is now in place,' the general declared. 'Anyone seen moving about outside the main house will be shot. No exceptions. Get to it!' he commanded his men.

And the police raced off in search of Joseph Green.

I was struggling to contain my anger. 'I don't know who the devil that man thinks he is,' I growled. I had poured myself a

194

large brandy from the decanter in the far corner of the dining room and sat myself on one of the chairs surrounding the central table. 'He's practically declared Marshal Law. He's acting like he owns the bloody place. Oh, forgive my language, Mrs Weiman.'

Susan Weiman was sitting opposite me, next to her husband. 'Susan, please. That's quite all right. It's been a very stressful day for all of us.'

'That's no excuse.' I shifted uncomfortably in my chair. 'Susan. You invited us here to your house and now all hell breaks lose. And it's that man's fault, more than anyone. General Tejada.'

'He's out of his depth,' Freddie suggested, taking a sip of brandy. 'That's why he's lashing out.' The Englishman was seated to my right. He had helped himself to a drink from the decanter too, with the Weimans' permission. Greta had brought in a pot of coffee for the owners, but the rest of us needed something a little more alcoholic. 'He only came here to rubber stamp an accident and now he's knee deep in corpses. Oh, sorry, Susan.'

Once again, Mrs Weiman declined to be offended. 'There's no point sugar coating the truth, Freddie. But Joseph...' Her brow furrowed. 'How did Joseph come to escape?'

'He was let out,' I said. 'Someone must have been hiding out there, by the sheds, waiting for their chance.'

'One of the labourers?' Freddie suggested.

'Very probably.' At this juncture, I did not feel inclined to tell anyone about Moses. I had no desire to get the boy into any more trouble than he was in already. 'They must have grabbed the keys from the overseer when he was out cold. But Green should have stayed where he was. He's signed his own death warrant, running away like that.' I took a slurp of brandy. 'They'll track him down like a wild animal and shoot him dead. No trial. And no real evidence against him.'

Gunther Weiman frowned. 'You believe he is innocent?'

'I do. In fact, I'm sure of it. He was nowhere near the hacienda last night. He was in that little cottage of his at the other end of the estate.'

'But the general said...'

'Oh, he got up for two minutes to answer a call of nature. That's what one of the labourers told Tejada. But I spoke to the man myself. Nathan. Sensible fellow, if I'm any judge. He said Green was only away for a couple of minutes. But the general will kill him all the same.'

That prospect troubled Mr Weiman greatly. 'But if he *didn't* kill Steven...'

'Then somebody else did,' I concluded. 'And most likely someone in this house.' I took a last swig of brandy and placed the tumbler back down on the table. There was a brief silence as the room digested my uncomfortable assertion.

Miss Bunting leaned forward. 'What was Mrs Montana searching for in the Talbots' bedroom?' she asked. She had taken a quick sip of coffee – without milk, this time – and used the brief pause to reflect upon the events of the last half an hour.

We were a sorry sight, the five of us, seeking refuge in the dining hall while the world was falling apart around us. Miss Bunting was sitting on the far side of Freddie, with the Weimans opposite us, pouring themselves another cup of coffee from the metal pot. I had helped Doctor Rubio settle Mr Langbroek in the living room and then left him to it, closing the intervening door to give the fellow a bit of privacy. The engineer, Gonzales, had gone out to help carry the body of Mrs Montana onto the porch, to lay her out respectfully. Arthur Montana was sitting with her now, mumbling to his dead wife and saying prayers for her soul. It was a pitiful sight. I would not have imagined the American man would have collapsed so readily, but collapse he had.

'She was looking for a banker's draft,' I replied, answering Miss Bunting's question. 'She found it too, in their suitcase. Nine thousand dollars.'

Freddie whistled appreciatively. 'That's a lot of money.'

'When I caught her at it, she ran for the window and tripped.'

'The poor woman,' Mrs Weiman breathed. 'Falling from the balcony like that. I can't believe she's dead. Do you

196

really think she was up to no good?'

'I can't say for certain. But the draft was drawn on the Anglo South American bank.' The bank that George Talbot had worked for.

That provoked a sudden thought from Miss Bunting. 'Crumbs! You don't think that might have been what was stolen from your flat last week? From the bureau?'

'That's exactly what I think. We had a robbery last week,' I explained, for the Weimans' benefit. 'From Giles Markham's apartment. The one he used before he....well, anyway, I'm convinced that that draft is the money he stole from our office. He must have deposited it in Talbot's bank little by little and then drawn it out shortly before he died.'

'And hid it away in the bureau for safe keeping,' Miss Bunting concluded.

'That's about the size of it. And someone else must have known it was there and broke in last week to collect it.'

'Goodness!' Mrs Weiman exclaimed. 'You surely don't think...Steven?'

I shrugged. 'It's possible. I do think the robbery had something to do with his death. He had financial problems, didn't he?'

'Not exactly,' Gunther Weiman replied. 'Steven did like to gamble, but it was never large amounts. He was certainly not in debt. Actually, he was saving up to purchase a small parcel of land, to start a farm of his own.' That must have been the bit of business they had been discussing the previous day. 'Not a coffee plantation,' the German added, taking a quick sip of his own brew. 'He wanted to grow *chicle*. Chewing gum. It is quite a big seller in the United States.'

I screwed up my face. 'Disgusting habit. But...he didn't have the funds to buy the land?'

'He thought he had. He was going to go into partnership with Giles.'

'Good lord.' That I hadn't known. I stood up and moved back to the side table to refill my tumbler. 'So Giles Markham was going to become a farmer?' I frowned. A British intelligence operative, throwing everything up to grow chewing gum? 'That's ridiculous.'

'The two of them were good friends,' Weiman explained. 'They had found a suitable plot of land to develop. Arthur – Mr Montana – had agreed to sell it to them. It was land that belonged to the company he works for.'

I grabbed the decanter and poured out a measure of brandy while Weiman continued his explanation.

'United Fruit has a lot of land it cannot use. Land not suitable for growing bananas, or even coffee. Normally, it likes to hold onto it as a bargaining chip, but sometimes small parcels are made available to favoured buyers. Steven and Giles put down a deposit together.'

'We were happy for him,' Mrs Weiman gushed, as I returned to the dining table. 'Steven was so sad after the death of his wife. And now he was finally getting his life back together.'

'He was confident they could pay off the balance,' Gunther Weiman continued. 'The payment was due at the end of April, I believe.'

Which presumably was why the cheque had been drawn up in March.

'But that doesn't make any sense,' I said. 'Markham couldn't have used government money to buy a plot of land. He'd never have got away with it. The books would have been checked and the money missed, especially if he resigned to go and work on the farm.'

'I cannot explain it,' Weiman admitted. 'We had no idea the money was stolen. Giles was a man of means, or so we believed, and the land was a legitimate purchase. George would not have allowed himself to become involved if he had thought there was anything untoward going on. He was acting as an intermediary, overseeing the contracts. He is...was a trained lawyer, as well as a banker. But then, when Giles committed suicide, the whole thing fell apart.'

'Steven didn't give up, though,' Susan Weiman said. 'He was convinced he could find the money and he asked Arthur to hold the deal open for another three months. Until...'

'Excuse me, madam.' The attention of the table shifted

to the far door, where the housekeeper, Greta, had slipped back into the dining room. She was an impressive barrel of a woman in her late fifties, with dark grey hair scraped back against her head.

'Yes? What is it Greta?'

'I am sorry to disturb you, madam.' The woman's expression was grave. 'But Moses has disappeared.'

The colour drained from Mrs Weiman's face. 'Disappeared?'

'I left him in the cottage, peeling potatoes.' The servants' cottage, adjacent to the main house. 'I just went to look and he is not there. He has not even started on the potatoes. He is nowhere to be found.'

'Oh God!' Susan Weiman lifted her hands to her face in horror. 'He's not running around outside? Not when there's a curfew in force!'

'Damn!' I exclaimed loudly. 'I thought...' My voice trailed away and I grimaced, as everyone turned to stare at me. 'I suppose you might as well know. It was Moses who let Joseph Green go.'

That elicited a horrified gasp from the Weimans.

'You saw him?' Gunther Weiman asked, his eyes flashing in alarm.

'I was upstairs. I couldn't do anything to stop him. But I thought once he'd unlocked the door and seen the man off he'd just come straight back here.' I hadn't for a minute supposed he would put himself in any danger.

'They must have run away together,' Mrs Weiman breathed. 'My poor boy. He'll be killed out there.' She let out a strangled sob. 'My poor little darling.' Her eyes were already wet with tears.

Miss Bunting regarded the woman in surprise. 'Your...*darling*?'

Weiman placed a restraining hand on his wife's arm. 'Liebling, don't...' he warned. But it was already too late. Freddie, Miss Bunting and I were all staring at the older woman. Hers was not the reaction of a concerned employer.

Susan Weiman raised a hand to wipe the tears from her

eyes. She glanced at her husband and took a nervous gulp of air. 'It's all right, darling. Moses...he's...' Her shoulders slumped as she met our eyes. 'There's no point pretending any more. Moses is my son,' she whispered, her hands trembling on the table top.

'Good grief,' I said.

Chapter Fourteen

Frederick Reeves was dumbfounded. 'Your *son...?*' he exclaimed, probably louder than he had intended. Miss Bunting, to his right, was wide eyed with surprise and I doubt I was looking any less flummoxed. 'That's not possible,' the Second Secretary breathed. 'I mean, he's *coloured*!'

'For heaven's sake, Freddie,' I hissed. For all the shock of the revelation, I had no difficulty grasping the mechanics of the situation. 'Do I have to draw you a diagram?'

Susan Weiman was staring down into her cup, her cheeks red with embarrassment. The admission had not come easily to her but – with her son's life on the line – it had become impossible for her to conceal the truth.

There was an awkward silence.

'So...who was the father?' I asked, eventually, keeping my voice low. 'One of the labourers?'

Mrs Weiman did not answer. She brought a hand to her face again and gently wiped her eyes. Her husband cut in, to save her any further distress. 'It was a long time ago,' he asserted, not wishing to answer the question directly. 'It is not important now.'

Freddie was still struggling to understand the logistics of the situation. 'But you must have...I mean, people must have noticed. That you were...well, with child?' The poor fool was tying himself in knots, trying to address the matter delicately, but in fairness it was not an easy subject to probe.

'We...we pretended that I had miscarried,' Mrs Weiman explained.

'The boy was found abandoned in a nearby village,' Mr Weiman added, 'some time afterwards. He was brought up with the other workers.'

'Does he know?' I asked. 'That you're his mother, I mean?'

Susan Weiman shook her head sadly. 'He has no idea. He doesn't even like me very much. He was spirited away as soon as he was born and then "discovered" a few weeks later.

Isabel's mother took charge of him. Mrs Collinson, God rest her soul. She was more of a mother to him than I've ever been.'

'And Joseph Green was a surrogate father. Or at least, an uncle,' I suggested. That was the way the lad himself had described it. 'Which presumably is why he helped him to escape.'

'Moses has always been impetuous,' Mrs Weiman said. 'It's a family trait. My father was the same. And so was Steven.' She smiled half-heartedly but then her face froze. 'Oh, God. What's going to happen to my poor little boy?'

Gunther Weiman could offer no words of comfort.

'He got a good head start,' I said, trying to look on the bright side. 'And it'll be getting dark soon. There are plenty of places on the estate the two of them could hide out.' The finca had its fair share of store houses, offices and other empty buildings. 'He'll be safe for now. If he's got any sense, he'll find somewhere to hide and then slip away after dark and head back to the house. As for Green...' I gazed down at my glass. 'I'm afraid he's beyond our help. That lunatic of a policeman won't let him get away.'

'Moses won't abandon him,' Mrs Weiman asserted anxiously. 'You don't know what he's like. He can be so stubborn. You should have seen him when Matthew died. He didn't speak for weeks.'

Mr Weiman was becoming as unsettled as his wife. 'Liebling...'

'I'm tired of concealing the truth, Gunther.' She closed her eyes for a moment. 'We should tell them about Matthew.'

Her husband let out a weary sigh. It was bad enough, I supposed, to have to admit that his wife had cuckolded him, all those years ago, but the death of Matthew Green at the hands of his cousin reflected even less well upon the family.

I saved them both from any further embarrassment. 'It's all right. I know all about Matthew Green. About how he died.'

'You know?' Weiman regarded me in surprise.

'I've heard the gossip. From Joseph Green, among others. He told me Mr Catesby threw his brother down the stairs.'

The German shook his head. 'No, that isn't quite what happened. Steven didn't kill Matthew Green.'

I shrugged. 'That's what I was told. You're not trying to suggest it was an accident?' There had been too many "accidents" already in this affair. I for one was getting heartily sick of them.

'No, it was not an accident.' Weiman glanced at his wife and then back at me, her anxiety mirrored in his face. 'Mr Buxton. Henry. Is there nothing we can do for Moses?'

I scratched the side of my lip. 'Nothing, I'm afraid. At least, not right now. But, look, don't be too concerned,' I said. 'Even Tejada wouldn't shoot an unarmed child. Can I get you both a brandy? Help steady the nerves?'

'No, thank you.' The Weimans shook their heads in unison. They were a very close couple, I could see. Even now, the two of them had their arms around each other, despite the awkwardness of the seating. Whatever foolishness had forced Mrs Weiman into the arms of another man – and a black man to boot – the matter had clearly been long forgiven.

'Look, honestly. They'll be fine, if they just sit tight. I could...maybe try to have a word with the general when he comes back to the house. Try to reason with him.' Even I could not make that suggestion sound plausible, but the couple did their best to take some comfort from the idea.

'We have no choice, liebling,' Weiman said. 'We must wait.'

I downed the last of the brandy in my tumbler. Freddie was thinking over what our hosts had just told us. 'But hang on a mo. If Steven didn't kill Matthew Green, then who did?' he asked. 'He did *fall* down the stairs?'

Weiman drew in a breath. 'Yes. I am afraid he did. But it wasn't Steven who pushed him. It was Giles.'

Freddie almost dropped his glass. '*Giles Markham* killed Matthew Green?' He exchanged a bewildered look with Emily Bunting. That was not what Alberto had told us.

'But we heard that Mr Markham...' I hesitated. 'Well, to put it bluntly, if you'll forgive the indelicacy, Mrs...Susan.' There was no easy way of phrasing this. 'We heard your cousin had found him and this Green fellow in bed together.' I cringed at the unfortunate words, even as I spoke them. Sodomy was not an easy subject to broach at the dinner table, but it seemed unlikely that Susan Weiman was in the dark on the matter and both of my colleagues already knew the truth. 'And he was so disgusted by it that he...'

'No, that's not quite how it happened,' Weiman observed, correcting me gently once again. 'It wasn't Steven who discovered Matthew in bed. It was....' He stopped and grimaced. 'Forgive me. This is a difficult matter for us to discuss.'

'I understand.'

'But Giles and Steven were not just close friends. They were...involved.'

Freddie had lost the thread of the conversation. 'Involved? How do you mean, involved?' I threw him a look and his face reddened. 'Oh! You mean...?'

'In an intimate way,' Weiman confirmed, with a shudder. The notion of two men sleeping together clearly unsettled him. It is surprising how few people are prepared to be broad-minded about such things.

'We knew nothing about it at the time,' Susan Weiman assured us, hastily. 'I had no idea my cousin had those...those kinds of feelings. He had been married, after all.'

'Old Giles.' Freddie stared at the table top. He had been shocked, the previous day, when Alberto had suggested Markham had been caught in bed with a labourer, but he had managed to convince himself it had been a one-off event. This new information suggested the behaviour was more entrenched and, like the Weimans, Freddie was having difficulty coming to terms with the idea. 'I worked with him for two and a half years,' he exclaimed, blowing out his cheeks. 'He was always flirting with the typists. They couldn't get enough of him. I can't believe he was...' His voice trailed off.

'It takes all sorts to make a world,' I said, with a half smile. Freddie was not quite as cosmopolitan as he liked to appear.

Miss Bunting evidently agreed with me. 'I thought you

were supposed to be a man of the world,' she teased.

'Yes, but...'

'Never mind that now,' I said. We were straying from the point. 'You're suggesting it was Giles Markham who killed Matthew Green?'

'That's right,' Weiman said. 'He came here that weekend, in March. We were away at the time, visiting friends. But Giles and Steven had some sort of argument, on the Sunday morning. I don't know what it was about. Giles went off to church with the other members of the household, but had a change of heart on the way down to the village and came back to the house. He found Steven and Matthew in bed together.'

'Lord,' I said.

'And he...well, he must have lost control of himself.' Weiman shuddered. 'He beat Matthew black and blue and then threw him down the stairs. Deliberately, as I understand it.'

'Bloody hell!' Freddie exclaimed. 'Giles? Giles did that?'

'I am afraid so. I cannot explain it. I suppose he must have felt betrayed. He lost his temper and killed the man in a jealous rage. But Steven took the blame for it. When we arrived back on Sunday evening, Giles had already left. We didn't even known he had been here. It was Steven who told us about Matthew. He said he had caught him stealing and had lost his temper. We believed him, of course. The fall had been an accident. Mr Langbroek helped him to cover it all up. I believe he was the one who suggested the story of the theft, though we only found that out later. The police came, but they had no interest in the death of a thief, especially a negro. It was all "brushed under the carpet". I believe that is the expression.'

'The policeman who came,' Miss Bunting asked. 'Was it the general?'

'No, it was a local man. I forget his name. Sadly, it was not considered an important matter. The law grants landowners the right to protect their property and that was what Steven claimed to have done.'

'What happened then?' I asked. 'I mean, between Catesby and Markham?'

The German sighed. 'As I understand it, Steven contacted Giles by telephone a few days later and begged him to forgive him. It must have been a difficult conversation. But he managed to persuade him to come up here again the following weekend.'

'And that was at the end of March? The weekend before Markham died?'

'Yes.' Weiman reached forward and took a final sip of coffee. 'At that point, you must remember, we knew nothing of his involvement in Matthew's death. Giles seemed no different to me when he arrived. We played cards and drank a little wine. He seemed in good spirits.'

'He was never one for showing his emotions,' Freddie agreed. 'Too busy having a good time.'

'But he must have been very hurt,' Weiman concluded. 'No matter how well he concealed it. He had been betrayed by a man I suppose he must have loved and then killed another man in a blind rage.'

'No wonder he topped himself!' Freddie exclaimed.

'The guilt must have been unbearable. He could not forgive himself for what he had done, any more than he could forgive Steven. I believe he only came here that weekend to tell Steven it was over, to break off their relationship once and for all. And of course there was no longer any question of them purchasing a farm together. Then, the following day, as you know, Giles took his own life.'

'We didn't hear about that until the Tuesday or Wednesday,' Susan Weiman put in. 'Steven was devastated.'

'Hardly surprising,' I muttered. 'In the circumstances.'

'He was distraught. I had never seen him so upset.' Gunther Weiman shifted his coffee cup sadly. He may not have liked the man but he had a natural sympathy for anyone in pain. 'And it was then we found out the truth. He told us everything. His relationship with Giles. There had been lots of rumours, of course, after the accident. That, I believe, was why the other workers did not protest when Matthew was killed.' They had been no more tolerant of a sodomite in their ranks than the Weimans had been. 'But nobody said anything directly to us.

206

The story, I think, soon became garbled. People said Giles and Matthew had been the ones discovered together and that Steven had killed Matthew. That was certainly the story that Mr Langbroek put about. And, for a time, that was what everyone believed.' Even the gossips in the village, like Alberto. 'After all, Steven had confessed to it, after a fashion.'

'So how did it make you feel, discovering the truth?' Miss Bunting asked.

'We were shocked, of course,' Mrs Weiman said. 'Bewildered, that he would involve himself in such an unnatural relationship. We had known they were close, but not...'

'He gave us no choice,' Weiman asserted. 'As soon as we found out, we told Steven he would have to leave. He could not continue as manager here. It would be too disruptive.'

'And what did he say to that?'

'He asked us for three months grace. He said he thought he could get the money to complete the purchase of the farm and we agreed he could stay on until the beginning of July. He went into town last week, with Mr Langbroek, to make the final arrangements. We thought he was organising some sort of loan.'

My eyes boggled. 'Langbroek came to town with him?' Freddie and I swapped looks. 'I didn't think Catesby even liked him.'

'No, I don't believe he did. But he found him to be an effective overseer. I confess I have always been a little uneasy about that man.' Weiman grimaced. 'He does not treat the workers well. It was Steven who insisted he stay on here and, as he was manager, I deferred to his judgement. I suppose he must have felt beholden to him. Mr Langbroek had been very helpful, covering up the incident with Matthew. I believe he would have followed Steven to the new farm, if that had ever happened.'

'So Langbroek must have been the bloke who broke into your flat,' Freddie concluded. 'If he was in town last week.'

'I wouldn't put it past him,' I agreed. 'And clobbered

my man too, the devil.'

As if on cue, a piercing scream erupted from another part of the house. Miss Bunting gave a start but I smiled with satisfaction. It was Langbroek, over in the living room. 'That'll be Doctor Rubio. Setting his leg for him.' Quite a painful procedure, by the sounds of it. Served the fellow right.

Freddie glanced back at the living room door. 'So, do you reckon Mr Langbroek could be our murderer?' he asked, the cogs in his mind whirring at an unprecedented speed. 'He might have killed Steven to get hold of that money.'

'It's possible,' I agreed. It was more than possible, in fact. 'Nine thousand dollars would be a hell of a temptation.'

There was one last grunt from the living room and then silence. Langbroek had probably fainted from the pain. For all his bulk, he did not strike me as a particularly brave man. Bullies never were.

'Perhaps he was behind everything,' Miss Bunting suggested, hopefully.

That would tie things up rather neatly, I thought. It would be nice, for a change, if there was a real bastard to blame for everything. 'He couldn't have killed Mr Talbot, though,' I realised, with some irritation. 'Whatever motive he might have had. Langbroek was out on the road when that happened. You remember, Freddie? We passed him by on the way back from the village, supervising the work party.'

The Englishman remembered. 'It couldn't have been him,' he agreed. 'Or Joseph. He was there too.'

'You think George may have been killed?' Mrs Weiman asked. 'As well as Steven?'

'I do,' I admitted sadly. 'It can't be a coincidence. Not if he was in possession of that banker's draft. It ties him in to everything else.'

Mrs Weiman shuddered, but her husband saw the logic in the argument. 'You are right. It cannot be a coincidence.'

'But your man Green couldn't have known anything about the money,' I said. 'Which means, whoever killed your cousin was someone in this house. It could even be one of us.'

Miss Bunting was thinking hard. 'Could it have been

Mrs Montana?' she wondered, reflecting on the events of the last hour. 'If she was searching the Talbots' bedroom?'

'The husband's a better bet,' Freddie thought. 'He might have had business dealings with Mr Talbot. Hey, didn't you say they'd had an argument yesterday afternoon?'

'That's right. Montana claimed they were arguing about an increase in transport costs.'

'That was a white lie,' Gunther Weiman admitted now. 'There *was* a discussion, a few weeks ago, but the argument yesterday was about the transfer of land. George had some concerns about the provenance of the money that Steven had provided. He was a very meticulous man.'

'Yes, so I've heard. But what had aroused his suspicions? He must have arranged the banker's draft months ago.'

'I would imagine so,' Weiman agreed. 'However, I think it may have been the conversation he had with you yesterday morning which gave him pause for thought. I believe you mentioned to him that Giles had embezzled a sum of money from your office. That was why he had committed suicide, you said.'

'Lord.' I did remember saying that, over breakfast.

'George would not allow the money to be paid to Arthur for the land if there was any possibility that it had been acquired illegally.'

'No. I'm surprised he didn't ask me anything more about it.'

'I gather he was intending to talk to you when you returned from the village. I doubt he would have had the opportunity earlier in the day.'

'No, I suppose not. I do remember Mrs Talbot saying he wanted a word with me, when I arrived back at the house. That was just before...well, before the accident.'

Weiman peered at me intently. 'But you now believe it was not an accident?'

'No, I'm afraid not. I wish you had told me the truth about that argument earlier on,' I remarked testily.

The German was apologetic. 'Arthur is very protective

209

of his business dealings,' he explained, with some embarrassment. 'And at that time there was no reason to believe George's death was anything other than an accident.'

'You still should have told me the truth.'

Miss Bunting had finished her coffee. 'So do you think it might have been Mr Montana who pushed Mr Talbot down the stairs?' she asked.

'I have no idea. I didn't see him anywhere near the scene of the crime. And you thought Mr Catesby was to blame.'

The girl flushed. 'Yes, I did.'

'We...suspected something untoward might have happened there, right from the word go,' I explained to the Weimans.

Freddie smiled. 'Henry has some experience, investigating this kind of thing.' I shot him a warning look but the man was not to be deterred. 'We couldn't be in safer hands.'

'Freddie's exaggerating.' I growled. 'As always.'

'But if Joseph was not involved in either of these deaths,' Weiman said, 'then who *was* responsible?'

'Well, that's the question,' I agreed. 'It must have been somebody closer to home. And you're not the only who's told a few white lies over the course of the last few hours.' I stared pointedly at Miss Bunting. The girl was looking just as perplexed as the rest of us, and now that the possibilities seemed to be exploding in every direction, it struck me that it was high time she came clean on a few matters as well. 'Miss Bunting. Is there anything you would like to tell us?' I asked. She blinked uncertainly. 'About last night?'

Frederick Reeves was horrified. 'You can't seriously think...?'

I gritted my teeth. I had a feeling I would regret bringing this up, but if we were ever to get to the bottom of this affair then the matter of Miss Bunting's nocturnal expedition needed to be cleared up; and after the revelations of the last few minutes I was beginning to think that perhaps my secretary was not quite as involved in events as I had first supposed. 'I saw you creeping about the house last night,' I informed her calmly. 'I was up answering a call of nature and I saw you heading across the landing in the direction of Mr Catesby's bedroom.'

Miss Bunting brought a hand to her mouth. 'I...'

'But when I asked you this morning if you had got up during the night you denied it. You lied to my face.'

'Look here, Henry,' Freddie protested.

Miss Bunting raised a hand. 'It's all right, Freddie. Yes, I was up and about. And I'm afraid I did lie to you.' Her voice was a girlish whisper. 'But you don't really believe I could have killed Mr Catesby?'

'I don't know what to believe. That earring of yours.' I pointed a finger. 'The one you lost yesterday. The little flower. I didn't find it out on the landing. It was over by the window in Mr Catesby's bedroom. I found it there when I discovered his body this morning.'

There was a shocked silence. Everyone was now staring at the young Englishwoman. The earring was back in place, the clasp having been fixed. 'I didn't kill him,' Miss Bunting mumbled softly, her hand rising reflexively to that ear. 'Crumbs, I wouldn't kill anyone.'

'Of course you wouldn't!' Freddie agreed at once. 'Henry, what on earth are you thinking?'

'She was in his room,' I stated firmly. 'And she is definitely concealing something. You knew about that draft, didn't you?' There was no answer. 'Well, didn't you?'

The girl sighed and gave a quiet nod. 'Yes, I knew.'

Freddie stared at her in bewilderment. 'You knew?' he breathed. 'But how on earth...?'

'I wanted to tell you, Freddie,' she insisted. 'I really did. But every time I came close...' Her voice faltered.

'Perhaps you'd better start from the beginning,' I said.

Miss Bunting closed her eyes and took a moment to gather her thoughts. For all her shock at the sudden accusation, she was not acting with the air of a cornered fugitive; more like a schoolgirl confessing to a prank that had gone awry. 'It was just an accident,' she explained to us mournfully. 'I moved into that flat, shortly after Mr Markham killed himself. There was a bureau in there. A big mahogany thing.' Everything in this part of the world was made of mahogany. It was one of the regions big exports. 'My mother had one just like it back in England. I didn't pay any attention to it for the first few days. I was too busy getting everything else sorted out and settling into my new job. But then one day I glanced at it and I remembered, my mother's bureau had a secret compartment. She had showed it to me once. You'd never find it if you didn't know where to look. Even daddy didn't know about it. And the bureau in the apartment was exactly the same. So I opened the flap one evening and I gave it a try.'

'And you found the banker's draft?'

Miss Bunting looked down at her lap. 'Yes. A draft for nine thousand dollars. I couldn't believe it. Just stumbling across it like that.'

Gunther Weiman was intrigued. 'And this was the money Giles intended to invest in Steven's farm?'

The girl nodded. 'Yes. He must have hidden it there. Although I had no idea about that at the time. I didn't know what it was for.'

'But, hang on a mo,' Freddie said. 'You must have known that was the money Giles had stolen from the office.'

Miss Bunting dipped her head. 'I knew. Well, not at first. It was a week or two before we worked out exactly how much had gone missing. Mr Markham had only just killed himself and it was William who handled the accountancy side after his death.'

That was true. William Battersby had given the books a thorough going over in the wake of Mr Markham's suicide and it was only then that the scale of the theft had been identified. That was why everyone had assumed Markham had had serious gambling debts. Bits of money had been diverted from the office over an extended period. Markham must have deposited the money in his account little by little to avoid suspicion, and then finally got the draft written out, when he had enough to pay out for the land. How he planned to cover the loss and leave work without being caught I had no idea.

'I didn't know what to do with the thing,' Miss Bunting continued. 'There was nobody in charge at the office. William was snowed under with work, all on his own. I was just learning the ropes and I didn't really know anybody, apart from William and a couple of the girls. I didn't know who to tell. So I just, well...I left it there. I put it back where I found it.'

'That was a daft thing to do,' Freddie admonished.

I had a less charitable interpretation. 'You thought you'd just leave it where it was for a few months, until everyone had forgotten about Giles Markham and then collect it and cash it in.'

'No!' Miss Bunting's eyes bulged in horror.

'That was why you held onto the key,' I suggested.

'No! At least...not really. Perhaps the thought did cross my mind,' she confessed, her eyes downcast. 'But I didn't...I would never have acted on the impulse. I'm not a thief, Mr Buxton. Honestly. We all have silly thoughts at one time or another.'

'Don't we just,' I agreed, pursing my lips. Mind you, if she had really been intent on cashing in the cheque herself, she could simply have taken it with her when she had vacated the flat.

'I decided to hang on until you arrived,' she said. 'I wanted to wait until there was a proper authority figure in the office. But then, when you did come, so much happened so quickly. I had to move out of the flat and you moved in. And I forgot to give back the key. That was an honest mistake,' she added, taking note of my sceptical expression. 'But once that had happened, it was difficult to know how I could broach the subject. The longer I left it, the more difficult it became. Then, when the flat was burgled last week, I knew I had to come clean. I didn't want William to know about it, though. He would have been so disappointed in me.' She did have a soft spot for that boy, after all, even if she preferred Freddie. 'So I came to visit you that evening, to tell you everything. But then, well...' She looked up at last and smiled at me. 'Events rather ran away with themselves, and it slipped my mind completely.'

Freddie was incredulous. 'How on earth could something like that slip your mind?'

'Ah.' I cut in rapidly. 'Best not go into that.' We had so far managed to avoid any reference to more personal matters. I

213

had been taking a serious risk, confronting Miss Bunting in this manner, but seeing her reactions so far I was prepared to push it a little further. 'You still haven't explained what you were doing up and about last night. And don't pretend it was a call of nature. You were nowhere near the hall stairs.'

She flinched at my unkind tone. 'No, you're right. I didn't need the bathroom. I did...I did visit Mr Catesby's bedroom.'

'Emily!' Freddie cried.

'Not last night,' she added hastily. 'Yesterday afternoon, when you were both down in the village; and when Mr Catesby was out on the estate. You see, I had convinced myself that he was the one who had broken into your flat.'

'Why would you think that?' I asked.

'Well, Freddie had said he and Mr Markham had been good friends. It occurred to me that *he* might know about the draft, if anyone did. And then at lunch, we found out he had been in Guatemala City last week, on the Wednesday and Thursday, when your flat was burgled. So I thought he might have been the one who broke into the bureau and took the draft.'

'And you decided to play detective, to see if he had it stashed away somewhere in his bedroom?'

'I thought it was worth having a look, after all that Freddie had told me. I slipped into his room and had a quick ruffle around, but there was nothing of any interest in there that I could see. Nothing relating to Mr Markham, anyway. I suppose my earring must have dropped off then, brushing up against one of those shutters. I didn't realise it was gone until the evening, when I was dressing for dinner. But by then Mr Talbot had had his accident and the house was too crowded to risk going back and having a look. Crumbs, I was so relieved when you found it and said it had been out on the landing.'

Freddie threw me a questioning look.

'I didn't want to accuse her outright,' I explained. 'Not without further evidence. But what were you doing, later on, creeping about? You weren't answering a call of nature,' I repeated.

'No. I couldn't sleep. I couldn't stop thinking about poor Mr Talbot, about the way he died. I didn't believe it could possibly have been an accident. Not after what I'd seen on the terrace; or thought I saw.'

'A figure moving about?'

'That's right. So I...well, I thought I might as well get up and have another look around.'

'In the middle of the night?'

'Yes. Don't ask me to explain it. My mind was in a bit of a whirl. But it was too dark to see anything properly. I walked down the stairs – the terrace stairs, where he fell – and then...then I had a look at Mr Talbot's body.'

'You wanted to go through his pockets, before the police gave him the once over this morning.' That did make sense. 'You were searching for the draft!'

'I just thought, if Mr Catesby didn't have it and Mr Talbot was his banker...'

'You might find it on him and relieve him of it.'

'Not for myself!' she protested. 'But to see if that might have been a motive for...for killing him.'

I scoffed. 'If he'd been killed for the money then the killer wouldn't have left it on him, even if he did have it.'

'No, I suppose not. I wasn't really thinking.' She stared down at her lap, shame-faced.

'You should have told me all this in the first place,' I barked.

'I know. I wanted to. But the longer I left it, the more difficult it became.' She looked up then, an impish gleam in her eye. 'And we all have our secrets, don't we, Hilary?'

Freddie was perplexed by the name. '*Hilary*?'

'It's a...private joke,' I covered hastily. 'Yes, we all have secrets. It's the nature of our job. But this has nothing to do with work, Miss Bunting. I'm sorry to have to say this, but you have behaved abominably.'

'Steady on!' Freddie protested.

'I'm sorry. It has to be said.'

'He's right. I have behaved very badly,' the girl agreed. 'I'm very sorry, Mr Buxton. But I've told you the truth now.'

215

Gunther Weiman was more interested in the references to his banking friend. 'So you believe it was Steven who killed George?' The German did not sound quite as surprised as I would have expected.

Miss Bunting shrugged. 'I don't know. What reason would he have had?'

Weiman glanced at his wife and then back across the table. 'Steven was due to pay the balance on the purchase of the land this weekend. George was overseeing the details. But when he learnt from Mr Buxton here that the money had been stolen, he requisitioned the banker's draft and refused to allow the transaction to go through.'

I lifted an eyebrow. So Talbot must have nipped into Catesby's room first and confiscated the draft, while the rest of the household were out on the guided tour. That would not have gone down well with the farm manager, I realised. Or Mr Montana. 'And so Catesby lost his temper and pushed him down the stairs?' I considered that briefly. 'I suppose that's plausible.'

'I can't believe Steven would kill anyone,' Mrs Weiman said. 'He had a temper, but he never lashed out. Not physically.'

'It might just have been an accident,' Miss Bunting suggested.

'But whoever *was* responsible,' Weiman concluded, 'it could not have been Joseph Green.' He rose to his feet. 'I should inform the general. We cannot allow him to shoot an innocent man.'

Mrs Weiman grabbed her husband's arm. 'Gunther, you can't go out there!'

'It's not a good idea, Mr Weiman,' I agreed.

'We have to do something!' the German exclaimed.

Chapter Fifteen

Maurice had been hovering for some moments at the far door of the dining room, waiting for the right moment to interrupt. The door to the hallway had been left open by the housekeeper Greta who, having passed on her concerns about Moses, had then taken away the metal coffee pot to organise a refill. I was not sure how much of the conversation my man had overheard. At least the general had not been standing out there or one of his many underlings. The valet brought a hand to his mouth and made a discreet coughing noise. Gunther Weiman had already resumed his seat, at our insistence. I caught Maurice's eye and made my apologies to the table, rising up and hurrying across to speak to him. 'What is it, Morris?' I asked, pulling the dining room door shut behind me and drawing him across to the stairwell.

'I have packed your suitcase, Monsieur, as requested.' Freddie had passed on the message, as I had asked. 'You are intending for us to leave this evening?'

I shook my head. 'I don't think it's going to be possible. Not now our lord and master has declared Martial Law. Just a contingency plan. Thought we might need to break out the alternative passports.'

'Because of what happened to Madame Montana?'

'Exactly.' I jerked a thumb in the direction of the dining room. 'How much did you hear?'

'A little, Monsieur.' Maurice hesitated. As a matter of professional pride, he did not wish to admit to eavesdropping.

'It's all getting damned complicated,' I muttered. 'But I was right about Miss Bunting. She was holding something back.' I filled him in briefly on what my young secretary had told me. 'It's a bit of a lame story, all things considered.'

The valet's expression had not altered. 'You still believe Mademoiselle Bunting may have been responsible for Monsieur Catesby's death?'

I threw up my hands. 'That's the thing of it, Morris. I have no idea. It could be any one of them in there. Miss

Bunting's not the only one holding things back. Mr Weiman's told me a fair few lies as well, and we know he had no particular love for Mr Catesby.'

'There was that argument in the generator room last night, before Monsieur Catesby went to bed.'

'Well, exactly. And then there's Mrs Weiman.' I scratched my nose. 'Did you know Moses was her child?'

'I had an inkling, Monsieur.'

I frowned. 'An inkling?'

'Yes, Monsieur. When Joseph Green was arrested on the front lawn, her eyes were on the boy and not on Monsieur Green.' Greta had held the lad back, I recalled, to prevent him interfering with the arrest; with good reason, it now transpired. 'The expression on Madame Weiman's face, it was not that of a dispassionate employer.'

'No, it wasn't.' I rubbed my chin. 'Do you think Catesby might have been blackmailing her?' Could that have been a motive for murder?

'It is a possibility, Monsieur. As a relative, he may well have known about the child.'

'And he would certainly have needed to raise a bit of cash for that new business of his. Oh, you won't have heard about that.' I quickly sketched in the details. 'And if he couldn't use Markham's money – with Mr Talbot having a moral crisis – he might have decided to look elsewhere.'

'To Madame Weiman?'

'Exactly. Of course, he might have been blackmailing her already. You'd need a lot of money to start a business from scratch like that. As I understand it, the draft only covered the cost of the land.' I frowned again. 'But if he *was* blackmailing Susan, how would he have gone about it? What exactly would he have said? "I'll tell the world you shared a bed with a negro and bore him a child?"' I scratched my head. 'Not really the stuff of newspaper headlines. Rather a minor scandal, I would have thought.' It was hardly an unusual occurrence in this part of the world. 'Oh, there'd be plenty of gossip, but it would all blow over. And if anyone could weather the storm it would be Mr and Mrs Weiman. Their business is fairly solid, so far as I can see.' I gestured vaguely to the house. 'Even with the economic downturn. It wouldn't do them much damage in the long run.'

'No, Monsieur. But the reputation of Madame Weiman would be destroyed. That would not be an easy thing for her to come to terms with. Also, we cannot underestimate what a mother would be prepared to do to protect her child.'

'Yes. Maternal bonds and all that.' It was not an emotion I had ever felt, but I knew such things could have a powerful effect. 'Still, I can't see an Englishwoman attacking her own cousin with a razor blade. Any more than I can picture Miss Bunting doing it, come to that.'

'Madame Weiman would have known the razor was there, Monsieur.'

'I suppose so. As would Mr Weiman. And Miss Bunting too, if she had a good poke around his bedroom yesterday afternoon.'

'And then there is Madame Talbot.'

I grimaced. 'Jane Talbot?' I had already dismissed that idea. 'I don't think she's a credible suspect. She was too busy grieving for her husband.'

'But Monsieur Talbot must have retrieved the banker's draft from Monsieur Catesby's bedroom. The Madame may have known of this. And soon afterwards, Monsieur Catesby died.'

'What, you think Mrs Talbot might have blamed Catesby for her husband's death and bumped him off?'

'It is a possibility, Monsieur.'

'Nonsense. She was out for the count. And if she did have any knowledge of that draft, why would she leave it behind?'

'The first instinct of a murderer is always to fly the scene of the crime,' Maurice said. That was true. It had always been my first instinct, when things got tricky. 'And Madame Talbot left the estate at the first opportunity.'

'Ah. Yes, I see your point.' I pulled out my fob watch. I wondered if Mrs Talbot was still waiting down in the village. Somehow, I doubted it. If she intended to get home at a reasonable hour she would have to head off before it got dark. 'But a murderess.' I closed the watch and returned it to my waistcoat. 'I can't see it, Morris. Mrs Talbot is far too sensible to want to kill anybody.'

'If you say so, Monsieur.' The valet changed tack. 'Then, of course, there are the members of the domestic staff.'

I rolled my eyes. 'The staff? What, you mean Isabel and Moses?'

'And the housekeeper, Greta. They would all have access to Monsieur's Catesby's bedroom.'

I saw what he was getting at. 'Yes, and I suppose they would know about the razor too. But what motive would any of them have?'

'Monsieur Catesby was not popular below stairs.'

'Yes, I remember you saying. Why is that? Did he flog them?'

'No, Monsieur, but he had a short temper. He was not tolerant of mistakes. And, as I understand it, Moses was rather upset about Monsieur Green's punishment yesterday afternoon.'

'The whipping? Yes, he must have been.' I scratched the side of my chin. 'And at that age boys do tend to over-react to things. But, even so, murder...?'

'People have been killed for less, Monsieur.'

'Yes, I'm aware of that, Morris,' I responded irritably. 'I suppose he could have been the one who damaged the generator.'

'Yes, Monsieur.'

'And he was very upset about the death of Matthew Green, back in March. He probably blamed Catesby for that as well. Lord, the resentment could have been building up for months,' Another plausible theory. I growled. It seemed like we were awash with the things. 'Dammit, it could be any one of them.' I flicked my eyes skywards. 'Or somebody we haven't even thought of yet.' That was more likely, if I was being honest. 'You know what my track record is like with this type of thing.'

Maurice nodded gravely. 'Yes, Monsieur.'

Over the last couple of years I had been involved in several murders and each time the identity of the murderer had come as a complete surprise to me. With the best will in the world, I was a hopeless detective. Freddie was deluding himself if he thought I had any chance of getting to the bottom of this affair. For goodness sake, I didn't even want to *be* a detective. And yet here I was, once again, forced into the role. 'There is at least one person I think we can say is definitely involved.'

'Monsieur?'

'That overseer fellow, Mr Langbroek. He was in town with Mr Catesby last week. I'm pretty sure he was the one who clobbered you the other day in the flat.'

Maurice did not blink. 'He was in Guatemala City?'

'Apparently. On Wednesday evening; with Mr Catesby. They must have conspired together to retrieve the banker's draft, although Mr Langbroek would have done the actual deed. He must have been the blackguard who crowned you.'

'But how would the two of them have known the banker's draft was there?'

I shrugged. 'Markham must have told Catesby, before they fell out. He was the one who stashed it there, after all. One thing I don't understand, though, is how he planned to get away with it all. I mean, before he took his own life. If he was intending to run away with Catesby and become a farmer. He must have known the money would be missed and we would come looking for him. It makes no sense.'

'A man in love, Monsieur.'

'Yes, but even so. He must have had some plan to cover it up. And whatever it was, Catesby must have known about it. He certainly knew about the draft. Though why he waited so long to pick it up...'

'Perhaps he was biding his time, Monsieur, until matters had settled down.'

'I suppose so. And then roping in Mr Langbroek with the promise of a job on the new farm, and perhaps a share of the loot.' The overseer would have been happy to play burglar. 'He's got his comeuppance now though.' I smirked. That broken leg. 'I really ought to have a quiet word with the fellow, when I get the chance. I have a feeling he knows more about all this than anyone.'

'He is with Doctor Rubio at the moment, in the living room.'

'Yes, I know. I'll need to get him on his own, though. Get the thumbscrews out.' I smiled again. I had no qualms about getting awkward with a man who could not fight back.

'If Monsieur Langbroek was in league with Monsieur Catesby,' Maurice pointed out, 'then that means he is unlikely to be the murderer.'

'No, I suppose not. Unless the two of them fell out for some reason. Or Langbroek got greedy. He couldn't have had anything to do with Mr Talbot's death. That much I do know. Perhaps Catesby killed Talbot and then Mr Langbroek killed Catesby.'

'There is another possibility, Monsieur. A suspect we have not considered as yet.'

'Another one?' I sighed, peering across at him. 'Go on.'

'Monsieur Gonzales. The engineer.'

I coughed in surprise. 'You think *he* might be involved?' Maurice was right. The thought had not even entered my head. 'But he wouldn't hurt a fly. The fellow's a mouse. And he's absolutely in terror of the general.'

'Yes, Monsieur. But I was speaking to the maid, Isabel, earlier today, regarding the telephone in the main hall.'

I didn't follow. 'The telephone?'

'I was curious to know how long it had been out of order.'

That was an interesting question. Something else I hadn't considered. 'What, you think it might have been cut off deliberately?'

'It occurred to me that it was a possibility, Monsieur. According to the maid, the telephone was last used on Monday evening. The fault was discovered late the following day. There was a storm that afternoon and it was assumed that this was the cause of the failure.'

'They must have a dedicated line, all the way out here,' I guessed. 'It wouldn't take much to bring it down. And the

222

storm was quite a bad one?'

'Yes, Monsieur. On Tuesday afternoon. But earlier that day Isabel went down to the village, to buy some groceries for the kitchen. On the way back, she noticed that a motor-bicycle with a sidecar had been parked a little way off from the road.'

My eyes widened. 'Was it Gonzales' bicycle?'

'She could not say for certain. There did not appear to be anyone about. But the bicycle was parked next to a telegraph pole.'

'I see. You mean, one of the ones that carries the phone line to the hacienda?'

'Yes Monsieur.' Presumably, the Weimans had hitched a ride on the existing telegraph line and then run their own cable up to the house.

'And this was the pole that came down in the storm?'

'No, Monsieur.'

I scowled. 'Then what the blazes are you talking about?'

Maurice was unperturbed. 'The pole that came down was only a short distance away, and *that* was the first dedicated pole leading towards the farm.'

'I see.' That was why they had had such a job getting it fixed. The telegraph company would be out pretty sharpish to repair its own line, but it wouldn't care about a private auxiliary line running off from it. 'And you think Gonzales might have nobbled it?'

'I do not know, Monsieur. Isabel had not given the matter much thought. It is only in the light of the tragic events of this weekend that she remembered it at all. But it is probably nothing. As I have said, she is not certain if the motor-bicycle did belong to Monsieur Gonzales.'

'And he might well have just stopped off for a spot of lunch in any case,' I agreed. 'Still, it's worth thinking about. It could tie in with something else I heard, from our Mr Battersby this afternoon.'

'Monsieur?'

I told the valet briefly about the professional connection that had existed between Giles Markham and George Talbot.

223

'That is most interesting, Monsieur.'

'I get the feeling he was going to tell me himself, before he died. If Talbot was ruffling feathers about police corruption, then General Tejada might have good reason to want to get him out of the way.'

'Indeed, Monsieur. But how would a banker like Monsieur Talbot know of such things?'

'Money laundering. Criminals and policemen stashing their ill gotten gains. If Talbot was as much of a stuffed shirt as William suggests, he might have caused one hell of a stink, if he caught even a whiff of anything like that.'

'And so the general arranged to have Monsieur Talbot killed?'

'It would make sense of him coming here. Why would a high ranking policeman come all this way down from the capital to investigate the case of a man accidentally falling down the stairs? Unless he wanted to make sure there was no possibility of anyone crying foul.'

'But he could not have killed Monsieur Talbot himself.'

'Of course not. Don't be daft, Morris. He would have had an agent acting on his behalf. You know as well as I do the police have informers in every village in this god-forsaken country. And who better to act as an informer than a road engineer, who goes up and down the country as part of his job? He must have passed on the news that Talbot was going to be here this weekend and was then told to disable the phones.'

'But would he then murder the man, Monsieur, in cold blood?'

'Don't ask me. It's your theory, Morris.'

'Monsieur Gonzales does not strike me as a violent man.'

'No, me neither. He was looking fairly shifty, though, when he came down the stairs shortly afterwards. That might just have been shock I suppose. But it's certainly a plausible idea, if that girl was right about the bicycle.'

'Yes, Monsieur.'

'And the general has been suspiciously keen to ignore any possibility of foul play regarding Mr Talbot's death. And, now I come to think of it, it was Gonzales who went down to the village to call him in in the first place. Perhaps he wanted to make the phone call himself, to make sure it was Tejada who got the summons, rather than some local bod.'

'That does fit the facts, Monsieur.'

Well, not all of them, I thought. 'But how would that tie in with the second murder? How would Catesby be involved?'

'I believe it would be better to remain in the house, Monsieur.'

'I'm sorry?' I blinked, suddenly unsure what my man was talking about. His eyes were staring pointedly across my shoulder. I wheeled around, just in time to catch Mr and Mrs Gonzales descending the stairs. The engineer was carrying a suitcase. His wife had a light travel bag hanging from her shoulder.

'Talk of the devil,' I declared, attempting to brazen things out. 'We were just saying, how lucky it was you had your own transport.'

Maurice was eyeing the luggage the Guatemalan couple were carrying. 'You are leaving us, Monsieur?' he enquired of the engineer.

It was Consuela Gonzales who answered. 'Ricardo is hoping we will be able to leave this evening. But we have to wait for permission from the general.' She smiled sadly. The woman had dark, penetrating eyes and a rather wistful air.

'Yes, best not to step outside just yet,' I agreed. 'Not with all those constables on the prowl. Coffee's being served in the dining room, if you're feeling parched.'

'That would be very nice,' Mrs Gonzales said.

The engineer was happy to be directed. 'We can leave the luggage here,' he suggested, placing his suitcase by the side of the stairs. 'How is Señor Montana?'

'I'm not sure.' The last time I had seen the American he had been sitting out on the front porch, staring at his wife's body and knocking back a bottle of scotch which Isabel had fetched from his room. 'He's had a terrible shock.'

'His poor wife,' Mrs Gonzales breathed.

'Is there any news of Señor Green?' Mr Gonzales

225

enquired.

'No, I'm afraid not. But no news is good news, as they say.' I looked across the courtyard to the front of the house. The sun was just setting, out of view to the west. 'It'll be dark shortly.' That would provide some protection for the two fugitives.

Doctor Rubio was emerging from the living room on the far side of the courtyard. My eyes lit up. Now might be the time to have that quiet word with Mr Langbroek. I left Maurice to hustle the Guatemalans into the dining room and darted across the square to intercept the doctor.

'How's the patient?' I asked, meeting him half way.

'He is recovering,' Rubio responded gravely. He clipped up his medical bag and placed it on a nearby table. 'I am going to the kitchen to fetch him a light snack. It will do him good to eat something. Then I will try to find Señor Montana. He was looking a little distressed earlier on.'

'That's hardly surprising,' I said.

The door to the living room was wide open. The overseer was propped up on the sofa, his left leg sticking out, the foot resting on the coffee table, with two bits of wood serving as a makeshift splint. Langbroek had a sour look on his face, as well he might, but he was alert now and regarded my entrance with some suspicion. 'What do you want?' he growled. He had a rounded, pasty face – nondescript rather than ugly – and short cropped hair. It was the first time I had seen him without a hat. He wore a casual shirt, part of which was stained red; from Mrs Montana, presumably.

'Just wanted a quick word, while I have you alone.' I closed the door, moved across the room and pulled up a chair, settling myself on his side of the sofa.

'You think I want to talk to you?' he snarled. 'From what I hear, it's your bloody fault that woman fell on me.'

'After a fashion. It must make a change, you getting clobbered like that.'

His piggy eyes narrowed to the point of invisibility.

'What are you talking about?'

I leaned in closely. 'Don't think I don't know what you did to my man, you filthy swine. You broke into my flat last week and coshed Maurice. It was lucky he wasn't seriously hurt.'

Langbroek's eyes widened a fraction of an inch. 'I don't know what you're talking about.'

'Don't deny it, you blackguard.' The gall of the fellow, sitting there, trying to look innocent. 'You broke in and stole that banker's draft from the bureau. The one Mrs Montana found in the Talbots' bedroom.'

Langbroek laughed. 'You're out of your mind. I'm an honest, law-abiding citizen. You should watch your bloody mouth, throwing accusations around.'

In ordinary circumstances, a threat like that might have given me pause for thought – Langbroek was clearly a man who knew how to look after himself – but luckily for me he was not in a position to threaten anybody just now.

'Look, Mr Langbroek,' I said, adopting a more reasonable tone. 'I have no interest in you. I have no intention of informing the authorities about anything you may or may not have done. I am only interested in finding out the truth, about the murders of Steven Catesby and George Talbot.'

'I don't know anything about that.'

'Oh, I think you do. Maybe not the murders themselves, but certainly the circumstances that led up to them. Particularly the comings and goings of Mr Giles Markham.'

His eyes narrowed again. 'Mr Markham?'

'My predecessor. You knew him rather well, didn't you?'

The overseer shrugged. 'I met him a couple of times.'

'Don't lie to me, Mr Langbroek. You knew him every bit as well as you knew Steven Catesby.'

'Maybe.' He glowered at me. 'Why the bloody hell should I tell you anything?'

I gazed down at his splint. 'As I understand it, that leg of yours needs to be kept very still. Any undue pressure and you could be crippled for life.'

Langbroek laughed humourlessly. 'Don't try to threaten me, you little bastard,' he hissed. 'You're just a bloody pen-pusher. You haven't got the guts to hurt anyone.'

I lifted my shoe and placed it firmly on the edge of the coffee table. 'I assure you, Mr Langbroek, appearances can be deceptive. After what you did to my man, it would give me the greatest pleasure to cause you pain.' I met his eye and made sure he could see that I meant it. One swift kick and his leg would go flying.

His eyes flicked nervously to my foot. 'All right,' he grunted. As I had thought, when it came down to it the man was a coward. 'Just one question. Off the record.'

'Off the record,' I agreed. 'Giles Markham. He was stealing money. Spiriting it away from my office.'

'So what if he was?'

'Between the visa receipts, the money in the safe and the outgoings, nearly two thousand pounds went missing.'

'I'll take your word for it.'

'Now Markham wasn't a fool. He was intending to purchase a patch of land with Steven Catesby. But he couldn't have walked out of that office with nine thousand dollars in his pocket. He might have been in charge of the books but the discrepancy would have been noticed eventually. One of the secretaries was already starting to become suspicious. So how did he think he was going to get away with it? He must have had some plan. How was he going to cover himself?'

A slow smile spread across Mr Langbroek's face. 'Piece of cake. Just between you and me,' he said.

'Of course.'

The overseer chuckled. 'I was going to blow the safe.'

I blanched. 'I'm sorry?'

'Blow the safe in the office. Stage a robbery. Steal the money.' He grinned again. 'Except there wasn't any money there.'

'You were going to break into the office? The visa office?'

'I just said so, didn't I? Nip in there, mess things up a bit, leave the safe wide open. No-one would know the money

228

had never been in there. They'd think I'd nicked it all.'

'But the police...'

Langbroek scoffed. 'The police would do what they always do. They'd arrest some bloody idiot, fit him up and sling him in jail. Case closed. But the money would never be found. And Mr Markham could resign a few months later without any fuss.'

'Good lord.' So Markham *had* intended to quit his job and walk away. He had a lot of nerve, I thought, if that was really what he had been planning. A departure like that would have raised quite a few eyebrows in Whitehall, though in practical terms nobody would have been able to stop him.

'It would have been perfect,' Langbroek asserted. 'If the bastard hadn't topped himself. Bloody fool.'

I nodded slowly. It was all starting to make sense. 'Why did you leave it so long to retrieve the banker's draft, after he died?'

'You're trying to trick me now. You've had your question.'

'Oh, for heaven's sake. I've told you, I don't care if you stole the draft. I just want to know the truth.'

'All right, look. Mr Catesby was in a right state, for weeks afterwards. He was in love, the daft sod. Took him time to get his head together, didn't it? And I thought it was better to hold off, anyway, to let things calm down a bit. It all worked out in my favour, in the end. In exchange for me breaking into Mr Markham's flat, Mr Catesby offered me a half share of the farm. We were going to go in it together.'

'So him dying like that...'

'Was the last bloody thing I wanted, believe me.' He met my eye firmly. 'I didn't kill Mr Catesby, no matter what you think. And I'd happily throttle the bastard who did.'

I peered at the fellow curiously. Here was a man, if ever there was one, who seemed entirely capable of murder. But on the issue of Steven Catesby's death, strangely, I believed him.

A clunk behind me signalled the return of Doctor Rubio. The grey-haired man was carrying a jug of wine on a tray with a small serving of bread and cheese. I rose up to greet him as he entered the living room and, as I did so, I knocked the coffee table away from underneath Mr Langbroek's leg. He let out a loud scream.

'Oh, I'm terribly sorry. How clumsy of me!'

'You BASTARD!!' he yelled.

I leaned in quickly to right his leg. '*That* was for my man Maurice,' I hissed, as Doctor Rubio rushed across the room.

The valet was silhouetted in the archway on the southern side of the courtyard, staring out onto the front terrace. I caught sight of him at once as I moved into the square. The sky was already beginning to darken above us. Night tends to fall rather quickly in the tropics. 'Morris? What the devil are you doing?'

'I thought I heard something, Monsieur.'

I laughed. 'That was Mr Langbroek screaming. His leg fell off the table.'

'No, Monsieur, before that. I heard something out on the terrace.'

I shuffled across and together we stepped out onto the front porch. It took us barely a second to establish the source of the noise. One of the policemen was sprawled out across the landing to our right. Someone had thumped him from behind. I moved closer and peered down at the fellow, who was lying at the foot of the exterior stairs. 'He's been belted pretty thoroughly,' I observed, crouching beside him. I recognised the man. It was one of the two officers who had come up to the house that afternoon on horseback; the one who had sworn at me when Gonzales had blown his horn. He had been sent off by Tejada to search the labourers' cottages; not a particularly time consuming task. It was no surprise that he had been the first to report back. And then a bottle had been smashed over his head. I reached out a hand. There was glass scattered everywhere and the wooden surface was damp beneath my feet; but there was no sign of an assailant. 'He's still breathing,' I said. 'No damage done that I can see.' I looked back along the terrace. Apart from a couple of chairs and a hammock, the area was notably devoid of life. The body of Mrs Montana had been laid out respectfully to the right of the dining room windows, some distance away, but there was nothing else in view. I stood up and glanced at Maurice. 'You'd better fetch Doctor Rubio, have him give the fellow the once over.'

The valet hesitated, observing the unconscious body with a keener eye than me. 'Monsieur, his revolver has been removed from its holster.'

I looked down in alarm. 'Lord, you're right.'

'Could Monsieur Green have done this?'

'I doubt it.' I had a horrible feeling I knew exactly who was responsible. I could already smell the whisky in the air. 'Where's Mr Montana?' I wondered.

The barrel of a gun clicked into place and a figure emerged from the gloom of the stairwell. 'Right here,' the American replied in a harsh drawl.

Chapter Sixteen

Before I had time to react, Arthur Montana stepped forward and struck Maurice a savage blow across the back of the neck. The valet let out a moan and crumpled to the ground, in front of the unconscious policeman. I cried out in surprise as the American raised the revolver and aimed it squarely at my head. He must have dipped out of sight underneath the stairs when he had heard the two of us coming; but now there was only him and me. His eyes were red and his hands were trembling as he pointed the revolver.

I raised my own hands warily. It was not the first time somebody had pointed a gun at me, but it was not an experience I would ever become used to. 'Look, Mr Montana,' I said, trying to keep my voice as calm as I could. 'You've had a terrible shock. Your wife...I'm so sorry about what happened.' I didn't need to fake the regret in my voice. 'But you mustn't...you mustn't do anything rash.'

'Don't you talk to me,' he snapped back, his whole body shaking with rage. 'Don't you dare talk to me!'

'I...I...' My voice faded away. I was the one trembling now. I could see the fury in Montana's eyes, the vicious, alcohol-fuelled determination. My God, I thought, he intends to kill me. I swallowed hard and did my best to keep my bowels under control.

'Turn around,' he barked.

I did as I was instructed. All at once, I felt the man's cold breath on the back of my neck. I could smell the whisky there. He grabbed my arm with his free hand and pulled it tightly behind my back. The other hand pressed the revolver against the nape of my neck. Abruptly, I found myself propelled past the stairs towards the entrance hall on the west side of the house. We moved through the door and along a dark corridor – no-one had been out with the lamps as yet – stumbling past the telephone and the WC. Where on earth was he taking me? I wondered. Out into the back garden? Or just away from the body of Mrs Montana?

'I loved my wife,' the American declared drunkenly. 'Anita. We were childhood sweethearts. She was the most beautiful girl I ever saw. Everything I ever did, I did for her. And now she's dead. You son of a bitch. She's dead and you killed her.'

I swallowed again. There was nothing I could say to that.

'My beautiful, beautiful girl. We only came here for the weekend. Seeing old pals. A bit of business on the side. But you ruined that, Mr Buxton. Ruined the business. And killed the only woman in the world who ever meant a damn to me.'

Again, I had nothing to say in reply. Everything seemed to be happening in such a whirl. We reached the far end of the hall and I found myself propelled sideways and through a far arch out onto the back terrace.

'And now,' Montana declared, 'I'm going to kill you.'

Before I could respond, I felt a hard shove from behind and staggered forward down the steps, out onto the muddy grass of the back lawn. I lost my footing on the wet earth and crashed to the ground. This is it, I thought. I am going to die here, in some god-forsaken backwater in the middle of nowhere. 'You don't have to do this!' I called out desperately, scrabbling onto my knees and trying to turn around. 'You're a God fearing man. You know this is wrong!'

Montana had clomped down the stairs behind me. 'I *am* a God fearing man,' he agreed with a sudden, chilling calm. 'I read the bible every day. I know every syllable of that holy book. An eye for an eye, Mr Buxton. Exodus Chapter 21 Verse 24. An eye for an eye, it says, a tooth for a tooth. So make your peace with the world.' He stepped forward and pressed the nub of the revolver firmly against my head.

I closed my eyes and mumbled a desperate, half-forgotten prayer.

And a single shot rang out across the lawn.

I don't know what I was expecting to happen next. A Holy Chorus, perhaps. The Archangel Gabriel beckoning me through the pearly gates; or more likely Old Nick dragging me down into the fires of Hell. What I got instead was a heavy thud, as Arthur Montana crashed forward, a dead weight collapsing on top of me. I had no time to move aside. I was knocked forward from the kneeling position, my legs buckling underneath me and my face abruptly colliding with a layer of soft mud. Winded and disorientated – with the sudden heavy bulk of an American pressing down on top of me – I was momentarily too stunned to move. Montana's head flopped and I found myself staring at his face, which had come to rest barely eight inches away from me on the grass. The man's eyes were glassy and unfocused. There was a neat red hole in the side of his head. I flinched at the sight of the blood dripping down from it. My own head was bloody too. I fumbled a hand to check the back of my neck and felt the stickiness there. I slid my fingers in front of my face and realised it was not blood at all. It was...my God, it was bits of Arthur Montana's brain. I gagged. I could not help myself, throwing up over the grass to my left, some of the spittle splattering Mr Montana's corpse. I had seen a lot of death in my time, but I had never been quite so thoroughly covered in it before.

The shot that had rang out had caught the attention of the house and elicited cries of alarm from the hacienda. I could hear people scrabbling out onto the terrace. Footsteps were padding towards me across the lawn. My attention, however, was focused on those glassy eyes, resting so close to me. Arthur Montana shot dead at the exact moment he had intended to kill me. I should have felt relief, I should have felt joy at my own survival. But instead, all I felt was a gut wrenching terror; the horrible realisation of just how close I had come to death. Nausea swept through me and I retched a second time, on this occasion producing very little except a deeply uncomfortable sensation in my throat. And still the blood and brains continued to drip from the head opposite me and I continued to stare.

A pair of boots thudded into view, coming to a halt just to the left of Arthur Montana's body. Military boots. I tried to move, to get a better view of my unlikely saviour, but a flash of pain shot through my twisted legs. The lower half of Montana's body was still pressing down on me and I was too disorientated to wriggle free. The boots were in a better place than I was. One of them prodded Montana's shoulder, pushing his head to one side, to make sure he was really dead. I had managed to shift my head back a little bit. I slid a hand up to my mouth and wiped it awkwardly, making a concerted effort to get a grip on my senses. I followed the line of the boot up the uniformed leg, past the holster, the swagger stick and the tightly creased military shirt, to the rounded, dark face of General Julio Tejada. I stared up at the man, speechless. He was still holding the revolver in his right hand. With some difficulty, I managed to retrieve my legs from underneath the corpse and then flip over and raise myself up onto an elbow. Montana's lower torso settled behind me and I regarded the policeman in understandable confusion. His thick eyebrows were creased together in an expression of absolute fury. 'I said nobody was to leave the house!' he barked, though whether at me or at the world in general I had no idea.

I coughed the last remnants of lunch from my mouth. 'You...you shot Mr Montana?' I croaked, barely able to articulate the question. My throat felt as raw as a sand-blasted stone. Out of the corner of my eye, in the last of the twilight, I could see the other guests staring at me from the safety of the terrace. Mr and Mrs Gonzales huddled together with Gunther and Susan Weiman; Freddie Reeves and Emily Bunting to their right, observing the scene with open-mouthed astonishment.

Tejada followed my gaze and growled at the spectators. 'There's nothing to see here!' he snapped. He had no time for sight-seers. 'Get back inside, all of you!' He pointed his revolver skywards and the house guests rushed to do his bidding. Only when they were gone did he deign to drop his hand and glance down at me. He did not holster the weapon, however, and made no effort to help me up; but that was scarcely any reason to complain.

'You...you saved my life,' I breathed, in disbelief.

Tejada shrugged. 'I shot an armed fugitive. He assaulted one of my officers and stole his revolver.' He gestured to the abandoned weapon, which had come to a rest close to the body of the deceased United Fruit executive. The policeman must have been heading back to the house just as Montana was dragging me off. 'He had it coming to him.'

I stared down sadly at the American. 'I suppose there was no way to disarm him before...'

'I would have shot him whatever he was doing,' Tejada cut in bluntly. 'He made his choice when he attacked my deputy.'

I rose unsteadily onto my knees. 'His wife had just died,' I mumbled, finding myself in the bizarre position of defending a man who had just tried to kill me. 'He was drunk. He didn't know what he was doing.'

The general regarded me coldly. 'You would rather I had let him kill you?'

'No. Lord, no.' I swallowed again. 'You did the right thing. Thank you. Thank you for saving my life.' Tejada grunted and I took a moment to steady myself. I was covered in mud and blood and much else besides, some of which I tried to scrape off now as best I could, but at least I was alive. The policeman loomed over me, his back to the house. The daylight had evaporated, but a few lamps had now been lit in the dining room off to the left and there was just enough of a glow from them to make out his stern face. I hesitated, swaying on my knees, and looking back once again at the dead American. A sudden mad thought occurred to me. Montana's demise could well be a blessing in disguise. My own brush with death had brought me a moment of sudden clarity. Why not blame the American for everything? I almost laughed at the thought. It was the perfect solution. Why not pretend Arthur Montana had killed Steven Catesby? Heaven knows, it might even be true. That would get Joseph Green off the hook and solve all our problems in a single stroke. And it wasn't as if the American or his wife were in any position to object.

I took a moment to collect my thoughts. I still had the taste of bile in my mouth. I coughed and brought a hand up to my face, giving myself an extra second or two to work the matter through. 'It was him all along,' I declared at last, gesturing to the corpse. 'Arthur Montana. He killed George

Talbot. He pushed him down the stairs.'

General Tejada regarded me suspiciously.

'That draft you confiscated. The banker's draft. Mr Talbot took it from Steven Catesby's bedroom.' That much at least was true. 'Talbot refused to allow the money to be handed over, funds that Catesby had promised to Mr Montana.' Bizarrely, now that I was speaking the words, it did seem to make a kind of sense. 'Talbot thought it was dirty money. They had an argument about it and then Talbot fell down the stairs. It probably wasn't intentional. Just a shove at the wrong moment.' I was making this up as I was going along, but it did sound vaguely plausible. 'Catesby knew what Mr Montana had done and was going to tell the police about it when they arrived this morning. So Montana killed him too.' I was babbling now, saying the first thing that came into my head, but with both the American and the Englishman dead I was not about to be sued for slander. If I could convince Tejada that Montana was his man, then Joseph Green might be saved from the gallows and everyone could live happily ever after. 'Mr Montana confessed it all to me,' I said, getting rather carried away with the lie. 'Boasted about it, he did, when he was dragging me out here. So you see, he was behind everything. He's your murderer, not Joseph Green.' I stopped gabbling, looking up at the general, to see if my words were having any effect, but the man's expression was unreadable. He had been regarding me impassively for some moments. Now he lifted up his cane and struck me hard across the face with it.

I howled and fell backwards onto the grass.

'I do not like liars,' Tejada declared forcefully.

I stared up at him, too shocked to respond. That stick of his was lethal. The side of my face felt like it was on fire and I could feel fresh blood dripping down from my nose. My head, too, had fallen back into the same patch of mud which I had previously vomited all over. That, however, was the least of my concerns. 'No, honestly,' I mumbled at last, desperately pulling myself back onto my elbows. 'I'm telling the truth.' This time my voice lacked any conviction. A smack across the face does that to a person. 'The man just tried to kill me. Why would I lie

237

about that?'

Tejada gazed down at me scornfully. 'Montana tried to kill you because you had just killed his wife. I would have done the same in his position.'

'But...' I rose up again onto my knees and fumbled for the handkerchief in my breast pocket.

'Señor Montana was not responsible for the death of Señor Talbot.'

'But he was, I assure you. He said...'

The general raised his cane again and I trembled at the sight of it, almost falling backwards without him even having to hit me. 'Do not lie to me, señor. Do not ever lie to me. Arthur Montana was not responsible for the death of George Talbot.'

'But...but how can you be so sure?' I stopped and met the man's gaze. He did seem very certain of what he was saying. Worryingly certain. His mouth formed into a tight smile – a *knowing* smile – and all at once I realised the truth: he knew because *he* had been responsible. I blanched, my hand frozen to the side of my cheek. 'You killed him,' I breathed, in horror. 'You killed George Talbot.' I dropped my handkerchief. 'Or arranged to have him killed.'

Julio Tejada was not about to admit anything. 'I came here to investigate an accident,' he asserted crisply. 'Nothing more. It should have been a simple affair. Then you arrived, señor, and things became more complicated.' He regarded my blood spattered body with contempt. 'Look at you. The grand Englishman. I should kill you now. Put you out of your misery.' He observed me grimly for a second and then, without ceremony, he thrust his cane into the muddy earth, twisting the top of it to form a short "T". I flinched again as he perched down on the top of the blunt cross and then moved his face close to mine. 'Luckily for you, señor, you can still be of some use to me.' He wrinkled his nose at the smell of the vomit and shifted his head back a fraction. 'That is the only reason you are still alive.' His hands were toying with his revolver. He was trying his damnedest to unnerve me and it was working.

'George Talbot.' I was still trying to make sense of that look in his eye. 'Did you...did you really have him killed?'

Tejada curled his lip. 'Talbot was interfering in my affairs. He was drawing attention to things that were none of his concern.'

Police corruption. That was what William had told me on the phone. Extortion. Money laundering. 'He was kicking up a fuss about your financial affairs?' I rubbed my nose nervously.

'He tried to. Mine and those of my fellow officers. So I drew his concerns to the attention of my brother-in-law. The general agreed with me that the man was making too much of a nuisance.'

Lord. I shuddered. If the chief of police had got involved then this was deep water indeed. George Talbot could not have fully understood what he was up against.

'And so...you arranged to have him killed?' My eyes dipped a little as I asked the question, but this time Tejada did not deny it. In fact, he did not say anything at all. His eyes were fixed on my face and I could see the calculation there. He knew he had nothing to fear from me. He could tell me anything he liked. I took a chance and asked the obvious follow up question. 'How did you do it?'

He smiled coldly. 'I have eyes and ears everywhere. People to do my bidding.' He lifted the revolver for emphasis. 'Whether they wish to or not.'

'But how did you know Mr Talbot was coming here this weekend?' I was struggling to understand the logistics of it all.

'I just told you,' he snapped. 'I have eyes and ears everywhere.'

'And you arranged for him to be...pushed down the stairs?'

The general laughed. It was not a pleasant sound. 'Accidents happen,' he declared. It was as close to an admission of guilt as I was likely to get.

'And that's why you came here in person? To investigate his death. To make sure it was all covered up.'

'You're not a complete fool then,' Tejada conceded.

'But who...who did the actual deed? Who pushed him down the stairs?'

'That is none of your concern.'

It didn't matter. I was pretty sure I already knew the answer. 'It was the engineer, wasn't it? Mr Gonzales?' He was the one who had gone down to the village to summon the authorities in the first place. 'He called you in'

'That idiot?' The bushy eyebrows furrowed.

'And he must have cut the telephone lines for you too.'

That got a reaction. 'How do you know about the telephone?'

'Er...just guesswork.'

The policeman grunted; but it was of no consequence. 'Sergeant Velázquez cut the line. He borrowed my motor-bicycle and drove out here last week.' So that was the vehicle Isabel had seen. The two were rather similar.

'But it *was* Mr Gonzales who called you in?'

Tejada shook his head. 'That fool has nothing to do with any of this. I have a man in the post office. He made sure the call was put through to me.' The general really did have eyes everywhere.

'And what about Mr Catesby? Steven?' I scarcely dared to ask. 'Did you...did you arrange his death too?'

He scowled. 'I have no interest in Señor Catesby, alive or dead. The man is nothing to me. Though his death has caused me a lot of unnecessary trouble.'

That I could believe. I had been in the bedroom when he had first caught sight of the body. 'But you do know who killed him though?' I couldn't resist posing the question, curiosity trumping my usual caution.

The general's response was unequivocal. 'Joseph Green killed him.'

'But he couldn't have done. You know that as well as...'

'I know nothing of the sort,' he growled. 'It doesn't matter what you or anybody else thinks. I did not come here to investigate a murder.'

'No, you just wanted to cover everything up.'

Again, the man did not deny it. 'And Joseph Green is a convenient scapegoat. Nobody will be surprised at a coloured man killing his employer, not when he has just been whipped.

There will be no awkward questions.'

Tejada would see a man hang, just for the sake of convenience. What kind of a policeman was he? A very successful one, it appeared. 'But how are you going to explain the other deaths? Mrs and Mrs Montana?'

'That has made things rather more complicated,' he admitted tersely. 'I hold you responsible for that. But I do not think it will be difficult to explain.' He jabbed a finger at my left shoulder. 'You killed Señora Montana. Her husband assaulted one of my officers and tried to kill you. I shot the man dead. That is all.'

His confidence was worrying. Was he intending to arrest me for the murder of Mrs Montana? Having just saved my life? 'But...but if you want to cover all this up...I mean, no-one's going to believe these deaths are just a coincidence. A man falling down the stairs.' I waved my hand for emphasis. 'Another having his throat cut. A woman dropping off a balcony and then another man being shot while resisting arrest. You can't seriously believe no-one's going to question any of that?'

The general sat back on his cane and regarded me with something akin to amusement. 'It does not matter what anyone believes. I am the law here. The truth is whatever I say it is.' He looked down at his revolver, which he had still not put away. Idly, he clicked open the barrel and checked the ammunition. There were still five bullets in there. He was probably right, I thought. His brother-in-law would back up anything he said and make sure there were no embarrassing consequences. 'All you have to consider, Señor Buxton,' he declared, closing up the barrel, 'is your own skin. Do you wish to die now, resisting arrest, like that fool down there?' He gestured contemptuously to the man he had just killed. 'Or do you wish to go free?'

I frowned, not sure what he was getting at. 'Free?'

Tejada leaned in again. This time his eyes were intense. 'Joseph Green. You heard him confess to the murder of Steven Catesby. He spoke to you and admitted entering his bedroom and cutting his throat. You will make a statement to that effect. And then you will live.'

I stared at the fellow in disbelief. 'You want me to incriminate Green?'

'That is exactly what I want you to do.' That was why he had pulled up a seat out in the garden; why he was bothering to talk to me at all. For all his brutality, he was a clever, calculating man. 'And in return, I will conclude that Señora Montana's death was an unfortunate accident. And Sergeant Velázquez will confirm it.'

'But...but....' I stammered. 'You can't....I mean...I can't let an innocent man hang.'

'It is your choice,' Tejada stated grimly. He lifted his revolver and rested the barrel of the gun against my temple. 'You have ten seconds to decide.' His finger tightened around the trigger.

'No, but...' I stuttered. My head was spinning. This was all too much to take in.

'One...' he began.

For a moment, I was unable to breathe. I had no doubt that the general would carry out his threat. If I didn't agree to his plan, he would shoot me dead; not at some future date, but right now, this instant, out here on the lawn. If I refused to incriminate Green then I would not live another minute; and while I had no desire to see the labourer hang, I valued my own life too. I stared blindly at the revolver, just out of focus above my eyebrows. I could feel the pressure of it against my temple and I shuddered. Was I prepared to give my life to save Joseph Green? Even if I did, could I be sure Tejada wouldn't just kill him anyway? Better to save my own neck, surely? At least agree for the time being?

'Six....seven...'

I was just on the point of articulating my complete capitulation when a flicker of movement from the far side of the garden caught the general's attention. The foliage was rustling, just beyond the gate. He abandoned the count and raised the gun from my temple. 'You there!' he bellowed, jumping to his feet. 'Stay where you are!'

My head whipped round and I caught sight of a slim figure on the dark pathway leading away from the house.

242

Tejada took careful aim with his revolver. 'Move forward where I can see you,' he barked. But the figure ignored his instructions and the general opened fire. The shot went wide, though only because the retreating figure had ducked down as he had scuttled away. I had a moment of déjà vu, watching him go. This, I felt inexplicably certain, was the same fellow I had seen rushing across the lawn on Saturday evening; and though I could scarcely make out anything in the all-consuming darkness between the trees, I was convinced I knew who it was. The house boy Moses. He was the one who had spiked the generator.

Tejada did not get the chance to take a second shot. Instead, I heard a loud clang and, looking back in surprise, I saw the policeman freeze, his mouth framed into an abrupt 'O'. Then, with grim inevitability, his body began to fall towards me. I leapt sideways as the general crumpled to his knees. He clipped the back of my legs and lurched to the ground. Behind him stood a formidable middle-aged German. It was the housekeeper, Greta. In her hand was a large metal coffee pot. She had been carrying it back to the kitchen for another refill, but seeing what the general was about to do she had crept down the steps and struck Tejada from behind. Now she regarded his body in horror, spread-eagled as it was alongside the corpse of Arthur Montana. I could read her expression and the same thought echoed inside my own battered head: what on earth had she done?

'I could not let him shoot Moses,' the housekeeper mumbled, in her thick German accent. She too had recognised the lad in silhouette. 'I could not.'

'It's all right,' I reassured her, as she dropped the coffee pot to the ground. 'Everything's going to be fine.' But I was lying. Things were far from fine, and any joy I might have felt at seeing a brute like Tejada clobbered from behind had already been tempered by the realisation that such an assault would have serious repercussions. I stared down at the uniformed figure. The general had offered me a way out of this mess – albeit a rather dishonourable one – but that offer had evaporated the moment Greta had hit him. I would probably be blamed for her actions, if he was still alive. He would say...my god. *If* he was alive. I looked down at the bulky figure in sudden panic. Please god, don't let him be dead, I thought.

Greta had had the same thought. Her hands were shaking at the enormity of what she had done. 'Is he...?'

'I don't know,' I admitted, my own body shuddering as I shuffled across on my knees to examine him. If Tejada was dead then that was the end of everything. It wouldn't just be my life that was over. Nobody here would be safe. A senior policeman dying in the middle of an investigation. It was unthinkable. There would be reprisals. His brother-in-law would see to that. No one here would escape. The labourers, the house guests, the owners. It would be nothing short of a massacre.

The weight of the world was pressing down on my shoulders as I reached out and tentatively placed a hand on the back of his head, where the coffee pot had struck him. There was no brain matter or blood there, except the dull smudge already on my fingertips from Arthur Montana; and now that I was close to him, I could see the gentle rise and fall of his chest. I shut my eyes momentarily, the relief shuddering through me. 'He's still alive,' I breathed. I opened my eyes and smiled weakly up at the housekeeper. 'He's out cold, though. You must have hit him pretty hard.'

'My boy...' she muttered again, in half-hearted explanation.

The general's revolver had flown from his hand and skittered across the lawn. I pushed myself up onto my feet, wincing slightly as the life finally returned to my legs, and moved across to retrieve the weapon. Two guns, in fact. Montana's stolen revolver was lying next to Tejada's. I picked them both up and stuffed them into my jacket pockets. Better to get them both out of circulation.

Lord, what a mess, I thought, straightening myself up. Four men clobbered in the space of fifteen minutes and one of them now dead. It was too much to take in. I had come here for a quiet weekend, but in the last hour I had been held at gunpoint twice and had only managed to survive by the skin of my teeth. The worst of it was, it was not over yet. I looked down at my sodden clothes and took a moment to wipe some of the mud from my trousers. The suit was completely ruined. Maurice would have a fit. And as soon as Tejada woke up, my life would be at an end. Greta would be put up against a wall and shot; and the same would probably happen to me too. What the hell was I going to do?

Behind us, Susan Weiman had returned to the terrace. 'Moses!' she called out, across the lawn. She too had recognised her son.

'It's all right!' I shouted, peering through the gloom beyond the garden gate. 'The general's out cold. You can come back to the house now. It's safe.'

General Tejada took that moment to let out a muffled groan, giving the lie to my reassurance. Lord, he was beginning to come round.

Greta's reactions were quicker than mine. She dipped low, retrieved the coffee pot and clouted the general a second time across the back of the head. My mouth fell open as the man slumped back into the mud, instantly unconscious.

'For heaven sake!' I hissed, glaring at the housekeeper. 'What the devil did you do that for?'

'Moses...' she muttered, gesturing across to the gate. I could see the anger in her eyes as well as the fear. She would not allow any harm to come to her adopted son.

I squatted down next to the policeman, to make sure she hadn't done any permanent damage. 'We need Tejada alive!' I declared. Thankfully, he did not appear to be seriously injured. I stood up anyway and grabbed hold of the housekeeper. 'Do you understand? If he dies, we all die.' My hands gripped her shoulders tightly and my eyes bored into her. 'You cannot lay another finger on him.'

She nodded stiffly, unable to meet my gaze. Susan Weiman stepped down from the terrace to join us. I took the coffee pot from the housekeeper's grasp and handed it to her mistress. Greta stared down at the unconscious figure, her face quivering with fear and hatred.

Moses was now moving back towards the garden. The

245

light was so dim I could barely make him out, but I could hear the rustle of the trees. Isabel had brought a couple of lamps out onto the terrace, illuminating the grim tableaux and serving to reassure the young lad that everything was all right. With our encouragement, he pulled open the gate and sprinted across the grass, skipping around the two prone figures. Greta threw open her arms and Moses leapt into her embrace, hugging her as tightly as he could. The housekeeper had tears streaming down her face.

Mrs Weiman stood back, numbly, watching the display of affection but unable to join in. The relief in her eyes, however, was more than adequate compensation. She clutched the coffee pot to her breast instead. The devil's brew, more use out here than it had ever been in the dining room.

I moved across to the boy. 'It's all right, you're safe now,' I reassured him. He pulled back from the housekeeper and looked up at me. Safe. That was another lie, but a necessary one. The last thing I needed was him taking fright and running off again. The necessity of reassuring the lad also served to ground me a little and, for the time being, I was able to contain my own panic. Perhaps I did have a little of the maternal instinct in me after all. 'Where's Joseph?' I asked.

Moses gave me a toothy grin. 'He is back there.' He gestured to the gate. 'Up the lane. One of the policemen found us. There was a fight. Joseph was hurt.'

'And the policeman?'

Moses grinned. 'He is unconscious now.'

'Did he see you?' Mrs Weiman asked, fearfully. 'The policeman?' Did he know who had helped Green to escape?

'No. But Joseph knocked him out and we used his own handcuffs to tie him up.'

'Good for you,' I said, ruffling the boy's hair.

The other guests were coming back onto the terrace, staring down numbly at the bizarre scene. Handcuffs, I thought. That was a good idea. If we could tie the policemen up and dump them somewhere quiet, that would give us a bit of a breathing space; some time to work out what the hell to do next. 'Where's Morris?' I called across to the assembled group.

If any of us were to get out of this alive, we needed someone with half a brain.

'I am here, Monsieur,' the valet replied, emerging from the back hall, clutching the side of his battered bonce.

'Are you all right?' It was not often I saw the man out of sorts.

'Yes, Monsieur,' he replied, without elaboration. That was the second time this week he had been sloshed from behind. It was becoming a habit. Luckily for him, Montana's thwack had done no serious damage, though it had floored him for a couple of minutes. Now, the valet moved down the steps towards me and took in the scene.

'What the devil are we going to do?' I hissed, briefly summarizing events.

Maurice took a moment to think. 'The bags are packed, Monsieur. It might be better if we were to leave here as soon as possible.'

I nodded sadly. He was right. It was our only option. Things had gone too far now to negotiate any kind of settlement. We would have to scarper. But if we were to escape the scene completely, we would need to have a decent head start and that meant preventing anybody here from raising the alarm.

Joseph Green had popped up tentatively at the garden gate. I waved him forward. 'It's all right,' I said. 'It's safe now.' He too was covered in mud and blood. His bewildered expression matched that of my own, though with a fair degree of fear added to the mix. This time it was Moses who provided the reassurance. He disentangled himself from Greta and rushed across to the older man. If the housekeeper was effectively his mother, then Green was definitely the father figure. Poor devil. He was every bit as entangled in this affair as I was, through no fault of his own. Well, some fault, I reflected. If he hadn't arranged to meet me like that when he was meant to be working then things might have played out a little differently. But this was no time for recriminations. The fellow looked exhausted. Even a couple of hours on the run had taken its toll. He would have to come with us, I realised abruptly, if he was to stand any chance of avoiding the noose. Green hugged the boy and the two of them stepped back towards the house.

'Moses said you thumped one of the policemen,' I observed.

The man nodded uneasily. 'Yes, mister. I had no choice.'

'He hurt you?' The labourer had a slight limp, I noticed.

'My leg. It is nothing.'

'But he's out cold? The policeman?' That was the important point.

'Yes, mister. I hit him quite hard. I...don't know my own strength.'

I waved away his concern. 'You don't have to explain.' That was three out of the four policemen accounted for. 'Where is he?'

'Just along the lane there. What happened?' He gestured to the bodies.

'A god awful cock up,' I replied, as honestly as I could. 'Have you ever handled a gun?' I fumbled in my jacket for Montana's revolver.

Green eyes widened in surprise as I whipped it out. 'No, mister.'

'Well, now's the time to start. We need to get shot of the police.' He regarded my hand in alarm as I proffered the weapon. 'Sorry, bad choice of words. I mean, we need to lock them up, get them out of the way. Which one found you? Was it the sergeant, Velázquez?'

'No, mister. I don't know the man.'

'Damn. So Vela...'

'Henry, look out!' Freddie Reeves was standing on the terrace. He pointed a finger eastward, to the far side of the house. A bright light flitted out from the pathway, by the store houses where Green had been incarcerated. There was our fourth man, I realised. Velázquez, doubtless hurrying back from the edge of the estate to investigate the sound of gunfire.

I had no time to find a defensive position. I took out the second revolver and placed my legs firmly either side of the unconscious general. I aimed the pistol down at him as Sergeant Velázquez barrelled into view. I took a deep breath and then called out, 'Stop right there!' as authoritatively as I could. 'Drop your weapon!' I added, with slightly less vigour, before the sergeant had time to take in the scene.

Joseph Green was covering him with the other revolver. He had moved closer to the house and his heavy frame was bathed in the terrace lamp light. Two against one. The boggle eyed sergeant boggled even more at the sight of the armed fugitive than he did at me, though in truth poor old Green was shaking like a leaf. He had never held a gun on anyone before. Thankfully, Velázquez proved to be an abject coward. He raised his hands without a second glance and slowly bobbed down to place his revolver on the grass in front of him. He dropped his torch, too, for good measure. The government did not pay him enough to risk his neck in this kind of stand-off. At my direction, he kicked the revolver across.

I signalled Green forward. 'Joseph. If you wouldn't mind?' The labourer took a moment to gather himself and then darted over to collect the gun. Afterwards, with greater confidence, he directed the sergeant across to me.

'On your knees,' I said, with more authority than I felt. Green handed me the second revolver. 'Morris?'

'Monsieur?' The valet stepped forward.

This was as far as my planning had come. 'What the hell do I do now?' I whispered, my authority abruptly deflating.

'Keep calm, Monsieur,' Maurice advised. He strode across to the sergeant and removed the handcuffs from the fellow's waist. He grabbed the keys too and then pulled the policeman's arms behind his back. The manacles were quickly clicked into position. 'We will lock them up,' he suggested, 'in the outhouse over there.' The generator room, where Moses had shoved that thick branch yesterday evening.

'Good idea,' I agreed. The valet moved back to me and I handed him the sergeant's gun. 'Can you take care of that fellow Montana clobbered? Out on the front terrace?'

'Of course, Monsieur. I will bring him here.'

'And Doctor Rubio, too.' There was no telling whose

side the elderly doctor would be on. The valet departed to round up the stragglers.

'Freddie,' I called across. 'Would you go with Green here and get the other officer? He's up there in the lane somewhere.'

Frederick Reeves had been observing the whole affair in some confusion. 'You want me to...?' Every diplomatic bone in his body was screaming out not to get involved. 'I don't think I should...'

'Freddie, just help him!' Miss Bunting snapped.

I had no time for pussyfooting around either. 'If it helps,' I said, 'just imagine I'm pointing a gun at you.' I pointed a gun at him, just to emphasize the point. 'And be quick about it, there's a good fellow.'

Freddie rushed off to do as he was bidden, with the armed Joseph Green in tow. Moses returned to the embrace of Greta, who had stepped back onto the terrace now and was standing next to Mr and Mrs Weiman. Gunther seemed to have aged several hundred years in the last few minutes. I knew exactly how he felt.

Sergeant Velázquez was on his knees in front of me, looking across at Tejada's unconscious body. 'Is he dead?' he asked me now.

'No. He was knocked out, but he's still alive.'

His face lit up in a cruel grin. 'You want *me* to kill him?'

'No! Lord no!' Evidently there was no love lost between the two men. 'If *he* dies, we all die.' That probably included the sergeant too. 'Miss Bunting! Would you mind awfully opening up the generator room for me? My hands are a bit full at the moment.'

'Yes, of course,' the girl agreed, tripping down the steps into the garden.

'And we might need a bit of rope....'

Chapter Seventeen

It took about twenty minutes to get Tejada and his men tied up. The light was gone completely now so we had to borrow the policemen's torches to help us. No-one had had time to repair the generator and the lamps from the hacienda proved rather underwhelming away from the house.

The policemen were not the only ones who needed to be locked up. There was also the overseer, Mr Langbroek. Even with that broken leg of his, he could not be left to his own devices in the living room. 'What the bloody hell is this?' the man muttered as Maurice prepared the stretcher.

'Keep quiet and you won't get hurt,' I said, brandishing my revolver. The overseer was not about to argue with an armed man, but neither was he happy when he discovered we were going to tie him up. Doctor Rubio made a token protest on his behalf, but agreed nonetheless to give Maurice a hand transporting him across to the outhouse. Rubio was a genial old buffer but he would have to be tied up as well. I could not be certain where his loyalties lay. We had four sets of handcuffs and some hefty rope. 'I think we can forego the gag, in your case,' I told the doctor. The cotton bedsheets Miss Bunting had ripped up would only go so far. 'If you give me your word you won't try to wake the general.'

'You have my word,' he said.

Sergeant Velázquez was glaring at us from the far corner of the outhouse. He was the first one we had gagged. His arms had been threaded through one of the wheels of the generator – just below the splintered branch – before we had attached the handcuffs, to prevent him moving about. The general, who was still out for the count, was also tightly bound. Greta must have thumped him pretty hard that second time, though the doctor seemed to think he had suffered no permanent damage.

At last, after a quick mercy trip to the bushes for Doctor Rubio, we had the six men exactly where we wanted them, in the darkness of the generator room. I closed the door myself and locked it up, with my valet and Joseph Green standing either side of me as I did so. We had been careful to make sure we were the only ones any of them had seen brandishing weapons. That had been Maurice's idea. Better, he said, that the three of us should be seen to be in control of the situation, with the rest of the household reluctantly doing our bidding. That way, we could minimise the repercussions for them when the police were eventually freed.

Maurice and I had had a short but intense discussion of our options. It was not just a question of fleeing the scene. As wanted men, there would be nowhere safe for us in the whole of Guatemala. Ideally, we needed to get out of the country as quickly as we could. And, if we were to save his life, we would have to take Joseph Green with us.

The labourer was astonished when we suggested the idea. 'But this is my home,' he protested. 'My life. My friends. My family. I cannot leave.'

'It's not safe for you here,' I told him calmly. 'If you stay, you'll be hanged for murder.'

Green could not deny the truth of that; but that was not the only consideration. His good name mattered to him too. 'If I leave, people will think I am guilty.'

'The police already think you're guilty. Look, we don't have time to discuss this...'

'And the real murderer...'

'Is probably already dead. Listen Green, I understand how difficult this is for you, but we really have no choice. If you stay, General Tejada will see you hang. Far better to come with us and live to fight another day.'

Reluctantly, the man accepted the force of the argument. Escape was the only practical option available to him.

'That's the spirit. Now go and get yourself cleaned up. Isabel can dig out some fresh clothes for you. We need to leave within the hour.'

I bundled him off into the house.

There were two motor-bicycles at our disposal, parked out front of the hacienda. We would only need one of them – the sidecar would provide space for an additional passenger –

and I had already grabbed the keys to Mr Gonzales' vehicle from the general's top pocket. 'You've ridden a motor-bicycle before, haven't you?' I asked Maurice.

'Yes, Monsieur. As a young man.'

That was that then. We would motor down to the village and then make for British Honduras, the nearest safe haven. Unfortunately, there was no accessible road border. Transport links between the two countries were severely limited. 'I'm afraid our only option is to head to Puerto Barrios. We'll have to catch a boat.'

'A boat, Monsieur?' Maurice paled. He must have realised that would be on the cards, but he could not disguise his concern. My valet had an abject fear of the sea. I had only got him to accompany me to the Americas in the first place because I had managed to get tickets on board an airship.

'Do you think you'll be able to manage it?' I asked, with some concern.

'I do not know,' he answered honestly.

'Look, if there were any other way...' I waved my hands. 'As soon as the general is released from that shack, there'll be no safe place for either of us in the whole of Guatemala. And there's no other country we could get to in the time. It'll only be a short hop. A few hours at most.' Still the valet did not look happy. 'Perhaps we can find you some sleeping pills, knock you out for the duration. We've got no other option, Morris. The general was all set to shoot me, even before that damned woman clobbered him. And it's not as if I'll be able to go back to the office on Monday morning. When news of all this breaks, Mr Richards will have my head on a plate. We have no choice.'

Maurice steeled himself. 'Very well, Monsieur.'

'You'll do it?'

'Yes, Monsieur.'

I slapped him on the back. 'Good man. Oh, I meant what I said about the sleeping tablets. Better to knock you out on the boat if we can. Perhaps we can find some here before we leave.'

'I believe there may be a bottle in the kitchen,

253

Monsieur,' the valet said, after a moment's thought. 'Madame Talbot was given some tablets last night to help her sleep.'

'Oh, yes. I remember.' After her husband had died. She had needed a good dose of something to knock her out. 'Good lord.' I blinked.

'Monsieur?'

'That's it!' The explanation suddenly dropped into my mind. 'That's how it was done.' My face lit up in surprise as the details slotted into place. 'Sleeping tablets. That's why Catesby didn't struggle. That's how someone was able to slit his throat in the middle of the night without him waking up or reacting at all. He must have taken a sleeping draft. There was a glass by the bed. And every room has a jug of water.'

The valet nodded carefully. 'That is a reasonable hypothesis, Monsieur.'

'It's not a hypothesis,' I snapped. 'It's a cast iron certainty. But did he take it himself or was it forced upon him?' Could one of the servants have done the deed, rather than one of the guests?

'I do not know, Monsieur. Perhaps we can discuss this further once we have left the hacienda? I need to check up on the motor-bicycle.'

'Yes, yes, of course. You're right.' There was no time to play the detective now. We had more important things to worry about. I tossed him the keys. 'Make sure we've got plenty of petrol. It's going to be a long journey. Syphon off a bit from the other one if needs be.'

'Of course, Monsieur.'

'And we'll have to nobble Tejada's bicycle as well,' I realised. 'Don't want him speeding after us.' The general could damn well walk down to the village, when the time came. Or take a horse. He would have to go to the post office or Alberto's bar if he wanted to alert the rest of the police force. Hoist on his own petard. Served him right for cutting the phone line to the hacienda. 'I'd better go and have a quiet word with Miss Bunting,' I said. 'And then I'll need to speak to the rest of the household...'

'It's never going to work,' Freddie Reeves said, when I explained the plan to him. 'It's madness. Why not just head back to the capital? Hide out at the legation. You may not have diplomatic immunity, but they can't arrest you if you're camped out at a British consulate.'

I laughed sourly. 'You really think the minister will protect me? When the national police force comes knocking at the door, enquiring into the death of Mrs Montana?'

His shoulders slumped. 'No, I don't suppose he would. But, hey look, everyone knows that was an accident.'

'You know it was an accident and I know it was an accident. And General Tejada knows it too. But do you really think that will make any difference? The general will be gunning for me now. I have no choice. I have to get out of the country.'

'To British Honduras?'

'It's the only place I can go. We've got the passports. All I need is a few hours grace to get to Puerto Barrios and onto a boat. That's why we have to lock everyone up. You included.' The house guests would be incarcerated in the servants' cottage for the duration. 'So nobody gets it into their heads to let the police out before tomorrow morning.'

Freddie scratched his chin. 'But what will you do when you get to Belize?'

'Contact the governor. Get a message to London, telling them my side of the story. I have a few connections back home. I'll get a fair hearing from them, if not from the minister.' I would throw myself on the mercy of my real bosses.

'I know a couple of blokes in the governor's office in British Honduras. I could probably put in a word for you.'

'That would be appreciated.'

'You'll like it there. It's a nice place. Got a really relaxed feel to it.' Freddie grinned. 'But hey, what about the people back home? In the Foreign Office? If the government of Guatemala makes an official complaint, they'll hit the roof!'

'It won't come to that. Tejada came here to cover up his own wrong doing. He won't want to draw attention to events.

255

It'll look bad for him, especially if he had the man responsible under lock and key and let him escape.'

Freddie was sceptical. 'You're really going to take Joseph Green with you?'

'What choice do I have? He's a dead man if I leave him behind. He has to come with us. But to be honest, it's the boy Moses I'm really worried about. You know it was him who spiked the generator.'

'You're joking!' Freddie laughed. 'The little tyke!'

'He's stronger than he looks.' The boy must have found a suitable branch on Saturday afternoon and stashed it somewhere close by, before skipping out after dark to nobble the generator. It had been his way of getting his own back on the family after Joseph Green had been whipped. 'But if the general realises it was him who released Green...well, it doesn't bear thinking about. You've got to make sure he doesn't make the connection. It was my man Maurice who let Green out of that hut, at my insistence.'

'Of course it was.' Freddie grinned again. 'Blimey, you've got it all worked out.' He shook his head, dumbfounded. 'I can't believe you're being so calm about it all.'

'I don't *feel* calm,' I said. 'But when your neck is on the line it does focus the mind somewhat. I'm relying on you, Freddie. You have to keep Moses out of it.'

'Are you sure the general didn't recognise him, when he fired at the gate?'

'I'm fairly sure. It was too dark for him to know who he was shooting at. He'll assume it was Green. And, so far as anybody here is concerned, it was my man Maurice who crept up and clobbered him from behind. You've got to make sure everybody understands that. We don't want to get the housekeeper into any trouble, for protecting that lad of hers.'

'Don't worry,' Freddie said. 'You can rely on me. I'll make sure they stick to the story.'

I had already given a brief pep talk to the other householders. Once we had dealt with the police and carried the body of Mr Montana to the front of the house, where he was laid out respectfully next to his wife, I had shuffled them across to the servants' cottage and told them everything they needed to know. My man and I – and Joseph Green – were responsible for everything that had happened in the last few hours. It was a bare faced lie, of course, and most of them knew it, but I did my best to impress on them the value of sticking to the story. To my surprise, the group accepted the idea – and even the necessity of being locked up for the night – with little complaint. 'It's for your own protection,' I assured them. 'If the general thinks you were complicit in his incarceration then you'll all be up against the wall as soon as the sun's over the horizon tomorrow morning. Just stick to the story. We were the ones who were armed. You were just following orders.'

'And for god's sake,' I added now, to Freddie, 'make sure you keep them inside that cottage until at least nine am.'

This time, there was no necessity for handcuffs or gags. Freddie and Miss Bunting could keep an eye on the rest of the householders through the early hours. Neither was there any need to withhold the regular comforts. Mrs Weiman had accompanied Greta to the kitchen to prepare a bit of cold food to see them all through the night. I had taken a few minutes then to get myself cleaned up, washing away the mud and blood of the last hour – and pouring myself a large glass of whisky – before finalizing the arrangements for our departure.

'I'll keep them quiet,' Freddie agreed. 'But what do you think will happen when we let the general out in the morning? I'm not worried for myself,' he added hastily, lest I should think him a coward, 'I'm thinking about Emily. What happens if he takes out his anger on us?'

'It is a possibility,' I conceded. 'I can't pretend otherwise.' As fellow members of the British legation, they might reasonably expect to be in the firing line. Tejada had no great love of the British. 'Look, you'd better release him yourself. Smash a window in the cottage, pretend you broke out, then open up the generator room and untie him yourself. That should get you in his good books.'

'Let's hope so!' Freddie grinned nervously.

'I don't think you need worry, though. He's more likely to take out his anger on his own men. Just...feel free to say

257

what you like about me. The nastier the better. The general will be more concerned with chasing Green and me than hanging around here to batter any of you.'

'And when he finds out you've left the country?'

I shrugged. 'Then I imagine he'll be looking to limit the fallout. He may be a brute but he's not a fool. He's not going to do anything that casts himself in a bad light. He's got four dead bodies in hand. He can concoct any explanation he likes. I'm sure Mr and Mrs Weiman will back any story he puts out, if it means they are left alone. And that's all he needs.'

'So he'll get away with it, then?' Freddie said. 'Arranging George Talbot's death?' I had told the Englishman all about the general's confession.

'Probably,' I admitted, with some distaste. 'But he'll get his comeuppance one day. That sort always does.'

'And what am I going to say to the minister, when me and Emily get back to Guatemala City?'

I chuckled, picturing Mr Richard's face turning a bright shade of puce when he heard all the details. Part of me wished I could be there to see it. If I had to abandon the damn job, I was happy to cause maximum embarrassment to the head of the mission. That said, I had no desire to hurt Freddie's career prospects, even if it had been his foolishness that had brought me to this point. 'Tell him you were caught up in events. You had no idea what was going on. I got myself involved out of a misplaced sense of duty and ended up implicating myself. But essentially it was a domestic dispute; and you being here was just bad luck. The same for Miss Bunting. Ah, speak of the devil.'

Emily Bunting was descending the hall stairs, carrying a small brown holdall. She wore a quiet smile, as she arrived at the bottom. 'I borrowed the bag from your room, Freddie. I hope you don't mind.' The blond man waved away the inconvenience. 'I hope this will do. It's the best I could manage.' Her eyes were twinkling as she as handed it over.

Freddie was in on the idea. He looked from the holdall to me in amusement. 'It's never going to work.' He laughed. 'You'll never get away with it.'

Miss Bunting wiped a fleck of dust from my suit. 'I'm sure you'll do very well.' She beamed.

'It's only for a few hours,' I said, pulling out my pocket watch and coughing with embarrassment. 'And the passports are genuine, if nothing else.' No customs official would look twice at them. 'There are some advantages to being a passport control officer.'

'You certainly think ahead,' Freddie observed, with a smirk. 'What will you do about Joseph?'

'I've got a blank passport he can use. Maurice has already filled it out. There shouldn't be any problem passing him off as a British subject. Jamaican stock and all that.'

'But you'll need a photograph, won't you?'

'We'll cut and paste the one from his identity card. It's not ideal but it'll serve, if they don't look too closely.' I smiled, glancing down at the holdall. 'Thank you for this, Miss Bunting.'

'It's the least I can do, Mr Buxton.' The girl was grinning from ear to ear.

'Give us a minute, will you Freddie?' I asked. 'I need to have a quick word with your girlfriend.'

'Oh. Right. I'll...er...I'll head back to the servants' cottage.' Freddie waved a hand and moved out of the hall.

For a moment Miss Bunting and I stood alone, quietly observing each other. 'Is there anything else I can do for you?' she asked, at length.

'Yes.' I lowered my voice. 'Send a coded message to London. Tell them my cover was blown and I had to flee. Get them to send you out a replacement as soon as possible.'

She smiled shyly. 'The office won't be the same without you...Hilary.'

'Probably just as well,' I said. 'But I'm happy to let some other poor sap take the reins. You and William will have to manage things in the meantime, though.'

'I'm sure we'll be able to handle it.'

'I'd recommend you as replacement, but...well.' I sucked in my cheeks. 'A woman as passport control officer. They'd never stomach it.'

She laughed. 'If only they knew.' All at once, her face fell. 'I'm so sorry that I didn't...that I wasn't more honest with you about...everything.' She looked up. 'Did you...did you really think I might have murdered Steven Catesby?'

'I didn't know what to think,' I told her, honestly. Her eyes dropped again. She was putting a brave face on it, but my suspicions had clearly hurt her feelings. 'I hoped not, anyway. You didn't seem...well, you don't strike me as a murderess.'

'Will we ever know who really did it?' she wondered.

'Tejada was responsible for Mr Talbot's death. That much I do know. But as for Catesby...'

'Do you think it might have been Mr Montana who killed him?'

'It's possible.' I shrugged. My gabbled explanation to the general might not have been completely wide of the mark. 'Probably better if everyone believes that, anyway. Officially, of course, Green will be held to blame. That's why he has to come with us. The poor fellow. He won't even get the chance to say goodbye to his friends.' The other labourers had been instructed by the police to remain in their homes after Green had made his escape and the less they knew about subsequent events the less chance there would be for any gossip to spread. For once, even Alberto would be in the dark.

'Moses will be very sad to see him go,' Miss Bunting said.

'I dare say. But it's for the best. For him and for me.'

'It's been such a dreadful weekend. All these horrible deaths. All these lives ruined. I shall be glad to get home to the legation.'

'Yes, give my love to the minister,' I commented, dryly. 'He'll be glad to see the back of me.' I picked up the holdall and unstrapped the top, taking a quick peek inside.

'You must be careful on that motor-bicycle,' Miss Bunting said. 'It looks awfully dangerous.'

'Don't worry. Maurice will keep a steady pace.'

'It's not safe, though, travelling these roads at night. You hear such stories...'

'Actually, I'm more concerned about the road blocks

than bandits,' I confessed. 'But we should be all right. Safety in numbers and all that.'

'And when you get to Belize, how will you get by? For money I mean?'

I grinned and patted my breast pocket. 'Oh, I have some funds set aside...'

Her eyes glittered in surprise. 'You don't mean...?'

I laughed. 'Well, I wasn't about to leave it with the general, was I?' I had slipped the banker's draft out of Tejada's top pocket when I had handcuffed him.

Miss Bunting giggled with delight.

'It should set me up nicely in the Port of Belize, if I decide to stay there.' A banker's draft was as good as cash and I would have no trouble converting it. Luckily, most bankers – unlike Mr Talbot – knew not to ask too many questions. 'And I dare say I can spare a few coppers for Mr Green too, to help him set himself up somewhere. Unless you have any objections?'

'No, no.' She beamed again. 'You deserve it. Crumbs, I wish I had never found that dratted piece of paper. You must think me such a wicked creature, keeping it all from you like that. And even considering the possibility of...of keeping the money.'

'Don't be too hard on yourself, Miss Bunting. Emily. We're all human. We're all open to temptation. The important thing is, you didn't yield to it.'

'Unlike you...' she teased.

'Well. Only in exceptional circumstances.' I coughed. 'In any case, as far as the office is concerned, the money's already been written off.' Giles Markham had taken the blame for that and he was beyond the reach of the law.

Miss Bunting turned her attention to more practical matters. 'What on earth will you do with yourself in British Honduras? Will you be able to find a job?'

'That remains to be seen. Freddie says he'll put in a good word. He knows a couple of people in the governor's office, apparently.'

She smiled at the thought of that. 'He can be very

261

considerate, sometimes.'

'Yes, he can. He's not a complete dolt, you know. And he's rather sweet on you.'

She nodded seriously. 'I'm rather sweet on him too. I think he would marry me, if I let him.'

I laughed. 'You'd make a fine couple.'

She grinned again. 'I'm not sure I'm ready to settle down yet. I wouldn't want to give up my career. Not just yet, anyway.' She glanced down at the bag. 'We'll come and visit you, in Belize. The two of us. When all the dust has settled. We wouldn't want to lose touch.'

'You won't,' I said. 'And thank you for...well, for keeping my secret too.'

She smiled and kissed me gently on the cheek.

'We've made you a few sandwiches to take with you,' Susan Weiman declared, handing across a small package in brown paper. 'You're bound to get hungry, driving all through the night.'

'That's very kind of you,' I said, accepting the gift. 'It's a shame we won't be able to stop for dinner.' Actually, I was rather pleased to avoid another home cooked meal. Greta had been threatening us with stewed dumplings, according to Maurice. That and the foul coffee would just about have finished me off. The sandwiches were a nice thought, however, though I hesitated to ask what the filling might be. Greta, in any case, had been preoccupied preparing more elaborate food, which she and Isabel were now transporting across to the servants' cottage. I did not want the "prisoners" to go without sustenance during the night. Mrs Weiman and I followed the servants down the steps out onto the lawn. I was holding the general's large torch and providing the light for the company as they made their way through the west gate into the kitchen garden and then across to the cottage itself.

Mrs Weiman and I stopped for a moment at the gate, as the two servants made their way inside. Joseph Green was standing on the porch, a revolver tucked awkwardly into the back of his trousers. Moses was at his side, holding his hand, and the two were chatting animatedly. I was too far away to hear what they were saying but even outside the direct glare of the torch and with only minimal light from the lamps in the cottage I could tell it was a touching scene. Green would promise to stay in touch, of course, but realistically the two of them were unlikely ever to see each other again.

'He'll miss him terribly,' Susan Weiman lamented. 'Poor Moses.'

'He's young. He'll get over it.' I rested the torch on top of the gate post and slipped the packet of sandwiches into the pocket of my jacket; then I pulled out my cigarette case. 'And he's still got Greta.'

Mrs Weiman nodded sadly.

'Will you ever tell him?' I asked, grabbing a cigarette and closing up the case. 'That you're his real mother?'

'I don't think so. Better for him not to know. Though goodness knows how any of us are going to explain this weekend.'

'I don't think you need to worry about that.' I fumbled for my lighter and lit the cigarette. 'General Tejada will tell you what to think. Whatever damn fool story he comes up with, just accept it. Don't do anything to antagonize him. Blame it all on Green and me.' I pocketed the lighter and took a slow drag.

Mrs Weiman was uncomfortable with that idea. 'Moses will be very upset, if he hears me saying anything unkind about Joseph.'

'That can't be helped.' I exhaled a cloud of smoke. 'He'll understand, when he's a bit older.'

'And you, losing your job. I can't help feeling it's all my fault. This house.' She shivered, her face a pale glow in the torchlight. 'I think we must be cursed.'

'I've had quieter weekends,' I admitted, dryly. 'But don't worry about me. I'm used to starting afresh. It's the others I feel sorry for. Mr and Mrs Montana, did they...have children?' I hadn't thought to ask before now.

Mrs Weiman nodded. 'A boy and a girl. Both adults now.'

263

'Lord.' I took another drag of my cigarette. 'And Jane Talbot, with her daughter.' Another unknowing victim. Doubtless the Englishwoman would be halfway home by now. 'It's all been one god-awful mess,' I said.

'Do you...do you know if George really was murdered?' Mrs Weiman asked hesitantly.

'Oh, he was murdered all right. Tejada admitted it.'

'The general did?'

'He arranged it all. One of his agents, apparently.' I still hadn't worked out who.

'That horrible man! He really...?'

'I'm afraid so.'

'And...and Steven. Did he...?'

'No. The general had nothing to do with that. Although I think the two events were probably connected somehow.'

'Gunther was convinced Steven was responsible for George's death.'

'Was he?' I blew out another cloud of smoke. That was news to me. 'Hardly surprising, I suppose. All that business with the banker's draft. It was bound to cause a bit of ill feeling. Was that what the two of them were rowing about last night, in the generator room?' It had struck me at the time that there must have been more to it than just anger at the wrecking of the machine.

Mrs Weiman nodded numbly. 'Gunther accused Steven of pushing him down the stairs.'

'Good lord.' So that was it. 'And how did your cousin react to that?'

'He was very upset. He couldn't believe my husband would think him capable of murdering anybody, especially a friend of the family. Steven and Gunther...they never really got on. And it all came to a head last night.' Mrs Weiman shuddered. 'I thought they might come to blows.'

Perhaps one of them did, I thought suddenly; but I kept that thought to myself. Weiman did not strike me as the violent type. 'It did sound like quite a nasty argument,' I said, tapping out a bit of ash from the end of my cigarette.

'Gunther threatened to go to the police – to tell the

authorities what Steven had done; or what he thought he had done. And Steven...Steven threatened to tell everyone about...about...' She gestured across the lawn to the cottage.

'About Moses?' I coughed awkwardly. 'He knew about that?'

'Yes. He couldn't help but know. Moses...his face. He's the spitting image of my mother.' The woman who had taken that family portrait in the living room. 'As soon as Steven came here, he knew. He's never liked the boy. But...but last night, he was so angry. I had never seen him like that before. I didn't know what he was going to do. He stormed off to his room. I tried to calm Gunther down, but he was convinced Steven was guilty of murder; was adamant the police would have to be told. And Steven was equally determined to retaliate.' She clasped the side of her head, her voice suddenly strained. 'I didn't know what to do. Everything was falling apart. Both of them seemed hell bent on destroying everything we had built here.'

'So what *did* you do?' I asked.

'I tried to talk to him. To calm him down.'

'You went up to his *room*?' A sudden chill began to descend upon me.

'Before dinner, yes. But he wouldn't listen. His mind was made up, just like Gunther's...' Her voice was really starting to waver now, the distress bubbling up.

'So you...what? Offered him a glass of water?' My hands were starting to feel cold and clammy. 'And then slipped in a couple of sleeping tablets?'

Mrs Weiman's eyes flashed at the mention of the tablets. 'I...'

'Or asked him to take them,' I breathed. 'And then...and then later, in the dead of night...' My right hand slid down quietly into my jacket pocket and grasped the revolver. I could not believe what I was about to suggest. 'You crept into his bedroom and...'

'No!' she exclaimed. 'I couldn't...I wouldn't...'

But she was lying; I knew she was lying. The cigarette dropped from my lips and hit the grass without a sound. 'You killed him,' I declared, with sudden conviction. 'You killed

Steven Catesby.'

Chapter Eighteen

Susan Weiman let out a strangled sob. Her body shuddered and she gripped hard on the wooden fence to stop herself from fainting. 'Yes, I killed him,' she whispered abruptly, unable to stop herself. Tears were already streaming down her face, the guilt bursting forth in a sudden avalanche of uncontrolled emotion. She had managed to keep herself in check for the better part of a day, but now the woman could control herself no longer. 'My own cousin,' she sobbed again. 'Little Stevie.' Her body was shaking uncontrollably. 'I didn't know...I didn't know what else to do. My family...he was going to destroy everything.'

'And so you...you killed him?' I regarded the woman in astonishment.

'I was in a daze.' She sobbed again. 'I didn't know what I was doing.'

'But...you crept into his bedroom? And grabbed hold of the razor?'

Her hands were still gripping tightly to the fence. 'It was on the bedside table. He always kept it there. I picked it up with my handkerchief and...and...oh, God forgive me.' She closed her eyes, her face a mosaic of despair. 'The blood came oozing out, as soon as I cut through the vein. But he didn't...he didn't struggle. That was the awful thing. He had no idea what was happening. And he looked...he looked so peaceful. Afterwards, I mean. As if he were asleep. And that made it so much worse.'

'And the razor? You dropped that on the floor.'

'I put it there. I thought...I don't know what I thought. Maybe we could blame it on an intruder. One of the workers perhaps. That's what Gunther thought, when the body was discovered.'

I blanched. 'You *intended* to blame his death on Joseph Green?'

'I wasn't really thinking. I just...I wish Steven had never come here. Had never...had never met my son.'

'Was he...blackmailing you?' I asked, trying desperately to make some sense of what she was saying. That had been my first thought, when Maurice and I had discussed the matter earlier in the evening.

'He needed money to start a new life.' Mrs Weiman lifted a hand to wipe the moisture from her eyes. 'At first, it was just a favour. A request. A little extra cash, on top of his wages, to help him build up funds for this new business of his. Gunther and I had a bit of money set aside, from before the crash, and we were happy to help out. It meant that Steven would be back on his feet and away from us. There was never any mention of Moses. Well, not to begin with. When he first arrived here, Steven was too caught up in his own grief to even think of doing anything like that.' Catesby's wife had died, of course, back in Panama. 'Steven was precocious but he was never spiteful. I hadn't seen him since he left Havana, though we did exchange letters from time to time. After Margaret died, we invited him to come and stay with us for a while. Then he met Giles Markham and gradually his depression lifted. In many ways, it was good for him, even with...with another man. Not that we knew about that at the time. We thought they were just good friends and we were happy he had found a comrade in arms. And then, when the two of them hatched this scheme of buying a plot of land, we were happy to encourage them.'

'But they needed more money than they had expected?'

'It's always the way with new businesses. But he made no demands of us. Not at the beginning anyway. As I say, he just asked us to help out, to build up his funds. Gunther was content to go along with that.'

'Even though he didn't like Mr Catesby very much?'

'Oh, he always treated him well, for my sake. And then, when Giles died, Steven fell apart. He became fixated on the land. He wanted to get away from here, as much as my husband wanted him gone. But to do that, he needed more and more money. He thought he could pay the balance for the land himself – from Giles as it turns out, although we had no idea about that until this weekend – but that alone wouldn't be enough. And so he demanded more support from Gunther and I.

268

It was becoming difficult for us, our own business wasn't doing very well. We had set aside some money a few years ago to invest in some new machinery. My husband has always been a fervent believer in new technology. But after the economic downturn, we were forced to use a part of that money to support the existing business. It was a safety net, helping to keep us afloat. We could afford to let Steven have a little, but nowhere near as much as he felt he needed.' She grimaced. 'That was when Moses came into the equation.'

'He threatened to tell?'

'It...it was never a direct threat, it was always implied. But we were left in no doubt as to what he meant.'

'So what did you do?'

Mrs Weiman shrugged. 'We tried to meet his terms as best we could. It wouldn't be forever. He had promised to leave by the end of July. This weekend was supposed to be the beginning of the end. Arthur was coming here to collect the balance for the land.'

'But then I came along and put my foot in it?'

Mrs Weiman nodded and at last she met my eye. She had calmed down a little now, but her hands were still gripping the fence. Her confession, it seemed, was proving cathartic. 'When George discovered the money Giles and Steven had deposited in their account had been obtained dishonestly, he put his foot down. He refused to countenance the transaction. Arthur was furious and so was Steven. Then, when George died...fell down the stairs...my husband, well, he thought that Steven must have been responsible. Some sort of...altercation at the top of the stairs, like the one between Giles and Matthew Green. I didn't believe it, of course. Steven had a temper, but he was not a violent man. But Gunther was certain. He was convinced Steven was guilty. And so the two of them rowed.'

'And Catesby stormed off,' I said.

'Gunther had had enough. I tried to calm him down. He's not a man to show his feelings much but I could see how rattled he was. Nothing I could say would dissuade him. He was going to inform the police, tell them everything that had happened. The blackmail, George's death, the death of Matthew

Green. Every sordid little detail and the devil take the consequences.'

'And Catesby?'

'He was just as angry with my husband. He was furious to be accused like that, of murder. To be thought capable of it.'

'Wrongly, as it turns out.'

'He...he said he had had enough. He was going to tell everyone about Moses and me; about who and what I was. You must understand, we would have been ruined.'

'*What* you were? I don't follow.'

'I...'

'Was there more to it than Moses?' Did Catesby have something else on the woman? 'I know you...had an affair with a coloured man, but that in itself would hardly....'

'There was no affair.' Mrs Weiman looked away in embarrassment.

'Well, a liaison then.'

'Not even that,' she sniffled. 'Whatever else you may think of me, Mr...Henry, I would never be unfaithful to my husband. Gunther means the world to me. I would never hurt him in that way.'

'But...' I was struggling to understand. Not for the first time in this conversation, I was feeling somewhat on the back foot. 'You mean...Moses *isn't* your son?'

'Oh, no. He *is* my son. Of course he is. My darling boy.'

'But...'

'And Gunther is his father.'

I blinked. Now I was really confused. 'But how can you *both* be his parents?' I said. 'Moses is...well, he's a negro. Gunther isn't black and neither are...' I stopped, suddenly remembering that photograph and Susan's Weiman's absent mother. My jaw fell open. So *that* was it.

The woman drew in a heavy breath. 'My mother was black,' she admitted finally, 'although my father was white. He was an English gentleman. But he fell in love with a negress. My mother, Betty, who worked on the estate. He married her for love and it very nearly ruined him.'

'Good god,' I exclaimed. No wonder Weiman had been

so cagey about the subject earlier on. 'I would never have guessed.' I peered at the woman in the reflected light of the torch. 'I mean, your skin is whiter than mine.'

Mrs Weiman sighed. 'It happens that way sometimes, with mixed marriages. One child will be black, another one white or something in between. My father only had the one child and I was born like this.' She held up her hand and examined it for a moment, as if she were seeing it for the first time. 'You would never guess, unless you had met my mother.'

'But Catesby knew?'

'Yes, he knew. Of course he knew. We grew up together. He often teased me about it, as boys do. But he was never spiteful. At least, not then. He worked on my father's estate when he was a young man, helped to keep the business from sliding under. That was...partly why I felt indebted to him.' Why she had invited him here after his wife had died.

'And your husband? Does he know? About your...heritage, I mean?'

'He knows. We met in Havana, just before the war. He was there on business. He met my father and through him he met me. And we fell in love, just like my parents did. Gunther brought me back here, to Guatemala, and nobody in this country knew anything of my past. I was educated in England, like Steven. As far as the people here were concerned, I was a white Englishwoman. We didn't dare tell them anything different. How could we? You know how people of colour are regarded in this part of the world. It's ridiculous,' she asserted bitterly. 'We are all the same, under the skin.'

'And...and Moses?' I asked.

Mrs Weiman took a moment to gather her strength before replying. 'Gunther and I never intended to have a child. It would have been too much of a risk. But accidents happen. We thought...well, my husband was white and I had fair skin. The child was bound to be white too.' Her face fell. 'But he wasn't.'

'Lord,' I muttered, with some sympathy. 'That must have been a shock for you.'

'It was. Greta helped us. She was the only one who

271

knew the truth. She's lived in these parts longer than Gunther. I pretended to miscarry and the child was spirited away. Later, he was found abandoned in a nearby village and we arranged for Isabel's mother to adopt him. That much of what I told you was true.'

'And Catesby knew all this?'

'He guessed it, as soon as he came here. He saw the resemblance. I should have realised that would happen, but it didn't occur to me. And he was family, after all. But if he had told anyone about it, that would have been the end of everything. We would have been ruined. The estate, the workers, Moses. I had to protect my family.' She gazed at me earnestly. 'You do believe me? I had no choice.'

'Oh, I believe you,' I agreed. My hand had loosened its grip on the revolver momentarily but I clutched it again now, as it nestled in my pocket, just to be on the safe side. 'I can't really blame you for killing Mr Catesby. I dare say he deserved it, if he really was blackmailing you. But you would have let Joseph Green take the blame for his death. You were happy to see him hang in your place. And that, frankly, is unforgivable.'

'I...'

'Don't try to pretend it wasn't planned. You engineered things so that he would be the obvious suspect. You placed that razor there deliberately, knowing the conclusions that would be drawn.' I raised my free hand, to forestall any attempt at denial. 'It was a cold and calculated decision, Susan. You set him up and didn't say a word when Tejada had him arrested.' Despite her distress, she had known exactly what she was doing. 'Any judge worth his salt would see you hang.'

Mrs Weiman brought her hands up to her mouth. 'You're not...what are you...what are you going to do?'

I shrugged. I was not sure what I *could* do. 'I could inform the general, I suppose. I could wake him up and tell him everything you've just told me. It wouldn't affect my plans. I could still make my escape, leave him tied up, but knowing the truth.' I fingered the revolver again. 'Can you give me one reason why I shouldn't?'

Mrs Weiman quivered. 'I...Moses,' she breathed, her

eyes flashing with fear. 'And my husband.'

'You should have thought of that before.' I shook my head. Poor old Gunther Weiman, caught up in the middle of all this. The mild-mannered German, trying to do the right thing, even if he had been wrong about Mr Catesby. 'Does he know? Your husband? Does he know what you did?'

'He has no idea,' Mrs Weiman confessed. 'He wouldn't think me capable of it.'

'He must have noticed how distressed you've been?'

'Yes, of course. But on a day like this, who wouldn't be? Gunther trusts me. He always has. He is the kindest, most gentle man I have ever met. He would never suspect me of...of anything like murder. The thought wouldn't even enter his head.'

I was not so sure about that. 'He didn't notice you creeping out of bed, last night?'

'No, he was dead to the world. I was very careful. The sleeping tablets...they belong to him. Doctor Rubio prescribed them. Gunther hasn't been sleeping well of late, because of...everything that's been going on.'

'So who does he think was responsible for your cousin's death?'

Mrs Weiman sighed. 'At first, he thought it was an intruder. Then Joseph, of course, when he was arrested. But now, after what Arthur did...what Arthur tried to do to you, and what you said to us in the cottage, he believes Arthur Montana must be behind it all.'

I had rather pinned the blame on the American, when I had addressed the householders. It had been the easiest thing to say; and I didn't want them all at each others' throats after I had fled the estate.

'And what would he think if he discovered the truth?'

'He must never find out the truth.' Mrs Weiman trembled. 'It would destroy him. It would destroy us both. I couldn't bear it. It would be the end of us. He would never forgive me.' Her hands were shaking once again. 'So what...what *are* you going to do?' she asked a second time.

I closed my eyes. What *could* I do? 'Nothing,' I replied,

at length. 'Oh, I could tell the general, but I doubt he'd believe me. And even if he did, he wouldn't care. I could tell your husband, destroy your marriage. But what would be the point?' I grabbed the torch from the top of the fence post. 'All the labourers here who depend on you. The farm workers. Greta and Isabel. They'd be destitute if this business of yours failed. So what am I going to do, Susan?' I sighed. 'There's nothing I can do. It's your mess. You sort it out. I am going to put as much distance between myself and this god-awful place as I possibly can.'

Susan Weiman shuddered one last time. 'Thank you,' she said.

'Don't thank me.' I grunted. 'You underestimate your husband. He's an intelligent fellow. He'll work it out eventually. And then, heaven help you.'

I looked up. Joseph Green was making his way across the lawn towards us. Greta was taking care of Moses, her arms enveloping the boy protectively in the door of the cottage as they watched the labourer depart.

'All done?' I called out, as the man came within earshot.

'Yes, mister.' He bobbed his head, acknowledging his mistress; then he noticed her red eyes and frowned. 'Are you all right, Mrs Weiman?'

She wiped her eyes again. 'Just a bit over-wrought, thank you, Joseph. It's been a rather trying day.'

'Maybe things will be better from now on,' he suggested, hopefully.

'I do hope so.' Mrs Weiman was busily pulling herself together. 'We'll be sorry to see you go,' she declared, with apparent sincerity.

'Thank you Mrs Weiman. I am sorry to go. This has been my home. I have been very happy here.'

'The place won't be the same without you.' She held out her hand and Green grabbed it eagerly. I bit my lip, ignoring the hypocrisy. 'Thank you for all your hard work.' She stepped aside, to allow the man to pass through the gate. 'I wish you well in the future. You too, Henry. Thank you for...your consideration. Godspeed to you both.' And with that, she made her way hurriedly across the garden towards the cottage.

Green hovered at the gate, reluctant to make a final move.

'We'd better get on,' I told him.

Chapter Nineteen

The officer at the checkpoint had a rifle slung casually over his shoulder. He was an odd looking cove, wide and muscular, with a three day stubble and enough creases in his shirt to keep an iron busy for the better part of a week. He looked down at the passport and then up at me suspiciously. It was not the first time I had fled the scene of a crime in somebody else's clothing and I doubted it would be the last. I had covered the back of my head with a large bonnet, to disguise my short hair, but I was not sure if that would be enough. In the passport photograph, which Maurice had taken some weeks earlier, I had been wearing a wig.

Joseph Green's eyes were out on stalks the first time he caught sight of me in Miss Bunting's floral dress. Despite the tension of the situation, his face had broken into a wide smile. 'Mister,' he grinned, taking in my secretary's rather bright travel clothes, 'do you think maybe *I* should wear the dress?'

We had left the hacienda at eight thirty on Sunday evening. Maurice had proved surprisingly competent at the wheel of the motor-bicycle, in Gonzales' borrowed goggles and helmet. Green had taken the back seat, while I was shoe-horned into the bullet shaped sidecar. Thankfully, my valet was a better driver than the engineer, but I had still been treated to an unwelcome reprise of my earlier bone-crunching descent as we made our way slowly down the mountainside.

We by-passed the village and drove for some time before pulling up to change into our new clothes. Maurice had thought it better for us to be well clear of the estate before I struggled into Miss Bunting's ill-fitting garments. I had wanted to stop off in the village first, to nobble the police van in the square, but my valet had talked me out of it. 'If the general reaches the village,' he suggested gravely, 'he will have no need of a motor vehicle.' That, sadly, was true enough. Tejada could knock up the postmaster at any hour and send a telegram ahead, warning the authorities of our escape. Fortunately, any such alert would be for three men rather than two men and a woman.

Maurice had conferred with Ricardo Gonzales regarding the route we should take. The engineer had been disconcerted to discover that we would be borrowing his motor-bicycle for the journey, but I had promised him faithfully that we would find a way to return it. Gonzales could not provide us with anything like a map – the roads hereabouts were too new for that – but he did give us some comprehensive directions. There were so few proper roads anyway that we were unlikely to get lost. The big concern would be the check points between the hacienda and the port. At least three of them, Gonzales had reckoned, and every one a potential disaster.

We dipped the bicycle into a small clearing away from the road and I broke out the sandwiches, anxious to keep Maurice's strength up for the night ahead. Green was looking rather pensive, the enormity of what we were doing only now beginning to sink in. Events had overtaken him somewhat, the poor fellow.

'I found out what happened to your brother,' I told him, as we sat on the grass to eat. We had brought a lamp with us and placed it on the ground in the darkened forest. Thankfully, it was rather a warm night. The insects buzzed around us but they did not seem in the mood for biting. 'It wasn't Mr Catesby who killed him,' I explained, opening up the pack of sandwiches. 'It was Giles Markham.' Green's eyes widened in surprise. That was news to him. 'They had some kind of argument that day, the day your brother died, at least according to Mr and Mrs Weiman. I don't know what it was about. Your Mr Langbroek, perhaps. The extent to which he was becoming involved in their scheme. Mr Catesby wasn't altogether fond of him, I gather.'

'That is true, mister,' Green acknowledged, examining the sandwich I had given him. The filling was roast beef, left over from Saturday lunch. 'Nobody likes Mr Langbroek. He is a cruel man.'

'He's certainly that,' I agreed. Cruel and unpopular. It was only later, when Langbroek had helped Catesby to cover up Matthew Green's death, that the farm manager had come to see the value of the fellow.

Joseph Green knew little of the plans the men had had to buy a farm, so I filled in a few of the details for him now.

'Anyway, Markham stormed off to church that morning and Catesby sought solace with...with your brother.'

'I understand.' Green did not sound surprised.

'You knew about his...unorthodox predilections?'

'I knew, mister. Most of us knew. Apart from Moses. He was too young. But the others.' Green shook his head sadly. 'They did not understand. They thought it was unnatural. An affront to God. But they were wrong. Matthew was different, not better or worse. He was a good man, mister. A kind man.'

'I'm sure he was.'

'But I did not know that he had slept with Mr Catesby.' Green frowned, struggling to digest the idea. 'There were rumours, after he died. That my brother was a thief. That he had been in bed with Mr Markham and Mr Catesby had found them together.'

'Yes, that was Mr Langbroek's doing, deliberately confusing the issue.'

'But I did not believe it. That is why, when you came here, I wanted to talk to you. I thought you would be able to discover the truth. Moses told me that you were here to investigate the death of Mr Markham.'

'Well, after a fashion,' I agreed. 'But the rumours were wrong. It was Markham who discovered Catesby in bed, not the other way round. He came back early and found them together. He must have flipped. I don't think he meant to kill your brother. It was a jealous rage. He lost control, started beating him and then pushed him down the stairs. There was not much more to it than that.' I leaned back against the tree trunk. 'So, really, what you heard at the time wasn't that far from the truth.'

'I would not have believed it. I thought Mr Markham was a decent man.'

'Love does funny things to people. Sorry, that's probably not much consolation.'

'I wanted to know the truth. But I am sorry that I

278

involved you in this, mister. It was wrong of me.'

'Oh, don't concern yourself.' I took a munch of one of Greta's sandwiches and winced. The beef was chewier than ever. 'It's only natural you would want to know what happened to your brother. It was Freddie who dragged me down here for the weekend. He's to blame if anyone. And he's the one who's going to have to explain it all to the minister tomorrow.'

'All these deaths,' Green lamented, brushing away an insect that had landed on his shirt sleeve. 'It is a terrible thing.'

'Mrs Montana. It's my fault she died,' I said. I could still see her body, sprawled out on top of Mr Langbroek.

'That was an accident, mister. It was not your fault.'

'Doesn't make it any easier. And Mr Montana. I can't really blame him for what he tried to do. He didn't deserve to die either.'

'All these people dead.' Green shook his head. 'Mr Talbot, Mr Catesby. Mr and Mrs Montana. And no-one held to account.'

He was right. It was a dreadful injustice. Julio Tejada had set in chain a horrific sequence of events, without any thought for the consequences, and other people had paid the price. 'You're a good fellow, Green. But the world's not a fair place. We just do what little we can. At least we've kept you safe. Prevented a further injustice.'

'You are right, mister. I am grateful.'

'Henry, please. We might as well dispense with the formalities, now that we're both on the run.' I smiled at him briefly. 'Oh, but not when we get to the boat.' Green had agreed to take on the role of manservant for that journey. 'And it will have to "sir" rather than "mister". Or "madam" in my case.' I would be posing as Maurice's wife and Green would be our servant. It was not an ideal set-up, but there had not been time to think of anything better.

'I understand, mis...Henry.' Green munched on his sandwich disconsolately. 'I will miss the farm, though. My friends. It has been my life.' He struggled to swallow a mouthful of the beef. 'What will happen to Mr and Mrs Weiman?'

I shrugged. In truth, I had no idea. 'They should be all right, if they keep their heads down.'

'They were good to me. I would not want anything bad to happen to them.'

'They'll be fine,' I assured him, with greater conviction than I felt.

A brief silence descended. The insects continued to buzz but like me they seemed to have no interest in the sandwiches.

'Do you think Mr Montana was responsible for the death of Mr Catesby?' Green asked. That was what I had been telling everybody back at the hacienda.

'Who knows?' I shrugged again, refusing to be drawn. The fewer people who knew about Mrs Weiman's involvement, the better for everyone. 'Very probably,' I added.

'I did not like him. Mr Catesby. I did not trust him. I thought he was responsible for my brother's death. But he did not deserve to die like that.'

'No, he didn't. And neither did Mr Talbot.'

'Was General Tejada responsible for *his* death?'

I nodded grimly. 'Yes, he was. He admitted it to me, the callous brute. He didn't do it himself, of course. He must have had somebody there ahead of time, acting on his behalf. I can't think who it might have been. I thought perhaps Mr Gonzales, but he denied that flat out.'

Maurice had been tightening up a couple of nuts on the front wheel of the motor-bicycle, but had been listening to our conversation. 'I believe I may know who it was, Monsieur,' he said, belatedly throwing his twopenn'orth in.

'Oh?' I offered him the last of the sandwiches as he came over and sat himself down. He took one look at the filling and waved it away.

'It had to be someone who had been at the house for some time. Someone who knew the family well, but was not of the family.'

I frowned. 'What, if they were to be an informer, you mean?'

'Yes, Monsieur. As we know, the government has ears

everywhere, in every town and village.'

'That is true,' Green said. 'People have to be careful what they say.'

'And it occurred to me that the most likely suspect would be the housekeeper, Greta.'

I snorted loudly. 'Don't be ridiculous, Morris! She wouldn't work for General Tejada. She hated the fellow.'

Joseph Green agreed with me. 'She does not like the police. She is afraid of them, as we all are.'

'And she was the one who clobbered him,' I pointed out.

'Yes, Monsieur. With some force, I understand.'

'Well, that's hardly a surprise. Tejada was taking pot shots at her boy. It was natural that she would try to protect him.'

'Yes, Monsieur. But I believe there may be more to it than that.' The woman had been been very angry when she had hit him, I recalled, as well as being scared. 'I believe the madame may have had a long lasting hatred for the police and for the general in particular. Imagine if, for years, she had been an informer; had earned a small amount of money, passing on information about the family and the community she lived in, like many people hereabouts. That information would have been filed away somewhere, unnoticed, until it became relevant or useful.'

'She knew all about Mrs Weiman,' I reflected. 'About Moses. You think she would have told them about that?'

'I am sure she would, Monsieur.'

Green was looking a little confused. He had not been privy to that particular fact and I was not about to enlighten him.

'The information would have been recorded and locked away,' Maurice added.

'Until it became useful to someone on high. Like the general?'

'Yes, Monsieur. General Tejada had decided to get rid of Monsieur Talbot, a thorn in his side. He knew the man was friends with the Weimans. The finca would be the perfect place to dispose of him. A quiet estate in the middle of nowhere; and a family who would not dare to complain.'

'Yes, I understand that. But you think *Greta* did the actual deed?' I could not hide the incredulity in my voice. 'That he just rocked up and said, thanks for all the intelligence over the years, by the way, could you push a man down the stairs for me? Don't be absurd, Morris.'

'It would not be a request, Monsieur.'

'He threatened her, you mean? Or one of his underlings did?'

'Threatened her and the boy, I suspect; and the family and the farm. General Tejada has it in his power to destroy them all. If he had wanted to make a house boy disappear, it would be easy enough to arrange. Many people in this country disappear at the hands of the police. Madame Greta would know he was making no idle threat.'

'In that case, he should have just "disappeared" Mr Talbot,' I muttered. But the banker had been too prominent a citizen for that. 'Why would Greta care so much, though? If she'd already been betraying the family for all those years?'

'She probably believed the information she provided was too trivial ever to be used. It was nothing of national importance. It was just a little extra money for her. But after living on the farm for so many years, she became attached to the family. She watched the boy growing up. She looked after him. A second mother, Madame Weiman said, after Isabel's mother had died. And, as we know, a mother will do anything to protect her son.'

'I suppose so.' It had certainly been true in Mrs Weiman's case.

'It is just a theory, Monsieur. I could of course be completely wrong.'

'Yes, very probably.' I grunted. But thinking about it, I could just picture Greta at the top of the stairs, pruning the flowers in those baskets as the rain eased off, waiting for George Talbot to come by. It wouldn't take much of a shove to ensure he didn't survive the fall. Those outside stairs were lethal. Then she could have sped along the terrace to the west side, nipping into the Gonzales' bedroom just as the engineer had come out the other side. That must have been the blur Miss Bunting had seen. Yes, it was all horribly plausible. Another woman doing what she had to do to protect her own. 'I don't suppose it matters now either way,' I said, gazing down at the remnants of my discarded sandwich.

'No, Monsieur,' Maurice agreed. He peered at his wristwatch. 'It is getting late. Perhaps we should move on?'

I nodded. 'Just as soon as we've changed clothes.' I stood up and walked across to the motor-bicycle, to retrieve Miss Bunting's holdall. Joseph Green would need to change too, and while he was fiddling with some of Maurice's clothes, my valet helped me quietly into the flowery dress. We kept our distance from Green as I changed, Maurice masking my body as much as possible, so that he did not catch sight of the bandages laying beneath the shirt and tie.

When the labourer finally saw me in my dress, my shawl and my over-sized bonnet, his eyes boggled and it was then that he had started laughing. We had already outlined the plan to him but the details were only now beginning to sink in. After a quick mutual inspection, the three of us were ready to assume our new roles: Mr and Mrs Harold Bannerman and Mr John Johnson, our servant, heading for a new life in British Honduras. If we could get past the road blocks.

We were lucky to begin with. The policeman at the first checkpoint waved us through without a second glance. This was at ten thirty in the evening. The second road block, in the early hours, had been abandoned for the night. It was only when we approached the third, shortly before dawn, that our luck gave out.

A policeman stepped out from behind a makeshift barrier – two oil drums and a plank of wood – and signalled for us to draw to one side. My hands were shaking as the officer approached. 'Out of the vehicle,' he commanded, in Spanish.

Maurice had to help me up from the sidecar.

'Passports,' the man snapped. He could see at a glance that we were not locals. Maurice, as the husband, handed them across. The officer examined each one in turn and then scrutinised the three of us with his beady eye. I tried not to stare at the rifle he was carrying. We had kept one of the revolvers with us, but that was buried away in the depths of the sidecar and was of no use to us here. The policeman frowned, scanning my absurdly bright attire. With the best will in the world, a square jaw does not sit happily atop a summer dress. It is one of the many ironies of my life that, despite having been born a woman, whenever I am forced to wear women's clothing I end up looking like a man in drag. But my passport at least was in order. There was even an entry stamp in there, courtesy of Giles Markham. The office back in Guatemala City had a large collection of counterfeit stamps, to aid in our secret service work. My only real concern was the photograph in Joseph Green's passport, which had been pasted into place in rather a hurry. Thankfully, the officer did not look twice at his documentation. 'Where are you going?' he asked curtly.

That was a damn fool question. We were on the road to Puerto Barrios. There was nowhere else we could be going. But I bit my lip and answered politely.

'A bit early to be up and about,' he observed.

'We wanted to catch the early boat.'

His eyes narrowed. 'Coming from Guatemala City?'

'That's right.' We were now on the main road between the two towns.

'What time's your boat?' the policeman asked, checking his wristwatch.

Hell. I had no idea. It wasn't as if we had booked a ticket in advance. 'Er...nine o'clock, I think.'

He frowned. 'You mean nine thirty?'

'Er...yes, that's right,' I agreed, a little too quickly.

The officer peered at me again. I felt sure I had aroused his suspicion. Perhaps he was playing with us. Had the general somehow escaped from the generator room and telegraphed ahead? An agonising pause followed and then the policeman gave a slight nod and handed Maurice back the passports. 'All right, on you go,' he said. I climbed back into the sidecar, my heart pounding, and watched as the officer moved aside the plank of wood and allowed us through.

'That was too close for comfort,' I muttered, as the vehicle chugged slowly away.

We arrived at the port shortly after that. It was a squalid, bustling place, dirty and over populated. We found a quiet corner to abandon the motor-bicycle – shoving the keys into a letter box belonging to a business associate of Gunther Weimans – and then joined a surprisingly long early morning queue for tickets. The customs man nodded us through with barely a moment's thought.

And so here we were at last, on the jetty, surrounded by crates, preparing to board a banana boat for the Port of Belize and safety.

'Almost there,' I whispered, as loudly as I dared. The gang plank had been lowered and a small bundle of passengers were preparing to board the decrepit, rust bucket of a steamer. Maurice regarded the vessel in horror. The boat was alarmingly low in the water. 'It'll be perfectly safe,' I assured him, with dubious authority. 'That's our ticket out of here.'

The valet nodded and stiffened himself. I would get the fellow below decks as quickly as I could. We would be sharing a cabin, unfortunately, as we had on the Zeppelin out to America. There had been no option but to book a double berth, since we were supposed to be married. In fact, that had been the only ticket we could get, at this late hour. Joseph Green would have to bunk with a stranger.

The labourer was standing to our left, awestruck, not by the boat but by the future it represented to all of us. 'A new life,' he breathed.

'Got quite a Caribbean feel to the place, British Honduras,' I said, 'so Freddie tells me. We'll be on the coast too, the Port of Belize. You'll fit in well there, I'm sure.' There would be no secret police, no government corruption and no damned coffee. Just happy, well-treated natives, efficient British civil servants and the occasional pot of tea. An oasis of calm in an unstable region, that's how somebody had once described it. 'Just the place to settle down for a few months,' I told Maurice, as we stepped towards the gangplank.

For once, my heart felt light.

NEWS IN BRIEF

ACCIDENTAL DEATH IN GUATEMALA
From Our Own Correspondent

The wife of a German coffee plantation owner in Guatemala has died after taking an overdose of barbiturates. The Englishwoman, Mrs. Susan Weiman, 41, who was born in Havana, Cuba, is believed to have been receiving treatment for a nervous disorder. It is the second tragedy to strike the Finca Weiman plantation in recent months. In July, a crazed worker attacked and killed the estate manager, Mr. Steven Catesby, a relative of Mrs. Weiman. Two house guests, Mr. & Mrs. Arthur Montana, from the United States, were also killed. The attacker, Mr. Joseph Green, a coloured man, was reportedly shot and wounded by police as he fled the scene.

HURRICANE IN WEST INDIES
From Our Own Correspondent

A telegram from Tampa, Florida, the headquarters of Pan-American Airways, reports that a hurricane and great wave devastated Belize, British Honduras, yesterday afternoon...

– The Times, September 1931

Acknowledgements

The Devil's Brew is a light mystery novel, not a serious work of historical fiction. I have nevertheless endeavoured to portray the times as accurately as I can, particularly with regards to the social attitudes of the period. The following books have been particularly helpful: *The Business Of Empire – United Fruit, Race and US Expansion in Central America* by Jason M Colby (Cornell University Press 2011); *Guatemalan Caudillo – The Regime of Jorge Ubico* by Kenneth J Grieb (Ohio University Press 1979); *Bananas – How the United Fruit Company Shaped The World* by Peter Chapman (Canongate Books 2007). Thanks to my beta-readers for their keen eyes and constructive criticism; and to my family for their continued support and encouragement.

Jack Treby

The Pineapple Republic
by
Jack Treby

Democracy is coming to the Central American Republic of San Doloroso. But it won't be staying long...

The year is 1990. Ace reporter Daniel Parr has been injured in a freak surfing accident, just as the provisional government of San Doloroso has announced the country's first democratic elections.

The Daily Herald needs a man on the spot and in desperation they turn to Patrick Malone, a feckless junior reporter who just happens to speak a few words of Spanish.

Despatched to Central America to get the inside story, our Man in Toronja finds himself at the mercy of a corrupt and brutal administration that is determined to win the election at any cost...

www.jacktreby.com

Also Available On This Imprint

Murder At Flaxton Isle
by
Greg Wilson

A remote Scottish island plays host to a deadly reunion...

It should be a lot of fun, meeting up for a long weekend in a rented lighthouse on a chunk of rock miles from anywhere. There will be drinks and games and all sorts of other amusements. It is ten years since the last get-together and twenty years since Nadia and her friends graduated from university. But not everything goes according to plan. One of the group has a more sinister agenda and, as events begin to spiral out of control, it becomes clear that not everyone will get off the island alive...

Also Available On This Imprint

The Gunpowder Treason
by
Michael Dax

"If I had thought there was the least sin in the plot, I would not have been in it for all the world..."

Robert Catesby is a man in despair. His father is dead and his wife is burning in the fires of Hell – his punishment from God for marrying a Protestant. A new king presents a new hope but the persecution of Catholics in England continues unabated and Catesby can tolerate it no longer. King James bears responsibility but the whole government must be eradicated if anything is to really change. And Catesby has a plan...

The Gunpowder Treason is a fast-paced historical thriller. Every character is based on a real person and almost every scene is derived from eye-witness accounts. This is the story of the Gunpowder Plot, as told by the people who were there...